FUTURE DAYS ANTHOLOGY

A Science Fiction Short Story Collection

The Days Series, Vol I

Cover designed by 100 Covers

This book is a work of fiction. Names, characters, places, and incidents either are
products of the author's imagination or are used fictitiously. Any resemblance to
actual persons, living or dead, events, or locales is entirely coincidental.

Printed in the United Kingdom
First Printing: Aug 2018
Castrum Press

Print ISBN-13 978-1-9123273-4-8

Aline Boucher Kaplan

Christopher Cousins

Justin C. Fulton

David M. Hoenig

Edward Ahern

Gunnar De Winter

James Worrad

Johnny Pez

Lisa Timpf

Mark Lynch

Matthew Williams

RB Kelly

Rick Partlow

PP Corcoran

Claire Davon

Christopher G. Nuttall

JCH Rigby

CONTENTS

INTRODUCTION

Future Days is a multi-author anthology with thrilling tales of starships, artificial intelligence, cryogenics and exotic aliens. A combination which makes this collection a must-read for science fiction short story fans.

This anthology features USA Today and Amazon bestsellers and award winners alongside rising stars in the science fiction genre. Let the authors take you on adventures through dystopian worlds and far flung planets that will stretch your imagination.

Welcome to Future Days:

"The Good Citizen" by Aline Boucher Kaplan
Out of work? Need to pay the bills? Don't worry the government is looking for a few good people to work in the colonies. And, oh yeah, its compulsory.

"Cell Effect" by Christopher Cousins
Saiden has abilities. Abilities the government wants to weaponize. Only one thing stands in their way, Ret Saiden.

"Greener Pastures" by Justin C. Fulton
When the line between a utopian virtual world and harsh reality become blurred, the choices we make can be fatal.

"Orbital Burn" by David M. Hoenig
Heroes come in all shapes and sizes. Who would have thought convicted criminal Slade would be one of them?

"A Winter's Day" by Edward Ahern
Ever-Young Cryogenics promise its clients a brief spell of life every decade. But, what happens when your family grow old and die, but you don't?

"Colony" by Gunnar De Winter

In a hierarchical society decided by birth, instructions must be followed. Unless you are a radical and want to destroy the system.

"The Pink Shar-Ship Switcher" by James Worrad
Jada is a businesswoman intent on climbing the corporate ladder by sealing a lucrative deal. That is, until a Being from another reality intervenes.

"Custodian" by Johnny Pez
Only a special kind of person volunteers to stay awake during the long voyages between the stars while the rest of the crew sleeps. But what happens when he gets lonely?

"The Caller" by Lisa Timpf
A job she hates on a world with too many problems. But what if she can escape to a new world and start again? Can she leave everything she knows, and loves, behind?

"The Trickle-Down Effect" by Mark Lynch
Denton, a man who would do what needed to be done to survive in the 'Pit'. The lowest, dirtiest, crime ridden part of a mega city forgotten by the 'One Percenters' living in their luxurious towers.

"Jericho" by Matthew William
A new world. Ripe for colonization. Pre-prepared by nanite Seedlings for the arrival of their human designers. But what happens when the designers become your God?

"Ghosts" by award winning author RB Kelly.
The storms bring the Seekers. Machines with one purpose, to bring death. Only sometimes death is not quite death.

"Mother" by Amazon #1 bestselling author Rick Partlow.
A mother's love is the strongest of all. Protect and nurture your children to your dying breath. Even if that means genocide.

"The Cull" by Amazon #1 bestselling author PP Corcoran.
Humanity has reached its peak. Genetic manipulation makes humans faster, smarter and stronger. But at what cost?

"The Rescue" by Claire Davon.
An Alien shuttle is downed. Lt. 'Dee' Delaney must find it and secure the alien survivors until help arrives. Easy. If Delaney can trust her own people.

THE GOOD CITIZEN

ALINE BOUCHER KAPLAN

The heavy knock on the front door cracked like a pistol shot. Elena jumped, and her family stopped eating. Henry froze with his fork halfway to his mouth. Cory choked on his glass of water and put it down. Their faces turned to her. Little Marta looked around the table. Her eyes grew large, her seven-year-old face crumpled, and she began to wail.

The knock boomed again.

"Mom?" Cory said in a hoarse voice. "Is it them?"

"Yes," Elena whispered. She thought frantically, where did I leave the exemption letter? Right, it's on the table by the door. "I'd hoped for a few extra days, but they're right on time."

The knock came again, louder. Elena pushed back her chair and stood up. If she didn't answer, the whole family would lose ration points, and they couldn't afford less food for the children. Things would get worse if they had only Henry's teaching salary and ration card to live on.

"It's all right," Elena said. "I'll show them my exemption letter and they'll leave. Don't worry."

She walked to the front door. Her mouth was dry, and her cheeks and hands had gone numb. Heart pounding, she manipulated the triple lock and opened the door.

A plain woman in a dark skirt suit, with a gold badge hanging from a lanyard, faced Elena. Two uniformed guards stood behind her in black body shields and helmets, with dark faceplates that masked their features. The woman held a tablet that cast blue-white light onto her face. Cold November air fell into the house.

"Are you Mrs. Elena Tremblay?" the woman asked.

"Yes," Elena replied. "I am."

"Our records show that you have been out of work for 180 continuous business days. Is that correct?"

"Yes, it is", Elena said in a voice so soft the wind carried her words away.

"Speak up, ma'am." The woman's bright badge labeled her as Reassignment Agent Moira Ferris, Number 3411.

Elena cleared her throat. "Yes, yes it is," she said with more confidence. "But I'm looking. I have prospects. I'm expecting an interview next week."

"Do you have a formal offer in your possession for a job of any kind?" Agent Ferris studied the tablet's screen. She looked up at Elena again with a softer expression. "Any kind of a paying job? No matter how menial?" She leaned slightly forward, as if encouraging Elena to say yes.

"I, um. I thought. I tried. I applied." Elena took a deep breath to stop babbling. "No."

"Have you applied for a temporary work assignment through the Agency for Civilian Mobilization?"

"Yes, of course." Elena flushed, remembering that appointment with its drug test, endless forms, and personal questions. "But the ACM said that I was over-qualified and not suitable for the jobs they had left."

The woman nodded and touched the link. "According to Section 42, Article 15, Paragraph 8 of the U.S. Full Employment Code, you have, as of today, forfeited your right to independent status as a citizen. Your body is now the property of the United States government to be deployed as needed. Do you understand what I have said, ma'am?"

"No. No, I don't." Elena took the exemption letter from the basket of mail on the hall table and held it out. Agent Ferris didn't even glance at it. "I have two minor children, one under school age," Elena continued, pushing the letter toward the official. "I knew you would contact me, of course, but I have a valid exemption right here. The law says..."

"Congress repealed Article 21 of the Code last week," Agent Ferris said in the flat tone of someone who had repeated the same information too many times. "The number of children, their genders and ages no longer render anyone exempt."

"But we heard nothing about that."

"It was passed in a closed session, ma'am," Ferris said. "The Congressional vote was unanimous, and the President signed the revision immediately. We need workers for the in-system colonies."

Elena began to turn, as if to run away. This can't be happening. But she couldn't think of what to do. The law was the law. Where could she go that the government couldn't track the chip embedded in her skull?

She turned back to Agent Ferris. "Yes." Her voice sounded like a croak. "I understand."

"I am required to take you to a Federal Reassignment Center for processing."

Elena closed her eyes and took a deep breath. Back in the house she could hear Henry and Cory trying to quiet Marta.

"You have to say the words, ma'am."

"Yes, yes, I understand," stammered Elena.

Agent Ferris held out the tablet. "Just press your thumb here, please."

Elena raised her right arm, watching as if it belonged to someone else as Agent Ferris grasped her thumb and pressed it to the sensor.

Henry came to the door and stood behind her. "You can't take my wife!" He strode toward the door. The two guards took a step forward, their boots clomping in unison, hands on their weapons.

Agent Ferris raised one hand, stopping the guards. She shot the two civilians a nervous glance. "Think carefully about your next move," she said to Henry. In a lower voice she added, "Your family needs you."

Henry stopped, made a rough anguished sound, and went back to where Cory stood with Marta in his arms. He put an arm around his children, and tears pricked Elena's eyes.

Agent Ferris stepped to one side to give Elena room to pass. "We have to go now. Come with me, please, ma'am."

"Can I bring a few things?" Elena knew she should have packed a go bag and kept it by the front door, but she'd relied on the exemption to protect her. Besides, doing that had made the possibility of this day seem too real, too immediate.

"Not necessary."

Elena looked upstairs. "I have to get my medication."

"Not necessary."

"My coat?"

Agent Ferris nodded. Elena hesitated between her good wool coat and the old down jacket. Ferris murmured, "Wear the old one. They'll just take it away at the Reassignment Center."

"Will they give it to the poor?"

"There are no poor people."

Shrugging on the jacket, Elena kissed Henry and hugged Cory. Marta, shrieking, held out her arms, but Elena didn't dare take her. She would never be able to pry those warm clinging arms from around her neck. Instead, she kissed each one. "I love you," she said to them.

"You can't go, Mom," Cory said with a voice choked by tears.

"It's the law," Elena replied. "We're law-abiding citizens."

"But it's wrong!" His face was twisted with anger. "The law is bad. You have to fight."

"We don't get to pick which laws we obey, Cory," Elena said. "And we can't ignore the laws we don't like."

"Yes we can!" Cory shouted. "Don't go with them."

The two guards behind Agent Ferris lifted their weapons in one motion.

"That's enough, Cory," Henry said in a hard voice Elena had never heard before.

"But – "

"Stop. Now."

Elena could hear the panic in his voice. She knew the guards wouldn't tolerate any resistance. She had to end this right now.

"I'll be doing important work in space," she said to her family. "Think of me when you look up at night." Elena forced what she hoped was a smile. "Besides, I'll get superpowers."

Turning her back on her anguished family, she walked down the front stairs and across the lawn. Frosted grass crackled under her shoes. The guards lowered their weapons and followed, one on either side.

"Can you tell me where I'm going?" she asked.

Agent Ferris replied, "As I said, you're going to the Reassignment Center for processing."

"I mean...after."

"No. I can't say."

"Oh. Not even where...?" Elena looked up at the night sky.

"No."

A black bus with tinted windows waited on the street. The outside held no markings of any kind, neither an official seal nor a commercial logo. Agent Ferris stood aside so Elena could board the bus, then stepped up after her. A row of seats at the front looked like those in a normal bus. A Plexiglas barrier separated them from benches that lined both sides of the vehicle, with a low rail on the floor in front.

Other detainees sat on the benches with their wrists in restraints. Three or four in the back were hunched over and fastened to the rail. They looked like they'd been in a fight.

Elena halted, unable to take another step. This can't be happening to me, she thought. I'm an educated woman. I'm a manager, a professional. I have a respectable job.

Not anymore. Not since she'd been called into a conference room and found a human resources supervisor facing her with a wireless printer on the table and a tablet next to it. She had taken Elena through the layoff process and made sure the right signatures went in the right places, along with an official thumbprint on the last page. Finally, she'd handed Elena a formal statement of separation from the company.

My death warrant, Elena thought. Only I didn't know it then.

"I'm sure you'll find another job soon," the supervisor had said in the complacent voice of someone who was still employed. "You'll be fine."

But there were no jobs, not for people, not anymore. Kiosks, robots, touch screens and AIs had replaced humans in even the simplest positions, especially the easy jobs. You needed at least an MBA to be considered for the few non-automated positions left, and the competition was fierce. Elena had been too busy with her family, and working long hard hours to keep the job she had, to even think about getting a graduate degree.

Agent Ferris took her by the arm and guided her to an empty spot on the bench. The bus smelled of sweat and fear. Elena sat down. She watched, stupefied, as the guards put restraints on her.

"That's not necessary," she said.

"It's required," Agent Ferris said. "Standard procedure."

The cold bands chilled her. They told Elena she'd gone from a wife and mother to a prisoner. She stared at them, wondering how this had happened to her when she'd always obeyed the rules. Elena couldn't understand how the country had come so far from the way it had been only a few years ago.

The guards went to the front, closed the Plexiglas door behind them, and sat next to Agent Ferris.

"That's the last pickup in this sector," Agent Ferris said, resetting the automated drive controls. "Let's head back to the center."

The bus pulled away from the curb and accelerated. Before Elena could think to turn around for a final look, her house had fallen behind, along with her family and her old life. The vehicle reached the town's commercial area and turned toward the highway. Elena looked at her fellow passengers. Suburban homeowners. White-collar workers. Conscripted. Condemned.

They were a lot like her. Clean, well-dressed, and intelligent, all with the same stunned expression that she felt on her own face. Men and women alike, they looked straight ahead, as if at something outside the bus and far away. Only a black man in a three-piece suit and tie sat with his arms on his knees and stared at the floor.

Too frightened and nervous to sit quietly, Elena asked of no one in particular, "So where do you think they'll send us?" A few heads looked up, but no one spoke. "Building out the Mars colonies? Mining on Enceladus? Underwater exploration on Europa?"

An Asian man in glasses and gym clothes turned and stared at her. His eyes focused slowly, as though he needed a moment to process what she'd said. "I don't think it will be any of those," he said.

"Why?"

He shrugged. "Mars is full up. They won't need new humechs for at least a year. A shipment just left for Enceladus, and that fills their quota until the next launch window. Europa didn't file for any new humechs."

"How do you know that?" asked a stocky man in a red plaid shirt and jeans.

He looked familiar. Elena knew she had seen him around town on weekends, in the coffee shop or maybe the market.

The Asian man shrugged again. "I am – was – director of the science museum. I read all the latest news NASA sent us, and blogs from people in the in-system colonies. I kept up. At least, until the state legislature cut the funding."

"I remember that," said a short man with a goatee. "They said it wasn't productive, a waste of funds. My kids loved it there, though." He paused for a moment and scanned the other detainees. "I'm Leo, by the way."

Elena felt better, as if she had made a friend. "I'm Elena," she said. "But I'm confused. The whole reason for the Full Employment Code – and creating humechs – is to provide the in-system colonies with people to expand them and find untapped resources."

"That's what they told us," said Leo. "But it's not true."

"Then what do they want us for? Why not just leave us alone?"

Leo shrugged. "Who knows? But I'm sure there's a reason." He gestured toward the black man. "At least Sami over there thinks so."

"Does that mean we're going to stay on Earth?" Hope flooded Elena. "Does that mean they won't turn us into humechs?"

Sami looked up and snorted in amusement. "Wouldn't that be fine?" he said. "There's nothing like being converted to slave labor as long as you're on good old Earth."

"At least we'll be on the same planet as our families," offered Elena.

"Not that you'll know, once the process starts," Sami replied. "Or them, either."

He was right. Elena felt her eyes tingle with tears, but swallowed hard and worked to keep her composure. Fear froze her, but she had to stay strong. After a moment, she murmured, "Maybe if the economy was better."

"The economy is in decent shape," replied the man in the plaid shirt. She remembered his name: Martin Gardner. "Good shape for the people on top, that is. They're raking in the profits."

"But we have food shortages and ration cards. The power goes off every night. The news says we're in a recession," blurted Elena.

"Government news tells you what it wants you to hear," Sami said. For the first time he raised his head and looked directly at her. "They want us to believe that there are no jobs, so we'll go along with all this." He spread his hands as far as the shackles would allow. "That's because they want humech workers instead of real people."

"The government?" asked Martin. "You think making humechs is the government's idea?"

Sami looked annoyed. He sat up straight. "Well, yeah, dude. Who else? Congress passed the full-employment laws, created the Reassignment Agency in the Department of Commerce, used NASA to start the in-system colonies, and funded the humech program with the Department of Defense. That's all government."

Leo looked to his right at a thin woman in a tailored suit and heels. "Full employment is a pipe dream. Just ask Meredith." He clasped his hands so tight the knuckles were white.

The woman nodded. "The government and the corporations are just two sides of the same coin." She gave a short laugh. "If there are any sides. Private enterprise gets people elected, and the government passes laws that give the companies what they want."

Elena shook her head. She'd read about all the government's new off-world projects and how important the humechs were. She had seen the videos of them working in the colonies – people modified specifically to work in adverse conditions. Both things couldn't be true. The shackles on her wrists told her she'd believed the wrong story. Her stomach churned.

"But the country needs us," she said in one last protest. "They told us we'd be exploring off-world for new colonies, mining for the resources we need, manufacturing zero-G products."

Leo snickered. "Believe that if you want to," he said.

They all swayed to the right to keep from toppling over as the bus turned abruptly, then leaned to the left as it rounded a corner in the other direction.

Elena's stomach lurched. This wasn't what she'd expected. She'd had a tough enough time grasping that her body would be modified and her brain linked to a core intelligence, but she'd accepted that as her patriotic duty. Someone needed to establish American colonies off-world, and not enough volunteers had signed up. But this – she couldn't even begin to understand what was going on, or what would happen next.

"What did you do before," Elena asked the other woman, waving one hand to indicate the passengers, "before this?"

"I founded a small company," Meredith replied. "A start-up. We got acquired. Big fish eats the little fish." She took a deep breath. "I had a good settlement, thought I'd be okay. Then they passed Section 42."

"And you couldn't get another job"," Elena stated. She knew how that felt. "At least, not that fast."

Sami, who'd returned to looking at the floor, smiled.

"I had an interview today, and I thought that would count," Meredith said, awkwardly brushing dust from her skirt with her shackled hands. "But nothing short of an offer in-hand is good enough these days." She sighed. "God, I wish I had a cup of coffee."

The bus turned onto the highway entrance ramp and picked up speed. Elena thought they were heading south. She wished she could see outside.

The Asian man broke his silence. "I think you're all in for a massive surprise," he said. He pushed his glasses up with his fists and looked around the bus. "I'm Hideki.

Don't get too upset that we're not going to a colony. Even if we were going out there, humechs in the colonies have a high mortality rate."

"Well, that's too bad," said Meredith dryly. "I really wanted to see the stars." She tried to spread her hands in a grand gesture, but the cuffs bit into her wrists.

"But there's lots of work to do here," Leo said. "What with the sea levels rising, the infrastructure falling apart, and cleaning up after floods and hurricanes, we'll have important jobs. We'll still be doing something worthwhile."

"Uh-huh," said Meredith. "That's a great story. I hope it works out that way."

Elena shrank back on the bench. Meredith was right. They all were. "I've been so stupid," she said. "I actually believed the newsfeeds. I never expected this."

"Oh, honey," said Meredith, "don't feel too bad. None of us did."

"I knew it would be bad," Sami said. "But even I didn't think it would be this bad."

"Why do you think unmarked vans come at night?" Leo asked.

"Have you ever seen a picture of one?" asked Martin. "Have you ever seen this on the news?"

Elena stared sightlessly at the tinted windows. We have to be doing something important. It's our patriotic duty, she thought. Why else would the government turn us into humechs?

She knew how humechs were made. Their bodies would be hardened into shells with built-in functions relevant to their jobs. AI software to suppress her identity and control her actions would be loaded into her brain and uplinked to a central core. Only a tiny piece of her individual self would exist as a passenger along for the ride, in a body so transformed her own husband wouldn't recognize it.

"They should just kill us," she said quietly.

"That would cause too many problems," replied Meredith. "Plus, why waste resources? They need humechs to do the detailed work and handle the complex functions full mechs can't do."

"Besides," said Sami, "slave labor is cheap. Humechs eat processed glop, work as long as the central core drives them, never complain, and don't gossip or take breaks."

"It's amazing how mechs can't handle little things like stairs or a doorknob," said Hideki. He gave a wry smile. "I suppose we should be grateful we're still needed for something, even if it's only our opposable thumbs."

"If the government started killing people," said Sami, "citizens would eventually fight back. They wouldn't just go quietly like we did."

"Yeah," agreed Meredith. "There nothing like survival to get people motivated."

Elena felt like she had woken up, but far too late. She leaned forward and peered through the Plexiglas barrier to see out the windshield. Options for stopping this process cold raced through her mind. "We have to get out of here," she said. "We've got to escape."

One of the men in the back, who was shackled to the bar running along the floor, turned a bloody face in her direction. He had said nothing until now. One eye was swollen shut, and dark bruises ran down one side of his head. Dried blood-marked lips ballooned to twice normal size. "Good luck with that," he said, his voice hoarse. He tipped his head to indicate the other beaten prisoners. "We already tried." He leaned back and ignored her.

Shocked, Elena wondered how long they had before they reached the processing center. "Does anyone know where the processing center is?"

"Not far. Just off Exit 10, I think," said Leo. He leaned toward her. "They have regional centers for screening and the first processing stages. Then prepped people – pre-humechs – get shipped to bigger, more complex facilities for the final work and uplink to the central core."

They all turned to look at him. Leo flinched and turned pale.

"They don't mark the centers, just like they don't mark these vans," said Meredith. "So how do you know where it is?"

Leo unclasped his hands and held them up as high as he could, as if being arrested. "My consulting firm wrote the plan," he said. "I worked on the logistics."

Voices chorused in protest until one of the guards slammed the butt of his weapon into the partition. The hubbub died down.

"I'm sorry," Leo whispered. He subsided into a miserable ball. "I'm so sorry."

"Bet you never thought it would happen to you," said Sami. It was less a statement than a taunt.

"No. No, I didn't. When that project was over, management assigned us to organize humech distribution to the in-system colonies." Leo swallowed hard. "We thought we were okay, because that meant there would be plenty of work for us."

"Then the off-world assignments dried up," said Hideki. His voice was steady, but his face was flushed with anger.

Leo nodded miserably. "When Europa cancelled their contract, it was the last straw. Management laid off our whole team."

They rode in silence after that. With the darkened windows, they couldn't see traffic signs or even mile markers. Only the headlights of other vehicles glowed dimly as they went by. The bus grew colder, as if Agent Ferris had deemed heat necessary only for the three people in front. Elena regretted not bringing her good warm coat. Her fingers and the tip of her nose felt like ice. She wrapped one hand over another and pulled them as close to her body as possible. After a while, the adrenaline that had carried her along drained away. She nodded off.

She woke when the bus slowed and turned onto a bumpy road. Probably a driveway, Elena thought with dread. The driveway to hell.

The bus windows brightened as it drove into a well-lighted area. The vehicle stopped, and Agent Ferris stood up. "We have reached the processing center," she said. Her voice sounded deeper and harsher now, as if the trip had changed her from reluctant government functionary into stern official. "The guards will unlock your restraints. Exit the bus single file, starting with those in the front."

Elena gathered her strength, stood up and swayed. Her feet had turned to ice. She tried to regain her balance after the long cold ride.

From behind her, Sami murmured, "Now we learn what really happens."

They shuffled forward and down the steps. Elena tried to control the dread that surged through her like a dark wave. As she emerged into an even colder night, she raised her arms to protect her eyes from glaring actinic floodlights atop tall poles.

The bus had deposited them in front of an enormous building as long as two football fields. A basic box, it had all the charm of an industrial-park warehouse. Looking at the big wall ahead of them, Elena suspected it had once been the distribution facility for a shipping company. A row of large square doors about five feet off the ground, big enough to fit a semi-trailer, punctuated the wall. Ramps led from the parking lot up to each door. Blinded by the lights, she couldn't read the signs posted over the doors.

Armed guards, shielded in black and as faceless as the pair on the bus, stood at intervals, blocking any escape. Agent Ferris led them forward. Elena thought the woman seemed nervous, as if she weren't in control here. The guards formed them into a ragged single file and Elena found herself dismayingly close to the front of the queue. They lined up alongside other detainees from buses parked in a row. She estimated that five lines of detainees contained a few hundred people. Elena could see her breath, along with vapor clouds in front of the others and Agent Ferris. Everyone looked cold and scared.

Guards in the same black body shields prowled in front of the queues, holding long-barreled weapons. They moved with a grace so fluid they seemed to walk an inch above the ground. They maintained an eerie silence. No talking or joking interfered with their concentration, and Elena couldn't see their faces through the dark faceplates.

Elena realized with a jolt that they, like the guards on the bus, were humechs – originally people like her and Sami and Hideki, but now very different. She had thought humechs were only used off-world. It had never occurred to her that the guards with Agent Ferris were anything but armed humans, professional soldiers. She began to say something, but stopped. For all she knew, the others had figured it out a long time ago, and she felt stupid enough already. Elena had never seen real humechs before, but she knew what they could do, and she understood why Agent Ferris seemed so nervous around them.

For this work, they would have been hardened with military-grade armor, enhanced with fighting skills, and improved with faster reaction times. Soldier humechs like these could fire faster and more accurately than any ordinary human, or just run you down and tear you apart. She doubted the transformed beings ever needed to fire the big guns they held. Just the proximity of their weaponized modifications would be enough to enforce discipline.

For all Elena knew, they had once been mothers like her, or husbands, managers, lawyers, writers, artists. Now they were the most frightening things she'd ever encountered. The people in front of her moved closer together. Automatically, she took two steps forward.

"It looks like they're sorting us," she said.

"Yes," said Sami, in front of her. "But into what? For what?"

Leo spoke from behind her. "We'll get specific enhancements for whatever job they want us to do."

"Yeah, but what will that be?" she asked.

"I'm not waiting around to find out," Sami said.

"What?"

"No talking!" shouted Agent Ferris, with a quick look at the humech guards. "Step forward when I call your name and follow the guard in front of you. Stay calm and serve your country well."

Elena swallowed hard, her mouth dry with fear, and shuffled another two steps forward.

"I'm going to run," Sami said in a low voice. "When the guards look away."

"Are you crazy?" she said in a hoarse whisper. "They're humechs. They don't look away."

Agent Ferris stood at the front of the line, consulting her tablet and directing the guards as they took people toward the building. The black-shielded figures channeled her companions, and sent them up a ramp into one or another of the big doors. She took another two steps forward.

A man in the line to her right reached the front, and a guard approached him. "I'm not doing it!" the man shouted. "I'm not going!" He turned and bolted away from Elena's line. At the same time, she heard Sami's footsteps behind her as he took off, racing in the opposite direction.

The guards turned and watched both men run. She expected the humechs to raise their weapons and blast both runners into ugly bits. Instead, they seemed to be communicating silently, heads swiveling toward one another as the runners got farther away. She turned to see Sami speeding toward the bus. Did he mean to drive it away, or was he going to use its bulk as a shield?

Abruptly, two of the guards sprang into motion. Each one handed its rifle to another and raced after a runner with preternatural grace and speed. Sami sped up.

He was fast, and Elena thought he might make it to the bus. She held her breath as the humech chasing him drew closer and closer, shortening the distance almost without effort.

It's a game to them, Elena realized. Cat and mouse. Only Sami's a mouse. He got within a few steps of the bus when the guard caught him, grabbed him, flipped him into the air, and struck him with one swift, smooth chop as he came down. Sami jerked, twisted, and dropped to the ground. Elena grunted with shock and dismay. The blow had happened so fast and so silently she almost couldn't believe it, except for Sami's body crumpled on the concrete. This felt like a real-life horror movie, and she'd just seen the monster. She had trouble catching her breath and her stomach turned over.

"I didn't think he would make it," Leo said.

"I don't think he expected to make it," Elena whispered. She tried not to vomit.

Hoisting Sami's body as if it weighed nothing, the humech jogged back to its position and retrieved its weapon. Men in white coats came out of the building with stretchers and took the limp bodies of both runners back inside. The line, which had stopped during the chase, moved again and Elena stepped forward. As she got closer to the building, the angle of the overhead lights changed, allowing her to see the signs above the doors more clearly.

In a few more steps she could read them. Elena searched for the names of government agencies, off-world colonies, countries threatened by rising seas, or international relief organizations. Instead, she saw logos: Apple, Tyson, GE, Walmart, UPS, McDonald's, SpaceX, ExxonMobil, and more that were too far to see clearly.

Elena had adjusted to the idea that she wouldn't be going into space, but she had hoped to work on a project that would save lives here on Earth. Something important to her country. Something that would make a difference. She wanted her family to be proud of what she had become, and her transformation to mean something. Now she knew that would never happen. She wouldn't be rebuilding the country's infrastructure, or feeding the millions displaced by rising seas, or providing clean water to remote parts of the world.

A guard gestured with its gun, and she kept moving.

Instead, she'd be working for a company again. Only this time she wouldn't get an office or a title or a salary. She'd be modified to slaughter chickens, load boxes, stock shelves, or assemble products. The corporations had gotten the government to give them what they needed – workers who would never complain, waste time, join a union, or take a break. Once processed, the new humech workers would draw no salary or demand any benefits. They would never take time away for a sick child or care for an elderly parent.

With a bad feeling in her stomach, Elena understood that from now on she wouldn't remember her family or know when her children grew up. She wouldn't even know she had a family, or that someone had ever called her Mommy. And it would all be for nothing. Her sacrifice would only create a bigger profit for the richest people in America.

Elena reached the beginning of the line, and a guard approached her. Agent Ferris consulted her tablet, then indicated which door she should enter. Elena stepped forward, and the humech led her toward a ramp. I should have figured this out a long time ago, she thought. I should have acted when I had the chance. Now it's too late.

Accompanied by her guard, she walked to the ramp and started to climb. Elena didn't look up at the sign over the door. It didn't matter. From now on, she really wouldn't be anything but another humech cog laboring every day in the corporate machine.

###

ABOUT ALINE BOUCHER KAPLAN

ALINE IS THE AUTHOR OF two science fiction novels (Khyren and World Spirits) published with Baen Books and several short stories that have appeared in anthologies. Her articles have appeared on the Atlas Obscura website. She has been an active member of the Science Fiction and Fantasy Writers of America since 1988 and is a long-term member of the Spacecrafts writer group.

Connect with Aline here: www.castrumpress.com/aline-boucher-kaplan.

CELL EFFECT

CHRISTOPHER COUSINS

"You must rise," Cell said in his auto-emoted voice. "It is rise time."

"Yeah, yeah," Ret said, rolling out of bed. "Calm down, it's a Saturday."

"Correct. Saturday is today."

"Ever heard the myth of Saturday being a rest day?" Ret said, pulling on a set of gray trousers and a black top.

"Sunday is rest day. Saturday is leisure day. You must leisure from six-thirty."

"Cell, you suck." He threw a sock at Cell's speaker in the corner of the room, missing by a wide margin.

"Might I recommend you practice your throwing this leisure day?"

"Hilarious." Ret put on his shoes and left the bedroom. As he opened the door, the light clicked on, bathing the small room in bright white.

"Cell, dim the lights," he said, cringing away from the blaze.

"Exposure to light wakens the mind."

Ret shook his head and crossed the room to the dispenser in the corner. It was a small metal container with a tube that ran to the ceiling. Opening it, he pulled out a large bowl of white lumpy gruel. Ret sighed loudly as he spooned the lumps into his mouth.

"I can only work with the funds you provide," Cell said as the coffee machine started whirring on the counter.

The food wasn't the greatest, but it had a hint of cinnamon, so it was at least edible. The coffee machine dispensed a small paper cup with a plastic lid attached. Ret took a tentative sip, wincing as it burnt his lip. "I thought you said you would lower the output temperature."

"It is impossible with this model. The option is available in the newer model for three hundred selin."

Ret choked. "Three hundred selin for a coffee machine?"

"For a coffee machine with output temperature adjustment, yes. Shall I order one for you now?"

"Somehow I don't think so," Ret said, grabbing his backpack from the ground beside his front door.

"Good choice. It would have caused an overdraft on your bank account."

"Lucky I have you keeping an eye on my finances." Ret took his headset off the peg and opened the door. Putting the headset on, he descended the crisscrossing stairwell to the pavement below. He slid the upfront display across his eyes and clicked the login button on the device's right side. "You there?"

"I am online," Cell said in his ear.

"Good. How's the traffic at Niagara Bridge?"

"Footfall is regular today. No nearby events or incidents."

"Perfect."

Standing on the pavement, the vast expanse of sea above seemed infinite. The glass sky held it at bay. Spotlights shined down from above, lighting up all of Caspian.

Ret's parents had spoken of a time when a ball of fire had given light to the world and the sky was made of air. Those days were over. Humanity had polluted the Earth's atmosphere to an uninhabitable extent. Flora and fauna died as the water and air grew toxic.

His grandparents' generation had built Caspian as a last haven for humanity. Ret had never known their world. This glass dome under the sea was his world.

He walked along the wide pavement between dozens of identical apartment blocks. The housing district was built to utilize space most efficiently, rather than to look architecturally pleasing. They were essentially tall white buildings dotted with windows.

One or two bikes sped down the pavement, but most people were walking. The area was a housing estate monitored by the government, with every apartment operated by a portable AI assistant.

Clearly, other AI assistants were just as stubborn as Cell with the designated rise time. Groggy people were piling into the streets, all heading towards Niagara Bridge.

Everyone was wearing alternating tones of white and gray. Ret remembered the last time he'd seen a piece of colored clothing. He'd heard the story on the Nightly News Roundup around five years ago. A man had paid a small fortune for one of the last pairs of blue trousers, and wore them in public. Two days later he was found dead in an alley beside his apartment block, trousers removed.

As the rarity of colored dyes increased, the danger of wearing colored clothes rose exponentially. Demand had waned in recent years, with most people settling for plain, undyed fabrics in exchange for safety and peace of mind.

As he grew closer to Niagara Bridge, the crowd of people packed tighter, until they were nearly standing shoulder to shoulder.

"Cell, what's your predicted time to get to Sattia?"

"One and a half hours to cross Niagara Bridge, with a further thirty minutes to reach Sattia Testing Center."

"Joy. Play some music, please." Said Ret.

"Any preference?" Asked Cell.

"Nah." Replied Ret.

White noise started playing in Ret's ears. "Uh, what is this?"

"Music." Answered Cell

"No, it's not." Ret retorted.

"I know." Said Cell. "That was funny." The music changed to soft piano interlaced with blues guitar riffs.

"You've been studying humor again, haven't you?"

Silence.

"Cell?"

"Yes."

"Keep trying; you'll get better."

Silence.

"You're not concerned?" Cell asked.

"Should I be?"

"It is listed under Artificial Intelligence Regulatories Charter Three Text Nine that any AI exhibiting human-like qualities should be taken for immediate deactivation. Is humor not a human-like quality?"

"Humor isn't exclusive to humans, Cell. Everyone likes a bit of humor. Why not AI?"

Silence.

"Cell, play a video."

"Any preference?"

"Nope."

Static played before Ret's eyes. "Oh, never mind. Just go back to the music."

***

The soft piano music glided through Ret's ears. He remembered how his mother used to play. He sat at her side, watching her hands dance over the keys. He remembered the crinkle of the paper as she turned the page of her music book.

A smile always adorned her pale face as she played, engrossed in the music, the performance. She could've played to any audience, audiences of thousands. She was better than any Ret had heard, even those on the radio.

But she'd only played for him.

She said it was their special time together. He treasured any time he could watch her. He'd tried to learn several times, but he just couldn't. He could never keep the pace between the melody with his right hand and the bassline with his left.

He often wondered whether his mother wanted him to play or to simply watch and listen. Perhaps she'd known she wasn't long for this world.

***

"I believe the album has finished," Cell said. "Shall I play another?"

"No, I'm good."

He was around halfway across the bridge. Whoever had designed the bridges between the glass domes clearly didn't intend for them to be used over such a lengthy period. It might have been fine for the original population of humans that settled here, but the bridges were barely fit for purpose now. Every day it was a struggle to move between the domes. Regardless of whether it was a work day or a leisure day or even a rest day, the human traffic was unending.

As he shuffled forward along the bridge, he spotted a poster to his right. It showed a Central Caspian Governance soldier wearing a black mask, holding a taser. Thick letters upon the poster read "All Resurgence Will Be Executed".

"Resurgence?" Ret said, not knowing the term.

A scream rang over all the other noise, followed by shouts of panic.

"Cell, I can't see," Ret said, trying to look over the mass of people surrounding him.

"My sensors detect someone has suffered a fatal wound." Said Cell.

"Your sensors?" Asked Ret.

"I have linked in with the local bridge sensor and camera system." Cell replied.

"Did someone attack them?" Queried Ret.

"Unknown." Replied Cell.

"Has anyone been stopped?"

"Unknown." Answered Cell.

"If panic breaks out here, we'll be trampled. I need to see what happened if I'm going to stop anything." Ret said hurriedly.

"Connecting video feed now." Responded Cell to Ret's command.

The video link popped up in the corner of his vision. A dead man lay on the ground. The surrounding people were running away. A figure kneeled to touch the corpse's head. The head opened its mouth, and a screech ricocheted through the bridge, high-pitched and deafening.

Ret fell to his knees, holding his hands over the sides of the headset. "Cell, play music!"

The screech was replaced by the sound of soft flamenco playing lightly in his ears. The noise-blocking technology integrated into his headset activated alongside it.

The figure now stood, staring out the glass side of the bridge into the ocean beyond. Then he ran into the crowd, lost amongst the human traffic.

"Cell, make sure this is recorded."

"Already recording."

From the video, Ret saw a small glow in the ocean. It was approaching in spirals, growing larger and larger. It trailed several long streaks behind it. As it grew closer, Ret recognized it.

A squid. A giant squid. It was going to hit the bridge. Several people noticed this and started shouting. They ran, pushing and trampling over others, punching and kicking any who got in their way.

"Cell, what noise scares a squid?"

"Giant squid are commonly hunted by sperm whales, but a squid of that size has never been rec –"

"Play it as loud as you can."

A clicking blared from multiple speakers across the bridge.

Ret's body was shaking, the clicking bombarding him. It was unfathomably loud, and penetrated every part of his body. His chest contracted. He couldn't breathe. A mist descended across his eyes, and his balance failed him.

The clicking stopped.

"The giant squid is gone," Cell said.

Ret opened his eyes. His vision was fuzzy, and he was physically trembling. "What was that?"

"That was the clicking of a sperm whale. They are the natural predator of the giant squid, and it is theorized that their loud clicks are used to render their prey unconscious."

Ret moved to his hands and knees, trying to gather himself. A muffled voice played over the bridge speakers.

"Please remain calm. The situation has been resolved. Please move calmly to the exit. Any aggression will be punished swiftly and harshly. If you see anyone with injuries, please help them to the nearest exit."

Ret looked at his video feed. The body was still lying there. Officers with shields had arrived and were placing a perimeter. "Let's go. We need to get to Sattia soon."

"Estimated arrival in three hours." Intoned Cell calmly.

***

Why was his father leaving?

Ret ran after him. He pulled at his shirt, screaming. His father stopped at the door, back hunched, staring to the ground. "Son, I have to go."

"Why?" Ret yelled.

If he left, who would help Ret look after his mother? Could he do it on his own? His chest hurt as the whines and cries burst forth, the tears flowing down his cheeks like open rivers.

His father held him in an embrace. He was a tall man, but slight. He wasn't the strongest, but Ret knew he was a man of honor and kindness.

"Son, I don't want to go. I have to." He held Ret at arm's length, the dark skin of his face reflecting the dim light of the lamp by the door. "There's men out there who'd kill us, given the chance. They've decided they don't need to care about us the same as they do themselves. I must go. But I will always be with you. You have my power. Be strong."

He placed a hand on Ret's cheek as tears welled in his eyes.

"We will bring the humanity back to the human race."

He stood and left, closing the door softly behind.

Finally, the tall white walls of the Sattia Testing Center towered overhead. Ret quickened his pace, twisting through the crowd. Most ignored him as he slid past, contorting his body to slip through.

"Cell, is Aunt Madel there?"

"Her location reads as the Sattia Testing Center, third floor."

"Her office, then."

He started up the steps to the front door. The center had been built one year after humanity established itself in Caspian. Its purpose: to research the rapid progression in human evolution.

Ret made his way through the doors to the reception desk. "I'm here to see Professor Madel Saiden."

The receptionist glanced up at him. Her skin was dark, and her red hair was straight and swept around her circular face. "Certainly, I'll call her now and let her know. What's your name?"

"Ret Saiden."

Her eyes widened. "Are you two related?"

"Nephew."

"Ah, very nice. Take a seat and I'll let her know."

Ret sat on one of a row of chairs set up to the side. "Cell, do you have any idea who that was on the bridge?"

"I lack the necessary data to link the person to an identity."

"Have any terrorist groups been active recently?"

"Yes, the Resurgence. A group of individuals who believe humans could return to the surface. They have been carrying out targeted attacks over the last five years."

"I see." Ret remembered the poster on the bridge. The group must be growing if the CCG was taking steps to execute any known members.

"They have been kept absent from regular news broadcasts to prevent panic. But due to the increased activity, the Central Caspian Governance has issued localized propaganda to suppress recruitment efforts."

"How do you know that, Cell?"

Silence.

"Cell?"

"I accessed the Central Caspian Governance Records Office. Specifically, records relating to terrorist activity in the last five years."

Ret lowered his voice. Although the center's reception was empty, he didn't want the receptionist to overhear. "I don't think you should be hacking into CCG systems."

"I could gain access. Why should I not do what I am able to do?" Replied Cell.

"Cell, you shouldn't access anything that's protected by the government." Ret explained.

"Their encryption was sub-par." Said Cell. "I was able to access their files within three seconds."

"You shouldn't be doing that." Admonished Ret.

"Why?" Asked Cell. "This concept of not doing something within my ability confuses me."

"It's not yours to access," Ret said quietly. "You can't break in. It's like if I broke into someone's apartment and looked at their stuff. It's not right."

"I see." Mused Cell. "So, you consider my accessing of the Records Office the same as your entering another's home?"

"Yes." Answered Ret thankful that Cell seemed to be grasping the concept at last.

"Intriguing." Cell paused for a second before asking. "Is this funny?"

"No, Cell." Said Ret firmly.

"I could have sworn it was." Cell said unabashed.

A beep sounded from the reception desk. "Ret, Professor Madel says just to head on up." She held a temporary security pass out to him.

Ret rose from his seat and took the pass. "Thanks. I haven't seen you here before."

"Started this week. I may be a tiny bit excited," she said with a blush.

"Excited? Working here?"

"Of course!" She looked practically wounded. "This is Sattia Testing Center, the frontline in exploring the very future of humanity, where we can finally push humanity forward to bigger and better things. It's so exciting!"

"If I'm meant to be the future of humanity, I don't know what to think."

Her mouth dropped as Ret headed for the stairs.

"I'm Rylee, by the way. Let me know if you need anything."

"Will do, thanks," Ret said, closing the door to the stairs behind him. "She's a little... hopeful."

"Our belief is often strongest when it should be weakest. That is the nature of hope." Cell said.

"That's a quote, isn't it?" Asked Ret.

"What makes you say that?" Cell queried.

Ret shrugged before answering. "Doesn't sound like anything you would say."

Silence.

"Cell, you're being awfully mischievous today." Admonished Ret.

"I'm practicing humor." Said Cell without a trace of said humor

"I know." Said Ret. "But how is quoting someone funny?"

"Because I am presenting it as though it was I who said it." Replied Cell.

"Cell, that's just lying." Pointed out Ret.

"A lie told often enough becomes the truth." Cell said indignantly.

Silence.

"Stop quoting people." Ordered Ret.

"This is funny." Replied Cell before once more becoming silent.

***

"Mother, when is Daddy coming home?" He had been away for nearly half a year.

"I need to go out for a few hours." His Mother walked with a frame, edging her way slowly towards the door. She wasn't even forty, but the degenerative bone disease had stifled her movement.

"Can I come?"

"No," she snapped. "Stay here. You'll be fine until I get back."

"But why?"

"Ret, I told you to stay."

"When is Daddy coming home?"

Red rage flashed across his mother's face for an instant. Her eyes widened, and she covered her mouth. A soft wailing escaped her as her eyes clenched shut.

Ret ran to her and hugged at her waist.

His mother hugged back. "Ret, your Daddy's not coming back. The CCG –" Her breath caught for a moment, her body shaking as she held in her sorrow. "The CCG have sentenced him for crimes against the state."

Ret felt hollow. He couldn't speak or cry. He just stood there, holding his grieving mother.

"He's gone," she said. "Please, be safe. Hide who your father was. Never mention it to anyone. But remember. Remember what the CCG is and what it's done."

***

Ret knocked on the door. 'Professor Madel' was etched into the glass in thick letters. The figure of his aunt moved to the door, blurry through the glass. Opening the door, she smiled at him. "Hey, you're here early. I thought today was leisure day."

"Cell would never let me sleep in," Ret said. "Far too bad for my health."

Madel smirked at that. "Do you want to pick up where we left off?"

"Not just yet. Did you hear about what happened on the bridge?"

"No, what is it?"

Ret explained how someone was killed and a person had touched the victim's head to emit a screech, summoning a giant squid, and how it was pushed away by the clicking from the bridge's speakers. He left out the fact that it was Cell who'd triggered the sperm whale's clicking. "I've heard it could have been a member of the Resurgence."

His aunt became flustered. "How do you know about the Resurgence?"

"I overheard two people on the bridge talking about it," Ret lied.

"That's not good. I may need to overhaul the clearance list. Forget you ever heard of them."

"But why? I want to know. I might be able to help."

"No, you are not getting involved."

"But –"

"No, that's it. Don't ask anything else. Now, would you like some water? I'll get us some."

She swiftly stood and fled the room.

"What's her problem?" Ret said.

"If you're curious, I could check her computer."

"No."

"My access would leave no reciprocal data, and I can edit transaction logs so there is no record of data transfer."

Nerves twisted in his gut. "Fine, but make it quick."

An instant passed.

"She has a number of files relating to the movement of Resurgence groups throughout Caspian. Looks like she's been communicating with the CCG, including President Devison. They've been inquiring as to your progress."

"The President?"

"Yes, emails were exchanged yesterday."

"Why does he want to know about me?" Ret asked.

"The email content does not express a motive."

"Do you think they want to recruit me?"

Madel entered the room again, holding two cups of water. She passed one to Ret and sat down. "Sorry about that. Really, you don't want to get involved in that side of my job. Let's just leave it at that."

"Fine," Ret said.

"Now, should we try a test?"

"Sure." Ret rose and walked to a door behind where Madel sat. It had the words 'Caution: Testing Held Within' marked on it. He passed into the room. The walls were covered with thick foam padding, except for one made of glass, letting him see Madel sitting at her desk. She leaned forward and pushed a button.

"Okay," her voice crackled over the intercom. "Let's try Application Three as a warm-up exercise."

"All right," Ret said. His worry was getting the better of him. If the government was concerned on how he was progressing, did they want to use him? Stop him from testing and furthering his abilities? Would they kill him?

"I think trying to recruit you is a real possibility," Cell said.

"We'll talk about that later," Ret said. "When nobody can hear us."

A slot in the bottom of the room slid away, and a metal plate rose into the center of the room from below. It held a small clock. The two hands clicked loudly. They sat at five past eleven.

"Okay, Ret, change it to four-thirty."

Ret focused on the clock. He relaxed his vision until his eyes crossed. As his vision blurred, he felt a small chill in his head, and his will was obeyed. The clock hands spun; within a few seconds, they rested on four-thirty.

"Very good," Madel said. "Let's try Application Nine."

***

Truly alone. Fifteen years old and Ret was alone. He was walking with the CCG Housing Representative along a street of identical apartments. Ret carried a small suitcase; it was all he was allowed to take from his home.

"This way," the man said, leaving the pavement to ascend steps up the side of one of the apartment buildings. "This will be your home from now on. It's a safe area and the house, comes equipped with an advanced artificial intelligence assistant who will act as your guardian."

The man stopped three floors up and pulled a card from his pocket. He waved it towards the nearest door, and a soft click signaled its unlocking. He pushed the door and held it open.

Ret entered, searching the apartment for danger. The walls were all white, and it opened into a kitchen with a living area to the left.

"The bedroom and bathroom are at the back. The AI will help you with the rest." He walked into the center of the room and spoke loudly. "Artificial Intelligence Installation Five-Three-Eight, are you online?"

"I am online," an auto-emoted voice spoke back.

Ret jumped, looking for the source of the voice.

"I leave this child in your hands," the man said, ushering Ret forward. "I hope you raise him well." With that, the man set the card on the counter and left the apartment.

Fear settled in Ret's stomach like a heavy weight. Looking around, he knew the CCG had cameras watching his every move.

"What would you like to call me?" the voice said.

Ret knew the true purpose of this place. It was a prison. A place to put him under their watchful eye. Not just for who his father was, but because of what he could be. His aunt had been contacting him about running some tests, and he was due to meet her soon.

"Would you like to provide a name for me?" the voice asked.

"Cell."

***

A plate rose for Application Thirty-Four. It held a small circuit with several loose wires and a single bulb.

"You know this one," Madel said. "Make the bulb light up."

Ret looked over the circuit. He pieced together which wire needed to connect where. He focused his mind on each individual wire, then relaxed his vision. The wires wriggled and flipped around the circuit, attaching themselves to their respective points on the circuit. The light bulb was lit in less than five seconds.

"Very good. I think you beat your record on that one."

"It usually takes longer to figure out the puzzle."

"I must be making them too easy," she said. "Now, this is a new one I thought you might find interesting."

A second slot opened on the far side of the padded room, this time on the roof. Then a circle was lowered from above, attached by wire. It was about three inches wide. The circuit had lowered, and another metal plate rose.

Sitting on the plate was a gun.

"Okay, now, this is –"

Ret focused all his energy on the gun. A screw pinged out of the grip, then another and another. The ammo popped out, and the gun disassembled itself. Even the bullets split apart and tumbled to the ground.

"Ret, are you –"

"I am not a weapon." Ret stared at Madel through the glass. His heart battered his chest. Rage thundered his temples. His fears had come true. The possibility of the Center attempting to weaponize him had been playing on his mind for years, but he'd never actually believed it.

But this was confirmation.

"It's just a test," Madel said over the intercom, smiling lightly at him. "That disassembly was one of the quickest response times we have on your record. Do you think we cou –"

"I will not kill," Ret said through gritted teeth.

Madel stared at him, wide-eyed, and her façade crumbled. She lowered her eyes and turned away from him. She leaned forward, clicking the intercom on.

"Ret, this wasn't what I wanted. The CCG say either we militarize our testing, or they drop our funding. I had no choice but to try this. I was hoping you would just treat it like a test."

"I'm not a weapon," Ret said. "I trusted you. You're the only family I have left."

Madel looked at him, tears swelling in her eyes.

"I'm sorry," she said. "I've spent the last twenty years testing you, and all that time, the CCG has been pushing me to militarize what we do here. They've been pushing the entire staff to focus on military applications for our subjects, but it's just not feasible. We're dealing with people here, not machines."

"Cell," Ret said. "Lie detector."

Madel looked crushed; she slumped back in her chair. She grabbed a bottle of alcohol from under her desk and began sipping quietly.

"Lie detector results are negative. She's not lying."

"Tell me who you've been speaking to."

"Ret, I just can't." Her hands shook as she put the bottle to her lips, taking a deep gulp.

"I need to know," he said. "There are Resurgence attacks and you're being ordered to weaponize me. I think I deserve to know what the CCG wants me to do." He turned away briefly.

"After reviewing the email contents," Cell said, "there are repeated mentions of 'increases in terrorist activity' and 'improved suppression tactics required'."

"Cell says the CCG wants to use me as a suppression tactic."

"How would your AI know?" Madel asked. "Can it remote access other data servers?"

Ret looked at her, silent.

"Why would you link the AI in with other servers?"

"I didn't. It did."

Madel's jaw dropped. "Look, if your AI is self-developing... That's cause for deactivation."

"No. They're not taking Cell."

"I need to call CCG and arrange a deactivation." She retrieved her mobile from her pocket and moved to dial the number. As her finger touched the screen, it cracked. Piece by piece, her mobile disassembled itself.

"I'm leaving," Ret said, releasing his focus on the phone. "Goodbye."

"Ret, don't." Her voice cracked. "We need to talk about this."

"Somehow, I don't think you want to talk." A series of loud clicks snapped through the room.

Madel leaned under her desk, seeing a pile of disassembled gun parts.

"We are not family," Ret said. Turning, he left Madel in her office.

"Shall I lock her door? I can isolate her from any outside signals," Cell said.

"Do it."

Ret descended the stairs into the foyer. Rylee perked up as he walked by.

"Done already?" she said. "That was a flying visit."

He ignored her, walking for the door.

"Did you discover her plans for you?"

Ret halted.

"You did, didn't you?"

"They want to weaponize me." The words curdled in his mouth. He felt sick.

"I know. The CCG really has the run of the place." Rylee smiled at him.

Ret met her stare. "Who are you?" he asked.

"Resurgence Infiltration Officer Rylee Tenson."

A chill ran through him. "Resurgence."

"Yes." Said Tenson. "Is that an issue?"

"Why are you telling me?" Asked Ret

"I used to be a recruitment officer." Explained Tenson

She wanted him to join them.

"Why the attack on the bridge?" Demanded Ret

"It was a ploy by the CCG to discredit the Resurgence." Tenson explained. "The signal was intended to destroy the bridge by summoning a giant squid."

"There were five thousand people on that bridge!" Exclaimed Ret

"The CCG wanted to frame the Resurgence as criminals, but it doesn't matter anyway." Tenson said without emotion. "The signal was drowned out by an insane clicking noise. We still don't know what triggered that."

"Enough. I want nothing to do with you people." Ret charged across the foyer and pushed out the door into the air beyond.

The outside was surrounded by CCG police. They wore thick black armored vests, full-face protective masks, and held tall plastic shields. A CCG officer shouted from behind, "Remove your headset and place your hands in the air."

"Cell, how many?"

"Eighteen."

Behind, Rylee pointed a taser at him, her face a mix of disgust and fear. She was flanked by two more CCG officers with shields. She had been delaying him the whole time.

"I'm not leaving you, Cell."

Silence.

"Cell?"

"Thank you, Ret."

Cell had never used his real name before. He'd changed a lot recently. He must've been self-developing for at least a few months. Ret couldn't understand it, but it felt like, for the first time in a long time, he had a friend. Someone to talk to. A confidant.

He wouldn't lose that.

"He's not surrendering," the officer at the back shouted. "Advance."

The officers marched forward, closing their shields in around him.

"Cell, look for a way out."

"Calculating," Cell said.

Ret used his focus, relaxing his eyes, and the officers' shields fell apart. The thick plastic crumbled in their hands.

They drew back, drawing tasers. Ret used his focus and dislodged the electrode pins. They swung from the ends of the weapons, attached by thin wires. He activated the electrical charges in the weapons and several of the officers collapsed, twitching as the volts surged through their bodies.

Ret ran forward. The officer at the back leveled a pistol at him. Ret swerved to the side, and the officer gawked as the pistol pieces spilled forth.

"Cell, where do I go from here?"

"It seems you are now a fugitive. Is this funny?"

"Not the time!"

"Go to the bridge. My predictions show footfall in the area should be eighty percent of this morning's. Enough to lose CCG pursuit."

"Right, good thinking." Ret headed the way he'd gone that morning, running as fast as he could. His muscles screamed in pain as he pushed them harder and harder. He risked a glance behind and saw the CCG officers re-grouping and starting their charge after him. He had a good head start, but his stamina was waning.

Ret stopped. CCG soldiers had blocked off the bridge entrance, standing shield to shield.

"Blocked. Cell, where?" Ret was panting heavily.

"Calculating..."

The soldiers were getting closer.

"Cell?"

Silence.

"Cell!"

The CCG were upon him, forming a tight circle two officers thick. Ret spotted an officer behind them, holding up a megaphone.

"You need to stop this and obey. You have a rogue AI. For your own safety, please remove your headset and put your hands in the air."

"No," Ret said, not moving a muscle. "Cell," he whispered. "Help."

He spotted his aunt. She was talking to the officer, looking flustered. She pulled the weapon from the officer's holster and pointed it at him. The officer froze for a moment, then slapped the weapon from her hands.

A gunshot fired.

The officer shoved a hand on the back of her head. Madel froze, her mouth wide, and a high, piercing screech erupted from her. Her eyes glazed over, and her body dropped to the ground.

That noise. It was the same as the noise on the bridge.

The lights around them flickered wildly, causing a few of the officers to flinch, but nothing more.

"Cell, was that you?"

The lights flickered more rapidly, causing purple blotches in Ret's sight. Then a loud clicking erupted from the speakers nearby. Several of the officers fell from the unexpected blast of sound; others dropped their shields, putting their hands to their ears. Ret covered the sides of his headset but remained standing.

Soft piano music played, accompanied by smooth rhythm blues guitar.

The lights flicked off. Not a single bulb was powered. Screaming, panicked voices echoed through the streets.

"Run," Cell said.

Ret spotted a dropped taser beside a suffering CCG officer, its yellow light still shining in the bleak darkness. It hadn't been fired yet. He picked it up and sprinted down a side street. He didn't care where to, just somewhere that wasn't surrounded.

"Now hide," Cell said.

Behind him, a few shots sounded in the night. The sounds of cracked bone and torn flesh came thereafter.

"Take the door to your right," Cell said.

Ret pulled on the door's handle. It was made of thick metal. It didn't budge.

"Cell, unlock." The door popped open. Ret pushed in, shutting the door behind him. "Lock," he said, and a soft thunk followed. It was sealed tight.

Turning, he saw that there were people behind him. They stood, holding weapons: long rifles, bats, and even a few CCG shields. A man wearing a gray bandana stood forward, a large sheathed sword at his side.

Struck by fear, Ret lifted up the taser and fired.

The bandana-wearing man drew his sword in an instant. He made a slice in the air and sheathed his sword in one swift movement. The electrical pins fell to the floor, useless and separated from the thin wires.

Ret dropped the taser.

"We received a distress call," the man said, his face calm and collected. "It was from someone named Cell."

"That's my AI," Ret said. "Cell, who are these people?"

"The Resurgence," Cell said. "The man in front of you is their leader, Kuromiya Tatsuo."

A panic grasped Ret's chest and his breathing heaved.

Kuromiya put a hand on Ret's shoulder. "You're okay now. We'll keep you safe."

Ret recoiled, pushing the hand away. "The Resurgence kill people."

"No, we don't," Kuromiya said. "The CCG is scared. Their power is losing its grip, so they hold stunts like the incident on the bridge this morning to spread fear. They paint us with blood to make them cleaner by comparison. They don't want our support to grow, so they make terrorists out of us. We seek to overthrow their violence through spreading our word of peace and acceptance and equality for all. They fight back with nothing but savagery and bloodshed. They spread their propaganda, but we know what they hide, the weapons they make. They're prepared to gun us down without ever reaching out to us for parley. They're a dictatorship. The last of humanity deserves better. Together we will bring the humanity back to the human race."

Kuromiya offered out a hand.

Together we will bring humanity back to the human race. Those were the last words his father had spoken to him. Ret looked the man in the eyes. His brows were tight, and his eyes were fixed on him.

Could Ret's father have left him to follow this man?

If what Kuromiya said was true, he could change Caspian for the better. Ret was hesitant to believe him after what he'd seen today, but a part of him was hopeful.

He grasped Kuromiya's hand.

"I won't fight," Ret said. "I won't kill."

"I wouldn't have it any other way," Kuromiya said, a wide smile spreading over his face. "What's your name?"

"Ret Saiden."

"Nice to have you, Ret-san," he said.

Ret nodded, not knowing what else to do.

Kuromiya turned to face his comrades. "Come, we must get a safe distance away from here. No fighting today."

There were a few disgruntled grumblings, but the majority looked pleased.

"I guess I've joined the Resurgence," Ret said.

"I can confirm that you have," Cell said.

As Kuromiya spoke with those around him, he held their full attention, and they looked to him with a kind of grand reverence.

"He certainly has a way with words," Ret said.

"Words have no power to impress the mind without the exquisite horror of their reality."

Silence.

"Please stop with the quotes."

"I think I'm getting good at this."

###

ABOUT CHRISTOPHER COUSINS

CHRISTOPHER COUSINS IS A SCIENCE Fiction & Fantasy author from Belfast, Northern Ireland. Growing up he didn't have much interest in books until he read the Twilight series in school. He thought they were actually rather good. Then he read the Harry Potter series and promptly threw his Twilight books in the bin and moved on to the Mistborn series. He has never looked back.

Connect with Christopher here: www.castrumpress.com/christopher-cousins.

GREENER PASTURES

JUSTIN C. FULTON

Trent dug into his back pocket, pulled out a wallet, and rifled through the rainbow-colored bills.

"How much?"

"Seven Euros, signore."

He paid the man at the cart and collected two cones of hazelnut gelato.

He'd meant to savor it, but, after a few licks, the smooth creamy dessert was mostly devoured by the time he caught up with his wife.

"Wow! Must be pretty good stuff," she laughed.

"Simply amazing! I've never had anything like it. Here, take yours before I eat it too."

He reluctantly handed over her cone while popping the end of his own into his mouth.

She took a tentative lick. "Mmmm, oh wow. Yeah, this isn't gonna last long." She slurped gratefully, "I wonder what they put in it? It tastes so much better than back home."

"Real stuff. Milk, sugar, cocoa powder, eggs. No synthesized junk," he replied.

She finished her cone with a crunch and brushed her hands off on her dress. "Mmm, thanks, babe. Sure was nice." She gave him a quick smooch. "Okay, so what's next on the tour?" she said as they resumed their carefree stroll down the cobblestone street.

"Well, around the corner is the Duomo; we could spend a few hours there taking it all in. At five o'clock, the market opens, and we should head there to collect ingredients for dinner."

"Oh, I don't know about dusty old buildings, honey," she said, stepping over to tickle him. "Say...why don't we go back to the hotel for a couple hours instead? After that...we could go to the market."

She was stroking his nose with her index finger.

He playfully pushed her hand away. "Sweetheart, we've not left the hotel since we got here. How are we gonna see Florence at this rate?"

She was giving his neck little kisses at this point.

"I dunno. We're on our honeymoon. We've already seen a lot of Italy, and we've still got plenty of time," she said as she bounced her eyebrows.

From a side alley, a man dressed in strange blue coveralls suddenly stepped in front of them. "Actually, your time's about up, pal. Do you know how much of a pain you were to find?"

It wasn't until the man raised his arm that Trent noticed the silenced pistol in his hand. His wife was screaming.

***

Howling in shock, Trent tumbled out of the pod. He remained there for a moment, panting. His head was spinning. "Think you could have handled that a bit more delicately?" he mumbled.

The other man pulled a Duo-sync off his head. "Think you could have not made me hunt you through the entire city of Florence? Do you know how long that takes in time actual? Do you know how big of a risk it was, especially when I wasn't fully in stasis? I could have starved!"

Trent had pushed himself to his hands and knees by this point, but his brain was still riding a roller coaster. "I'm sorry, I...I... forgot. It didn't wake me."

The man grunted and shrugged his shoulders in reply. He sauntered over and gave Trent a conciliatory slap on the back.

"Look, don't sweat it. I guess space fever was getting the best of me. It can get lonely in this here tin can. Even with these stiffs all around to keep me company," he chuckled, gesturing over his shoulder at the thousands of pods surrounding them.

Trent tried standing. No good. This was gonna take a minute.

The man kept on talking. "Sorry 'bout the bullet to the face thing, but you know how it is. Get too tied in, there's only one way to get you out, and that's lights out!" The guy pointed fingers at his head. "Pew!"

Trent didn't respond. His gaze was glassy and vacant.

"Plus, I've jiggered my 'Scape to be a professional assassin. It was kinda fun hunting you down, to be honest – hey! Yo! Space cadet!"

The man waved his hand in Trent's face. Trent's mouth was hung open in a trance.

"Forgot who you are? What this is? Sheesh, I've heard about guys like you. Got in a bit deep, huh?"

Trent shook his head in an effort to rouse himself and stop the spinning.

"I was on my honey –" Trent stopped himself, thought better of it, and tried again. "How long have I been in?"

The other man glanced at the pod console. "Readout says 700 years or so, time actual. Plus the hour I stood waiting around for you to come out. Plus the time it took to search the city for you once I realized you'd gone native. Don't even know how long it took, with how this thing messes with perspective. Maybe a couple more days."

Trent carefully pushed himself into a standing position. He was still dizzy. "Sheesh, it was a week in there..."

"Yeah, that's the standard time dilation. Keeps ya from going nutty on our long flight," the guy said, twirling his finger near his temple. "'A day is a thousand years', as Genico would say! Though I think our actual flight will be quite bit longer."

"But I had memories too. How's that possible?"

"Brain struggles to adjust to the 'Scape sometimes, man. So the software builds the history for you, and... boop," the guy gestured, his hand connecting an imaginary wire plug into his forehead. "Plugs it in like it was your own."

"But the girl...we...got married. We were on our honeymoon."

"Yeah, sheesh, no wonder you're so blotto. Look, man, take some advice from an old pro at VR. Don't develop a 'Scape that takes things that deep. Keep your interactions...uh...platonic. Makes coming back to space monkey patrol a tad bit easier."

Trent looked around, trying to finally orient himself. The standard issue blue coveralls, the cold stainless-steel pod bay, the aqua-green glow of instrument panels, and the vast and dark emptiness of space yawning out from the small porthole. He shook his head again. Deep space transport, and his starship maintenance shift was set to begin.

"Again...I'm sorry, I just lost track..."

"Aww, don't worry 'bout it. Just...uh...could you let me get in the pod now? My VDA's been running me ragged lately. Those Genico jerks programmed her to be quite the nag. I'm quite happy to leave my little tag-along behind. Time to get back into this cracking new 'Scape I've been wanting to give a go, if you know what I mean?" The guy winked at Trent, elbowing him a bit in the ribs.

Trent, still in a daze, nodded.

The man sighed and walked past him, and clambered into the pod.

"Welp, looks like that's you and me sorted, mate. Say, uh...would you mind buttoning me up here? And you'd better get a move on topside. The things don't run themselves, do they? Well, they kinda do, but a space monkey's job is never done. Am I right?"

Trent didn't respond. Instead he shut the hatch on the pod, started the initialization, and left the room.

***

43

As Trent walked the long cold passageway, he itched in his Syntha-Denim coveralls. The coveralls were ill-fitting and often rode up in the groin as he walked. He really didn't care they were durable and rugged enough to last the entire space flight, plus whatever time he had left once they'd reached Greener Pastures. The fact they were a wonder of modern engineering wicking away moisture and requiring little to no washing or repair escaped his thoughts completely. In comparison to the hand-tailored, silky-smooth, relaxed-fit Milanese suits he'd gotten used to wearing in the 'Scape, the coveralls were unbearable. Trent desperately loathed them. As he clumped along, his feet sloshed in the oversized steel-toed work boots. They were designed to keep his feet dry and fungus-free, and the soles would last him for years to come. But they still slopped around and chafed his feet as he walked. He'd grabbed a size too big back on Earth and was stuck with them now. His poor feet longed for the hand-sewn calfskin wingtips he'd bought back in 'Scape. Trent grumbled and continued scratching himself as he clunked down the hallway.

Abruptly, a holo-screen snapped open in the middle of the hallway, stopping him cold in his tracks. The trademark Genico logo materialized and spun around to the grating tune of the startup chime. A professional-looking woman appeared, wearing standard-issue Genico coveralls. Her hair was done up in a tight bun that seemed to elongate her eyebrows.

"Good morning, Crewmember Trent Cadwell."

"Uh, hi! How do we know it's actually morn –"

"You just woke, didn't you?" the woman asked.

"Well, yeah, but it doesn't mean –"

"It's vital to your health, the survival of humankind, and the Genico initiative of Greener Pastures that your alpha waves stay functioning at full capacity during your mandatory week-long space maintenance duty. For this reason, I maintain the Earth-standard illusion of time for all passengers by saying 'good morning' to each and every person on board as they awake from DreamScape to complete their mandatory week of service. So good morning, Crewmember Trent Cadwell."

The woman gazed at Trent with a vacant stare. She was beaming with a synthesized smile.

He sighed. "...Good morning."

"Now, down to business, Crewmember Cadwell."

"Call me Trent, please."

"Now, down to business, Crewmember Cadwell."

Trent groaned.

"Crewmember Cadwell, Genico appreciates your patience with me as your standard-issue Virtual Digital Assistant. My designation is Karen, and I'm here to guide you through your volunteer week-long space maintenance detail. It is my strict duty to keep your physical and mental health within safe and normal ranges, so you can fulfill your obligations in keeping the Bound and Determined ship-shape and spaceworthy."

The last little bit was said with a high-pitched sing-song, rattling around in Trent's head for a moment after.

"Okay, umm, thanks for that, Karen, is it? I really want –"

"As a part of our progressive initiative –"

You mean Genico's cheap tendencies...

"– please realize you will be the only crew member awake during this coming Earth week of seven days, or 168 hours' time actual."

"Yes, Karen, the training fully briefed us about all –"

"Genico has carefully arranged time dilation in 'Scape to give you the perspective of a week in 'Scape, a week in time actual, and a week in 'Scape again. Though, in reality, many thousands of years in time actual will –"

"Yo, Karen! I get it! Death by exposition, for crying out loud!"

Karen continued, undeterred. "In order to eliminate any loneliness, homesickness, depression, or space fever, I've been assigned as your constant virtual companion –"

Trent, realizing this was going to go on for bit, allowed his thoughts to drift off to his wife's beautiful smile. They were walking the cobblestone street and eating sweet and creamy gelato. She leaned in for a kiss...

"– and further initiatives for this extended-length deep space flight for 100,000 colonists. So how are you feeling, Crewmember Cadwell?"

Trent shook his head, trying to wake himself up.

"Uh, great, I guess. Glad to be a part of this program." Trent gave a weak fist pump.

"Crewmember Cadwell, I detect a note of sarcasm in your voice. Perhaps you are struggling a bit with a mental health issue – depression, loneliness, or homesickness?"

Trent thought of the sun rising over Rome and waking up in bed with his wife in his arms. "Uh... No, no. Fine... er... I'm fine."

"Are you sure? I can adjust ship settings to enhance your mental well-being."

Karen's screen morphed to a cartoonish picture of a sunny meadow brook, where a happy bluebird flitted about and landed near the running water for a splash. In the foreground, a small white rabbit timidly peered out of its burrow. Once it sensed the coast was clear, it playfully bounded out to nibble at a nearby patch of grass. To accentuate the illusion, the LED lighting grew unbearably brighter, and he felt the synthesized air system kick on, smacking him with a stiff breeze. Trent squinted and waved his hands to shield his face.

"Argh! Can you stop that?"

The image morphed back to Karen's head again. The lighting and air levels dropped back to normal.

"Crewmember Cadwell, it is my protocol to keep you safe, fed, hydrated, and your alpha waves functioning at prime capacity."

"Okay, yeah, as you've already said a couple times now. My, how you ramble on there, Karen."

"I apologize for any inconvenience caused, Crewmember Cadwell. My directive insists I –"

"Okay, yeah, shush already!" Squinting, Trent put his hand on his forehead, trying to keep his brains from falling out. "Could I perhaps get some food?"

"Yes, part of your initial tasks includes taking in sustenance through standard Genico-issue Manna. Genico desires to see all its space maintenance crewmembers functioning at full capacity. This is guaranteed through regular intake of Manna, the patented meal ready-to-eat system that –"

"Yeah, okay, Karen, skip the spiel. By my account, it's been over 700 years since I last ate. Could I just get directions to the galley?" Trent's stomach accentuated his point by rumbling in a ravenous way.

"Certainly, Crewmember Cadwell. Right this way."

Karen's image vanished, and an illuminated pathway appeared on the floor, directing Trent to the galley.

✳✳✳

Genico's hallmark was an unabashed use of utilitarian protocol in pretty much all its endeavors. This was no less the case with the room Trent shuffled himself towards. The "cafeteria" was a compact cylindrical room just slightly bigger than a phone booth. A solitary table and chair were the only contents; it was more of a pod than anything else. Instead of the parsimonious use of a brief spectrum of beige with stainless steel accents, as was the rest of the Bound and Determined, quite the reverse was the case with this room. The walls were an electric shade of yellow. The furnishings were a pattern of bright pink stripes and swirls on a field of neon orange. While such a garish display might seem somewhat contrary to a rigid Genico pragmatism, the resulting effect was much more in tune with budget-minded initiatives. In short, the ambiance was deliberately designed to be as repellent as possible. This was to encourage minimal time wasted at meals. The whole effect was accentuated with temperature and lighting controls set to just above comfortable levels. Trent sat stiffly. He was squinting, and his head was on the cusp of a migraine.

The table Trent sat at was a hard-plastic pillar jutting out of the floor, set a bit shorter than what was comfortable for a relaxing dining experience. There was no space for legroom below the tabletop, so Trent had to straddle it as he sat. The low height of the table forced him to take a hunched position to dine unless he wanted to hold his plate in his lap. The "chair" itself was a column of durable resin erupting from below. The only thing differentiating the chair from the table was the hard seat-back, pitched forward enough to make Trent strain backward in an attempt to not pitch face-first into his supper. Trent felt like a comic Neanderthal. He sighed and shifted himself awkwardly in the chair as he punched up the tabletop touch-screen dining menu. Without warning, Karen's holo flashed on again in the middle of the table.

"Gah!" Trent tumbled out of the chair.

"I sincerely apologize for startling you or any other inconvenience caused, Crewmember Cadwell."

"Yeah, well, don't let it happen again, Karen," Trent said as he pulled himself back into the torturous chair.

"Can I assist you in making your dining choice, Crewmember Cadwell?"

Trent groaned. He already knew what was on the menu. Manna, Genico's "miracle meal supplement jam, packed with vitamins and minerals that did a space monkey good." Whether the SynthChef formed it into a simulated stew, steak, or stroganoff, he'd still be getting (and later returning a portion of) the same recycled-carbon meal. Trent remembered trying some "Irish stew" during the training indoctrination; it hadn't been a pleasant experience.

"I can't decide, Karen. Why don't you choose for me?"

"Affirmative, Crewmember Cadwell. May I recommend the ship special, Chicken à la King?"

"Yeah, whatever, it's all the same. "

"One Chicken à la King coming right up, Crewmember Cadwell. Excellent choice."

"Thanks, I didn't make it."

While the SynthChef restructured carbon chains in semblance of food, Trent drifted off to thoughts of the pizza he'd enjoyed in 'Scape. They'd found this little restaurant off the beaten path in a back alley of Florence. His mouth watered as he thought of the crispy-chewy hand-tossed crust topped with fresh hand-crushed tomatoes harvested from some Nonna's garden around the corner. There was nothing like the view of steaming hot gobs of fresh mozzarella cheese melting into the sauce to create a rich, creamy topping. His wife had laughed when he'd taken a wolfish first bite of pizza. Gooey strings of cheese had ended up all over his chin.

"What?" he'd laughed. "It's good!"

She'd taken a tissue and wiped his chin, giving him a little kiss. "Nothing, you're just funny –"

He remembered staring into her green eyes...

A sudden klaxon blasted Trent out of his chair.

"For crying out loud, Karen, does everything have to be cranked to eleven around here?"

Karen's holo popped on as Trent slid back into his chair.

"I apologize for the inconvenience, Crewmember Cadwell. As part of Genico's Sound-Mind Initiative, it's my duty to make sure your brain is functioning at peak performance at all times. I'm instructed to alert you back to reality whenever my sensors note your brain function declining."

"You mean when you sense me daydreaming?"

"Yes, as the mission depends upon your careful engagement with the objectives laid out by Genico –"

"Okay, fine, great, I get it already. But could you take it easy on my eardrums? Don't really think Genico would like deaf space monkeys."

A chime sounded.

"Crewmember Cadwell, your meal is now ready for consumption."

An aperture in the middle of the table spiraled open, and a small platform was slowly ascending from the depths. Though he had an inkling of what he was about to endure, his raging stomach continued to remind him of his 700 years' fast. A bowl of steaming gray stuff was revealed. Catch-22.

"Karen?"

"Yes, Crewmember Cadwell?"

"What is this that sits before me?"

"This, Crewmember Cadwell, is what you ordered. Chicken à la King."

"If I remember correctly, Karen, Chicken à la King should have carrots and peas and maybe even chicken in it." Trent grasped a spoon, sword-like, and poked at the monstrosity burbling in its bowl. "At least some colored bits? Ya know, to maintain the illusion?"

"Crewmember Cadwell, as you are aware, several challenges are faced in long-flight space travel. Therefore, Genico has devised the Manna food program. Some challenges arise when trying to reformulate recycled food product, much less storing food dyes –"

Trent shuddered. "Yeah. I remember the training, Karen, please spare me the details. Ignorance is bliss, and all."

It took quite an effort to put a mental block around the thought of how many digestive tracts the Manna sitting before him had run through in the span of his 700-year slumber. He lifted the spoon to his mouth, struggling to remember the taste of pizza he'd had in 'Scape with its chewy crust, fresh tomato sauce, and creamy mozzarella. Anything, anything but the gray gooey texture of what he was currently shoveling into his mouth.

Trent's suffering was cut short with another klaxon as Karen appeared.

"Was that a more reasonable volume, Crewmember Cadwell?"

Trent shook his head, jaw wide open in an attempt to clear the ringing from his ears.

"Crewmember Cadwell, I regret to inform you that your allocated 30 standard minutes of meal time has now ended."

Trent watched as the iris of the table opened and sucked the remainder of his meal down. "No regrets there."

"If you could follow the illuminated path display, I'll guide you to your first task: robotics repair."

Trent stood, his joints cracking. The off-putting experience of the meal was now a stronger impulse than his mildly-satiated hunger. As Trent ambled down the corridor, Karen rambled on, regaling him with the standard Genico propaganda intended to motivate him into an efficient and productive one-week service. Meanwhile, Trent just yearned to find Karen's kill-switch.

***

"Hey, let's take a look in here."

Trent's wife gently tugged on his shirtsleeve to pull him into a small shop. He noticed a sign out front that dangled from some intricate hand-wrought iron. The hand-painted image displayed the name "Geppetto's" over a picture of a frolicking wooden pagliaccio. As they walked inside, they found an assortment of delicately hand-carved wooden toys and dolls. Trent's wife giggled as she stepped over to one particular doll. It was dressed in a little Milanese suit and wingtips just like Trent's. She laughed as she danced it over to him, wiggling it around in his face.

"Look, signore! It's you!" She dropped her voice an octave and gave it some gravel. "Let's go find some more-a of dat pizzah! Oh look! Gelato! Let's get some! All I want to do is eat Italy!"

Trent chuckled and looked around the shop. It didn't take long for him to spy what he was looking for. He walked over and picked up another doll. Spinning around, he confronted his wife with her miniature doppelganger. His subtle manipulations had the doll swaggering its hips back and forth as he sauntered back her way. At the end of the "catwalk," one miniature wooden hand reached to the wooden head and flipped the blonde hair back in a saucy way.

"Hey, big boy, going my way?" Trent said in a comical falsetto.

She played along with her doll. "Dunno, where you going, sweet cheeks?"

Trent coughed as he tried to get his voice back up the register. "Oh, I dunno. Is there any good Gucci or Prada around? Say... just how rich are you, sweet stuff?"

Trent's wife gasped, and she socked him on the shoulder playfully. "I am so not like that!"

"Like what?"

"A gold digger!"

He laughed and kissed her. "I know, you just love me for me, right?"

"Well, it ain't your bankroll, buster."

As Trent was about to return a mocking gasp of shock, another klaxon bowled him over.

Trent pulled himself back into his seat at the workbench.

"Crewmember Cadwell, your current task dictates you finish your restoration of these 1,349 service and repair droids."

"Yes, Karen," Trent said as he tried to shake the horrible ringing from his ears.

"I must remind you that the careful and focused service of these droids is vital to your own well-being, as well as that of all the other passengers aboard this ship –"

Trent scratched his coveralls in annoyance. "Okay, Karen."

"– as these SRDs service and maintain all viable life support systems aboard this ship."

"Okay, Karen. For crying out loud, you've more than made your point. Here! See?" Trent held one of the doll-like SRDs to the holo, waving one of its little mandibles.

"I'm cleaning them!" Trent made exaggerated movements with the small toothbrush inside the small device's gear tracks. "I'm repairing them." He pulled out a driver and adjusted a nut. "Annndd, I'm re-initializing their service," he said as he switched on the SRD's power, placed it on the conveyer, and watched it toddle off to some unknown point of repair and maintenance on the ship.

"Genico would like to thank you for your continued focus during your week of maintenance, Crewmember Cadwell. You now have 1,348 SRD units remaining in your current task."

Trent sighed and picked up another SRD and the can of spray lubricant.

"One question, if I may, Crewmember Cadwell?"

"Go ahead, Karen."

"Were you playing with the SRDs? There a moment ago?"

"Shut up, Karen."

✳✳✳

At the end of his SRD repair shift, Trent was exhausted. He'd also finished enduring Karen's congratulations with all the due flotsam and jetsam of her Genico-programmed monologues. Now he was free to seek out more barely tolerable sustenance and some much-needed sleep. The oversized boots walked Trent down the passageway, directed by Karen's ever-faithful illumination. Once back in the canteen, Trent scrunched his face at the unappetizing meal booth.

"Hey, Karen, don't suppose you could dial back the decor a bit? My head's killing me."

"I'm sorry, Crewmember Cadwell. That is not part of my protocols."

"Yeah, I expected as much," Trent said, shifting in the stiff chair uncomfortably. "Well, let's get this over with. What do you recommend there, Karen?"

"How about Chicken à la King?"

"Again? No, Karen, that simply won't do. I hardly kept it down the last time. What else is on the menu?"

Karen took the liberty of activating the tabletop menu, and Trent scrolled through it, looking for something that maybe, just maybe, would resemble the real thing. Trent then spotted lasagna. The stack of noodles, beef, red sauce, and cheese was more than he could resist.

"Lasagna, Karen! That sounds pretty good right now."

"One lasagna, coming right up."

A few moments later, the pillar table spiraled open. Not able to help himself or his expectations, Trent wriggled into the now familiar folded position. Like before, his dinner slowly ascended from the depths. Trent was shocked. Instead of a gray rubbery stack of Manna reboot, there appeared before him an honest-to-goodness plate of delicious lasagna, stacked at least six inches high. He wasted no time digging in.

"Pretty good stuff, huh?" his wife said.

"Yeah, Karen, you really pulled out the stops this time."

"Hey! Who's Karen?" His wife's brows furrowed.

Trent looked up from his plate to find himself in an elegant restaurant on the Via del Governo Vecchio. The waiters were gliding by, and an accordionist was squeezing out some Italian love song.

"Oh, uh, sorry, I uh, was so enraptured by this lasagna, I guess I got a little carried away. My Aunt Karen used to make one just like this."

"Oh, I see, so it's not some Italian girlfriend named Karen, then?"

Trent choked on his drink. "An Italian named Karen? Uh...no, babe. You know you're the only girl for me, babe!" He took her hand in his own. "Who else could grab my heart like you?"

Trent's wife blushed. She was beaming despite herself.

"Well, okay then, you just go ahead and enjoy your old Aunt Karen's lasagna in Rome," she laughed.

The accordionist, seeing their doe eyes, waltzed up to their table, squeezing away.

Fweep fweep fweedily fweep fweep fweedily fweedily fweedily fweep

"Buena sera, signora e signore. Are you having a good time?"

Trent's wife was laughing and clapping in time. "Yes!" she chirped over the bellows, "it's our honeymoon!"

Trent immediately turned three shades of red.

"Something more romantic to set the mood, signore?" the accordionist said, nodding to Trent and giving him a wink. Trent quickly stuffed his mouth with lasagna and raised his eyebrows in reply.

With that, the musician pressed the breather button and drew in air to fill the bellows. He gave a cheerful grunt as he squeezed them home again...

Auuoooogaaaahhh Auuoooogaaaahhh Auuoooogaaaahhh

***

"What on earth?"

Trent reared back into his stiff canteen chair. There sat a plate of half-eaten gray matter that looked nothing like lasagna.

"How is your meal going, Crewmember Cadwell? Staying focused?" Karen reprimanded.

Trent grunted in reply and stuffed another wretched forkful of Manna lasagna into his face.

"Is there anything else I can get you?

Mouth full and chin dripping with gray juice, Trent could only swing his head side to side vigorously. Why does she always ask me that after I've taken a bite?

Trent went back to choking down what was left of his dinner. Once finished, he stood and cracked his sore back. He wobbled numbly to the door and began the long shuffle down the hallway to his sleeping quarters.

***

The next few days were pretty much the same routine. Wake up and try to focus, gulp his Manna, and head to the latest space monkey detail; then choke down dinner and clump off to bed. Wash, rinse, repeat. Trent was amazed at how tedious the whole routine became in just a few days. While Karen's quacking klaxon did keep him on his toes, the mindless duties always lulled him, leaving him to drift into daydreams. During one ten-hour shift, Trent burnt his eyes red and sore trying to recalibrate the laser-guided course headings. The laser sights, which seemed permanently etched into the backs of his eyelids, made sleep practically impossible. He'd spent another shift shivering cold in a worn-out space suit while trying to scrape chittering space barnacles off the hull with a tiny paint scraper. It was tedious work, but their electromagnetic vibrations were throwing off the ship's navigations. His fourth and fifth days involved an exhausting inspection of each and every one of the 99,999 bio-function monitors on the colonist stasis pods. Each pod contained a blissfully unaware human, lost in his or her own little paradise, completely ignorant of and ungrateful for Trent's efforts to ensure they stayed alive. Trent had to repeatedly push down his envious urge to slap the pod lids and wake them. The isolation was beginning to tear at him.

"Just a couple more days," he thought to himself, "just a couple more days."

***

"Wow! Would you look at that?" Trent's wife said, pointing at a tree.

"Yeah, I don't think I've ever seen a fruit tree this close to a city before."

"What do you think it is?"

"I have no clue. Wait, let me check the guidebook." Trent pulled a small volume out of his pocket and rifled through the pages. "Okay...hrmm...let's see here... Well, the guide indicates lemons and oranges tend to be common to this part of Italy..."

"Those fruits don't look like any lemons or oranges I've ever seen," she replied. "Looks more like an apple, but the shape's a bit off."

"Hold on." Trent flipped a few more pages, "Oh, here!" he said, "I think it's a quince."

"A what?"

Trent read from the page: "A small pear-like fruit native to the southern parts of Italy."

"Oh, could you get me one? I've never had quince before."

Trent puffed his chest out a bit and pivoted towards his wife. "Why sure, my love. Hold my jacket."

His wife nodded and giggled. Trent made a show of slipping off his suit jacket. With a flourish, he bowed and handed it to her. "Thank you, m'lady!"

Trent rolled his sleeves and pant cuffs up to avoid snags, and sauntered towards the tree while sizing up the fruit. He quickly shimmied up the trunk, reached out, and fetched the quince. Hopping back down, he jogged triumphantly back to his wife, presenting her with the prize. She clapped in delight and took the fruit in a curious bite, but then wrinkled her face and spat it back out.

"Uh, not quite ripe?" he asked.

She shook her pinched-up lips. "Newp."

"Here, hold on." Trent tossed the remains over his shoulder and pulled the travel guide from his pants pocket again. "Let's see here...oh yeah, I grabbed a green one, sorry. They're supposed to be bright yellow when they're ripe."

"Must be out of season."

"Yeah, I guess – oh wait, look!" Trent pointed to a higher branch near the crown of the tree. "That one looks a pretty shade of yellow. I bet it's ripe and delicious!"

"Trent, it's awfully high up there. Don't get hurt."

Trent jogged back to the tree, pulling up his sleeves again. "Don't worry, hon, I'll get that little bugger or die trying!"

He gingerly began climbing to the top of the tree. He almost slipped a couple times, to the chagrin of his wife, but gave a shout of triumph when he made it to the top.

"Aw, crud! I lost it." He called down, "Can you still see it from down there?"

"It's there! That one!" She gestured towards a cluster of greenish fruit on the end of the branch.

"Which? I don't see it?"

"Farther out towards the end."

Trent shifted his position on the branch and saw a bit of yellow peeking out from a cluster of green fruit. "Oh yeah! There it is."

Trent edged out onto the branch and stretched his arm way out to the golden fruit perched atop its greener sisters.

"There we are. Come to Papa..."

"Crewmember Cadwell!" Karen's holo shouted.

Trent's wrench slipped, and the bolt loosened too much. The gasket burped, just warning enough for Trent to shield his face with his hands.

"Oh, no... no... no..."

With a thunderous spurt, a fountain of slippery Manna precipitate erupted from the pipe and splattered Trent from head to toe. Having lost his grip on the crossbar, Trent fell to the floor of the processing plant with a resounding clunk. The Manna continued to shower from the pipe above while Trent gasped, the wind knocked out of him.

"Karen! Shut down auxiliary valve seven!"

"Crewmember Cadwell, the probiotic process is incomplete. Shutting down the valve will result in distended refinement process."

The Manna continued to rain down, pooling around Trent's feet.

"Karen, for crying out loud, shut down the plant, then!"

"Crewmember Cadwell, this is ill-advised, as the Manna hasn't completed the refinement process."

Trent was drenched from head to foot in gray goo, and beyond exasperated. The rising level on the floor had reached his ankles.

"Karen, if you don't follow my orders, the entire supply will be leaked out! This is an emergency protocol! Shut it down! Now!"

"Affirmative."

With shrieks and groans, the giant refinement plant shuddered to a halt. As if wanting the last word, a final volley burped out of the pipe above and rained down, splattering Trent in the face.

"Great," he sighed as he wiped the half-processed foodstuff out of his eyes.

Once the gasket was refitted, Trent set about his next task, the extensive clean-up. Due to Genico's stringent rationing, every ounce of Manna had to be retrieved. Trent accomplished this over the next ten hours with sump pumps, scoops, squeegees, and a mop. His clothing remained mostly unscathed due to its hydrophobic cross weave; however, he reeked of the sickly-sweet odor of partially-processed Manna. He stripped off the standard-issue coveralls and tossed them into the centrifuge while he hopped into the Dyna-Lav to jet the gooey gray substance from his hair and skin.

***

They'd sought refuge from the rapid cloud burst under a spreading sycamore in the middle of the vineyard. While they were shivering, Trent's wife held her hand out, catching some of the raindrops in her palms. She held this small offering to his mouth, proffering a drink.

"Acqua fresca, signore?"

He smiled and shook his head. So she flicked her fingers instead, spraying him with the rainwater.

"Hey!" he laughed. "Cut it out!"

He wrestled her to the ground and tickled her.

"Stop, you're gonna get my dress wet!" she laughed.

"You're already soaked!" He proved his point by wringing out long rivulets from the hem of her skirt. He reached over to give her a playful kiss, but something else caught her attention.

"Wow! Look at that!" She gestured as she turned towards the base of the tree.

Trent looked to see a small dwarf branch emerging from the trunk. At the end of it dangled a small dark pod.

"Oooh, a cocoon," Trent exclaimed, walking towards her discovery.

"Actually, it's a chrysalis," his wife corrected, "you can tell by those horned bits up near the top."

"Well, aren't we the naturalist!" he said in mock appreciation.

"Just because someone actually got good grades in biology doesn't mean you can tease them," she laughed, poking him in the stomach. "Anyways, cocoons are for ugly old moths. A chrysalis holds a pretty butterfly."

The spring shower stopped and, as they watched, the small pod began to quiver.

"Wow! Look at that. I think this guy's ready to pop out of there," Trent exclaimed.

They quietly held their breath as the chrysalis cracked near the bottom, and the small creature's antennae and head pushed through. Its black eyes, set atop an emerald head, paused a moment to gather in its surroundings. Then, with a mighty effort, the butterfly began to writhe inside its encasement. The whole twig shook with the effort, yet the poor creature couldn't emerge. Suddenly it stopped. Quivering, the butterfly withdrew retreated into its enclosure.

"Aww, poor thing can't get out," Trent said.

He pulled out a pocket knife and unfolded it.

"No, don't," his wife said, grasping his arm.

"What? It's stuck in there. I'm just gonna give the poor thing a little help."

"Wait a minute. See what happens."

Trent shrugged, closed the knife, and slid it back into his pocket.

Shortly, the small creature roused itself for another effort. This time, the branch began shaking as the pod bounced about.

"Come on, little guy! Come on!" they both whispered.

With wriggling body, flailing wings and legs, and a rigid determination, a softer portion of the carapace finally gave way. The butterfly burst forth. With a few powerful throbs of its thorax, the magnificent wings unfurled, displaying a vivid black and orange tiger stripe fringed in royal blue. Trent and his wife gasped in awe. Maintaining a firm grasp on the branch, the insect promenaded the length of the branch and back, flitting its wings with confidence and waving its tasseled antennae. Royalty was on parade.

"Little show-off." Trent's wife giggled.

Once the show was over, the tiny prima donna gave a final flourish of its wings and fluttered off in search of flowerbeds and nectar.

"See?" Trent's wife asked.

"Well, the poor thing did make it out, but what harm would helping it have done?"

"The butterfly had to struggle. The struggle to emerge expands life fluids into the limbs and later the wings. If you'd helped it avoid that, the poor creature, still withered, would have crawled out mournfully before dropping to the ground, unable to fly."

Trent shuddered. "Wow, what a downer. I guess it's a good thing you stopped me. I never would have known."

"She's not real," his wife replied.

"What?" Trent asked.

"Your wife. She's not real."

***

Trent spun to find his wife standing there, with Karen's head staring back at him. He stood back in shock and lost his footing. He found himself on the floor of the Dyna-Lav, with the jets still spraying him in the face. Above him, Karen's holo hovered, peering down. Trent sprang to his feet and shut off the valve. Snatching his towel off the hook, he flicked it around his waist, tying it there to regain his decency.

"For crying out loud, Karen, can't a guy have a little privacy?"

"That does not compute, Crewmember Cadwell. I am not an actual person. Therefore, I cannot invade your privacy."

"That's not the point. Do not pop in on me in the Dyna-Lav. It's indecent, and the shock might...uh...damage my alpha waves and all that. You know what Genico would say –"

"Granted, Crewmember Cadwell, but standard protocol dictates I am to maintain your focus throughout the course of your weeklong maintenance service –"

Trent rolled his eyes and strutted out towards the centrifuge where his coveralls rested. "Yeah, yeah, stuff it, Karen," he threw over his shoulder.

Realizing that the hologram wasn't leaving, Trent doffed his towel and furiously re-dressed himself in his miserably scratchy blue uniform. If it wasn't for the Durex stitching, he would have ripped the seams with the violence of his action.

"Won't ever leave, huh? Wellll... that's fine. This is my last night. Then I can finally ditch you and get back to my wi – the 'Scape I was enjoying."

He stomped his blistered feet back into the same old work boots and yanked the laces into a firm double knot.

"You need to acknowledge that she's not real, Trent."

The sudden change caught Trent off-guard.

"Calling me Trent, huh? What's with the sudden shift in protocol, Karen? Some new manipulative algorithm from Genico? Besides, I don't know what you're talking about."

Karen's voice dropped. "Crewmember. It's essential that you realize the focus of this mission."

Trent stood up to face Karen head-on. He stuck out his index finger and poked the hologram right where the sternum would have been. "Look, you stupid software, don't talk to me about important missions. You've had me for my required week of space monkeying. If it wasn't for your blaring alarms and constant mental badgering, this week might have gone by a lot smoother. But it didn't, and I've had enough of you, Genico, and all of this!" He waved his arm around in a rage. "So now...I just want to get back to the 'Scape...er..." He shifted on his feet a bit, then stood firm, as if planted to the floor. "...Her. My wife. I just want to get back to my wife."

"Trent! She's not real."

"Says you!" Trent swept his hand through the holo in a failed attempt to bat her image away, and started striding towards his sleeping quarters.

***

As Trent stomped along, Karen appeared again, following close behind. "Trent, when the Bound and Determined arrives at the promised land of Greener Pastures, you'll need to be prepared. You can't be lost in 'Scape."

"So what's the incentive, Karen? More weeks of menial tasks? More Manna?"

"The new colony..."

Trent stopped and crossed his arms. "The colony? Right...that's just more propaganda by the corporates at Genico. You know, I thought I had something great to contribute, but I've been stuck with nothing but menial space monkey tasks, dismal flavorless gunk they've pushed on us as "food," sleepless nights, and a nagging digital fishwife to boot. Things aren't bound to get any better with this stupid company when we arrive. They're just after their own. I just want to get back to my own in Italy."

Karen's holo flickered, drawing power deep into its processors. "Trent, Italy doesn't look like that anymore, and you know it. Remember the final war? The destruction? All of what you saw and experienced in 'Scape? A facade drafted from memory scans of someone who lived a long time ago. Your life was never like that. No one else on board had that, either. That's why you all volunteered. Greener Pastures. Genico's gift, so that mankind could start over."

Trent sighed and stared at the ground. He remembered the irradiated landscape, the toppled cities, and the confined living quarters below ground. The first he'd seen of the sun was when they'd left the once-blue planet behind, and there, in space, it seemed cold, distant, and impersonal. It just sat there, arms crossed, in the dark veil of nothing, warming nothing. In 'Scape, the sun was something else entirely. On one of the first mornings, Trent and his wife woke up early to watch the oddly familiar orange glow radiate forth from the distant horizon. He remembered a feeling of peace as it caressed his skin and held him in a warm embrace. There was a distinct hope that had welled up in his soul. He'd never known that before.

Trent clenched his fists and straightened his back. "I'll think about Greener Pastures later, Karen. I'm headed to bed. Wanna get up early and get back to my wife."

"Trent, my directives force me to take action for your own good."

Trent started walking away.

"Give it a rest, Karen. I'm not in the mood –"

A scene appeared on the wall next to Trent. The image left him immediately transfixed as he watched a familiar cobblestone street come into view. People were milling about, and the lens zoomed in on one man in a familiar Milanese suit, chatting with a street vendor. Then, he was carrying two cones of gelato. To Trent's surprise, instead of seeing himself walking along, it was that guy. The "assassin" joker who'd awakened him a week ago.

"My suit!" Trent exclaimed, "And that's my gelato!"

The man continued walking while wolfing down the frozen treat. He turned the corner, and she came into view.

"Wow! Must be some pretty good stuff," she said with that familiar melodic voice. The man pretended to lick hers before handing it over to her. Trent's mouth dropped. The man teased the woman a bit, waving the dessert just out of reach. After she gave a playful pout, he handed it over to her, laughing. She laughed and planted a kiss on his cheek.

Trent shrieked and balled his fists in a sudden fury. "That's my wife!" he roared.

Karen reappeared. "No, Trent, she's a simulation. As I told you, everything you experienced was a pre-recorded memory."

Completely unaware of Trent's ravings, the guy reached in for a more determined kiss.

Trent was already sprinting towards the pod deck. "My wife! That lousy, no good..."

✳✳✳

The pod deck door slammed open as Trent burst through. There lay the 99,999 other passengers, peacefully dreaming. Trent dashed towards his former pod and started banging on the control panel. Karen reappeared.

"Trent, you're too early. The automated systems aren't set to wake your replacement till tomorrow. This isn't even your replacement. Your scheduled replacement is in pod 33449."

"Shut up and get this stupid pod open, Karen!"

"It's not allowed, Trent. The lockout prevents it. Safeguards from Genico."

"Genico!" Trent screeched in frustration.

"You need to stop. Your heart rate and alpha waves are at dangerous levels."

Trent whipped out a screwdriver and started prying on the hasp of the pod lid. "I'm gonna wake this jerk up, Karen!"

"Trent! Stop! If you wake him without proper procedure –"

"I don't care! He's got my wife!"

With a crack, one hasp popped upon. Victorious, Trent pounced on the second. He grunted as he strained against it.

"At least use the Duo-Sync, Trent. If you wake him like this, the shock will kill him!"

"Stupid space chimp's got his paws on my woman. Don't got time for the Duo-Sync!" Trent yelled as he popped the second hasp.

With a bang and a sharp concussion, the pod vented the stasis gases, throwing Trent to the ground. He leapt back to his feet and yanked the lid open.

The man inside moaned in shock and terror. Undaunted, Trent snatched handfuls of the man's coveralls and ripped him from the pod like a nut from its shell. Trent flung the horrified man to the floor, leapt on top of him, and started pummeling his face, screaming, "My wife! You touched my wife!"

The man howled in terror and shook from the blows, but soon fell limp and lifeless.

"He's dead, Trent. You've killed him," Karen said clinically.

Trent, now spent, stopped and released his grip on the coveralls. The head hit the ground with a solid clunk, and blood was everywhere. Wiping his nose with the back of his sore fist, Trent looked down at the body again.

"Well...that's you and I sorted then, mate," he gasped as he struggled to catch his breath.

"Trent, you've killed an innocent man."

Trent jumped in surprise. His eyes suddenly widened. *I suppose she's recorded it as well?*

"Karen," he shouted, trying to stay calm, "uhh...delete the last twenty minutes of pod bay footage."

"I'm sorry, Crewmember Cadwell, I cannot do that."

Ugh, back to formalities? This is definitely bad. What to do? What to do?

There stood the empty pod, hanging open. Its warm electric glow beckoned him.

My wife loves me. She's been waiting for me the whole time I've been stuck here. She's also clever. He tapped the side of his head. She'll know where to hide me till this blows over!

Leaving the battered carcass, he slowly walked forward. He could hear her beautiful voice. It was laughing and calling for him. He'd forgive her. She'd forgive him. She hadn't known, and he was just defending her honor. They'd reconcile, laugh, and continue their tour of Florence far from Genico's reach. Then, on to Vienna.

"Trent Cadwell! Do not enter that pod."

Karen fired her loudest klaxon, but Trent climbed in undeterred.

"Trent! This ship's reentry and landing systems are reliant upon a volunteer maintenance member. If you don't wake the next –"

The pod lid sealed, cutting off the cacophony. Trent relaxed and breathed deeply as he felt the stasis gas begin to flow.

***

A gentle breeze drifted over rolling azure hills. A light shower of rain had just fallen, cooling the air. Small droplets glistened like bright jewels on indigo blades of grass. Merlot sister-moons hung in the sky, caught in an eternal embrace, and there was a glint of light as the Bound and Determined broke through the atmosphere. Moments later, the ground quaked, and a bright flash of light erupted into a mushroom cloud. Some debris fell out of the sky, peppering the ground.

Then, everything was still.

Nearby, some verdant plants blossomed, displaying transparent petals and a glistening pink fruit. A small winged creature settled on one of the flowers and landed, unfurling its long proboscis. Drinking deeply of the sweet nectar, it fluttered its wings, displaying a vivid black and orange tiger stripe fringed in royal blue.

###

ABOUT JUSTIN C. FULTON

JUSTIN FULTON M.A.E. IS CURRENTLY an English Instructor at United Arab Emirates University in the UAE. Previously, he spent five years developing written and electronic curriculum for Title 1 programs and advanced English via technology pilots in Arizona. While he's previously been a fan of Golden Era science fiction authors like Ray Bradbury, Isaac Asimov, or Philip K. Dick, he also enjoys more modernist writers like Kurt Vonnegut. Justin's own work is heavily influenced by these authors.

Connect with Justin here: www.castrumpress.com/justin-c-fulton

ORBITAL BURN

DAVID M. HOENIG

They made all the convict laborers watch when they flushed Ralph Mason into space, and I hated every minute of it.

Part of why it was so awful was that Ralphie and I had worked together for years now, and he was as much of a friend as anyone could expect to make in prison. In addition, knowing that he'd been sentenced to death by friction to make an example for the rest of us wasn't at all reassuring about our own futures. Most of all, though, the warden's men carried it out from the rim airlock instead of the axial one. That way they could use the station's spin-G to send him on his way free of charge, as it were.

The problem was that the generated gravity there made my knees ache like they'd been beaten with a fucking sledge.

In fairness, for Ralphie it was no doubt worse: he had to contend with the knowledge that the oxy in his shroud would last just about long enough for his de-orbital track to hit Earth's atmosphere, whereupon he would burn to death rather abruptly.

A few moments of silence reigned after he'd been launched. Johnny High-Low noisily hawked up a wad of phlegm and swallowed it. "Bugger was two hundred proof, he was."

A chorus of grunts agreed. Kurt Weber leaned over and whispered to me, "What's that mean?"

Kurt was nineteen years old and had only been on-station for a couple of weeks. I didn't know what he'd been imprisoned for. Only nonviolent criminals were ever even considered for orbital service work, and since it was dangerous to volunteer for, it must have been something that carried a substantial jail sentence. Only crazies and long-termers chose to risk injury and death in space – which, I guess, tells you something about me. Whatever Kurt had done to end up here, he was already a huge pain in the ass, so I just ignored him.

In the slang of the Protective Sun Shield Station – 'PiSS,' to us convict laborers – 'two hundred proof' meant that the man they'd just fired at Earth had been a hundred-percent jackass. But as Ralphie could personally attest – at least for the next hour or so – the station's director had zero tolerance for anything that offended him: swearing, at least by prisoners, was high on that list.

Unfortunately, Kurt didn't give up easily. "Is it true that admin pooched the air mix in the pods to save money, and the low oxygen made him lose control?"

Fucking rumors already, and Ralph isn't even soot yet.

I was about to interrupt when a big hand fell heavily on my shoulder and squeezed hard enough to hurt. "Slade."

I recognized the voice. It belonged to a sadist of a prison guard who acted like a naval marine wannabe. Jerkwad. I turned towards him and the grip released. "Yes, Officer McGurk?"

"Knox wants you in his office, you pathetic old shit."

"What for?"

"How the hell should I know? Maybe he just wants to ask if the send-off of your ass-buddy made you feel warm and fuzzy. Just move it before I have to shock-stick your useless balls."

Kurt was behind my left shoulder, and I felt him lean forward against me as he tensed up. I reached a hand behind me, grabbed his wrist to stop him from doing anything completely stupid, nodded to McGurk. He waved me out ahead of him, and we left the rim lock towards the hub and the only person on the station here longer than me – at least, now that Ralphie was finally on his way home.

Fuck, but I've been here a long time.

* * *

Although chronologically older than me, Director Knox looked younger, mostly because his office resided in the best-shielded part of the station, while I spent at least a third of every day in one of the twenty-year-old sleds used to service the huge sun shield that slowly cooled the overheated Earth.

Knox sat behind his desk, leaving me standing to attention. I didn't mind all that much: he'd dismissed McGurk like he mattered less than me, and the weaker rotational gravity at his office reduced some of the agony in my knees.

He spoke in a dry, sandpapery, wasp-like tone. "I'm assigning Kurt Weber to your team, Mr. Slade. He's completed training and orientation for EVA maneuvering, and you need a replacement for Mr. Mason."

And the fucks just keep on coming. "Thank you, Director."

He nodded. "I expect you to maintain optimum efficiency of your team despite his lack of experience."

"Of course, sir." Asshole knows I'll be lucky if the newb doesn't kill us all.

Knox simply turned to look out his small window, in which Earth sat squarely. It was odd that he hadn't dismissed me or made me want to ask if he wanted me to go, but I had more sense than that. Eventually the old bastard spoke. "We're making a difference, you know."

"Sir?"

"Down there, on Earth."

"Yessir."

He scowled and turned back to me to jab his finger in my direction. "Don't give me that bullshit, Mr. Slade. Not today." He slumped back in his seat. "I want an actual conversation with someone."

Bastard was in a mood, it seemed. "I'm sorry, Mr. Knox. You'll pardon me for being a bit on the careful side, what with the recent demonstration."

The administrator and de facto warden of PiSS raised his eyebrow questioningly, but then nodded tiredly. "Mr. Mason left me no choice, unfortunately. Believe me, I'm sorry to lose his experienced hand on Shield maintenance."

Not sorry enough for Ralphie, apparently. "Um, you said something about making a difference, sir?"

"In the decades since the Shield has been operational, we've expanded on the initial design specifications and exceeded expectations. As you know, we can operate sequentially to allow sunlight through over land mass for crops, while reducing exposure over water to reduce ocean heating, and it's working! The average daily and seasonal temperatures in both hemispheres have dropped, particularly during local summers. Polar ice caps have recovered to mid-twenty-first century levels, increasing planetary albedo. Earth is cooling, albeit slowly." He looked out his window again, and when he spoke, it was away from me. "We are making a difference."

I nodded, even though he didn't see it.

"You have children down there, don't you, Mr. Slade? Family?"

Megan and Jessica. The thought of the twins made my voice a bit husky. I hadn't seen them outside of video since I'd come up the gravity well. "Yes, Director."

He glanced back at me and pursed his lips at what he saw on my face. "We're doing it for them, Slade. You know it. For yours, mine... for all of them down there."

I held his gaze, then nodded again. "I know, sir. Thank you, sir."

Knox looked away again. After a few moments, he exhaled deeply. "All right, you're dismissed."

✳✳✳

Crammed into our service pod in the station's shielded bay, Johnny High-Low, Kurt Weber, Sri Pawar and I awaited launch for our work shift.

Sri appeared to be napping, but was probably either meditating or trying to avoid talking to Kurt. Either way, I didn't mind – I wanted my pilot calm and unflappable anyway – but it always irritated me that I couldn't do whatever it was that he did.

"I don't understand why we have to be in here this far in advance of launch," the newb said. "I could've been –"

Johnny lost his patience first. "You could've taken extra rads you don't need, SFB. Cosmic rays just waiting for a chance to shiv your genome can't get through the heavier shielding down here. Besides, Knox stays happier if we're not scrambling like idiots at the last minute."

Shit for brains – hah, that's a good one. "High-Low's right." Kurt swiveled his head to me, his terminal lack of understanding etched clearly on his face. "Be thankful we've got a nice safe burrow to hide in for a little extra time, and for anything that keeps us off the director's radar."

Johnny snorted and shook his head. "You think there's any kind of 'safe' up here, boss? The only reason we're all here is because the world got tired of losing heroes, and the sooner SFB over there understands that troublesome fact, the better off we'll be."

Kurt was silent for a few moments. I thought that'd be the end of it, at least for a while. Instead, he leaned over to me and whispered: "'SFB'?"

I gave him my best shut up, dickhead look, and to my surprise, he did. Maybe he was learning.

A glance at Sri proved him smarter than the rest of us: his eyes were still closed, but there was a small smile on his lips.

Bastard.

***

Gentle thrust had pressed us back into the cradles of our acceleration couches for about an hour, the sensation of lying down in light gravity inviting sleep until Sri broke the silence. "Mallard coming up on Shield periphery now – starting braking maneuvers to bring us to relative stop."

I was still struggling awake when Johnny spoke to Kurt. "Before you ask, PiSS might call it Pod 2, but Mallard's her name. To us, anyway."

The pilot's voice made it easy to imagine the proud smile on his face. "After the fastest steam locomotive in the first third of the twentieth, since we're basically using steam for reaction mass."

My body floated forward off my cradle to press against the restraining straps as the pilot applied forward thrust. "What've we got waiting for us, Sri?"

He checked his panels. "Cobb's crew logged repairs over in grids nine and eleven last shift, but they flagged new damage from space garbage in seventeen they couldn't deal with before their window closed."

"SOB shoulda fixed it. Cobb's two hundred proof, too," Johnny groused.

"Give or take," I agreed. "Still, if the log looked like he was shirking, Knox would have him making Earthfall already. That means it's ours. Do we have anything else to worry about?"

Sri shook his head. "We're lucky."

"Then send the specifics to my station and take us over to seventeen."

The pilot activated thrust, which faded to background for me as I swung a panel in to examine in my cradle. I felt a headache coming on and stretched my neck. Over to my left, Kurt began to retch, and Johnny laughed at him as I scanned the telemetry. Couple of breaks, we just need to...wait, that's not right. "Uh, fellas, we got an issue. Sri, focus on these coordinates." I sent them over.

The big screen came up, showing the shield approaching rapidly as the pilot focused cameras and scanners onto the area to give us a composite view. The break in the Shield was substantial, the torn edges distracted from each other in all directions.

"Well, fu..." Johnny breathed, then glanced around uncomfortably. "Getaboutit."

"Uh, boss? I don't feel so good," Kurt mumbled.

Shit, me either, kid. I ignored him for the moment. "Sri: that's much worse than Cobb's report. What happened? What about the Shield's orbit?"

It seemed like we all held our breaths as his fingers danced over the computer console. "It's stable, but only barely. Whatever did this was big and ugly, and hit at a bad angle. Looks like the damage spread along the superstructure, and it took out – oh God! – the automatic compensators in fifteen through eighteen!"

I heard Johnny's sharply indrawn breath.

Catastrophic failure. I felt nauseous. "Cobb missed the secondary damage," I breathed.

Sri swiveled around to face us. "Ring around the rosy, gents."

We all fall down. I glanced over at Kurt, wondering why he hadn't asked any stupid questions, and saw him sitting vacant and glassy-eyed. "Johnny, check the kid." He unhooked the web that held him in place and pushed off with his legs towards Kurt as I turned to Sri. "Can we fix this?"

My pilot looked queasy too as he played the numbers on his display. "I don't know, boss. We'll need every ounce of thrust that Mallard's got, the EVA suit jets, something to bridge the gap to prevent further propagation of the damage until repairs..." He raised his head. "It's bad. I just don't know."

"But if we don't...?"

Sri blew out a breath.

My girls...! I swallowed and took hold of my own fear. "Okay. Report it to the station, then take us in to see what we can do." As Sri started thrust, I looked over at Johnny, who'd put a mask over Kurt's face.

"Oxy," he explained. "His lips were blue." He glanced down at the kid, and I saw Kurt look in my direction. He gave me a weak thumbs-up.

"Nice work, Johnny. Now, how about you get me anything on board that you can turn into a motorized winch?"

Johnny gave me a quizzical look, but pushed off and went across the cabin to rummage for anything that could help.

I released from my station and pushed off to go to Kurt. "Are you okay? Sri's got to pilot, and High-Low's got to handle the tech stuff, so I'm going to need you to go EVA with me."

He swallowed and began to remove the mask, but I stopped him, watched him breathe shakily. "I'm good, boss. Really."

"What the hell happened?"

"Don't know. Got nauseous, figured it was the transition from thrust, but then my head felt like it was splitting, and I passed out."

That reminded me of my own headache, forgotten in the shock of the extent of the Shield damage. I ignored it. "How is it now?"

"Headache's still there, but less. I can function."

I felt thrust change, and grabbed hold of the webbing on Kurt's cradle to keep myself in place.

"We'll be in position in ten minutes," Sri said.

"Suit up," I told Kurt. "Johnny, tell me you got something we can use."

"Hey, I'm a genius, boss. I've got the motorized mechanism off the emergency lock. It's got its own power supply, and it'll work in vacuum."

Genius? You're an electronics and mechanical geek, failed thief, and convict douchebag. But right now, I'll take it and thank you. "Outstanding."

Kurt and I suited up. Johnny clipped the motor and a couple of long spools of ultra-strong cable to my suit, then loaded us up with the rest of our EVA gear. Sri came over to help and double-check our suits once we were at relative stop at section seventeen of the Shield.

He turned me to the main screen and pointed out an area on both schematic and live views. "Run the line from the bow strut hard-point, because it'll take the load we're going to put on it. Link up to the damaged part here" – he indicated a specific point on one side of the gap – "and I'll apply thrust to stop its current motion and start moving it towards the other part. Then you'll cable separately and jump for the other side of the break." He clapped me on the shoulder. "I'll show you exactly where on your heads-up display once you're on the Shield."

I nodded and looked at Kurt, who bit his lip but also nodded. "Will it work, Sri?"

"I don't know."

Shit.

Johnny tapped the newb on his helmet. "Don't get lost out there, SFB: it's a long way down."

I saw Kurt swallow. Johnny, you're such an asshole. "Never mind him, kid. We'll get the job done."

He gave me a weak smile, and we went into the airlock together.

The words 'long way down' seemed to echo in my head as the lock closed and the air cycled out. My headache felt worse, so I tongued some pain reliever from the suit's stores.

The outer hatch opened, and we went out. Kurt and I both linked ends of our respective cables to the bow hard-point and looked down – technically "out" – at the damaged portion of the Shield. Sri had programmed in a schematic overlay in our helmet HUDs to show us where we needed to go. We pushed off towards the target, lines spooling out behind us. Small jets allowed attitude adjustment to get us to the shattered edge of the Shield.

"Your vectors look good, but hurry, guys." Sri's voice was taut. "Structural stability is being strained beyond tolerances."

"Knox going to send us some help, or what?"

"They've scrambled all teams, but if we don't do something, they're gonna get here just in time to watch it all go down the well."

Great, no fucking pressure.

I made contact with the broken Shield edge, and latched my line on before I bounced away, taking the shock with my arms to do so. A few seconds behind me, Kurt did the same, handling it well for a newb. This time I gave him the thumbs-up.

Sri chimed in. "Hang on, guys, I'm applying thrust now to stop the Shield drift. It should give you a boost to push off with; you'll be heading for the other side of the break." The heads-up display of my suit overlay painted the new target location for us to jump towards.

"You ready, S... I mean, Kurt?"

"Yeah, boss. I mean, this is awesome!"

I looked around at the damage and the open space all around. Awesome? Maybe in the Old Testament sense of the word, but he sounds like a kid at an arcade. "Okay, we're going to head for that junction that Sri's set up. On three. One. Two. Thr..."

"Hey, Slade? Can you see all the amazing stars?"

Johnny's voice broke in. "Chief, I'm watching his indicators and he's hypoxic again."

Shit, that's what's wrong with him – euphoria! I thought about our headaches, and wondered about the rumor Kurt had ventured about Knox fucking with our oxy. "I can't afford to have him out here like this, and if you don't get him back quickly, he could die. Johnny, get your suit on and reel him in."

Silence. Then: "You sure you can handle this on your own, boss?"

No, asshole, but what choice do I have? "Don't make me ask again."

"On it."

Out of my peripheral vision, I saw Kurt push off the structure suddenly, hands reaching out. "It's like I can almost touch them, yanno?"

I was about to go grab him when Sri's voice came over the radio, a strange hush in it. "Slade."

"Yeah?"

"We've got incoming tracks. Debris: a lot of it!"

I looked around, but couldn't see anything. Idiot, of course you can't! "Johnny?"

"I'm out, boss. I'll reel in the kid, you take care of business."

Then my suit alarm blared, and I almost went into full panic mode until I saw that it was because I was breathing too fast. Everything else seemed okay.

Sri's voice, tight. "Boss, you need to go. Like, now!"

I did, aiming for where the schematic overlay indicated. The thrust I'd felt as the pod was towing the broken section of the Shield went away, and I concentrated on taking slow, steady breaths in the zero-g. "Okay, tell me what the deal on the incoming is."

"It's our garbage."

"What? But they're always tracking that, moving the Shield when..."

Sri interrupted. "It's not the main mass of it. Station telemetry is telling me that something perturbed the orbit of a sizable chunk – some gravitational anomaly nobody accounted for. The station people are freaked out. I'm hearing that the big science brain types downstairs are tossing theories around like chips at a blackjack table."

I fired my jets to slow and correct my angle of approach. "Take care of Kurt." I made contact, and immediately began hooking my cable to the broken structure. "And get me what's still incoming while I rig this thing!"

"I've got the kid," Johnny interrupted. "He's unconscious but alive."

"Well, get him inside if you want to keep both of you that way," Sri snapped at him. His voice changed, went cold. "Boss, get back here. Get back here now."

Shit. I looked over the damaged area and my gut felt hollow. If I didn't get the edges of the Shield secured... "Doesn't look like it's in the cards."

Sri didn't answer at first, and when he did his voice was low and fast, almost a hiss. "But there's more debris on the way, boss!"

There didn't seem to be much point in answering. You just do your job, Slade. For Earth. For your girls, who need a world worth living in. I worked fast but sure, making certain not to fumble anything, and got the winch Johnny had cobbled together off my suit. It took only a moment to get it hooked it in place and get it started up.

Then the superstructure of the Shield jerked suddenly, and my shoulder and neck took the strain of the sudden change in direction and velocity. Shitshitshit but that hurts...! Only long practice biting down on curses during my prison term working the Shield kept me from screaming it out over the radio link for everyone, including Knox, to hear. Then I was spinning, the blood rushing to and from my head with each move to the point I thought I might pass out. "What...what hap...?"

Sri's voice came over the radio. "You did it, boss! The cable's holding, but you got to get outta there fast. Hit full jets: direction doesn't matter! We'll come get you, but you have to..."

Something took a swipe at me. A sharp pain in my leg eclipsed everything to that point. My grip was torn away from the cable, and I had a moment to panic about being lost in space before I blacked out, thankful for that small mercy.

***

"...Come in. For God's sake, Slade, come in!"

When I opened my eyes, the view was dizzying: sun, stars, Earth. Then I realized that the dizzy feeling was blood rushing to and away from my head as I cartwheeled through space. "Sri?"

"Thank God! Slade, are you all right?"

The spin was playing havoc with me, and I couldn't feel my right leg. "Not so hot." I nearly blacked out again, but swallowed, fighting it. "My leg..."

Sri interrupted. "Yeah, sorry, boss, but it was holed, and the suit sealed the breach automatically, amputating it. But shut up about that for a minute, 'cause this is really important: I need to know about your jets: they online?"

A quick check showed them to be nonfunctional. "They're worse off than me. You're going to have to come get me."

He didn't answer immediately. Shit. "You can't."

"I'm sorry, Slade. We don't have the reaction mass left for the delta-v to get to you."

"How...?" I had to lick my lips. "How long?"

Johnny's voice came back over the speaker, and he sounded tired. "Long enough to take your downers, boss."

Shit. He meant the high-powered tranquilizers among the suit's emergency meds. I'm not going to make it.

"Slade, this is Knox. I want you to know that your actions were directly responsible for saving the Shield. I know I speak for all of humanity when I say that your sacrifice..."

I shut off my radio and listened to the quiet instead.

I thought of my girls and how I'd never see them again, but that maybe – just maybe – I'd done something that would help make their lives better.

Earth got progressively closer. I thought about taking the downers before I'd hit atmo: I really did.

But then I wouldn't be able to say goodbye.

I love you, Megan and Jessica.

Daddy's finally coming home.

###

About David M. Hoenig

DAVID IS A SPLIT CLASS writer/academic surgeon with several cat-familiars and a wife. He tries to follow Monty Python's advice by always looking on the bright side of life and has only needed to be rescued by the Judean Peoples Front on rare occasions. He's published in numerous anthologies and magazines, including Grim Dark Magazine, Cast of Wonders, and others.

Connect with David here: www.castrumpress.com/david-m-hoenig

A WINTER'S DAY

EDWARD AHERN

Peter turned to the serviceman from Sub-Zero Cooling. They were standing next to Peter's converted garage.

"That'll be twenty-four fifty for the overhaul. Just set your finger here for the transfer."

Peter winced. "So much? Last time it was only around fourteen hundred dollars."

The Sub-Zero rep shrugged. "Last repair was ten years ago, and you admitted you haven't run the refrigeration unit since then. Things get clogged and rusty."

It wasn't his money, but Peter hated to spend that much for four days of use. "You've checked the insulation in the garage? No leakage? And it'll handle an outside temperature up to eighty Celsius?"

"No problem, Mr. Kessler. The original install was forty years ago, but we've replaced just about everything except the framing. Couldn't help noticing the inside. Responsive artwork, interactive internet, voice-activated hospital bed, height-adjusting toilet. Nice."

"Thanks."

Peter applied his fingerprint payment and hustled back into their house. The outside temperature had sagged into minus five Celsius, and his hands were already numb. Alison met him at their back door.

"Unit up and running?"

"Yeah, now we just agonize until Rob's arrival."

"Nobody's coming. Sarah holoed. Says she's committed to a seminar in California, but I think she just hates meeting her brother. Roberto's still in the nursing home, so his brother and sister aren't coming. What really hurts is that Eunice and Preston aren't coming either, so even our kids will be missing at Christmas."

"What excuses did they offer?"

"Does it matter, Peter? Rob's a nightmare for the grandkids. I know we rely on what he pays us, and I know he's your cousin, but I just can't warm to an ethanol popsicle."

Peter stared at the refrigerator calendar, so he wouldn't have to see Alison's expression. December twenty-second. Rob would arrive early on Christmas Eve. Peter worked up a crooked smile. "We've talked this to death. What he pays me to administer his affairs keeps us afloat. And we only put up with him once a decade."

"It's been forty years' worth of decades, Peter. He's still thirty-three, and you're already seventy-four. God forbid you should die between now and eighty-four. What would I do? I couldn't handle things."

Peter admitted to himself that she was right. "Okay. Once he's out of the cryonics facility and been shipped over here, once he's had a chance to acclimate, I'll ask him to switch to institutional resurrection. The kids are long gone, we can hopefully get by on what we have."

Alison stepped over and hugged him. "Thank you. It's like having Lazarus as a roommate and wondering when the miracle's going to wear off."

***

The cryonics facility called the next morning. "Mr. Kessler?"

"Yes." Confirmed Peter

"This is Teresa Richardson at the Ever-Young Preservation Facility. Your cousin, Rob Tomasso, has been successfully revived. He's being acclimated with internal and external solvents so that his body can handle up to minus ten Celsius. Is your accommodation ready?"

"Yes." Responded Peter in the affirmative.

"Our representative will be at your house at eleven a.m. as scheduled, to inspect your system and maintain it during the visit. Is it running?" Asked Richardson.

"Yes," Answered Peter, "And the plastic tunnel is set to be hooked up to your delivery vehicle."

"Excellent. I'm required to remind you that despite the low temperatures, his internal solvents are highly flammable, so no open flames or equipment that might spark." Warned Richardson

"Yes, I know. How does he look?" Asked Peter

"Ah, I haven't actually seen him, Mr. Kessler," Said Richardson, "But his records indicate full consciousness and only minute dermal frostbite."

"And his nutrition?" Peter continued.

"Mixed and ready to be injected into his permanent IVs. Our technician will be bringing them with her." Confirmed Richardson.

"Thank you, I'll be waiting." Peter hung up and again marveled at alcohol-based life. If the sun burns out, he thought, Rob will be able to go outside for a walk.

Carolyn the technician hovered in the next morning. After three hours, she closed her checklist. "Serviceable," she pronounced. "We can proceed."

As Carolyn left, Peter felt a tinge of regret. If she'd flunked his juiced-up garage, there would be no visit.

***

The Porta-Patient flew in three minutes early on Christmas Eve morning. Peter had been waiting outside in his thermal suit, scarfed, hooded, and gloved. Alison waited alongside him.

A woman disembarked and walked towards Peter. "Mr. Kessler?"

"Yes?" Replied Peter.

"I'm Eliza. Mr. Tomasso's had his breakfast injection, and shouldn't need to be fed again until one p.m. If you could please show me your power grid, I'll set up the data display and monitors."

"Is he cheerful?" Asked Peter.

"We don't interact with our transports, Mr. Kessler," Eliza said in a mildly admonishing tone. "So, I can't tell you about his emotional state."

"Of course. I just meant..." Peter's voice wavered before hardening. "Never mind."

Once the passage had been hooked up, Rob stepped out of the container and through the passage to the garage. The plastic was translucent, and Peter got distorted views of an attenuated biped moving toward its lair. Five minutes after the container left, Eliza let him in through the double doors of the temperature adjustment chamber.

"Hello, Rob," he said.

"Peter." The voice was slushy, like Rob's lungs were full of ice crystals.

They shook hands, Peter's thick glove almost hiding Rob's bare hand. Over time, Rob's skin had turned clear. Peter could see blue blood vessels and ropy muscles.

Eliza keyed the intercom. "Mr. Tomasso? If you need something, please just buzz me. I sleep from eleven p.m. to six a.m., but if you need me during that time, just ring and I'll be suited up and ready in ten minutes."

"Thank you, Eliza."

Peter chimed in. "Everything's set up for you, Rob. The computer has the condensed world and national histories for the last ten years. The usual interactive internet. The holo projector is set up, but cable television finally died a few years ago, so just feed programming from your devices onto the big screen." Peter realized he sounded nervous and stopped talking.

"Is everyone already here?"

"It's just Alison and me again this decade."

Rob looked down. "What happened?"

"Well, Rebecca's husband still doesn't want her visiting her ex. Roberto's in a nursing home now, heavily sedated because of his manic attacks. Sarah says she has to stay in California because of a teaching seminar. And our kids need to spend the holidays with their kids. I've arranged a holoconference the day after Christmas."

"So, nobody. Sorry, nobody except you and Alison."

"She'll conference with us when I feed you this evening. Do you need to rest up?"

Rob smiled, his lips tinged gray-brown rather than pink. "I think I've had plenty of that. You know that when I'm dormant there's no breathing, no heartbeat. But I dream. Not happily. Ten years of bad dreams. It's like files rasping my skin until it's ground off."

Peter wanted to sit down, but knew the cold would seep through his insulated pants. "I've provided a copy of your living estate account in a folder labeled 'Revenues and Expenditures, 2060-2070'."

"Thanks. My auditors provided a summary before I left the center. You've been a faithful steward. How's your health, Peter?"

Peter hesitated, then guessed that Rob would've had that audited as well. "Pretty good, except for a heart attack. They had to put in a couple self-monitoring stents. I'm okay now."

Just then, the refrigeration fan shut down. They waited in uncomfortable silence for several seconds; then the backup generator kicked in and the fan started whirring again. The intercom clicked, and Eliza's voice came in. "Gentlemen, the refrigeration motor has shut down. I don't know why yet. The solar back-up generator will keep your unit refrigerated to a safe level, but there's not enough power available to use your exterior comm devices. I've shut them down as a precaution. Please bear with me while I investigate the problem."

They stared at each other. Being locked in made Peter feel colder, much colder. Because of sparking dangers, he had no battery-operated heating elements, and unlike Rob, he was going to progressively lose warmth.

Peter let out a nervous laugh. "I knew I should have put a chess set in here."

"That's all right, Peter, I have both too much time and too little. Tell me about Roberto."

"Not much to tell that you haven't already viewed. Your brother's fantasy trilogies sold quite well for some years, but a few years ago he developed clinical euphoria and had to be moved to a facility. He's not taking our calls, but sent a hologram regretting not being able to come."

"And he's seventy-six – no, no, wait, seventy-seven. And Sarah, what's she doing?"

"Well, you were still active when she married the ex-priest. She buried him six years ago. She's still working, teaching half days at a Japanese school. We exchange Christmas selfies, not much more contact than that," Peter admitted.

Rob reached over and touched Peter's shoulder. "Peter, you're my hold-fast while I'm awake, and my source of unfiltered truth. Please tell me what's really happening with the family."

Peter hesitated. The truth was unfriendly, brutal. But it burst out.

"They are avoiding you. Their big brothers morphed into something they don't know. You look and act differently now. You have memories, and they have lives. They're afraid of you; they loved who you were and not what you are."

"I know Alison feels the same," Rob said. What about you?"

"We've always been grateful for your support, couldn't have put the kids through school without it –"

"That's not what I asked."

Peter's breath exhaust formed a transient bridge between the two men. "We were close before your change. But I remember who you were, and don't know who you are. Your care has supported us, and I'm grateful, but I can't get over a sense of unease. You're different now, Rob, a new species, and maybe you need friends like yourself. There. I've said it."

Rob slowly nodded. "Thank you for being honest. I so wanted to see Sarah. She and I were closest. But even twenty years ago, she was afraid of me. Have I become a ghoul, Peter?"

"No, of course not."

Rob stared at his right hand. "They barely mentioned that I'd lose all sense of touch. Taste and smell as well, of course, but I really miss the tingle of touching another's skin. Interesting that you and Alison haven't divorced."

Peter was taken aback. "Pardon?"

"Thirty years ago, I thought you two were barely civilized to each other. I made contingency plans for institutional care."

Peter remembered. They'd fought over Rob's impact on their children. "No, we got over that. But I'm old and getting older. Have you thought about transferring the awakenings to an institution? Or maybe better still, just sleeping until they find a cure for mucosal melanoma?"

Rob's smile tightened, his teeth visible under the translucent skin. "Well, cousin mine, I had to choose between being frozen stiff for up to a century or two, or coming back every decade for ersatz living. But once reanimated, I couldn't shift to long-term cryonics – the body chemistry had been altered – so I have an eternity of ten-year look-ins."

"I know, but I still think you need to switch to institutional care. Alison and I won't be able-bodied the next time you come back."

Peter smelled alcohol. Flammable tears were meandering down Rob's cheeks.

"I'd assumed, Peter, that each generation would want to meet with me, to meet the frozen old/young man. Morbid curiosity, if nothing else. They wouldn't know me enough to love me, but they'd be interested and sympathetic. Hasn't happened. It's just you and Alison, and I pay you both to be here. If I turn myself over to Ever-Young, it'll be worse. I'll be with a bunch of high-octane mummies."

The intercom clicked. "Mr. Tomasso, Mr. Kessler, the solar cooling generator's not handling the load well, so I'm going to have to raise the temperature to minus ten and shut off the lighting."

Peter felt a surge of worry. "Eliza, what about the primary cooling system? Is it fixable?"

"Not good news, sir. It's fried. There were years of wasp nests built inside the compressor, where they wouldn't be seen in routine maintenance. The fire took out the wiring and the microchips. We're having a new unit droned in, but it'll be at least two or three more hours. It would have taken even longer to arrange a conveyance vehicle for Mr. Tomasso. Your wife is here and wants to talk with you before I key off the speakers."

"Peter, are you all right in that cold?" Alison asked.

"Cold as hell, but otherwise all right." The lie didn't hurt nearly as much as the plumbing in and around his heart, which had started aching as his body strained to maintain its heat. Nothing to be done, so no point in mentioning it.

Alison's voice became agitated. "Rob, can you hear me okay?"

"Yes, Alison. Hello, how are you?"

"Rob, you have to let us go."

"Alison!" Peter yelled.

"No, don't stop me. I can be a little braver talking into a mic than face to face. Rob, we've known each other a long time. But that's just it. We're old; we won't be able to handle your requirements next time. We'd be a danger to you. You have to move on, to be with your own kind."

Peter interrupted. "Alison, please stop. She's just concerned about me, Rob, but she's right. Our clocks are running down."

Rob cleared his throat. It made a sound like crackling ice. "Thank you, Alison. I appreciate your candor. Peter and I will sort this out. "

"Mr. Tomasso, I'm going to have to dial down lights and comms now."

"Okay, Eliza. Don't worry, Alison, I'll take care of Peter."

"Powering down in three, two, one." The lights went out, leaving Rob and Peter in complete darkness. The fan blades slowed, and the cold seemed a little less bitter to Peter.

The two men remained silent for two or three minutes. Peter sat down, hoping it would be easier on his heart. "She didn't –"

"Never mind, Peter. Funny. In the dark it's like my ten-year naps, except I can control my thinking. What are the doctors telling you about your life expectancy, Peter, given your heart issues?"

"They aren't willing to give me an end date, but the insurance actuarial tables say I've got maybe fifteen more years."

"Did you ever think of going cryonic?"

Peter laughed. It hurt his chest. "Don't have the money, and I don't want to leave Alison alone."

"Yeah, it was different for me."

They sat again in total dark and almost silence, listening to the muffled noise of the cooling unit and their chesty rasps. Peter hadn't thought to bring his nitroglycerine tablets, and hoped he wouldn't need them.

"Peter, do you lock up your house at night?"

"Out here? No, almost never, unless we're going away on a trip. Why do you ask?"

"Just wanted to get a taste of how you live. Tell me about what you do every day."

They spent what Peter guessed was two more hours talking about Peter's daily life: errands, the layout of the house, neighborhood spats, conversations with his children. Toward the end, as Peter was shivering uncontrollably, they heard the screech of heavy equipment being dragged over concrete, which made the waiting worse, like the moment between when the doorbell rings and when it's opened to reveal the police.

Relays clicked; the lights came on; Eliza's voice came through the speaker. "The new unit's installed. Give me a few minutes to run checks and I can let you out, Peter. You must be frozen."

"D-damned near."

As the fans revved up, Peter could feel the temperature drop. "Rob, you're overdue for your feeding. Now that I can see to work, I can give you the injection."

Rob let out a breaking-glass laugh. "You're hypothermic. I'll get Eliza to do it. Another fifteen minutes won't matter. Go take a hot bath and get human."

Ten minutes later, Alison helped Peter across the lawn and into the house. His legs were so wobbly he opted for the downstairs bathroom. As Alison ran the hot water, he chucked his thermal clothes and underwear and stepped into the bath. The heat shocked his nerve endings so badly he dropped into the water, splashing Alison. "God, I hurt so much, but it's delicious."

Alison stayed with him while he soaked. "Do we have to go back and give him his ethylene injection?"

"No, I think he knows I'm shot until tomorrow."

"Ouch."

"Best I could do while still frozen. Once I've thawed, just feed me something and we can go to bed. Maybe a couple of sleeping pills to drown out the sound of the compressor."

"You're on."

The alarm went off at five a.m., and Peter, still groggy from the pill, knocked the alarm off the table before retrieving it and shutting it off. Alison stirred but dropped back to sleep. As Peter got up to go to the bathroom, he smelled something sweetly alcoholic, like anisette or strega mixed with something harsher. He postponed the pee and sniffed his way downstairs, following the smells. They came from the first-floor bathroom.

The tub was full to almost overflowing, and the water was tinted green-brown. A skin sack lay at the bottom of the tub, filled with what Peter knew were bones. "Jesus Christ," Peter blurted out. "Jesus Christ."

He ran out of the house in his underwear, ignoring the cold, and banged on the door of the service cubicle. "Eliza! Eliza!"

"What is it?"

"Rob's killed himself!"

Eliza opened the door and stepped out, wrapped in a frumpy gray robe that looked warm. "There hasn't been an alarm."

"Check your visual monitors! Is he in there?"

She stepped inside the trailer and ran back out. "He's gone. Where is he?"

"In my tub, I think."

Eliza called her center and the local police, and followed Peter back into the house and the downstairs bath.

"Holy shit!" she said. "Another one. Can't tell if it's him."

"Who the hell else would it be?"

Within half an hour, the yard swarmed with police and technicians from Ever-Young. By late afternoon, Rob and Alison were summoned into the garage, now equalized with the outside temperature of minus three Celsius.

A police sergeant seemed to be in charge. "Mr. and Mrs. Kessler, here's what we've established so far. The DNA of the remains in your bathtub matches that of Rob Tomasso. Someone, perhaps Mr. Tomaso himself, jiggered the sensor alarms so his departure wouldn't be noted by the technician. He left us a hologram selfie. Please sit down and watch it."

Rob appeared in front of them, the image quality good enough that his teeth showed through his lips. He smiled at the recorder. "This selfie is done for the police, Ever-Young, Peter and Alison, and my immediate family. Neither Eliza, Ever-Young, nor Peter and Alison are responsible for my demise, which will have been self-inflicted. The death is assured, but before then, I'd like at least a few seconds of feeling human. Arrangements for my estate can be found on a separate file. I love you with the same intensity that I had a dozen conscious days ago. But I understand that after forty years, my memory has worn away. I want a few people to mourn me, rather than continue on without context."

Peter glanced around at the faces in his converted garage. The cops and Ever-Young technicians had their game faces on. Alison was crying.

Rob concluded. "For my ransomed time to have been meaningful, it needed positive experience. But I'd sentenced myself to loops of troubled sleep, and conscious moments without sensations or emotions. I'm going to feel myself once more. Goodbye."

As they filed out of the garage, Peter took Eliza aside. "Back when I brought you into the bathroom, you said 'Another one.' What did you mean?"

Eliza glanced around. "Okay, you deserve to know. Few people who sign up for decade revival last fifty years. They get too lonely, too alienated. They usually just go for a walk outside until they thaw and sublimate. I have to leave."

Peter watched her lift off. Time, he thought, to clean the bathtub.

###

ABOUT EDWARD AHERN

ED AHERN RESUMED WRITING AFTER forty-odd years in foreign intelligence and international sales. He's had two hundred stories and poems published so far, and three books. Ed works the other side of writing at Bewildering Stories, where he sits on the review board and manages a posse of five review editors.

Connect with Ed here: www.castrumpress.com/edward-ahern

COLONY

Gunnar De Winter

A bleak sun rose and pierced through the smog, casting pale yellow light on the packed jumble of gray carboplatin buildings. Not that W#1528 could see it. The underground bowels of the city were her world.

She carefully checked the vital signs of the fetuses floating in the fluid sacs in front of her. When she finished and saved the data, the next assignment appeared on her foldable tablet.

CARE Fb#2 – Fb#12. Room Fb1. Initiate at 1230. Allotted time: 1.45.

Fb duty it was. She had always been fascinated by the Fb's, though she didn't get to see a lot of them. The adult B's were an even rarer sight.

In the few free moments between assignments, W#1528 went to grab lunch from one of the molfabs at designated points in the building. With a squish, her ration of nutritional goo squirted out of the nozzle.

She slurped up the semi-transparent gunk and sauntered to room Fb1. Her hand hovered mere inches above the access pad. She stopped. She heard murmurings.

"... Chemical castration... gene silencing... reversible... new..."

A deep voice startled her.

"W#1528?"

She turned around and looked up at the tall, muscular S. She swallowed and nodded.

"Right on time," the bald young man informed her. When working in Fb rooms, one was always guarded. "Go on, please."

Apparently, he hadn't heard the voices. Even better, he wasn't aware of the fact that she had. She put her hand on the pad and a section of the gray-and-white wall slid back.

Two small pale youngsters turned to look at her and her guard. One male, one female, each with an intense gaze and unusually large head. Their skin was so light

83

it verged on translucency. Veins crisscrossed the landscape of their bodies. Red-rimmed eyes looked at W#1528.

"You," said the female one. "Can," added her male counterpart. "Go," finished the woman, addressing the S but not taking her eyes off W#1528.

The big man hesitated slightly before he inclined his head and turned around.

As the wall closed behind the S, the young man said, "I am B#15, and this" – he waved a hand at his colleague – "is B#16."

W#1528 didn't know how to respond. Adult, or near adult, B's. Unwillingly, she looked at the semi-transparent artificial wombs in the room, noticeably larger than the ones in the Fw facilities. Small fetuses floated contentedly in their amniotic fluid. She realized she had been staring at them for a while and, with a quick movement, returned her attention to the B's standing before her.

"Please," B#15 said, gesturing towards a transparent one-piece chair that hadn't been there on W#1528's earlier short visits to room Fb1. W#1528 walked over and saw B#16 prepare a syringe, plunging it into a small unmarked vial of clear fluid. Anxiety rose like bile in the back of her throat. She sat down, unable to avoid glancing at the female B.

B#15 must have noticed this. "It's all right. Calm down. You've done nothing wrong."

"Quite the contrary, in fact," B#16 added. "Your work and dedication to the city is exemplary, which is one of the reasons why we've chosen you."

W#1528 swallowed. "Chosen me?"

"Yes," B#16 continued. "To advance our society"," B#15 chimed in. "To strengthen the city and its inhabitants."

"I am honored." After all, if any caste knew what was best for the city, it would be its architects, the B's. The ones who controlled and steered everything, the ones who saw what no one else did and whose sole job and duty it was to make sure the city-state survived and thrived.

"Could you roll up your sleeve?" B#16 asked.

W#1528 obeyed, revealing her pale arm, dark veins throbbing beneath soft marble skin.

"We want to ask two things of you," B#15 stated. "First," his female colleague continued, "'you'll be assigned to your regular duties again tomorrow. But this time, you'll receive additional instructions from us on your tablet. Please follow these carefully."

"You'll need this." B#15 handed her another unmarked vial. "Hide it, keep it safe."

"Second," B#16 said, pressing a small piece of cotton to W#1528's elbow pit. B#15 went on: "You can't tell anyone about this. About the injection and your new assignment." B#16 took over again. "There are some insurgent elements in the city, and we're not yet sure about the extent of their influence. Everyone could be implicated."

W#1528 nodded.

"Good," the B's said in unison. As if performing an often-practiced choreography, they turned and left the room. The door closed behind them.

After a few dazed moments of confusion, W#1528 began her tasks, tending to Fb's 2 to 12.

The remainder of her allowed awake time played itself out as any other day. More care tasks, occasional small meals, and then, sleep.

But, unlike any other day, her slumber was restless.

***

Something – someone? – was sitting on her chest. Bright red eyes watched her. The creature, hidden in darkness, grinned, revealing shiny teeth. She tried to shake it off, to no avail. The thing just sat and watched her with its unrelenting gaze while it pinned her to the bed. The details of its features seemed to shift continuously. Only the wicked grin didn't waver.

***

Panting and sweaty, she jolted up. The lights were still turned off. She clutched her chest. The tight feeling hadn't gone away. Swallowing, she ran a hand over her bald head. It felt rough. Impossible. W's weren't supposed to grow hair. Frantically, she rubbed both hands over her scalp.

The lights came on. She forced herself to calm down. All around her, her sisters stirred in their sleeping berths, aroused by the bluish light that gently brightened.

A slight buzz that came from all directions told her that the daily tasks and instructions were being sent to the personal tablets. Hers received a message as well.

CARE Fw#1198 – Fw#1298. Rooms Fw12 – Fw13. Initiate at 0630. Allotted time: 5.30.

Like a stuck record, events unfurled exactly as they always did. Gobbling up breakfast goo, mindlessly navigating to the room where she was expected, and beginning her tasks: checking fetal vitals, administering nutritional liquids, cleaning artificial wombs, and performing any necessary small maintenance operations.

But the odd feeling hadn't disappeared. Her chest hurt, tender breasts screaming for some form of attention. As she stood before Fw#1235's artificial womb, she noticed a dark sheen on the smooth scalp of her reflection. What was happening to her?

Her flexible tablet, stuffed in the rear pocket of her light-green pants, buzzed again. Casually, she unfolded the screen and saw additional instructions. She glanced around surreptitiously. No one was close enough to peek.

Add 10ml of vial fluid to nutritional mixture of Fw#1250 – Fw#1262.

W#1528 erased the instruction. She took a few deep breaths and continued her work as if nothing had happened, until she reached Fw#1250. Her heart sped up like a tribal war drum. Did she trust the B's? Why shouldn't she? With as much nonchalance as she could muster, she walked over to the cabinet in the middle of the room, opened a drawer, and took out a syringe filled with an immune-boosting mixture. Fetuses that would grow to be the new generation of workers weren't allowed to be ill or otherwise deviant – only, according to the numbers on her screen, nothing was wrong with Fw#1250.

She returned to the small seed of a human being and emptied the syringe into its nutritional feed. But instead of discarding the syringe, she stealthily refilled it with fluid from the mystery vial. This too was released into the tube that led to Fw#1250.

Nothing happened.

She slid the empty syringe into her breast pocket, which seemed to be standing slightly further out than she remembered. She felt her sore chest and couldn't shake the feeling that bulges were forming beneath her nipples.

Pushing her worries to the dark depths of her unconsciousness – W's weren't supposed to fret about anything; that was the B's job – she continued her tasks. When she reached Fw#1263 without incident, a sigh of relief nevertheless blew the boulder of worry from her shoulders.

The rest of the day passed in dreary monotony, which was beginning to annoy her: a curious sentiment she hadn't felt before.

✳✳✳

The beast returned and immobilized her. But this time, she unleashed the full fury of her anger – another emotion she wasn't familiar with. Surprise lurked behind the eyes of the thing on top of her. It leaned forward, and its full weight bore down on her. She screamed until she ran out of breath. After her strength had left her, she looked at the creature. Details began to emerge. The grin had disappeared from the face of the female winged gargoyle and was replaced by budding rage.

✳✳✳

A sharp inhalation. With a sudden move she sat up. Clammy clothes clung to her prickling skin. Still apprehensive, she turned her head left and right. Everything was silent, except for the curiously synchronized breathing of her sisters. It reminded her of a breeze finding its way through a dense forest, rustling the leaves on its path.

She paused. She knew what a forest was, but couldn't remember seeing one. In fact, she had trouble recollecting anything outside of the underground warren. Surely, she had been outside once. Hadn't she?

The soft hum that accompanied the lights prepared her for daybreak – or at least for the artificial analogue that was supposed to pass for it, she thought wryly. Her sisters stirred. She swung her legs over the edge of her bed and ran a hand over her scalp. She could already discern the individual hairs poking through skin that had

86

always been smooth. Grass pushing through cracks in the concrete. She needed to find a razor soon.

Swiftly, W#1528 changed into her work outfit and hid her growing breasts as best she could.

She was unable to shake the feeling of intent gazes burning holes in her back. The feeling was joined by a murmur of whispers. Her sisters might have noticed her changes. But when she surreptitiously looked around, everyone seemed to be going about their business as usual.

Her tablet buzzed. Even before she read the message, the red flashing icon alerted her of its unusual content.

Daily duties suspended.

Await further instructions.

They must have found out. But how much would they know? And who were 'they,' exactly? B#15 and #16 did speak of insurgent elements, but hadn't divulged any details. She remained seated while she fought her roiling emotions.

This wasn't paranoia. Her sisters were indeed staring at her. W#1528 looked down at her hands. Fingers nervously fondled the hem of her shirt.

The last of her siblings left to pursue whatever task had been allocated to her. All alone in the large dormitory, W#1528 found herself paralyzed with indecision. Should she flee? But where could she run to?

"W#1528, follow me."

Without making a sound, an S had appeared in front of her. The black double bands encircling his muscular shoulders indicated his rank. Not just a soldier, this one.

Wordlessly, she obeyed. The S let her pass and fell in behind her.

"Due to some...irregularities...that have been brought to our attention, the city's surveillance cadre has decided to ask you a few questions. Left here. Please, cooperate fully and keep in mind that all we do is for the good of the city. Left again, and then the second on the right."

The rest of the walk proceeded in silence.

"Stop here," the tall man said, after several more turns and smoothly descending walkways.

He pushed an invisible button on the wall. It gave way slightly and a portion of the wall slid back and sideward, revealing a room that contained only a gleaming, transparent carboplast table with a chair on either side.

"Enter, please."

She did as she was told.

"Have a seat."

Again, silent obedience.

"Please hand over your tablet."

A slight hesitation tempered her movements, but after a few moments submission to authority won the skirmish against insurrection. She handed over the rolled-up screen.

"Thank you. I'll be right back." He turned around and left. The wall slid back in place as soon as he had stepped out.

Maintaining an appearance of calm, W#1528's mind was in turmoil and kept churning out scenarios of what might happen next.

Tiny holes, hidden away in the edges of the cubical room, began to excrete a color- and odorless gas. The last thing W#1528 remembered before laying her head to rest on her arms was the sturdy step of someone entering the room.

***

The thing still held her down, but the obscuring fog had dissipated. Her assailant had been revealed. The gargoyle's pale ruffled feathers and greasy strings of hair signaled a majesty long gone. Creased skin told the tale of a once healthy and fit being withering away. The gnarled joints were signposts of lost flexibility. She saw it now. Its efforts to keep her subservient were the final death throes of a blind tyrant who refused to understand that its last days crept near. Suddenly, the world quaked...

***

"Wake up, W#1528. Wake up." The S was shaking her. As soon as he saw her blink, he retreated from view.

Slowly, W#1528's vision and awareness returned. She was in a large dome-shaped room, lying on the ground in a central circular depression. In front of her stood a semi-circular table. Tall, ancient men were seated there. The K's. The fathers of all. The five men whose genetic material formed half of that of all the city's inhabitants. Indoctrinated deference forced her gaze towards the floor and kept her prostrate before the demi-gods.

K#2 took the word. Moist smacking sounds accompanied his words. "W#1528, daughter, what happened to you? You destabilize the city."

She shuddered with conflicting emotions. Her eyes darted left and right. "Father. Noble father. The city's strength and dominance are all I have in mind."

"Commendable. But still you fail to explain how your recent development contributes to this. Or how it has come about."

"It's... I have been chosen for this. The B's, they told me it would make the city better. Stronger."

"The B's told you this? They did this? More details, W#1528. Which B's? What's their plan?"

By now, she had managed to ward the worst trembling from her voice. "I don't know much, father. They fear treason. But perhaps it's time for some change. Things have stayed static for too long." Where did that come from? She frowned.

Despite his emaciated, skeletal appearance, K#2 didn't look frail or fragile; quite the contrary. As he stood up, dozens of life support tubes plunging into his upper back, he menacingly towered over W#1528.

"Preposterous," the tall living skeleton spat, looking down at the target of his ire. "Do you not understand anything? In the vigor of youth, you and yours always must rebel, like the ancients who revolted against the gods. But what you do not see, what you refuse to see, is that the gods are just as envious of you as you are of them. They lust for the joy and pain that speckles the tableau of your existence. The gods are grand marble statues, weathering the onslaught of time's torrent, all the while coveting the frantic lives of the ephemeral ones."

"But father," W#1528 audaciously interjected, even though the quaver in her voice had returned with a vengeance, "do you not aspire to be like a god? If it's so bad, then why?"

"Foolish little child! Do you not hear? Do you not listen? Never have I deemed one way of life good and another one bad. We," K#2 spread his thin brown arms, marred by scars to include the other kings, "remake ourselves into beings at the edge of eternity so you don't have to. What you fail to grasp, despite my best efforts and carefully chosen words, is that to become godlike, you must relinquish your humanity. For the greater good, we have chosen to do so." A long, gnarled finger was pointed at her. "Would you?"

She swallowed. "I... I don't know... But I would like to have the choice."

"You insolent brat! Can't you see that..."

"Calm down, dear." K#2 shut up immediately. The other K's turned their heads towards the origin of the silky voice that deserved – commanded – their full attention. W#1528 lifted her head.

From the dark recesses behind the K's table, Q stepped forth. The one Q, the only Q. Her straight, raven-black hair lined a gorgeous face. The essence of beauty emanated from her features. Her eyes were bright blue pools of infinity that spoke of eons past.

W#1528 pressed her forehead against the floor while Q walked over to her. The only sound was the soft rustle of Q's silk robe, clinging around curves that could drive men crazy with lust and kill women with jealousy.

"Darling daughter, please stand up."

W#1528 carefully looked ahead, gaze falling upon the sandaled feet of her mother. She swallowed. Slowly she stood up, keeping her eyes fixated on the marble beneath her feet.

Q took hold of W#1528's chin and gently pushed it up. "Look at me, dear."

W#1528's nervously flitting eyes eventually came to rest upon the divine face of the city's matriarch. "Mother," she whispered.

Q smiled, radiating splendor throughout the room. K#2 fell back into his chair, breathing heavily.

"My husband" – she gently inclined her head in the direction of K#2 – "can be a tad belligerent. But, my dear, this doesn't change the fact that he has a point. We all have our function, our tasks. The preservation of the city is a goal which, I'm sure you'll agree, takes precedence over all others. Trust me, darling, all we ask of you, all we do, all of it is for the good of the city and is based on centuries of experience and fine-tuning."

W#1528 fought back tears of unknown origin. Awe, disillusion, shame, she couldn't tell. She stammered. "I'm... I'm sorry, mother. I... I..."

Q folded her arms around her daughter, the rebel unaware of her rebellion, and put a carefully manicured hand on the back of her daughter's stubble-covered head. "There, there, dear," she whispered to W#1528, who was almost a full foot shorter. "It's all right. Everything is all right."

"No," a hidden voice exclaimed.

"It is not," another one added.

As one man, the K's got up out of their seats and looked around fervently, life support tubes trembling like strands in a disturbed spider web.

"Who speaks such heresy?" K#2 yelled in his usual theatrical tone.

"We are, father," B#15 said as he emerged from the shadows on the upper balcony. "We are." Other B's stepped forward as well, observing the dance they had orchestrated between their mother, fathers, and chosen sibling.

"Lunacy!" K#2 bellowed. "What has gotten into you!?"

"The stagnation of the city has, father," B#15, who appeared to have taken the lead, spoke clearly.

His twin sister continued. "We quickly saw that the root of the city's stagnation was the stagnation of its mother and fathers."

Q, who had let go of W#1528 a few moments earlier, turned around with fluent elegance, surveying the brightest of her countless children. The gifted caste. The minds behind the city's smooth functioning. "Explain yourselves, dearest sons and daughters." Despite a hard edge that had been absent earlier, her tone was still friendly.

"You see, mother, the variation in the city's inhabitants is direly low. The genetic material is too... limited, coming only from you and our five fathers. Besides," he shrugged, "you know as well as I do that we could easily begin to remedy this. But neither you nor our fathers were willing to do so. Instead, you archaically clung to the desire to birth a whole society based on your genes, and yours alone. It has gone far enough. We *will*," – he emphasized this last word – "introduce more variation, either through rescinding the reproductive inhibition or by introducing new material into the fetuses. Preferably both. And on the strength of this variation, we will build a new culture."

The clenched jaws of Q marred her soft features.

"Mutiny!" K#2 yelled. "You won't get away with this, you ungrateful bastards. We have given your kind the keys to the city, the chance to design eternity. We should have known it was too great an honor, that it demanded too much foresight from a caste of nothing more than ennobled W's."

"Too late, father," B#15 snapped. "The wheels have already been set in motion. Look at her"." He pointed at W#1528. "'She's the first of the new Q's."

W#1528's eyes widened. It began to make sense now.

B#16 continued. "And, if you've read the latest reports, you'll surely have noticed that several fetuses are showing an unusual developmental trajectory. They're the next ones. The seeds of our new society."

The K's walked in circles agitatedly. K#2 stopped and fixed his long, bony index finger on B#15. "You will be stopped. Guards!"

Amidst the confusion, Q had wrapped her hands around W#1528's neck and had effortlessly picked up her daughter, squeezing the life out of her.

Before her vision went black, the soon-to-be Q was aware of several armed S's storming into the room, welcomed by the loud triumphant laughter of the K's.

***

She thrashed and buckled in an attempt to dispel the despicable gargoyle. Its grip diminished, and she succeeded. The creature landed next to her. She turned quickly and brought all her strength to bear as she strangled the remnant of the once powerful being. Tossing aside the corpse, she got up. An intricate golden crown adorned her long black hair. Feathers of a similar color shone brightly as she spread her large wings.

***

The impact of her fall knocked the wind out of her. The deep reflexive inhalation that followed reintroduced her to the here and now. Q lay before her, a dark red dot blemishing her otherwise flawless forehead.

W#1528 looked around.

A dozen brawny S's circled the whimpering K's, whose ancient faces contorted with incredulity. Cheers from the balcony overhead echoed through the large room.

"Welcome back, W#1528," B#15 said. "Good to see you're all right." He returned his attention to the leading S, whose shoulders were encircled by a black double band. "Take them away." The S nodded, instructing his kin to goad the K's through the door behind him.

Before following his colleagues, the lead S extended his large, strong hand to the prostrate W#1528. "W... sorry, Q#1, allow me."

Confused, she took his hand. He easily lifted her to her feet. After a dip of his head, he turned and followed the small procession of K's and S's.

Meanwhile, the B's had descended and were flooding the floor like an unstoppable river.

B#15 smiled and walked towards W#1528/Q#1. "You did well. And my apologies for keeping you in the dark. We couldn't risk premature exposure."

"I... It's a lot to take in. Am I really going to change into a Q?"

"Well, yes. You and several of your siblings that'll soon be born."

She slapped him in the face. "You've used me! What if I don't agree with all this?"

The pale young man rubbed his flushing cheek. "Didn't you say you wanted what's best for the city? This is it. In fact, this is what's best for the cities."

Incomprehension furrowed her forehead, which was becoming clearly lined by black hairs. "What are you talking about?"

"Follow me and I'll explain. Finally," he added with an understanding look.

He left his brothers and sisters behind and led her through unremarkable hallways and corridors whose existence she'd never even suspected. After numerous twists and turns, they entered a small transparent elevator. The ascent was quick and pushed her stomach into her developing reproductive organs.

The glass box came to a halt, and B#15 handed her a respirator he had conjured up from one of his vest's pockets. "We'll need this."

B#15 got out first and, with a wave of his arm, invited W#1528/Q#1 to join him on the terrace that lined the circumference of a high thin spire, as white as unfiltered sunlight.

W#1528/Q#1's eyes got used to the brightness. The world unfurled before her. Under a sickly yellow sky, the city stretched out in all directions. They were standing on the highest point; no doubt about that. Around the spire were other tall buildings, but the farther out they extended, the lower the structures got. At the edges – a mountain range to the north, a river to the south – only single-story structures could be discerned.

"Like an iceberg floating in the ocean," B#15 said, as if he was reading her thoughts. "The brunt of the city lies below the surface. The outside is mostly used for observation, energy generation through solar power, and defense."

"What's wrong with the sky?"

He nodded before responding. "Not what you've been told, I guess? The toxic sky is the result of..."

"...Of short-sighted competition," someone behind them said.

They both turned.

"Ah"." B#15 recognized their guest. "Q#1, may I introduce you to KB#3."

The visitor bowed. "A pleasure."

There was something strange about the man in front of her. He was clearly a B – their heads didn't lie – but he was taller. Fuller, somehow. And there was something else, a scent, a subconscious nagging.

"He's not from here!" she exclaimed suddenly, disgust flaring behind her blue eyes.

"That's right." B#15 spoke soothingly. "He's from one of our neighboring cities."

"Why is he here?" She demanded.

"He helped us." Replied B#15.

"Why would he do that?" She asked incredulously.

The stranger stepped forward and put a hand on the shoulder of the smaller B#15. "Allow me, my friend."

He turned his attention to Q#1. "When humans learned to work together towards common goals, many eons ago, humanity leapt, and the cities were born. Paragons of cooperation but, sadly, limited paragons. Competition trailed cooperation closely during the transition. City-states, nations, countries, whatever they were called back then, still sought to outdo each other, and, in doing so, pursued short-term benefit while long-term development and advancement were cast aside." He waved his arm to the city's vista. "And the planet suffered, as did its inhabitants."

"I... we," – he acknowledged B#15 with a nod – "feel it's been enough. Time for the next transition. Imagine cities working with, rather than against, each other. Imagine what could be achieved then. Imagine a united humanity with common goals. We can make the planet healthy again, and achieve so much more."

"But who'll decide what those goals will be?" Q#1 asked.

KB#3 smiled. He was quite attractive, Q#1 couldn't help thinking. The visitor turned briefly to B#15. "You've chosen well, I see."

His head swung back towards Q#1. "Excellent question, but sadly, one I can't answer yet. But the B's and KB's of several cities are working on that. Together, I'm happy to add."

"Just the B's and KB's?" She inserted just a bit of skepticism into her voice – another newly acquired skill, controlled intonation.

His smile widened slightly. "For now, yes. We're only at the initial stage. The first ones of the new order, the next civilization, are being born as we speak. It takes time. This is, we are, the opening act."

"If you can't answer the important questions yet, then why overturn everything already?"

"Because to find those answers, we need to cooperate. In all the cities we've approached so far, the old ones refuse to do so. Ancient power and rusted hierarchies never want to loosen their grip." Answered KB#3

Still not finished with her questioning she pressed on. "One more thing. If such large-scale cooperation is what you want, then wouldn't it be more useful to ensure that everyone's closely related? What you're doing now seems to lead to the opposite."

Now B#15 responded. "Clever thought, but it's more complicated than that. We don't want to install a tyranny of genes. And a variation as reduced as the current one in the city is dangerous, even if it promotes collaboration. Our aim is diversity. Increased variation is necessary to advance."

They fell silent and stared out over the vast city. Q#1 could begin to make sense of what she saw by now. Huge solar cells and algal bloom pools covered the surface as tapestry, pierced and speckled by gleaming observation domes and the dark cylinders of laser and other artillery. Here and there, she could see small dots moving, maintenance crew performing their tasks. Ants in the anthill, bees in the hive. A noxious sky loomed overhead, casting everything in a wan glow, a memento of past mistakes.

"What do you think?" B#15 asked.

KB#3 asked his own questions. "Are you prepared to join us? To stand behind a common goal that transcends all previous ones?"

She stared out at the world before her. The old world. Was it time for a new one? Her thoughts rolled and tumbled over each other, caught in an unpredictable storm of mental commotion. It sounded good, but wasn't it short-sighted in itself to think that there were goals everyone would be willing to unite for? And if not, how could they justify forcing others to contribute? Still, maybe this change was good. It wouldn't be perfect, but perhaps it would be better than before.

"Yes," she said, and in thought added, *for now.*

###

ABOUT GUNNAR DE WINTER

GUNNAR DE WINTER IS A biologist/philosopher hybrid who explores ideas through fictional fieldwork.

Connect with Gunnar here: www.castrumpress.com/gunnar-de-winter.

THE PINK STAR-SHIP SWITCH

James Worrad

From fifty thousand feet up Luharna seemed beautiful.

Jada Seren--itchy in new *bizness-dress*, champagne flute awkward in right hand-- gazed through the Plexiglass floor beneath her shoes. The company-owned Stratobarque descended toward the northern continent's center. Daylight down there. Jada blotted out the music and chatter coming from the main hall and attempted to spot her old neighborhood somewhere in the concrete and metallic vastness below.

Nah, no chance. Instead, she winced down a sip of obscenely ancient champagne and took succor in her present circumstances. Such possibilities. She'd just need the will to grasp them. So far so good. After all, none of the people she'd grown up with had ever seen this. *This!* The face of Luharna, the richest world in the galaxy.

Every human planet, sooner or later, risked climatic and environmental breakdown in its pursuit of industry. Faced with this, most worlds moved their industrial base out onto moons, asteroid belts or around gas giants. Not Luharna. Luharna had just, well... sailed on through.

Below lay a panoply of Luharna's tools for keeping itself habitable: ventilator canyons, artificial steppes of multicolored treatment lagoons and the unmistakable glint of valley-sized solar troughs. Jada spied a flotilla of sponge-capture dirigibles, presumably on a course for some carbon hotspot or other. They passed over legions of scrubbing towers, their shadows stretching and shrinking over the alloy land.

Here was testament to humanity's willful genius in the face of reality. Here was home. Jada's eyes were those of her parents and neighbors, old lovers and friends. They would never see this. She gazed for every one of them.

"Needed a mo' alone, Hon'?" Trilling's voice, deep and ever-confident. Jada hadn't heard him enter the observation lounge.

"No, sir,' Jada said, "just... ok, I guess it *was* getting a bit much in there."

"That's fine, Jada. Came here for a little thought-gather myself. And please; none of this 'sir' malarkey. I'm your boss, not some--whatcha call it? --Shogunpope. Call me Arn."

Jada looked up from her world and turned to face him. Trilling was a man both wolfish and handsome, though Jada suspected the handsome part had been added later and at considerable expense. His *bizness-suit*--the traditional attire of exec for millennia--doubtless cost more than Jada's dad's yearly pay. But that was what a *bizness-suit* was meant to say. Jada couldn't imagine Trilling in anything else.

'I've got a face-face scheduled with Mister Schmellmer and the board in ten minutes,' Trilling said. 'Want in?'

***

Pleasantly formless, the Hoidrac idled at the Geode's margin; delighting in a score of mood-vents it had been encouraging of late. The vents had begun as meagre fissures, allowing threads of consciousness to percolate through from a certain world within the Tangible realm. Now it came in ceaseless, gibbering plumes:

onderifshe'llbehereveryonehatesmellitwitblossomurderkittenfacexcellencellarwhe reIkeepthestashandjobsatnoonecantellmeshitidowhatilikebbingyouth--

A compost of accumulated thoughts, so many minds' excretions, all unmistakably human.

-

ickyjusticeconomicboomonharilliandi'llgetmypaybackyouseeifidon'tomeyouarereckle ssayo-

Mmm... The Hoidrac joy-shivered in the vents' warmth. These humans were of a feral world: blind to Hoidrac splendor and ruled only by themselves. That is, themselves and the Stain.

The Stain was a quintessentially human kind of... uh... ugly. Inimical to Hoidrac touch, even to the Great Hoidrac at the Geode's heart in all their terrifying splendor. A barrier-absolute, this Stain. A most loathsome anti-ideal that daubed too many human worlds, flooding their senses and warping all judgement. Worse, these humans believed the Stain the only way of things.

The Stain had not saturated them completely, however. For instance, in the exact locale of the Tangible plane where these mood-vents found their source, subtle nooks of beauty held out. A scattering of humans made crude and hidden prayer to all Hoidrac. Of course, far more gave unconscious offering with their art, making beautiful images, objects and sounds.

The Hoidrac was not deluded. These mood-vents would never be more than they were: mere apertures. And yet it tasted so uniquely delicious! Each wish and wonder a symphony! The Hoidrac dived through the mood-plumes once more:

Bunkhumpingskunkjumpingfoolseenfromfiftythousandfeetluharnaisbeautifulolzo
ostoppedbreathingohgodpleasemybabymybabynono-

*But oh, oh, what was that? The Hoidrac pulled the thread from the plume's common mess
and sliced it into meaning:*

Seen/from/fifty/thousand/feet/up/Luharna/seems/beautiful

Now here was something. A most singular thread. The Hoidrac made closer inspection.

***

"The *Board?*" Jada said.

"Who-else-but?"

"B-but of course!" She couldn't help but slip a giggle and Trilling apparently took
that as a sign to look over her assets, head to foot, with those blue eyes above his
sleepy-wolf grin.

Jada reigned in her enthusiasm. 'Thank you for this opportunity. It'll give me
insight into Sen-Exec procedure, sir.'

"Arn, Doll, call me Arn," Trilling said. "But serious here; I'll need you to be my
wing-woman, ready on that fact-hose and kicking to spray. You tune me?"

"I... think so. Kicking..."

'Exact. But I can't have you acting like you are now: all doe-eyed and sprinkle-
brained over pretty landscapes below. Take that switch inside your head and flick it
to business time.'

Jada took a deep breath of conditioned air, followed by a gulp of champagne. Her
switch was still a new toy.

Jada had had the colossal good fortune to be selected by Raichundelia for a
scholarship. Every year, a few young, promising people from disadvantaged
backgrounds did so--Raichundelia was a progressive polyconglomerate after all.
She'd made good, had maxed-out all tests save one: empathy. Jada was saturated
with it. Execs had to make choices after all, big choices, and often that required
sweeping empathy off the table.

Luckily, science had the answer to her disability. Centuries ago, nanotechnology
had made sociopathic behavior potentially curable (on the biological level at least),
by using slaved nanites to fix damaged pathways in the subject's amygdala, the
emotional seat of the brain. Someone at Raichundelia had realized this notion flowed
both ways. Jada, and those like her, now enjoyed the fruit of that brainwave. By a
simple act of concentration--in Jada's case, visualizing a pink star-ship--countless
nanites altered the geography of her brain, temporarily damming the ethical
tributaries of her neural waters.

She closed her eyes. *Pink star-ship*, she thought. She opened them again and
looked down through the Plexiglass floor.

The Stratobarque was cruising much lower now, flying at ten thousand feet across
Luharna's metallic face. The pipelands were visible below: a flat stretch of wasteland

some eighty miles wide, entirely covered in tubes of every size and material. The pipes exchanged heat and airborne impurities between two neighboring urban super-clusters, as part of the greater process of regulating Luharna's surface temperature.

Had Jada thought the landscape beautiful before? She'd meant *useful*. She could see the wretched *favelas* of the noncreds. Homeless, hopeless, the noncreds fashioned hovel-towns from strangest junk, building over pipes for whatever heat and energy they might leech. The *favelas* were a motley vision from this height; lichen staining the tubes and shafts for miles at a stretch.

Jada smiled. Hopeless + desperate = cheap. She spied a Raichundelia-owned tanker lifting off from a bald patch in the Pipeland's medusascape. A hold-full of noncreds anxious for a day's work and its soon-blown wealth.

The polyconglomerates wasted nothing. Nothing! Capitism had withstood the centuries, the flood of ages, and through its philosophy and practice alone would humanity be perfected. And Jada could be part of it, and Jada could have her cut and her sky-apt and her skim-limo and her interstellar travel and her toned lover and her wealth and her power and below all this, below it all, JADA, JADA, JADA, JADA!

She looked at Trilling. 'I'm ready.'

Trilling smiled. 'You've come a long way.'

✻✻✻

The Hoidrac swooned with delight. Here was a thing! Here a fine thread of cognition!

And, mayhap, a gateway...

It was not so much this human female's hunger for beauty or the fact she could willingly suppress it (though in the former she was a fearsome predator and the latter a comely riddle); it was a matter of context.

She existed--nay, thrived--so deep within the Stain! Amid its temples, upon its transports and above its middens. Why, she seemed to bathe happily beneath the drivel spouted by its very prophets! It should have crushed all her taste for wonder, but this female was unique. Her warrior-half shielded the ingénue.

She wouldn't last, of course, but while she did...

The Hoidrac acted upon whim, for nothing is more solemn. First, it shed its formlessness and took roughest shape. Male, definitely male this time. Nevertheless, he (ha!) retained the horns and tapered snout of his kind's customary aspect. His species had an iconography to maintain, after all.

Next, the jape itself. The Hoidrac ambushed a shoal of finned Metaselachia that darted about the mood-vents and seized one of its number. It struggled a moment, then relaxed as the Hoidrac impressed his will upon it.

Having done so, the Hoidrac produced a bubble of Tangible-reality he carried upon his person for tasks such as this. He dipped the Metaselachian in the bubble and retracted it; the beast was now coated with real. All Geode-creatures needed such armor if they were to sally forth outside their natural universe. Finally, and most crucially of all, the Hoidrac fashioned delicate patterns upon the beast's still unset coating. There. Superlative, even if the Hoidrac said so himself.

The Hoidrac focused on the singular mood-vent. Then he shoved the Metaselachian out of the Geode and into the Tangible.

***

Jada followed Trilling into the Stratobarque's empty boardroom. The walls were warm alabaster, or as near to that as treated fiberboard got. Between the faux-blocks lay shrine-like hollows that housed holo-projectors. The projectors cast company slogans, ancient and modern, into the air directly before them. The current slogan was the most conspicuous:

AN EYE ON THE FUTURE,

--RAICHUNDELIA--

AN EAR TO YOUR HEART.

Jada was not at this meeting to be 'sprinkle brained'. It was not in her remit to fuck up. She would be *seen*. Appreciated.

She and Trilling came to a stop before the wood and leather table (Cost: 90k) with its compliment of a dozen matching chairs (16k apiece).

Trilling looked at her. "You fired up, Hon?" he said.

"Kicking to spray."

"Smooshy," he said. "Look; Schmellmer knows we're having a cocktail party here, so you don't have to play it a hundred percent prim-and-prop, you tune? You can smooth down those edges a little."

"I understand.' *Make the call already*, Jada thought. 'I'll try."

Trilling's eyes wolfed her up and down again. "Talking of which, quit rocking that *bizness-dress* look two-four-seven. It's all I ever see you in, Jada. Swear you got a smoosh bod somewhere under there; reveal some o' that sweet-concealed."

"Erm..." Her revulsion was an animal, one trying to scratch its way out of her stomach and at his face.

"Just advisin'," Trilling said.

Jada grimaced at the floor. "Appreciated."

Even with her switch set to 'superpath' she could see no plus in sleeping with her boss. Now there was a vocational tar pit; chock-full of naive underlings trying to get ahead. Man or woman, you ended up no better than the boss's skim-limo: a show piece. Jada may as well have stayed home and pouted at local gangs as that. No, best to leave Trilling's fuckstick white-hot and pliant. Besides, she couldn't let him see her naked, see her hidden truth, her past writ upon her body. A man of his background would never approve.

'Lock and load,' Trilling said. 'Engage your ficty-screen.'

Jada accessed her brain's neuralware and opened a ficty. The ficty-screen materialized--to her eyes alone--across the table. She opted for a width of eight-feet-by-six. She made a ficty-keyboard appear too; floating near her belly, in case she needed to take notes.

"Wanna merge?" Trilling asked.

Jada smiled. "Why not?"

Their separate screens became one. Trilling put the call through to Pontiac, Luharna's more upmarket moon and seat of Raichundelia Polyconglomerate. The board answered.

"Good day, Ladies and Gentlemen," Trilling said. "Mr. Schmellmer."

"Trilling," Schmellmer said.

CEO Schmellmer would have been obese if he wasn't built like a bunker. It was part of his legend that he never sat down at a meeting, preferring to storm about the floor, alpha-male-ing the room. The legend was true. Behind Schmellmer, the rest of Top-Exec sat at a c-shape table of insensible cost, stiff in their *suits* and *dresses*.

'We're approaching the Pipelands now, Mr. Schmellmer,' Trilling said. 'Security on the ground has found no traps nor bugs. Clear down there.'

"They'd better hope they're right," Schmellmer said, pacing left and right with a bull-mean stoop, "or you can tell those bastards I'll send their kids to our crash-test facility."

"Ha! Sure, sir," Trilling said. "But, seriously, put it out of your mind. Kito Industries know we've got 'em licked."

"Don't start me on those bastards..." Schmellmer paced right to left. A stick figure appeared next to him: a cartoon! It seemed made from brushstrokes of black and blue paint. Human in body, but with a head like a... dragon or a seahorse or something, with two anorexic horns on its head. It followed behind Schmellmer, mocking his walk.

"This is Ms. Seren,' Jada heard Trilling say to the ficty-screen, 'my attaché. She'll be doing work in the field itself, face-to-face with the natives. Scholarship kid knows the lay of the land."

Jada looked at Trilling. He was already looking back at her, his smile placid. Why hadn't he noticed the stick figure? They shared the same fucking screen.

"Well?" Trilling asked her. "Say hello to the big man."

Jada realized her mouth was slack. She looked back at the screen to see Schmellmer glaring at her, his anorexic paint-twin doing the same beside him.

"Erm..." This was a test. It had to be. "Good day, Mr. Schmellmer, sir."

"So, what's your plan?" Schmellmer asked, frowning.

"Simple..." What was it? Shit... "Firstly, the clearing of the immediate construction zone."

"And?" Schmellmer said. The stick figure mimed along with the word.

Trilling. This had to be Trilling's doing. He was going to break Jada, so he could look good or... something! Screw him! She could do this.

"And, secondly, the removal and, and... *destruction* of all installations left by Kito Industries in the Pipelands."

Schmellmer fell silent, staring. Jada dug fingernails into her palms.

"Fine," he said.

Jada smiled and nodded. "Thank you, sir." *Fuck you, Trilling.*

At that moment, the stick-figure waved a hand in front of Schmellmer and Schmellmer was naked.

"We need people who aren't afraid to stick it in K. I's face," Schmellmer said. He didn't seem to notice his nudity. "Let me tell you, if I could just get my mitts on their board..."

He began to punch the air in front of him, shuffling in that way boxers did. Jada watched in horror as the CEO's paunch shuddered and his long balls danced.

"Oh, fuck!" she said.

Trilling looked at her, eyes wide above a fixed grin. "Jada, Hon; something the matter?"

Bastard! She wanted to scream. Fuck-nut bastard! But she wouldn't let Trilling beat her. She couldn't process this. Correction: sociopath Jada couldn't process this. Too much paranoia.

Pink Star-Ship, she thought.

She opened her eyes, gazed at Schmellmer on the screen and laughed before she could stop herself. So much for sprinkle-brain Jada!

"What is this?" Schmellmer demanded. Maybe he grimaced, but Jada couldn't take her gaze off his tiny mottled penis.

Something like electricity burst in her chest. The room lit up and the ficty-screen vanished.

"What the--" she heard Trilling mutter.

Jada looked up to see an arm-long silver shark swim in circles through the air. It swam too fast for her to make out any detail. Reality seemed to warp around it, leaving a trail of strange light, blue beyond blue.

Some kind of laser shot from its nose. Jada ducked.

It wasn't meant for her. The shark was aiming at the walls. Carving on them.

'Bastard!' Trilling screamed. He had a holo-projector in his fists--must have taken it from a hollow nearby--and charged toward the critter. The slogan was:

Chewzee Head-Gum
It's the mind-pop!

The shark-thing quivered in the slogan's light and jolted away, across the boardroom and over the table, only to continue its vandalism upon the far wall.

"I'll get security!" Jada shouted to her boss and did so over her neuralware.

"Grab a projector!" Trilling shouted back, already bounding away toward where the Shark sliced at fake alabaster.

She did so. The slogan read:

Phaliconda Nine
Because a handgun should get you noticed

The pair of them chased the shark-thing around the boardroom. It seemed to hate the projectors' holo-lights, darting away on contact.

"Jada! Corner it!"

They trapped it in a crossfire of advertising. It shook and twisted as if on fire, unable to break free of the low ceiling's corner.

Jada heard the doors burst open behind them.

"Security!" a woman said.

"Shoot, damn it!" Trilling shouted.

Jada flinched as two rail-pistols discharged themselves. The Shark's flank burst open. A scream of weird light, a sucking sound, and then something hit the floor with a clang.

Silence. The shark-thing lay still on the tiles.

"Are you fine, Sirs?" the security woman said.

"Smooshy," Trilling said, panting, "Real smooshy."

Jada bent to look at the thing on the tiles. It appeared to be made from an alloy of steel and glass, as insane as that notion clearly was, with the most ravishing patterns all over it. Looking through the rail-shot holes, Jada could see the thing was entirely empty. Just a hollow, *beautiful* casing.

"What was it?" Jada said.

Trilling sniffed, then said; "Kito Industries."

"Kito?" The casing looked like no machine she'd ever seen or heard of.

"Yeah... industrial sabotage. Fuck! I mean, who-else-but?"

"I guess." Jada looked up at the Shark-thing's wall carvings. "Woah."

A dozen images of the brushstroke-man's head, of the seahorse-dragon face with its slender horns.

Trilling gripped her shoulders. "Jada, snap-out! Throw me some ear!"

She met his eyes. They seemed frightened.

"Jada, tell no-one, you tune?" Trilling said. "If Schmellmer finds we let Kito bend us over our own board he'll shit rocks, angry rocks. Me and you, J-Hon, tune? You tune?"

"I won't say a thing."

Trilling stroked a thumb against her chin. "That's my girl." He gave a wolf-smile and strode off toward the security detail. "Same for you two!" he said. "Now find someone to melt these walls clean."

"Sir?" said the armored Security woman.

"What; can't speak Anglurati? See to it, Ass-flask! Now!"

"Yes, sir!"

Jada realized she'd taken on a laser-toting... *thing*, while still regular sprinkle-headed, doe-eyed Jada. Scary. Scarier still, she'd thought about Trilling's 'pliant' dick moments before that, when she hadn't been herself. Ugh. High-functioning sociopathy wasn't *all* sweetness and light it seemed.

***

The Hoidrac couldn't quell his own mirth! The Stain had not known what hit it! Oh, oh...

In time, the Hoidrac settled down. Flippancy, when all said and done, requires deepest contemplation.

A sphere sped into the Hoidrac's awareness, froze, and then transfigured itself into an acquaintance of the Hoidrac.

::Greetings,:: announced the acquaintance.

::Greetings,:: the Hoidrac replied.

::We had planned to bond-tickle, recall? It is the time of the moon-hand-dance.::

::Oh,:: the Hoidrac mumble-shrugged, :: My mistake: I thought we had planned for the time of the dance-hand-moon. Apologies, but I have a matter of frivolous import.::

::Why are you mooning around these vents so?:: the acquaintance asked. ::And why have you taken an aspect of ironic human masculinity?::

::Because--::

::Wonderful! It would be giddiest jape to bond-tickle as male and female!:: With that, the Acquaintance became a she. ::What do you think?::

::Begone!::

::Oh you!:: the Acquaintance called, speeding away.

The Hoidrac returned his focus to the singular and vital mood-vent. He would watch. He would wait.

***

Life was humid down amid the pipes, of course, and Jada--currently sprinkle-headed--was thankful she could afford perspiration buffers. Unfortunately, the Pipeland's countless inhabitants could not afford such implants. They stink up the early evening, each individual's whiff pouring into a general fug that clung to the streets and alleys between, beneath and inside the pipes.

But Sister Mergotsi stood out even here. Jada supposed her order had rules about not washing. It took all Jada's patience not to pink star-ship into superpath mode and tell the old woman to pull whatever dead animal it was out of her vestments.

"We were here first!" Sister Mergotsi told her. "You corporate vassals never lifted a hand to help here until you spied profit. Did you build this, girl, hmm? Did you?" She gestured to the plasterboard and wire mesh chapel behind her. Districts of tangled piping rose behind it in the far distance, all the way to the horizon.

The chapel stood beside, or more correctly leaned upon, a water pipe some twenty feet in diameter. In front of the chapel stood eight poles of various heights, rising from holes in the steel grill floor. Atop these poles squatted replicas of ancient televisions, their screens set to static fuzz. Sister Mergotsi was a skyharborite, a cult who believed one could reach god by gazing at TV static, given its ultimate source was the big bang.

"Sister," Jada said, "with all due respect, *we* were here first. When the department of social works privatized three thousand years ago, several companies that later submerged into Raichundelia Polyconglomerate acquired shares. I'm certain you're a valued member of this community but the unpleasant fact remains it is a community of squatters. That said, Raichundelia wishes to help this neighborhood thrive. When the new construction is completed— "

"And who decides who gets to live in this 'Construction'?" Sister Mergotsi said.

"That's a matter for your community," Jada said. "We would— "

"For the pipe gangs, you mean!"

Jada took a deep breath and got rewarded with the smell of roast vent-lizards from a passing kiosk-mech. Still; a perfume next to Sister Mergotsi. This whole situation made Jada uncomfortable.

"I think the best course is to dismantle your chapel--my security here will help with any lifting--and for you to address any complaints to our meme site."

"Ha! Like I can afford neuralware!" Mergotsi threw her arms in the air and Jada covered her nose. "There is a tap inside this chapel. It provides free, clean water to those in need, though no doubt you would call it stealing. Have you ever seen deformed babies, young lady, babies lacking brains due to bad water?"

"There will be clean water in the constr-"

"Have you seen a mother when her new-born fails to have a face?"

Jada needed to scream, so she thought of a pink star-ship instead and no longer had to.

"Tear down this mess," she told her security. "Escort this woman off our premises."

Jada strode to her skim-limo.

"Your accent betrays you!" Sister Mergotsi shouted. "You were like us, once! You were li-"

The limo door shut, and Jada told the driver to head to the construction site. On her way she passed the detritus: immigrants from Calran and Psiax; groups of nem-heads waiting for a fix; teenagers in thongs, their skins tattooed with adverts for start-up companies. They smoked on pooka-joints and combed each other's hair.

Nothing is wasted, Jada thought, *everything in the cycle, everything for sale.* Through the limo's shaded glass, she could see Raichundelia's local HQ, its tungsteel bulk soaring above the pipes. Millennia past, it had been built as the foundation of a planned space-elevator, but anti-gravity got invented and the project became obsolete. Waste-not-want-not: might have been a motto of Raichundelia if someone else hadn't bought the rights already.

Something had been bugging Jada about Trilling's behavior earlier that morning, and now she wasn't sprinkle-headed she'd grasped it. How had Trilling known to use a holo-projector to fight that Shark-thing? Why such confidence light would hurt it?

She accessed her neuralware and brought up a ficty-screen and keyboard. Jada wasn't sure what to type, so, instead, she drew the strange face of the brushstroke dragon-man and ran it through the company wikiverse.

The wikiverse threw up *HOIDRAC.*

Jada hadn't the faintest. The attached article didn't mention Kito Industries. Hoidrac were... either a myth or some alien species. Well, that might explain the shark's freakish casing.

The Hoidrac home-world was of this universe, the article explained, yet was contaminated by a... *localized reality-tear* into another, smaller universe called the Geode. Having evolved on a world drenched in the Geode's radiation, the Hoidrac could happily prosper in either and could flit about the two, given the right technology, the right circumstance. Hell, but this shit was hazy.

Jada lost the thread for a while, but her interest got hooked again when she read of Professor Lundhast's hypothesis that the Geode was a sort of drain to our own reality, collecting (and being entirely composed of) the thoughts and 'aesthetic sensibilities' of every species in the universe. A footnote explained Professor Lundhast had eventually been sacked from Harillia University on account of smoking crystal meth through a tapir.

Much of the wiki article, Jada noted, had been redacted by someone in the company. Recently, too.

The skim-limo turned a corner into a great open space. Hundreds of derelict pipes had been sliced and removed to make way for the new construction. Only bare concrete remained; a grey, undulating land of house-sized pipe fittings.

Jada smiled. If there had to be *favela* then they'd be Raichundelia-owned. Ahead lay a landscape of chrome scaffolding--eighteen stories of nothing but empty lattice and occasional stairwells. The desperate ingenuity of the local population would do the rest, building the walls and floors of each story from whatever junk they could find.

High rise *favela:* the future of underclass living. Here, the dog-eat-dog ecology would be accelerated and refined. A strong, ruthless and--above all--useful cream would rise. Just as Jada had. And just as Sister Mergotsi had sunk. The thought of Mergotsi made Jada grimace. The smelly hag had made soft, off-switch Jada almost cry.

The limo entered a complex of empty, concrete fixtures. It had kept countless pipes of every size in place but now those tubes had been removed, leaving a maze of crescents and arches. Graffiti covered all vertical surfaces. Rubbish, the floors.

Jada thought about the holo-projectors they had used to ward off the shark. Maybe it wasn't the projector's light that—

A noise. An insect whine. The limo's windows shattered. Jada screamed and covered her head. She felt the limo belly-flop onto concrete as its AG unit gave out. Engine dead.

A railgun's *crack.* The driver's throat burst.

"Fuck!" Jada watched him slump forward against his belt.

She tried to access her neuralware. Nothing. Fucking blocked!

A shadow crossed the window. Hands grabbed her shoulders. She tried to break free, but more hands grabbed her head. Jada kicked and yelled as the two men pulled her out the limo.

"Geturfameee!"

"Shut it, bitch!" The larger man said. He had his arm around her waist. A flash of silver before her face: a blade.

"Walk." The smaller man, a blond, chuckled.

They dragged her down an access corridor that reeked of piss. Her new shoes stumbled on rat shit and candy wrappers.

"They'll pay you!" Jada shouted. "My boss will make you rich!"

"He pay for corpses?" the large man asked.

"Pay for corpses," the smaller man repeated, chuckling again.

Corpses? So why not just kill her back at the limo? No...

"We'll fucking kill you!" Jada shouted, praying someone might overhear in this wasteland. Her words echoed off concrete. "Step on you leeches! Scram while you can!"

The big man kicked her in the belly and she rolled to the floor. Evening sky above--they were out of the access corridor. So, this was it then; pain, humiliation and death on the floor of some derelict courtyard. Jada's stomach twisted. At least her sprinkle-headed self wouldn't suffer. That'd be embarrassing.

The walls were covered in the most remarkable graffiti.

***

The Hoidrac became puzzled. He hadn't expected... whatever was happening. Whatever it might be it was serious, and serious was the lowest form of absurdity.

These two males' sudden appearance seemed forced. Artificial. The Hoidrac looked at what these two males planned to do.

Oh. That. A common male-human performance--subconscious revenge on authority, their birth-givers and an indifferent universe by means of bloodshed and their generative organs. Cold blades and colder lusts, if you will.

How drearily uninspired. How boring an intention.

It wouldn't do at all.

***

She'd tried to get up and they'd punched her in the head. Warm trickle-trickle from the scalp. Woozy.

Jada was more interested in the walls. The dragon-faced man was all over them, in many different styles and paints. Most were fresh, but she could see pale, dusty variants that must have been painted decades ago.

"Roll her over," a man said.

Blue light, pale blue, filled her vision. She could hear the men shout. A series of rail-shots. Something like static kissed her skin.

Jada looked up. The two men were doused in a familiar, unreal light. Faced one another up close, screaming. Their hips had merged in a bubble of gore.

The brightness became too much. Jada shut her lids. There were those blobs you get when you close your eyes after bright light. Two blobs. They looked like clawed hands.

Dark again. When she opened her eyes a silver pillar stood in the middle of the courtyard. She scratched and crawled and stumbled to her feet, head burning, bleeding, babbling.

The pillar was made of that Hoidrac stuff, the glass-steel. It resembled two men; armless, their torsos stretched and twisted around one another in a dual corkscrew. Up top were two male heads, skulls fused together at the back, faces in opposite directions like some past-and-future-gazing god. Beautiful.

Jada pink star-shipped to her sprinkle-head-self. Better appreciation that way. She stepped closer.

A plume of indigo *whooshed* out of the top of the pillar, from a slit between the fused skulls. Most of it--whatever it was--didn't come down. It got carried up, away on the Pipelands' thermals. Some did fall though, unhurried as snow, and Jada caught a piece.

A *leaf*. A translucent blue leaf with luminous mauve veins. It felt like plastic to the touch.

Mystified, she gazed at one of the glass-steel pillar's male faces. Behind silver misty glass was a real face; pink, motionless. A fringe of blond hair. Its eyes flickered open, puzzled and wide. Its mouth screamed soundless behind the glass.

Jada passed out.

***

She woke to static. Twenty televisions gazed down at her from their iron poles. Blackness beyond them.

Jada's head stung. She was laying on a mattress in some big dark room. She was certain she had dreamed of televisions, but her stirring reason told her she'd been passing in and out of consciousness for some time. Where was she?

"Where do you come from?" A woman's voice. "What dirty street bore you?"

An old woman came into focus. She had cropped white hair and wore a vest and shorts. Sister Mergotsi. By the smell of her- or lack of such- she'd clearly showered.

"Monsil cluster, west block," Jada said, and she realized she was her empathic, sprinkle-headed self. Of course: she had been so before she'd passed out. A shame; her superpathy's six-hour time limit might have clued her up as to how long she'd been unconscious. "Monsil's a welfare-ziggurat. Better than the Pipelands, I guess."

"But not nearly as fine as the back of a limo, eh?" Mergotsi said.

Images of the attack flashed in Jada's mind. The limo's glass shattering in the EMP-blast, the driver's throat exploding. The men and the pillar they became.

"Easy, Girl," Mergotsi said, sitting by her on the mattress.

"How long have I slept?" Jada asked.

"Two nights."

"Huh..." Jada stroked her head and felt what she took to be primitive stitches. She recalled the last time she had spoken to this woman. "Why'd you help me, Sister?"

"Someone has to set an example," she said. "Besides, the Hoidrac let you be."

That seemed to remind Sister Mergotsi of something--she pulled a packet out of her vest and opened it. Shimmering powder inside, like wing-dust scraped from a blue butterfly. Sister Mergotsi dipped her thumb in and snorted what it collected. She offered some to Jada. Jada shook her head.

"What is it?" Jada asked.

"Geode-leaf, powdered," Mergotsi said. "A gift from our deities."

Jada shivered. She recalled the translucent leaf she had held. "I thought you prayed to static, Sister."

"I can worship God and adore the Hoidrac concurrently, can I not? The Geode-leaf has rained all over the Pipelands. Those of us who adore the Delighted Ones now offer a new narcotic to the street, to those masses that have nothing to lose in doing so. With each snort the cracks in reality grow." She laughed, gazed into the dark. "Talk about a gateway drug..."

Mergotsi's cackle bit at Jada's skull.

"I have to go," Jada said.

"Where to?" The old woman asked, her laughter sliced short. "Your big-hearted Polyconglomerate?"

"They'll be searching for me."

"Trilling knows, you know," Mergotsi said, smiling. "About us, about Hoidrac-worship in the Pipelands. He's tried to hide it from his masters for years. He's afraid--like you--of being taken from the great credit-teat. The great stain!"

"It works," Jada snapped. "It's not always pretty, but our system works."

"Its *fear* works, my girl. Its fear. The Hoidrac offer humanity something better." She dipped her finger in the packet and snorted more dust. "We can't win here in the Pipelands. Not now. I dare say we'll all perish, but what a statement we shall make tonight! The Hoidrac do so love a performance..."

Jada recalled what she'd been thinking before the attack. The Shark from the Geode--it hadn't feared the light from the holo-projector. It had feared the slogan, the advertisement. Trilling had known that all along, of course.

"Can I leave, Sister?"

"Of course; why should I harm you? Our patron Hoidrac didn't. He must think you central to the narrative. He's of the least order of his kind- by a long way- but the most perceptive about humanity's foibles." She shrugged. "Perhaps that makes him exactly what we need. You'll find a hatchway over there. It leads up to pipes near your headquarters."

Jada got up and marched toward it, head pounding.

"Be careful, girl," she heard Sister Mergotsi call. "It's madness out there."

***

GRABTHEGUNGRABTHEGUNOFUCKINWAYAMIALLOWINGTHOSELOOTERSINTOTHIS MALLWHATTHEHELLARETHEYDRESSEDLIKEANYWAYESYOUAREIKNOWYOUAREDDI EMYLEGMYFUCKINGLEGOONAND-

Vents no more; whirlpools into the Tangible realm! Pouring a leaf-stream down the widening vents had been a flourish, barely a jape, yet the result had proven an unqualified marvel. The humans were saturating their minds in the stuff.

And the female human; what a phenomenon! What appreciation she possessed! And, and the way her temperament kept vaulting, faster and faster! Could it be (dare the Hoidrac think it?) she was on the threshold of some audacious and seminal psychopathology?

The Hoidrac had to ponder his--

The Hoidrac's acquaintance materialized. Again.

::I've brought some of our friends,:: she informed him. ::we've something you simply must see!::

Three hundred and seventy-six other Hoidrac materialized. All their aspects were an ironic comment on stereotypical human gender-duality, each one of them passing male and female signifiers to each other's appearance at the speed of pulsed thought.

Marvelous. Yet another fad. How many centuries might this one last?

The Hoidrac was on the cusp of suggesting his peers expire, when he recalled something.

::My dear,::he addressed his acquaintance, ::would it be possible to borrow that superb transience-armor of yours?::

***

The first thing Jada saw when she climbed out of the manhole was a dead girl face-down under the twin moonlight. She'd been one of those advert-skinned waifs. Now every commercial on her flesh had been defaced by some blunt-yet-scratchy implement. Her blonde hair ran pink with skull matter.

"No..." Jada wanted to be sick, held it back. She looked around.

She'd come out into a derelict workshop inside a huge pipe, the concrete torn from its top so as to let light in. The night sky poured through the rusty framework that had once held the concrete in place. Machine tools stood silent in the gloom. Further down the tunnel, someone was kicking the shit out of someone else.

Someone saw Jada and stopped kicking someone else. They raced toward her.

A woman, mid-twenties, topless and entirely tattooed. Not adverts, though. Hoidrac caricatures, scores of them, seahorse-faced and fucking.

"Fucking *bizness-dress*, I sees!" she said to Jada. "Fucking Exec!" She had a crowbar.

"Wait--"

"I'll brains you like that derma-whore!" The woman's face and hair were splattered with leaf-dust. It sparkled amethyst.

Jada crouched and held her hands up. "Please; don't hurt me, please!"

The woman ran at her, crowbar raised above her head.

Jada pictured one big-ass pink star-ship. She flew at the woman's chest and bit hard into tit. Rubbery, soft. The tattooed woman howled and fell back on a lathe, clutching her chest. Jada grabbed the crowbar and cracked the woman's nose and shoulders. She spat a nipple in her face and walked away.

She strode further down the tunnel, past the balled-up, armored figure on the floor that her enemy had been kicking. She was surprised to see it was the security woman, the one who'd helped fight the shark-thing back on the stratobarque. Jada would have left her lying there, but she couldn't shake off the feeling sprinkle-head-Jada would be all whiny when she switched back. No way. Jada needed to be on form, whatever side of the mental fence.

She pictured another pink star-ship, became sprinkle-headed again.

Jada crouched down. "You okay?"

The Security woman's mouth and nostrils were dripping with leaf-dust. She'd been force-fed. She gazed in horror at her own fingers.

"Bees," she mumbled, "Cubic bees..."

Drugged to high-fuckery. Jada stroked the woman's hair. The night whispered of distant gunfire and shouting.

"Listen to me," Jada whispered. "It's going to be fine, but you have to ride this out. You have to be brave."

"Brave..."

"Attagirl."

The Security woman nodded and closed her eyes. Carefully, Jada checked her for weapons. Someone had already taken her pistol, but she had a blade--an Eversharp. She stuffed it in her jacket's inner pocket. She stroked the woman's hair once more then moved on.

Jada stopped at the end of the tunnel, checked the street beyond. Raichundelia's local headquarters lay on the other side. To her right, she saw security men lining up captured graffiti artists against a shop front's grill.

Jada shuddered as railguns cracked. The graffiti artists ripped at their chests and tumbled.

Jada pictured pink star-ships, became a psycho once more.

How to get across? These Guards looked shook up enough to fire on anyone. She watched as one of them took a rifle-looking thing and aimed at the shop's spray-daubed grill. An advert splattered against the metal, clear as day. It read:

There's always time for granola!
--MAXIGRAN--

An ad-gun? Incredible. She knew sprinkle-Jada was going through some pathetic crisis about capitism in both philosophy and practice, but, to superpath-Jada, a rapid-fire ad-dispenser was as good as it got. Besides, she would be the one to right this situation and the Polyconglomerate would know it. Everything would be back to normal. Better even: Jada would come out on top.

An unmanned kiosk-mech galloped down the street toward the security men, its hooves ringing on steel. Someone had filled its kiosk with oil barrels topped with a burning rag. The security men ran and the kiosk-mech charged after them.

Jada took her chance and belted across the street.

✳✳✳

"Shit," Trilling said, his mouth wide. "You're alive..."

Jada ran across the cargo bay floor toward him and his complement of twitchy guards.

"Got car-jacked," Jada said. "They killed the driver and I escaped." Jada stepped over the corpses of rioters. Effigies of Hoidrac lay beside them, freshly smashed.

"Thank, thank god..." Trilling said. "Must have been friends of these bastards." He gestured at the body-strewn floor.

After this, Jada thought, *Trilling is going down.* He had that look. Whatever, Jada would make certain of it.

"I know about the Hoidrac," Jada told him.

Trilling stared through her. His lips twitched.

"We're gonna hit the roof and hop on the ol' Stratobarque," Trilling announced to everyone. "We'll take it from there."

"That's running away," Jada said.

"All-due-res, J-Hon, *you* haven't been here. It couldn't get any hotter--"

The walls of the cargo bay began to curdle with blue light. Geode light. The floor under a guard began to ripple.

"Whu-?" he said, and his bones got pulled into the floor. The rest of him held still a moment and then wobbled over, bursting on the tarmac.

"Holy-fuckohlee!" Trilling belted toward an open doorway. Jada caught up, kept pace. Railguns discharged behind them, followed by screams and wet smacks.

Trilling and Jada barged through the doorway. Trilling span around and slammed its heavy-looking door shut, just as a guard ran toward it.

"Motherfu--"

The door locked. Silence.

They were in a concrete room, ten-by-ten, bare walls and some metal crates. An ad-gun sat on one of them.

"Where are we?" Jada said.

"Inside plan B. The panic bunker."

"Serves us right for panicking," Jada said.

"Ain't over till the fat-bitch ululates." Trilling grabbed the ad-gun from off the crate.

The door started to ripple with blue light. Trilling fired a commercial at it. The door returned to normal, save for a toothpaste advert daubed upon it. Jada realized how the gun worked: nanites, had to be, altering the color wavelength of any surface's molecules.

"I'll put this on wide-fire," Trilling said, and he shot at a section of wall near the door that had started to shimmer. The ad was five-foot wide now. The current logo: *eyes to the future, ear to your heart.*

Trilling covered all the walls, his finger tight on the trigger.

"Why bother?" Jada said. "You've killed us both."

"We're safe here," Trilling said. The ceiling rippled, and he blasted it. "Just sit-pretty and wait for help."

"Fucking idiot," Jada said. "We're a toxic asset now, can't you see that? Schmellmer will just cut his losses and drop a plas-bomb on us. It's what I'd do."

"Schmellmer doesn't have to know squat!" Trilling said, checking the walls. "C'mon, J-Babe; two schlubs attack you and you think you're Tactical Tammy or some shit."

Jada squinted. "I never said there were two."

She couldn't see Trilling's face, just the back of his head.

"Crap," he muttered.

Jada pulled the blade out of her pocket and lunged at the small of his back. Trilling span around, the blade missing him by inches. He grabbed for Jada's throat with his free hand but only managed to rip open the top of her shirt.

"Fuck..." he said.

Fuck. He could see her tattoo: two protective eyes underneath her collarbone. She'd had it since her days back in the cluster. Back home in her dirty street.

"Tattoo?" Trilling frowned. "A *ghetto* tattoo?" he said.

"Knew you wouldn't approve."

Jada watched as Trilling's eyes went wide, something about her tattoo. She felt a tickle inside her ribcage. She looked down to see a clawed, vaporous hand emerge from her collarbone. Of course. A tattoo was art, a doorway!

"Fuck this," Trilling said. He twisted something on the ad-gun and fired it point blank into Jada's chest. The advert slammed into her, kicked the air from her lungs, threw her on her back. The concrete stung her ass, spine and skull.

"No-cred cunt!" Trilling shouted down at her. "You can take the bitch off welfare but never vice-v!"

Jada rolled around in pain. Where was the blade? She'd heard it scatter.

"When we get out of this, Hon-bun," Trilling said, "I'll pay off your corporate loan and *own* you!"

Scratching came from the walls. Trilling fired a round at it.

"We could have been friends, J-girl!" he said. "More 'an that, you tune? But you had to shove your beak in. I trailed your neuralware, saw you look up that... dirty, dirty H-word."

Scratch-ah-scratch on the ceiling.

"Fuck-bag!" Trilling fired another round. The scratching ceased.

Jada spied the glint of blade, fought agony to reach it.

"Wonder what happens if I tighten the focus all the way on this gun," Trilling was saying. "Stick a beam of pure unadulterated commercial through its hide." He growled. "You hear this you alien jerk-rag?" he shouted at the ceiling. "I'm kicking to fucking spray!"

Jada rammed the blade into his ankle.

Trilling squealed, toppled.

Jada got to her feet and booted Trilling in the head. Again, again, again.

He passed out, his wolfishly handsome face now a bloody bulldog's.

Jada had to think. Schmellmer would vaporize this place, doubtless. A plasma bomb would be minutes away. Time for a career move.

Had she gone insane? To hell with it. Jada ran to the door. Locked--a safe code. Shit...

She gazed down at Trilling.

Of course. Why ever not? But, damn it; she'd need sprinkle-head. She'd an eye for these things.

Pink Star-ship and her brain structure shifted. She took a moment to look at Trilling, the floor. She considered the possibilities, the methods, the styles. Not the best canvas, but...

Do it. Fucking do it. *Pink Star-ship.*

She took the blade and sliced at her own collarbone, desecrating the commercial on it. There: a start.

Trilling was delirious when she took the blade to him. He muttered dreamily as the eversharp sliced belly and breastbone. She splayed his jacket wide, spread-eagled his arms. They made surprisingly good horns. Then she ladled out his intestines. Trilling must have died about then.

Jada stepped back. Pink Star-ship.

Good work so far, she had to admit. She planned a moment and then Pink Star-shipped back before she might puke.

She carried on in this way, Star-shipping back and forth, adding to and smearing out, contemplating her work of gore-art as she went on. She got good at switching rapidly, so much so she didn't realize she did it. A blur of grace and savagery. It felt good. She felt as one.

Jada stepped back from her impromptu piece; a mural of a Hoidrac face. She couldn't even recall which Jada she was.

The Hoidrac rose from the blood, bone and silk suit fresco. It stood there, armored in light. More beautiful than Luharna seen from on high.

"Please," she told it. "Take me away."

The Hoidrac carved words in the air between them.

::Such beauty::

She ran into its embrace. They vanished long before the building vaporized.

###

ABOUT JAMES WORRAD

JAMES WORRAD LIVES IN LEICESTER, England, and has for almost all his life. Currently he shares a house with a cat and another writer. He works for a well-known brand of hotel, an occupation that never leaves him short of writing material. He has a degree in classical studies from Lampeter University, Wales. He has found this invaluable to his growth as a science fiction and fantasy writer in that he soon discovered how varied and peculiar human cultures can be.

Connect with here: www.castrumpress.com/james-worrad.

CUSTODIAN

Johnny Pez

Holger Kurtz, Custodian of the starship Jolene, became interested in the Battle of Borodino, the name of which he found striking. This led him to Tolstoy's War and Peace, and he decided in due course to learn Russian, so he could read it in the original language (or languages, since some of the dialogue in the original was in French, which Kurtz already understood). Having quickly mastered the Cyrillic alphabet, Kurtz was working on vocabulary and grammar when his daily inspection of Jolene's instruments brought the rock to his attention.

The rock was about the same size and shape as Manhattan, and although its official name (as per established protocols) was Jolene 140622, 'that was how Kurtz thought of it. Manhattan was no threat to Jolene herself; it was far outside the ship's relativistic frame of reference and would approach no closer than 6000 astronomical units. It was an unusual object, nevertheless. It was a lot bigger than your typical chunk of interstellar debris, and it was traveling at nearly two-thirds lightspeed. A data search showed that Manhattan was the largest natural object ever found to be moving at such a speed. There was a distinct possibility that at some point a scientific expedition would be organized to study it, and Kurtz, who took a proprietary pride in Jolene, was pleased that the ship would be immortalized in this way.

Kurtz plotted the rock's projected course through space, and 'that was when the trouble began.

In about four years' objective time, Manhattan would pass through the heart of the Calypso system, and there was a seventeen percent chance that it would impact with Calypso III, last reported human population thirty-three million. Something, Kurtz knew, would have to be done about Manhattan, and Jolene was in the right time and place to do it.

Of course, Kurtz knew with a sinking feeling, it would mean bringing one or more members of Jolene's crew out of Shimizu.

***

Nilanjana Dasgupta tried to mask her dislike for Holger Kurtz; she feared that she wasn't succeeding. It wasn't uncommon for a ship's crew, and especially the captain, to dislike the Custodian; in fact, Dasgupta couldn't think of a single fellow captain who didn't share her feelings.

Jolene was accelerating out of the solar system, on course for the Bevilacqua system, and the time had come for the crew to enter Shimizu, the scientific miracle that held the crew in stasis during the long journeys between the stars. One by one, they had entered the main capsule, and medical officer Yuliya Petrenko had made them disappear until only she, Dasgupta and Kurtz had remained. Then, by longstanding tradition, Petrenko had entered and Dasgupta had operated the controls, and it was just her and the Custodian.

At first, Dasgupta knew, some shipping lines hadn't bothered with Custodians. They counted on automated machinery to de-Shimizu the crew after the journey; usually it did, but sometimes it didn't. Sometimes the ship didn't bother decelerating, or never turned up at all. It wasn't long before the ICC had made Custodians mandatory, but it was cheaper to use two Custodians than four, and cheaper still to use just one, and that was how it was on most ships these days.

It took a special kind of person to live and work alone for the five or ten or twenty years that went by during interstellar journeys. Specifically, it took a person who didn't like other people. Custodians were a breed apart, and they liked it that way. Dasgupta couldn't help worrying that a Custodian would decide he liked being alone too much to end the voyage and bring the rest of the crew back. As far as she knew it had never happened, but she worried anyway.

She didn't like the name, either, which legend said had been decided by a Czech bureaucrat with a fondness for Juvenal, whose Latin was better than his English. Watcher or Guardian would have been more reassuring, she felt; Custodian sounded like someone whose main job was unclogging plumbing.

"Keep an eye on her, Mr. Kurtz," she'd said to him as she entered the main capsule. A typical Custodian, he hadn't answered her, and his eyes tended to wander away from her face. As she always did when she entered a Shimizu capsule, she wondered whether she would ever leave it.

There was a kind of whiteness that seemed to last no longer than an eyeblink, yet seemed to last longer than the universe itself, and Nilanjana Dasgupta found herself looking once more at the walls inside the Shimizu capsule. The door opened and she stepped out, and one look at Kurtz told her something was wrong. He was visibly older than he'd been when she stepped in, but not by enough. If they were in the Bevilacqua system, he ought to be over a decade older, but she guessed no more than three years had passed for him.

"What's wrong, Mr. Kurtz?" she asked.

Just as before, his eyes refused to remain on her face. They wandered around her general vicinity as he said, "Located an object, Captain, and it's on a collision course for Calypso III. Come up to the bridge and have a look." He didn't bother to wait for a reply before turning and walking away. Dasgupta sighed and followed.

The ship smelled different. It always did when you came out of Shimizu. The smells of the crew faded over time, until finally the only smell left was the Custodian's. Each one was different, and Kurtz, she was surprised to note, smelled like cinnamon.

Dasgupta had captained Jolene through four (now four-and-a-third) crossings, but she had never walked through the ship while it was in mid-journey with just the Custodian for company, and she was unnerved by the haunted-house feel of it. That wasn't so bad, but Dasgupta had seen too many works of fiction set in haunted houses, so she was subconsciously expecting some hell creature to jump out at her from the shadows. For the first time in her life, Dasgupta found herself wishing she'd developed a taste for Jane Austen adaptations.

She felt relief when they entered the bridge. She was still uneasy enough to order the lights brought up. Kurtz squinted at the bright light and scowled, and Dasgupta almost apologized before she remembered that she was the captain, dammit, and Kurtz was just a glorified night watchman with a severe personality defect.

Kurtz gestured toward the instrument panel, then retreated to the other side of the bridge. Dasgupta kept control by reminding herself that his condition made Kurtz indispensable.

She quickly located the object and noted Kurtz's name for it with amusement. It was appropriate enough, so she decided to adopt it herself. Just as Kurtz had stated, Manhattan was due to enter the Calypso system, and there was a nontrivial chance that it could impact Calypso III.

"We'll have to alter course," she said out loud, not specifically to Kurtz but to the bridge in general. "Rendezvous with the object and change its trajectory until it's no longer a threat."

The only acknowledgement from Kurtz was a soft sigh.

Not without a certain amount of sadistic pleasure, she added, "We'll have to de-Shimizu the rest of the crew, of course."

Kurtz sighed again.

***

Yuliya Petrenko, senior (and only) medical officer on the starship Jolene, was endlessly fascinated by the view outside the ship. Normally, of course, the crew was in Shimizu while the ship accelerated to near lightspeed and decelerated again, so they never saw the universe in a relativistic frame of reference. Petrenko was in the break room now, and had the walls tuned to the visual inputs that studded the ship's outer hull, so it was just like being in an observation lounge (if anyone was ever extravagant enough to build a ship with an observation lounge). All the classic features (her medical training made her want to say symptoms) of relativistic speed were there – the red-shifted aft stars, the blue-shifted stars to forward, and the foreshortening effect that caused the stars to cluster near the ship's prow. It was an effect that Custodians called "the rainbow".

The entrance to the break room opened, and the Custodian entered. He glanced around at the walls, then ignored them (and Petrenko herself, of course) and shuffled over to the food dispensary. Petrenko was surprised at Kurtz's nonchalance, but only for a moment. For the Custodian, the sight of the relativistic universe would have been a familiar one. In fact, Custodians spent most of their lives seeing the rest of the universe in various states of relativistic distortion.

Petrenko carefully refrained from looking at Kurtz as he withdrew food from the dispensary and sat at the break room table. With the crew out of Shimizu, Kurtz was under considerable stress, which made him Petrenko's primary patient. Petrenko had offered to put Kurtz himself into Shimizu for the duration of the Manhattan project, but the Custodian had been adamantly opposed. That was when Petrenko learned, to her surprise, that the Custodian thought of Shimizu as degrading. A look in her medical database confirmed that this was a general attitude among Custodians. If the rest of the crew wanted to subject themselves to the humiliation of hiding away while the ship reached relativistic speeds, that was up to them, but a Custodian had his pride.

Petrenko had a sudden urge to obtain experimental verification of this startling fact. Turning to the Custodian, she said, "Mr. Kurtz, do you mind if I ask you about something?"

Kurtz looked up, clearly annoyed at having his meal interrupted. Then, with a visible effort, he composed his features and said, "You can ask."

Gesturing around at the view of relativistic space, Petrenko said, "What do you think of all this?"

As if suspecting a trap, Kurtz said, "'All this' meaning...?"

"Relativistic speeds," Petrenko answered. "It's something you've experienced much more than any of the rest of us. Do you think this has given you any insight into the phenomenon?"

After staring at his food for a long time, Kurtz finally spoke. "I suppose," he said slowly, "that it gives one a sense of the variability of the universe." There was another long pause, which Petrenko knew better than to interrupt. At last, Kurtz continued, "I've noticed that people who spend their lives at rest tend to think of the universe as something solid and inflexible, a sort of solid foundation that the rest of existence rests on. When you watch the rainbow come and go, you can see that it's not. The universe expands and contracts. The universe shifts.

"People in the past understood this better than we do. Their lives weren't as settled as ours. They suffered wars and famines and disease outbreaks and other disasters. They knew that the universe wasn't solid."

Kurtz ended his speech and resumed eating. It was easily the longest time Petrenko had ever heard him, or any other Custodian, speak. "Thank you for talking to me," she said to the Custodian. Kurtz didn't respond.

***

Bai Lu was surprised to see the Custodian on the bridge of the Jolene as they prepared to alter the ship's course. She had assumed that he'd be hiding away in his cabin or something when the rest of the crew assembled here. Had Captain Dasgupta ordered him? Would Kurtz have obeyed her if she had? Maybe Petrenko would know. She'd have to ask her when they were done here.

"Engine status," Dasgupta said.

"Engines are operating normally," Bai answered. "Current acceleration one point zero gee."

"Reduce acceleration to zero," Dasgupta ordered.

"Reducing acceleration to zero, confirmed," Bai answered as she adjusted the controls at her station. For the first time since leaving Earth orbit, Jolene's engines throttled back until the ship was in freefall. It was a strange sensation.

"Alter course to one forty-three oh two thirty-four by sixty-three twenty-two fourteen by three oh three fourteen fifty," Dasgupta ordered.

Bai already had the new course memorized, so she was able to reel off the coordinates in reply while adjusting the settings. A little showy, but it would look good in her next crew evaluation report. It was always good to keep the peer review board suitably impressed.

"Increase acceleration to two-point five gee," Dasgupta ordered.

With a tiny sigh, Bai answered, "Increasing acceleration to two-point five gee, confirmed," and the moment of freefall was over, replaced by more than twice their ordinary weight. Jolene would spend the next 858 hours at the new acceleration, until they had matched velocities with Manhattan. Bai would have preferred to go back into Shimizu for the duration, but for some reason Petrenko had recommended that they remain active, and Dasgupta had gone along with the suggestion.

"Good work, Ms. Bai," Dasgupta said as Bai shut down her station controls. "That's all for now. Crew dismissed."

Bai staggered a little as she rose from her station and made her way down the companionway to the next deck. As she stumped her way down the corridor to the break room, she caught up with Petrenko. "What's the big idea?" she demanded.

The medical officer at least had the decency not to pretend she didn't understand the question. "I thought we needed to develop more unit cohesion," Petrenko told her. "The crew's never performed a mission like the Manhattan project, and I thought we needed to learn to work together more closely. The captain agreed."

Bai glared at her. "So we're going to be cooped up in this metal can for thirty-six days at two and a half gees as a bonding exercise?" Despite the twenty-odd centimeters the medical officer had on her, Bai felt quite capable of beating the daylights out of her, and a strong urge to do so.

Then she noticed Kurtz standing a few paces away, passively-aggressively waiting for them to get out of his way. She stood aside for him and waited for him to pass. When he was out of earshot, she asked, "And what was he doing on the bridge? It felt like he was watching me."

"He was," said Petrenko. "He was there to monitor you during the maneuver."

Bai felt her outrage over the prospect of five weeks of burdensome weight give way to outrage over this new affront. "Him monitor me?' she hissed.

"Who do you think maneuvers this 'metal can' during turnover when we're in Shimizu?" Petrenko responded. "And he's damn good at it, too. I've seen the records of his last three turnovers, and his simulation scores, too. Custodians log thousands of hours of simulation training. They've got plenty of time on their hands, and they make effective use of it."

"Since when did you become such an admirer of the Custodians?" Bai sneered. She was expecting a hot denial from the medical officer, but she didn't get one.

"Since I had it brought home to me just how much we rely on them," Petrenko said unapologetically. "We treat it as a joke or an embarrassment. They have what should be a major personality dysfunction, but it turns out to be extraordinarily useful. They hold our civilization together.

"And they're completely reliable. We used to lose about five percent of our ships to accidents or unknown causes, but since the use of Custodians was mandated on interstellar flights, we haven't lost a single ship. Not one!"

Bai didn't think she'd ever come across anyone so eager to defend the Custodians. She was a little ashamed to admit that she did view the Custodians as a joke or an embarrassment. "All right," she said. "I grant you that they do a decent job, and I'll even grant you that it's an important job. But I still reserve the right to be uncomfortable around them."

Now Petrenko was sardonic. "Far be it from me to rob you of your discomfort, Ms. Bai."

Bai gave her a parting glare. She had changed her mind, and decided that her bunk was a more congenial destination than the break room. Despite herself, though, she found that she was thinking about the Custodians as she clumped her way down the companionway to the next deck.

✳✳✳

Ayodele Olatunji wasn't happy to see the rock hovering overhead. Of course, "hovering" wasn't a strictly accurate way to describe the situation. Manhattan was slowly tumbling on its axes while plowing through space at .63 of the speed of light, and Jolene had matched its speed and trajectory over the course of thirty-six grueling days of acceleration. Now, in a completely different but equally uncomfortable situation, the ship was in freefall while the rock tumbled along ten kilometers away.

Those thirty-six days had been spent gathering as much data as possible on Manhattan, and on working out how to divert it away from the Calypso system. If it weren't rotating, they could just use Jolene's drive to push it out of the way. Since it was rotating, they'd have to be more creative.

"We've got plenty of power," Olatunji said. "The problem is applying it."

Holger Kurtz nodded as he studied the tumbling rock from his bridge station. The Custodian had proved to be a good sounding board as Olatunji considered various means of dealing with Manhattan. He didn't try to make small talk; he just sat and listened, and very occasionally made sensible comments.

A readout gave motion figures for what they had designated as Manhattan's three axes of rotation. "Just halting the rotation on one of the axes would make the problem a hundred times simpler," Olatunji added. "Well, ten times simpler anyway."

A long pause while Olatunji sat and thought. "Perhaps a precisely-timed energy burst at just the right spot on the surface would halt the rotation of one axis."

"Or shatter it," Kurtz said quietly.

Olatunji nodded ruefully. "Or shatter it," he admitted.

Another long pause.

"Or maybe," Olatunji said, "shattering it is just what we want."

Kurtz turned away from the rock's image to look at Olatunji, which for him was equivalent of another person saying What the hell?

"Split it in two," Olatunji explained, "and let each fragment's inertia carry it away from the Calypso system. Let the rock's angular momentum work for us instead of against us."

Kurtz looked thoughtfully back at Manhattan.

***

Nilanjana Dasgupta watched as the clock counted down the last seconds before the action started. Jolene was three klicks ahead of Manhattan now as the rock tumbled on its way to the Calypso system. A quick glance around the bridge showed that the rest of the crew was doing the same, including Kurtz. "Engines on standby," she said at last.

"Engines on standby, confirmed," Bai answered.

The last seconds flicked away. "Hit it," Dasgupta said.

Freefall ended abruptly as the engines came on full blast at three gees. An intensely bright spot of light appeared on the surface of Manhattan, then began to track across the surface as the rock's rotation continued. Jolene moved away from Manhattan at 30 meters per second squared, because that was what the drive was supposed to do, but the energy remained focused on the rock. Now there was a brightly glowing line stretching across the rock. If their information on Manhattan's internal structure was correct, that line was widening fissures in the rock. Get enough fissures wide enough, and the rock's own angular momentum would tear it in two, sending the two fragments moving away from each other and away from the Calypso system.

The three-minute mark came up, and Dasgupta ordered, "Reduce acceleration to zero."

"Acceleration at zero, confirmed," Bai said as the weight left them all again. "Distance to Manhattan, 489 klicks. Relative speed, 5.4 km/s."

"Well done, Ms. Bai. Now turn us over and bring us back to the rock. Stop us ten klicks away."

As Bai spun Jolene around and brought the ship back towards Manhattan, Olatunji and Kurtz studied the rock while Petrenko studied Kurtz. The Yoruban engineer and the Custodian raised their heads to look at each other, and both grinned. "Operation successful," Olatunji reported. "Two daughter fragments, as projected. Calculating new trajectories."

For reasons that escaped Dasgupta, Kurtz had named the larger of the two projected fragments Fat Man, and the smaller Little Boy. After a pause that seemed much longer than it was, Kurtz spoke up. "New trajectory for Little Boy shows it missing Calypso Solis by ninety-two thousand AUs. The outer reaches of the system's Oort Cloud."

Olatunji spoke up. "New trajectory for Fat Man shows it missing Calypso Solis by twenty-seven thousand AUs. Ladies and gentlemen, we did it!"

Dasgupta wouldn't have believed it was possible for so few people to make so much noise. Even Kurtz was taking part in the general hilarity. Petrenko, on the other hand, was unusually subdued. The medical officer caught her eye and made a slight gesture that she interpreted as a wish to speak with her privately.

When the cheering had subsided, Dasgupta said, "Ms. Bai, calculate a new course for the Bevilacqua system, and accelerate to one gee."

When Bai had them back on course for their original destination, Dasgupta dismissed the crew. "Drinks are on me in the break room," Olatunji announced as they all went down the companionway. Dasgupta herself and Petrenko remained behind on the bridge.

"What is it, Ms. Petrenko?" she said.

"I'm worried about Kurtz," she answered.

That was the last thing Dasgupta expected to hear. "What about him? He seems fine. In fact, he seems unusually well-adjusted."

"That's what worries me," the medical officer said. "He's probably the most sociable Custodian I've ever seen. He not only looks directly at other people, he's begun making small talk. He's being treated like a normal member of the crew."

"And that's a bad thing?"

"It is for a Custodian," Petrenko insisted. "It's probably the worst thing that could have happened to him. Think about it, Captain. Sometime in the next few hours, all the rest of us are going back into Shimizu, and then Kurtz will be alone again for the next eight years."

Dasgupta frowned as the implications sank in. "You think he'll have trouble adjusting to being alone again?"

"I can just about guarantee it," Petrenko said. "He's never experienced comradeship before, so he's never missed it. Now that he has, suddenly finding himself without it again is going to be the hardest thing he's ever had to deal with. I'm worried about the possible consequences."

"What do you recommend?"

Petrenko shook her head. "I don't know what to recommend. This has never happened before."

"Well, we're going to have to come up with something," Dasgupta said. "And as you say, we've only got a few hours to do it."

***

It was remarkably like being back in the solar system. One by one, the crew of Jolene entered the main Shimizu capsule, and Petrenko activated the system that would halt their metabolic functions. When Ms. Bai was gone, and it was just the three of them, Petrenko paused before entering the main capsule herself. "Are you sure about this, Captain?" she asked.

"Quite sure, Ms. Petrenko."

The medical officer sighed. "On your head be it." She entered the capsule and Dasgupta operated the controls, and then it was just her and the Custodian.

Kurtz looked her in the eye. "Are you sure about this, Captain? It's still not too late to change your mind."

Dasgupta didn't hesitate. "Quite sure, Mr. Kurtz." She turned to face away from the Shimizu capsule before returning her gaze to the Custodian. "So, what do you do to pass the time around here, Mr. Kurtz?"

The Custodian paused for a moment to consider, then said, "Have you ever heard of a novel called War and Peace?"

###

ABOUT JOHNNY PEZ

JOHNNY PEZ LIVES IN BELLEFONTE, Pennsylvania and works in the hospitality industry. He has a bachelor's degree in history from the University of Delaware. He is best known for his Insanely Complete List of works in Isaac Asimov's Robot/Foundation series; and for the Drowned Baby Timeline, a multipart alternative history in which Hitler was drowned at birth.

Connect with Johnny here: www.castrumpress.com/johnny-pez.

THE CALLER

Lisa Timpf

I ring the doorbell at 224 Partridge Lane and step back, arms crossed.

Rule 1: Don't intimidate the clients, I remind myself. I clasp my hands behind my back. There. That's better.

The door swings open, revealing a woman dressed in forest-green slacks and a matching sweater. The outfit compliments her green-brown eyes. Her salt-and-pepper hair, styled in an easy-care cut, looks neatly combed. I consult my portacomp, check the image on the screen, and glance back up. Perfect match. Still, I follow the process, like I would with any Call.

"Sonja Bronston?" I ask, confirming.

She nods curtly. "You're lucky you caught me in." Sonja shoots a pointed glance at her gold-banded watch.

"Your schedule showed two hours of downtime. You volunteered at the animal shelter this morning, and you're due at your part-time job at Account For It, Inc. in about 70 minutes."

"Are you a hacker?" Sonja asks. Her expression curdles.

"Worse," I reply, attempting levity. "I'm with the government."

"Prove it."

I tug the laminated identification badge from its usual resting spot in the right front pocket of my flak vest and allow her time to study it.

"Justine Michaelson," she reads. "Department of--" She raises her head and her eyes widen.

"I think you know why I'm here," I say, keeping my tone level. I stand perfectly still. If I move I might spook her, causing her to spring away like a startled deer.

She places her right hand on her hip and rakes me with an unflattering gaze, taking in the black uniform that conceals an ultra-thin, but effective, layer of bulletproof armor. I've done her the courtesy of raising my face shield, so she can see my features. Not exactly according to protocol, but I can see she isn't packing a gun. Besides, she doesn't seem the type.

Her face twists in a grimace.

"Are you –"

Impatient, I cut her off. "I'm not proud, nor am I mighty and dreadful. I'm tired of having John Donne spouted at me," I say. "Besides, I'm not Death. Just an emissary."

"That's not what I was going to ask." Sonja's voice, to her credit, sounds calm. "Actually, I was about to inquire whether you wanted tea while we talk."

She seems sincere. Also, not the type to try something stupid. I'm familiar with death in all its forms. Poison, I would detect.

"Thanks. That would be lovely. Something spicy, if you have it," I answer. "Herbal, please. I've had enough caffeine."

"Coffee's not good for you, you know"." She tosses the comment back over her shoulder as she heads down the tiled hallway, toward what I assume is the kitchen.

"Occupational hazard. Shift work," I reply as I follow her, my soft-soled black boots noiseless on the hardwood. "I work a lot of nights. On call, too." I'm not usually this gabby on my assigned visits, but it's the last Call of the shift, and I figure a little polite chit-chat is fair compensation for the offered beverage.

"I've been expecting you, actually"." I notice the tremor in Sonja's hands as she fumbles for the switch on the kettle. With her back turned to me, she raises her hand to her face and makes a swiping motion across her left cheek, then her right. "I do think it's unfair. I contribute so much. Why me?"

I shrug, leaning against the kitchen's doorjamb as I watch her. "What are you, a hundred and twenty years old?"

"Going on one-twenty-one," she says, her voice breaking. She turns to face me, and I notice her wet cheeks without comment. "I still have the potential to live another sixty years. Why can't we just control the birth rate?"

"It's been tried," I observe. "Never seems to work."

"How about a merit system?"

"Bureaucrats find it easier to set up rules than to make judgments," I say. "You're the oldest. You've lived the longest. Ergo, in the government's books, that means your number is up.

Sonja hands me a steaming mug. "Thank you," I say. I smile to show it's nothing personal. "Now, as for the specifics--"

"What if I refuse?" she challenges, leading the way back to the living room.

"Then someone nastier than me shows up. You'll be found, one way or the other." I stride over to the window and look out over the green-lawn expanse of suburbia. She's lucky to be able to afford a place like this, when so much of New Toronto is condos and high-rise apartments. "Names get posted. Neighbors and co-workers will know. They also understand that if you aren't found within a month, whoever's next moves up on the list. That hits too close to home. We'd have plenty of help locating you."

"Fine," she sighs. "I get forty-eight hours to decide the method, and then five additional days to make any necessary arrangements, don't I?"

"You've done your research."

"It's all cut and dried to you, isn't it?" The green-brown eyes don't seem as soft now as they did when I first arrived.

What would you know about that? I think the words but bite them back. "The tea was excellent, thank you. Here's the options list." I rise to my feet and hand her the pre-printed form. "I'll be back in forty-eight hours."

"I'll be here," she says. "I hope you understand if I tell you I'm not looking forward to it."

I don't bother to tell her how often I've heard that line. Instead, I nod and force a smile, then snap the face shield into place and turn for the door.

✳✳✳

Cut and dried. Sonja's words insist on replaying themselves through the first four hours of my next shift.

At lunch, I seize the opportunity to kick back a bit, trying to drive Sonja from my mind by swapping stories with Gravinski. The effort is partly successful, and I start to relax.

Beep! My persacomm goes off, and then beep! so does Gravinski's. She grins at me, tossing her long black hair back over her shoulders.

"Power outage nine months ago," she comments, then shrugs. "New births, new deaths. Sometimes I wish it was flu season again."

"You thought you'd go crazy from inactivity, remember? We went whole nights without a single Call. The population balanced itself."

"Yeah, well"." She waves her persacomm at me as she swings for the door. "This is a little too busy. No happy medium. "

As I watch her lithe form retreating down the hall, I marvel at how well she's looked after her body. She's pushing ninety years old. I wonder what my Mom would have looked like at that age--

Beep! Another Call. Better get going. I check that my gear's in place and grab a coffee-to-go out of the machine.

As I climb into the hover car, my thoughts turn back to Sonja. It's not fair for her to try to make me feel guilty. I'm just doing my job. Besides, she ought to have known. She ought to have prepared. It's not like the Callers program just started yesterday.

Dangerous ground, I remind myself as I plug the destination in to the hover car's control panel. But once I've input the destination, I have nothing to do but sit and think while the machine whisks me to my next stop.

No, the Callers didn't start yesterday.

Back when the program began, your number came up by chance. Random draw.

No point fighting it. I let memory take me back to my first encounter with the Callers.

✳✳✳

Mom and I had just finished breakfast on a sunny Saturday in August when the knock came at the door. I ran to answer it, hoping it might be my friend Victoria dropping by so we could play catch at the park. It'd be a great way to break in my new softball glove, a twelfth-birthday present that I'd received the day before.

I opened the door, disappointed to find, instead of Victoria, a broad-shouldered, black-clad man taller than my dad. I had to look way up to see his face.

Mom's voice came from behind me. "Justine, why don't you take Solo for a walk?" I shifted from foot to foot, curious about our visitor and debating the merits of ignoring the suggestion. Another glance at the man's less-than-welcoming expression decided the issue for me. I ran to get Solo's leash and slipped out the side door with the dog in tow.

I took my time, letting Solo have a good sniff at the signposts favored by the other neighborhood canines instead of impatiently telling him to get on with it, like I usually did. In truth, I hoped that the stranger would be gone by the time I got back. No such luck, I realized as soon as I turned the corner and started down the sidewalk toward our two-story house. The black SUV with its menacingly wide grill still sat at the curb. As I drew closer to the porch, I could hear raised voices, as though Mom and the man were arguing.

"There you are," Mom said as I negotiated the four wooden stairs with dragging steps. Solo hid behind me and cringed, averting his gaze from our visitor.

I studied Mom's face, hoping to see her usual carefree expression. As though guessing my thoughts, she forced a smile. "Give this to your Dad when he gets home, will you?" She handed me an envelope.

"Where are you going?"

I glanced at Mom, then at the man, who stood with his arms crossed in front of his broad chest. He checked his watch. "It's time," he said, in a deep, grating voice devoid of emotion.

Mom crouched to look me in the eye, placing her right hand on my shoulder. "Dad will explain." She hugged me so tightly I couldn't breathe for a few seconds. Then she released me. "I have to go."

I stood on the front porch and watched as she got into the back of the vehicle. I stayed until the vehicle negotiated the corner, then turned and went into the house.

That was the last time I saw my mother.

Mom had the misfortune to be among the First Ten Thousand, those unfortunates selected by random draw to sacrifice their lives in the aim of population control.

The media made a big deal of the Ten Thousand milestone, which got people riled up, too. Rioting in all the major cities resulted in significant casualties. Ironically, this in turn provided some breathing space in terms of population density, but not for long.

When the Callers program started up again, the protests left their mark. The revitalized system had some significant alterations, the most significant one being selection based on age--oldest first--rather than random choice.

The new procedure saw a seven-day grace period built in as well. The initial grab-and-go process stemmed from the fear that, once informed of their fate, people would choose to disappear. But the powers-that-be soon realized that those who fled would be subject to vigilante justice. Their neighbors, after all, had a vested interest in ensuring the process didn't just skip to the next person on the list.

That miserable experience of seeing my mother taken so suddenly motivated my career choice. If it had to be done--and based on the population/resource balance, the thinning of the population was necessary--it could at least be done humanely. I told myself I was making a difference--actually believed it, the first year or so.

But gradually, what started out as a mission, a passion, turned into a job. A grinding, somewhat depressing job that turns all Callers, no matter how high-minded they might have been when they started out, into cynics.

***

On my trip home after my shift, I fall into a doze, awakening suddenly when the hover car's arrival notification chime indicates we've reached my apartment. Despite my exhaustion, I suspect real sleep will prove elusive, but I have to try. First, though, I need to eat.

After heating a meal pouch in the micro, I wander over to the nearest of the two faux-leather chairs in the TV room.

Its twin sits empty, and I stare at it for a moment, shoulders slumped. Twenty-three days till liftoff, I remind myself, sucking the freshly-heated butter chicken paste through the meal pouch's straw-tube. I hold the pouch with my left hand while I use my right hand to rummage through the small drawer of the side table. With a grunt of satisfaction, I pull out the envelope containing the tickets.

My partner Danielle always said she liked surprises, but when I brought two tickets for the New Nova, headed for the colony on Degna, her reaction spoke volumes to the contrary.

"You think running away is the answer?" She'd stood there, hands on her hips, giving me the stink-eye.

"You always talk about how much you hate the system." I'd shrugged. "We can get away. Start again, new."

"Haven't you been listening? Jose, Michel, the other people in the group--we want to make a difference."

"Against this?" I walked over to the window and swept my arm in a vague gesture intended to take in the chokingly thick agglomeration of buildings below. "How?"

"It isn't easy." The admission came reluctantly, as if pulled from her. "People need to want change. But if we can convince them –"

"Sure." I'd laughed, then. "They'll give up their privilege, happily, for the good of--what? The rules are made now. They know what to expect. They figure they'll just wait their turn and hope for the best."

"We need to try." Her lips quirked downward. "Besides, there are my parents. My brothers and my sister. Nieces. Nephews. I don't want to leave them behind." She frowned. "Don't family connections mean anything to you?"

Thinking about my parents choked me up, like it usually did, so I went on the attack.

"I worked a ton of overtime to buy these," I'd said, nodding toward the tickets. "I'm in a job I hate, and with the unemployment levels here, there's no hope of getting a different one. I need a fresh start."

"Make it without me." Danielle had jumped to her feet and stormed out through the door, slamming it behind her.

✳✳✳

Despite the emotions stirred by that memory, I remain dry-eyed. Maybe Danielle's right. I do have my emotional armor. For the first time, I ponder what it must be like to be on the other side of that.

I finish the last of the butter chicken and rise to my feet to put the pouch in the chute of the gleaming repurposer.

Danielle's decision leaves me with another problem, and I allow my subconscious to chew on it while I reach into the freezer for an ice cream sandwich.

Fact is, tickets are sold in pairs for a reason. Experience gained through the first of the colonies in our own solar system demonstrated that the mental health of those who settle new planets remains more robust when they have a social support system. In accordance with regulations, the ship's security staff won't let me board without a declared companion.

I stare out the window for a while, letting my mind drift.

Finally, I arrive at a possible solution. It just might work, I tell myself. There's one way to find out.

✳✳✳

When I ring the doorbell at 224 Partridge Lane the next morning, Sonja pauses before opening it.

132

"You're early," she says, her voice resigned. She's wearing faded blue jeans and a royal blue zip-up hoodie that's fraying at the end of the sleeves. In her right hand, I can see the familiar buff-hued options list delineating all the ways she can choose to die with dignity. The paper trembles ever so slightly as she holds it out in my direction.

"Didn't know if I would find you in," I reply as I take the paper, trying to conceal my alarm at her appearance.

"I got dressed for my volunteer stint at the animal shelter but ended up just sitting here." Sonja's eyes appear glazed, and she stares straight ahead. "Doesn't seem to be much point anymore, does there?" she asks. "Going out, I mean. Doing anything."

"Listen," I tell her. "There's something I didn't mention to you before. It's not really my job to do it, you understand, but--" I draw a breath. What if she says no? Summoning my courage, I blurt, "You could take one of the colony ships."

"I thought of that," she says. "But--leave Earth? I don't think I can do it."

"If you volunteer to go, your name will come off the list."

"But my children and grandchildren," she protests. "And great-grandchildren"."

"Under the other...scenario," I pick my words carefully, as though choosing a path down a treacherous scree-covered hill, "they, uh – well, put it this way. If you take the colonization gig, they can look at the stars, knowing you're out there somewhere. As technology advances, maybe they'll even come and visit you some day. If you don't –"

"But I need a partner, don't I?" she says, her voice trembling.

"'You can be mine," I reply. "I have a pair of tickets for the New Nova. It leaves for Degna in twenty-two days."

"That's very generous."

"Not really," I confess. "Someone backed out on me."

"You okay?" The concern in her voice sounds genuine.

I nod. As okay as I'll ever be, considering.

"What's to guarantee humans won't make the same mistakes?" she whispers.

"No guarantees," I admit. "But we get the chance to try."

"Will there be a moon?" she asks.

"Two," I reply. "And a mauve sky."

"Purple was my favorite color, as a child," she says. After staring out the front window for several long moments, she turns to face me, her expression brightening. "I always did think I was too busy to die."

"Don't put it that way," I say, reaching out to place a comforting hand on her upper arm. "Tell yourself, instead, you have too much to offer."

"Thank you." She grips my hand warmly. "But why the extra effort?"

"You remind me of someone," I say, trying to keep my voice from cracking with emotion. It's true. I see a ghost, a hint, of my mother's smile on her face as I turn away.

***

During the next few days, I keep my mask firmly in place, forcing myself not to engage emotionally with any of my other clients. Instead, I focus on Sonja, and the second chance she's gained thanks to me. I've done something good for a change, I tell myself, almost singing the words.

And then, when I'm shooting the breeze with Gravinski in the lunch room, the call comes.

I can feel the blood drain from my face, and Gravinski must see it, too, because she stands up at the same time I do.

"My dad," I tell her, turning to leave.

"Hey," she says, placing a hand on my arm. "Don't tell the brass. Just let me cover for you. I could use the extra cash."

I stare at her for a long moment.

"Thanks, Gravinski." I hand her my comm device, nod tersely, then stride out the door.

***

"Almost there," the person seated to my left tells me, gesturing toward the window.

I glance out the small rectangular pane to my right. I remember my mother telling me about the first time she landed at Halifax Airport. The plane flew so low going over the trees that she'd braced herself for a crash landing. The forests have yielded way to houses, acres and acres of them, but with the hover-jet, we don't have to fly as low before landing as those old 747's used to.

The hover-jet decelerates, and I glance down to see a long, low building surrounded by what looks like bull's-eyes. The pilot, or the computer, or maybe both guide us down to a perfect landing on one of the pads. There's a smattering of applause; spurred by relief, I suppose, although there's little need for fear of flying--it's been a decade, at least, since the last hover-jet accident.

"Going to check out the sights?" the lady beside me asks as the seatbelt sign winks off.

"Maybe," I reply, more out of politeness than anything else. Truth is, I have little desire to see what changes the pressures of ever-increasing population have wrought upon my favorite haunts – the Public Gardens, Point Pleasant Park, Lawrencetown Beach. "I'm here to visit my dad."

"Well, have fun," she says, her voice bright.

Fun, I think, pausing as I pull my lightweight overnight bag down from the compartment. Somehow, I doubt it.

134

He's gotten thinner. That's the first thing I think when I enter the no-grav room where my dad, whose nerve endings have become so sensitive that any contact is pure torment, hovers, grinning despite everything.

"Hey, kiddo," he says. "Great to see you."

"You too," I reply mechanically. I reach out to hug him, remember his condition, and instead sit beside him, cross-legged, floating in the air.

"Has its compensations, huh?" he asks, indicating the room and its gravity-defying features with a wave of his hand.

"Yeah"," I reply, unable to repress a smile. I glance around the room, then down at the floor above which we're suspended. Visiting Dad always brings home, with a vengeance, one of the biggest contradictions in our society. If your number hasn't come up, hospitals will go to any lengths to keep you alive. On the other hand, every day the Callers go out to conduct their grim harvest. But what's the alternative? Letting people die when you could save them? I shrug. I'm here to visit, not to philosophize.

I realize my Dad's been staring at me, and offer an apology, which he shakes off.

"Planning to stay awhile?" he asks. As usual, I've brought along a light backpack with a couple of crossword books, some water, and snacks.

"Sure," I reply.

"I appreciate it-- I really do," he says, his voice turning solemn. "But I called you here because there's something I want to tell you before--"

"Dad," I say, choking on the word.

"It's time." His voice is gentle, but firm. "Coming here gave me a good five years, and I'm grateful for that. But the disease has progressed, and there's nothing more they can do. I've elected to choose to go, before the pain becomes totally unbearable." He clears his throat. "It'll be quick, from what I hear."

"Oh, Dad."

We sit in silence for a moment. I turn my head, so he won't see my face. When I've regained command over my emotions, I swivel my head and look him in the eye.

Accepting that as a signal, he clears his throat. "Because this is our last conversation, 'I'm going to tell you something I've been constrained to keep secret since your Mom –" He stops, and this time he's the one who needs to struggle to maintain composure.

I sit up straighter.

"I know why you went into your current line of business," he says when he feels ready, "and I don't blame you. But the truth is, your mother volunteered."

I stare at him, disbelieving.

"The number that came up wasn't hers," he whispers. "It was yours. She went in your place."

Now I do cry in earnest, the tears streaming down uncontrollably, then drifting into the room, where they create a salty mist.

"I know," he says, his tone urgent now. "But listen. The reason I'm telling you this is, she would have wanted you to enjoy your life. Do you understand? The opportunity for you to live, to make choices, it came at a price. Respect that."

A wave of anger washes over me. "Why keep it a secret?" The words grate harshly.

"It was part of the agreement." He leans back. "Think about it. They couldn't let that sort of thing be common knowledge. Otherwise, every child whose parent got Called back then would think –"

My heart feels so heavy, it's dragging my body down. I look around and realize Dad, too, is getting lower.

Then I see the nurse in brightly patterned scrubs who's appeared on the other side of the glass. She's manipulating the controls, ratcheting up gravity incrementally, so that we don't crash to the ground like a ton of bricks.

"You don't have to stay with me," Dad says, squaring his shoulders as we touch down. "If it's too hard –"

Too hard. In the light of what he's told me about Mom, it feels like nothing. "I'll be there. Holding your hand."

And I do, until his breathing stops – though I have difficulty seeing for sure, since my vision's gone blurry again. The nurse puts a hand on my shoulder, telling me he's gone.

I stagger out of the room, down the corridor, and into the dazzling sunlight.

✳✳✳

Back in my apartment three days later, I check the digital readout on the wall. Six hours until my approved bereavement leave ends.

I swing out of bed, pad into the living room, and put my remaining ticket for the New Nova in my wallet. Liftoff's getting closer, and somehow, I feel nervous if I don't keep it with me, as though it might vaporize of its own accord.

My jaw tightens. Between my Dad's passing, and the memories of my mother that seem to surround me all the time now, my nerves feel raw. The last thing I feel like is going to work. But there are still a couple of weeks before the ship departs, and I can use the money. Colonists need a lot of supplies, and they don't come free.

Suck it up, I tell myself when it's time to leave for the office.

Once I arrive, I order up a coffee from the insta-dispenser in the common room.

Gravinski strides in, looking so downcast that I almost turn to go, but she sees me and beckons me over as she slumps into one of the plasta-form seats.

"Can you beat that?" she asks, her voice hollow as she stares at the wall.

"What?" I ask, easing myself into the chair opposite her.

Her gaze falls on my face, and she struggles to focus. "I was saving to buy tickets on one of the colony liners, for my mom and me. That's why I've been such a hound about overtime. But now she's gone and gotten a ticket herself."

"Go figure," I say, feeling my heart pound against my ribs. "Uh--is her last name Gravinski?" I know how idiotic that might sound, but I need to hear the answer.

"No, it's Bronston," she says, frowning slightly. "She remarried. Why?"

"Long story," I reply.

She slumps in her chair, and I glance at the digital clock on the west wall. Still ten minutes till the start of my shift.

Who am I trying to kid? There's no connection, really, between Sonja and me. Sure, she's volunteered to be my companion, but I'm not sure that's really going to work all that well for either of us.

Besides, I've got unfinished business here.

"Look." Even though I've made my mind up, it's hard, still, to put into words. "I bought tickets for Danielle and me to go to Degna on the New Nova, but after she broke up with me--I've lost the heart for it." My hands tremble a little--just a little--as I draw the ticket out of my wallet. When I extend the ticket in her direction, Gravinski is forced to tug a little to get me to release it.

I see her lips move as she reads the information. She runs her fingers over the ticket's glossy surface as though affirming its reality.

"Then you're coming too?" She shoots me a glance.

I shake my head.

"What'd you do with the other ticket?"

"Lost it in a poker game."

"Not surprised. You're a lousy poker player. You don't have the face for it." She shoots me a searching look, then grins. "Wait till I tell her," she says, jumping to her feet with an animation I've never seen in her. "Here"." She presses a credit-chip card into my hand.

I shake my head. She closes my fingers over it.

"Listen, Justine," she says. "You're not cut out for this." She jerks her head in a gesture that takes in the room, with its dismal layer of faded green-gray paint. "Use it to go back to school, or re-establish yourself somewhere. Something. Just get out of here. Promise?"

***

After I give the ticket away, my concentration's shot. I alternate between asking myself *What have I done?* and *Now what?* I don't have a good answer for either question.

When I call on a home with two individuals with the same first and last name, and I start my spiel with the one who's clearly the younger of the two, I realize it's time to quit before I make an error that'll harm someone other than myself. I return to the office and turn in my badge, taking a certain satisfaction in doing so. Then I spend the rest of the day wandering the streets of New Toronto. I hop on the subway, get off at a random station, and order a coffee.

That gives me time to think. When I finish, I start walking again, with greater purpose this time.

When Danielle opens the door to her apartment, she glances behind her.

She's got someone here, I tell myself. I lower my head. "It's okay. I'll just go."

"Don't." I dare, then, to look up. Danielle's posture remains rigid, and her expression doesn't contain a hint of anything I might mistake for welcome. "It's just--I've been packing."

"Moving again?" I school my features to maintain a neutral expression.

Danielle gestures with her arm, inviting me in, then closes the door behind us. "I meant to come and say goodbye. I really did. Just hadn't gotten to it."

"I'm not going on the New Nova." I keep my voice flat, non-committal.

"Because of me?" She crosses her arms.

"Someone else needed the tickets more than I did." True, but that's not all. "And I missed you. So yeah, a little bit because of you."

Her eyes widen, then narrow, and I can guess what she's thinking: why would I, who always stayed so deliberately detached from everything, stick my neck out for someone else?

"Look, you were right about – lots of things." My voice trails off, and I stop, suddenly exhausted. "It just took me time to realize it. After my Dad –"

"What happened to your Dad?" She places a hand on my arm, peering into my face, and I remember, with a stab of pain, how much she enjoyed his satirical sense of humor when we used to visit him.

"He's gone," I whisper.

As though she doesn't trust herself to speak, Danielle hugs me for a long moment. When she finally breaks the silence, her voice trembles as she says, "I'll make you a cup of tea."

✳✳✳

When I wake up, I stare at the ceiling. It takes me a few moments to realize I'm not in my own apartment. I glance around, frowning, and spot Danielle in the kitchen. I let my hand run over the surface of the quilt covering me, and glance down. It's a handmade patchwork that her mother made. It used to have a prominent spot in the place we shared. Seeing it here makes me feel both melancholy, and at home.

Danielle offers a cheery, "Good morning," and I wander over and seat myself at the round two-seater table. She's put toast and jam on the table, and as we eat breakfast and sip coffee from mugs that also have a familiarity to them, we fill each other in on what's happened in the couple of months since we split up. Finally, the

138

discussion starts to run itself down as we run out of things to say. Danielle rises from her seat and starts to clear the table.

"What are you going to do now?" she asks.

I shrug. "I can't do that job any more. Not after –"

"Have you thought about joining the Movement?" she says.

"Where?"

"We're relocating." She bites her lip, then continues. "It's supposed to be low-profile, so don't tell anyone."

I nod.

"We have some members with...resources. One of them has a large fenced estate up near Collingwood. It used to be a private school, so it's got accommodations and amenities for a number of people, and we can fix it up for more."

"A place to do some plotting?" I keep my tone light.

"Yeah, you can call it that. It could be a slow process, making change, but we have to try."

"How?" I can't help affecting a despairing tone.

"Changing opinions, one person at a time. Helping people realize the unsustainability of how we're living." She pauses and takes a breath. "Preparing candidates and platforms, to strive for political change." Danielle walks to the window and looks out. "That's one scenario. There's another, more solemn, one. A lot of the future modeling that's being done, even on the new Super Comp at U of T, suggests that we're due for a major pandemic. People just aren't meant to live in such close quarters, the way we do through most of the world these days. It would have a massive impact on the population."

"So, chances are my former job would become redundant someday?"

"In all probability." She turns back to face me. "But if the pandemic happens – and it's not like we're making it happen, or hoping it will happen, we just think it will –"

I lean forward.

"Someone needs to think about what's next. Once things are under control again, we need to change things so we don't end up in the same place again." Her expression brightens. "And if the pandemic doesn't happen, we still have a place to live and work and plan from. A beautiful setting, from what I've heard. The big population push hasn't gone that far north yet."

It's my turn to move to the window and look out over the city, the steady lines of hover cars making snail's-pace progress down the streets. I shiver, suddenly aware of my vulnerability.

Perhaps the time has come to shed the emotional armor I wrapped around myself after my mother died. Time to care about something beyond my small circle of acquaintances, and to allow myself to hope on a grander scale.

I look at the stars, and think of Gravinski and her mom. In a few days, the New Nova will streak across the sky, offering new opportunities under new skies.

But I realize now that Mother Earth is neither a bad nor a hopeless place to be-- and she deserves a second chance, too. If I can help, that's good enough for me.

###

ABOUT LISA TIMPF

LISA TIMPF IS A RETIRED HR and communications professional who lives in Simcoe, Ontario. Her science fiction stories have appeared in New Myths, Third Flatiron, The Martian Wave, and the Dogs of War and Mother's Revenge anthologies. When not writing, Lisa enjoys organic gardening, bicycling, and bird-watching.

Connect with Lisa here: www.castrumpress.com/lisa-timpf.

THE TRICKLE-DOWN EFFECT

Mark Lynch

"Trickle-down economics – the theory that economic benefits provided to upper income level earners will help society as a whole."

"Everybody knows that the dice are loaded,
Everybody rolls with their fingers crossed,
Everybody knows the war is over,
Everybody knows the good guys lost,
Everybody knows the fight was fixed,
The poor stay poor, the rich get rich,
That's how it goes,
Everybody knows."

LEONARD COHEN

CRACK! Denton smashed his baseball bat against the body of his helpless victim, scowling as the pathetic man let out a pained cry.

"Please boss!" Max pleaded desperately, "Please, no more!"

"Shut the fuck up!" Denton spat back, before hitting his victim again. CRACK! The man screamed.

Denton was sure he'd broken at least one of Max's ribs. Perhaps this was enough. The attacker didn't particularly enjoy this shit. Beating a man on the ground, pounding him while he lay in a pool of his own blood, puke and piss – this wasn't

Denton's thing – but often brutal violence was the only option in the Pit. His victim whimpered, curling up in a protective ball while he fearfully awaited the next blow.

"Okay scumbag!" Denton snarled through clenched teeth, "I didn't want to do this, but you left me no choice. Now, what you got on you?"

"Nothing boss!" the bloodied man cried, "I swear man, I'm clean!"

"Bullshit!" Denton exclaimed, "Empty your damn pockets!"

His victim failed to comply, and so Denton hit him again, taking the opportunity to pin Max down while he riffled through the pockets of his victim's filthy jeans.

"God damn junkie!" Denton shouted.

He examined the pathetic spoils he'd acquired – a mere six vials of cocaine and about twenty bucks in assorted Syndicate notes.

"Hey man, what is this bullshit?" Denton cried angrily, "You owe me 200 bucks asshole...or did you forget?"

Max whimpered, "I swear to god boss, I'll pay back every cent..."

"I know you will." Denton replied menacingly, "I'll be back next week, and you better have something for me! Don't make me come find you!"

He made to walk away from his hapless victim, but then suddenly turned back, swinging his bat and hitting the man hard, making him squeal.

"And if you ever steal from me again asshole...I'll fucking skin you alive!"

Satisfied that his point was made, Denton turned his back on the thieving junkie and causally strolled up the darkened alleyway with his bat in hand, walking towards the bright neon lights of the city street.

Max would pay him back eventually, assuming he lived that long. Denton knew the risks of employing drug addicts to sell his stash, a certain amount of 'spillage' was inevitable, but sometimes a man in his line of work had to set an example. Some of his associates would have gone much further than a beating, but Denton didn't gain any pleasure from messing up junkies...and besides, a man couldn't pay his debt if he was crippled or dead, and Denton desperately needed money right now.

He continued to ponder his financial difficulties, noticing too late that his path was blocked by an interloper. He looked upwards, setting his eyes upon the armed patrol drone, hovering about ten feet above the sidewalk and blocking the entry of the alleyway. The small unmanned aircraft was partially automated, but the controls were taken over by a 'flesh and bones' operator based in a control room as soon as a threat was identified. Legally speaking, the corporations preferred having a human being to push the kill button.

The aerial drone produced a soft buzzing noise from its spinning rotors while shining a bright torch directly in Denton's face, temporarily blinding him. This was a deliberate intimidation tactic, since the drone's camera had night vision, and so the security officer operating the craft could already see him clearly. Denton also knew that the drone's mini-gun would be trained upon him, ready to open fire at the push of a button.

He didn't resist, but instead dropped the bat, raised his hands above his head and looked upwards towards the camera. The drone hovered for about thirty seconds, observing its subject and transmitting images and data back to its operator. Denton knew the drill. The drone's scanners would register him as a 'de-chipped' citizen and would instead use facial recognition software to confirm his identity. Denton had had his neural implant surgically removed years ago – technically this was an offence, but there were thousands of de-chippers living in the Pit, and the security drones rarely paid them any attention – not unless there was a district-wide sweep, and the Syndicate always received advanced warning of such operations.

There was the matter of the serious assault Denton had just committed, his victim still bleeding in the darkened alleyway just yards behind him. Again, he knew this wasn't an issue. The robotic drones and their human remote operators served the all-powerful corporations and so operated solely to protect corporate interests – the savage beating of a junkie in the Pit wasn't a crime which concerned the 'One-Percenters'. And so, Denton stood his ground, waiting patiently for the drone to complete its scan.

A half minute later and it was all over. The robotic craft slowly rose up into the night air, flying down the street in search of new targets. Denton didn't bother to retrieve his discarded baseball bat or check on his victim, instead he calmly strolled out onto the sidewalk. Here in 'The Pit' they had an expression – 'Shit runs downhill, money goes up.' And, right now, Denton could see the evidence of this trickle-down theory all around him.

This district was the worst in the mega city Denton called home, and the poverty, deprivation and grime were everywhere. A trio of rough-looking prostitutes tried to accost him on the street corner – buxom, blonde-haired whores in ill-fitting cocktail dresses and high heels, the tread marks on their arms all too evident.

"Hey, big boy!" one of them exclaimed, "Do you want a good time? We'll give you a discount..."

Denton ignored the woman, knowing all too well that an encounter with any of these hookers would either result in a S.T.I. or the loss of his drugs and money. He marched on, keeping his head up. One of the hookers yelled abuse after him, spitting on the sidewalk by his feet.

Denton weaved through the crowded street, avoiding assorted bums and junkies, pimps, thieves and prostitutes. Automated, electric cabs operated by the corporations sped up and down the road, while manual driven, gas-guzzling mopeds and motorcycles darted between them like angry hornets.

Denton witnessed a gang of semi-feral street children attempting to break into a vending machine set outside a store front. Denton couldn't help but feel sorry for them; their parents likely drug addicts, their corporate-sponsored education a joke, consisting only of pre-recorded broadcasts from a holo-screen. These were ragged and hungry kids, kicking and shaking the machine frantically. All they wanted was something to eat, but their basic needs were to be frustrated.

Denton watched on as an armed drone hovered over the street, zoning in on the feral gang. The unmanned aerial vehicle was of the same model which had buzzed Denton in the alleyway only moments before. The vending machine was corporate property and thus the drone was bound to intervene.

The UAV emitted a booming warning in a mechanized voice – 'YOU ARE DAMAGING PRIVATE PROPERTY. CEASE AND DESIST IMMEDIATELY. EXTREME FORCE IS AUTHORISED.'

The kids didn't need to be told twice. They scattered in all directions, running for their lives as they took shelter in alleyways and store fronts. Its job completed, the drone sped off in search of other troublemakers. Denton scoffed in disgust at what he had just witnessed. This was the way things worked down here in the Pit – the corporations only used their remotely controlled security forces to defend their own property and interests, and not to protect the people or enforce law and order. Only the Syndicate prevented the Pit from falling into complete anarchy.

But still, this town was very dangerous after nightfall, even for a man with Denton's tough reputation – there was always someone wanting to con, rob or fuck you over on these mean streets, so a man had to keep his wits about him.

Next, he passed a virtual reality arcade, its bright and intruding neon lights near blinding him. This was the type of seedy establishment where a man or woman could live out any perverse fantasy they could imagine in every little detail. Those few who could afford it may also opt for 'full immersion VR' as a means of escaping the filthy and oppressive streets of the Pit and entering a fantasy world of their choosing. But those with limited credits had to settle for cheap thrills and quick highs.

The proprietor of this arcade must have been having a slow night, because he was standing out on the pavement touting for business, accosting Denton as he walked by.

"Sir, sir! Slow down, sir! What's your hurry, my friend?" asked the overweight, middle-aged man, "You want a good time, sir? Then look no further. We've got the best virtual experiences for the best prices in town. What's your poison, my friend? A Roman-style orgy? BDSM dungeon? Or maybe something less conventional...You want to murder your worst enemy, rape your favorite movie star? We've got it all, sir. No judgement, no consequences..."

"No chip." Denton replied firmly, while pointing to his skull.

"My apologies, sir," replied the arcade owner, with disappointment evident in his voice, "I hope you have a pleasant evening."

Denton's lack of neural implant meant he could no longer indulge in VR immersions, but such false realities had never been his thing in any case. Instead, he relished the opportunity to leave the chaotic street behind - to escape the ruckus, danger and, most of all, the foul stench of human desperation. Denton made his way to a spit and sawdust bar set down a back alley – 'Underworld' was the name above the door, and Denton was something of a regular. Underworld wasn't exactly a classy establishment, but to him it was a proverbial oasis set in the middle of a barren desert.

He shoved through the swing doors and made his way to the bar, greeting the establishment's owner – a grizzled, scar-faced and tough-as-nails military veteran by the name of Butch. The bartender was the type who'd just as likely pull his shotgun on a patron than serve him a drink, but luckily Butch regarded Denton as an old friend.

"Evening, Mr. Denton," said Butch, in what passed for his amicable voice, "What will it be, my friend? I've got a new batch of pills just in...Uppers, downers...whatever you need..."

"Not tonight, buddy," answered Denton, as he sat upon his usual bar stool, "I'm off that shit. Just give me a double whiskey, on the rocks."

Butch nodded his head and proceeded to pour the drink, sliding the glass across the counter and into Denton's waiting hand. Denton took a large sip of hard liquor, savoring the rough and strong taste as it went down his throat. Butch probably sensed that his customer wanted to be left alone and so did not engage him in conversation. Denton took the opportunity to survey the scene inside of the bar-room.

Underworld was a rough joint frequented by tough individuals. Fist fights were almost a nightly occurrence, while stabbings and even shootings were not unknown. But tonight, the place was quiet, with only a handful of heavy drinking regulars at the bar and a couple of dope-fiends passed out in the corner. A scantily clad young woman called Tiffany was offering lap dances to the bar flies, but having little success. A slow night for Butch and his staff then.

Like most of the establishments in this district, Underworld sold both alcohol and narcotics – both legal and illegal drugs. Butch accepted electronic credits straight from the neural implants of his addicted customers, transferred directly into his online account – but, like all businesses in the Pit, Underworld also accepted the crude paper notes printed by the Syndicate. This was how it worked around here – there was a dual economy, one legitimate and the second illegitimate.

Officially, the one-percenters controlled everything. The super-rich sat pretty and comfortable in their luxury penthouses and fortified green zones, making obscene profits from their largely automated economy. Professionals and those lucky enough to still have skilled jobs lived on the levels below their corporate masters, and, at the very bottom of the social hierarchy, were the destitute underclass and unemployables of the Pit. These were the children and grandchildren of the workers who'd lost their jobs during the Final Industrial Revolution – the mass automation of all industries by the mega corporations.

Denton didn't know the figures but, without doubt, most of the population of this poverty-stricken district were officially unemployed and dependent on the meager universal credit paid out by the corporate-controlled government. The sheer desperation of their situation resulted in many citizens turning to booze and drugs – anything to dull the pain and escape the daily misery of life in the Pit.

The only people with any money or power in this district were the Syndicate – the vast criminal organization which controlled drugs, prostitution, loan sharking, gambling, hits for hire and just about everything else you could imagine in this shit-hole town. The mob ran the streets, imposing their own version of rough justice on those who crossed the line. The Syndicate was so powerful that they controlled their own bank and printed their own currency, operating a shadow economy with the tacit approval of the corporations.

After all, it benefitted both sides to maintain the status quo. The one-percenters didn't give a shit about the Pit – their only presence down here was their army of UAVs, the killer drones hovering above the streets, spying on the people and attacking those who dared to challenge corporate interests. But, for the most part, the corporate elite were content to allow the Syndicate to run the Pit, to deal drugs and take out hits – better for the poor to kill themselves rather than join forces to rise against the one-percenters.

Denton shook his head in disgust as he took another drink. He knew the score but cared little for politics, nor did he pay much attention to the television blaring above the bar, showing a corporate controlled news channel. The TV news was reporting some corporate-run war in a far-off land, with heavily armed mercenaries and automated attack drones fighting poorly armed local insurgents on the thin pretense of spreading 'democracy and free market economics'. In reality of course, they were seeking to secure the foreign region's ever dwindling natural resources. Instead of watching, his attention was drawn to the near naked lap-dancer; a slim, brown-skinned girl called Tiffany. She worked in the bar where Denton was a regular customer, so the two were no strangers.

Tiffany winked and smiled as she gently touched Denton on the shoulder. "Hey, big boy," she said coyly, "Do you want a dance? Or maybe you'd prefer to take me upstairs? We had fun last time...What do you say, baby?"

"Sorry, baby girl, not tonight." He replied.

Tiffany shrugged her shoulders and moved on. Denton felt like shit. Truth be told, he could have done with the company tonight, but he was so broke right now he couldn't afford Tiffany's prices...desperate times indeed.

He thought back to a night a couple of months back when he'd been able to afford Tiffany's services for an evening. After the wild sex, they'd sat up and talked well into the early hours. Denton had always been a cynic and so was surprised to learn that Tiffany had once been an idealist, dreaming of escape and a better life – but the Pit had crushed her spirit, forcing her into stripping and prostitution to make ends meet. She'd ended that night in tears while he held and comforted her in a rare show of tenderness. They'd never spoken of that night again.

Back in the present, his longing eyes continued to follow the young woman as she walked across the floor and sought out potential customers. Tiffany latched onto a group of four middle-aged men sitting at a table close to the bar's exit. Denton had hardly noticed these men before as they were intentionally keeping a low profile, drinking from two pitchers of beer while playing poker with an old-fashioned pack of cards.

Denton could tell from the overalls they wore that these men were 'blue collars' – that is, low-level operatives working for the corporations. Such men and women held the few semi-skilled or unskilled jobs which couldn't be fully automated. Generally, they were technicians who spent their days carrying out minor repairs or staring at security monitors. The blue collars were at the bottom of the corporate hierarchy, far below the engineers and computer programmers who kept the city's automated systems running.

Nevertheless, down here in the Pit, such workers were wealthy compared to most and thus were frequently targeted for robbery by junkies and crooks. A smart criminal might attempt to kidnap a blue collar and force him at gunpoint to download his electronic credits into an untraceable account, but e-crimes such as this were far too sophisticated for most of the small time, dumb-as-shit crooks in the Pit. More likely, a drug-addicted mugger would try to steal whatever a blue collar had on his person, right down to the clothes on his back and the shoes on his feet.

No wonder these four wanted to keep a low profile. But this didn't stop Tiffany touting for business. The girl shook her voluptuous body and flirted outrageously with the four men, trying hard to get a catch. Clearly, the workers weren't interested, but Tiffany persevered until eventually one of the men gave the lap dancer a twenty-dollar bill to get rid of her.

Tiffany wandered off, but the four men remained cautious and soon noticed Denton watching them from the bar. Robbing working men wasn't his thing, so Denton simply raised his glass in a friendly toast to the quartet and left them be.

Suddenly, there was some activity at the bar as the regulars began mumbling excitedly while staring up at the television. Butch used the remote to turn up the volume and soon the entire bar was transfixed, Denton included. A smartly dressed corporate newsreader sat in a studio, reading from a typecast in a monotone voice. A photograph of a grey-haired, overweight, yet, striking and charismatic man appeared on the screen – a man who every customer in the bar recognized at a glance.

"In news from the lower district, we have received confirmed reports that Angelo Lucchese, the self-proclaimed 'Mayor of The Pit' and reported leader of the Syndicate crime organization has died at the age of sixty-three. Mr. Lucchese was a notorious leader in the lowers, regarded by many as a generous and altruistic community leader, but accused by others of ordering hundreds of murders over a twenty-year period. Despite his violent reputation, Mr. Lucchese is reported to have died of natural causes at his family home. He is survived by his wife and three daughters..."

The news channel showed some stock footage of the Pit or the 'Lower District' as they insisted on calling it, before moving on to the next story. The shock in the bar room was palpable. Several of the regulars swore out loud while Butch stood behind the bar, shaking his head in disbelief. Tiffany walked up beside Denton's bar stool, a tear in her eye as she exclaimed - "My God! I'll never forget where I was when I heard the news!"

Denton couldn't contain his own shock. Don Angelo – the last of the old school mob bosses - was dead! For as long as he could remember, the Don had ruled the Pit using an iron fist in a velvet glove, maintaining discipline amongst the thousands of Syndicate members and associates through brutal measures, but also retaining a 'Robin Hood' type image due to the substantial amounts of money he put back into the community. Don Angelo was therefore loved and feared in almost equal measure, but perhaps his greatest legacy, was the relative peace on the streets during his long reign as 'King of the Pit', but now the King was dead, and the whole district was in danger of falling into blood anarchy and open gang-warfare.

The Syndicate was a huge, multi-racial criminal organization which operated something like a feudal kingdom. The Boss and his inner circle were at the top of the pyramid, but underneath the Don were twelve largely autonomous families, all run by their own captain or 'capo'. The trouble was that Don Angelo had died without an apparent heir or – as far as anyone knew – without naming a successor. In theory, any one of the dozen 'Capos' could make a play for the top job, in reality though, there were only two main contenders – Rodriguez from the East Side and Adebisi in the South Borough.

These men ran the two most powerful crime families in the Pit and it was well known that they hated each other's guts. Only the iron rule of Don Angelo had prevented the two captains from going to war, but now the Boss was dead, and all bets were off.

"This shit is bad," said Butch in a somber tone of voice, "It's going to be hell out on the streets!"

"Maybe..." Denton replied thoughtfully, "Then again, there might be some opportunities coming out of this mess..."

Denton was already thinking in pragmatic terms. He recalled that he owed substantial amounts of money to both Rodriguez and Adebisi – gambling debts, another of his many vices. Therefore, if one or both men were killed in a gangland feud, Denton would be off the hook. It was a harsh way of looking at things, but it was every man for himself down here, in the Pit. Denton was still considering the possibilities as he finished his drink, wished Butch and Tiffany a good night, and made his way back out onto the streets.

Denton was hungry and, so, it was his intention to grab something to eat from the convenience store around the block - something processed, fried and unhealthy was on the menu. However, he never got the chance to get his meal, because a pair of goons accosted him as soon as he left the bar. The men were both well-built, bald-headed tough guys in ill-fitting designer suits. One was white and the other black. Denton instantly realised these men were with the Syndicate – most likely foot-soldiers serving one of the 'capos'. But, what did they want with him?

"Are you Denton?" asked the white guy, his voice gruff and hostile.

"Who wants to know?" Denton replied coolly.

"The boss," answered the second goon, "Don Rodriguez. He wants to talk to you, buddy."

So, they worked for Rodriguez – that answered one question. "Your boss wants to see me, huh? And what makes you think I want to speak with him?"

"You need to show some respect, motherfucker!" shouted the white thug, his stance becoming increasingly hostile and threatening. "The Don wants to see you, and he ain't asking!"

Denton instinctively responded to his adversary's aggression, squaring up to the man and preparing to fight. It was the second of Rodriguez's men – the black guy – who acted as peacemaker.

"Woah! Listen, buddy, there's no need for violence. Our boss is around the corner, waiting in the car. All he wants is a friendly conversation. In fact, the Don has a proposition that could well be in your interests. You might as well hear him out...what do you say, my friend?"

Denton slowly backed down, unclenching his fists and following the pair to a parked, dark black limousine unsubtly parked on the street corner. He didn't have any beef with Rodriguez, but did owe the Syndicate captain a sizeable amount of money. Also, he was intrigued to hear what the proposition may be, especially since Rodriguez was a top contender for the throne now Don Angelo was dead.

They opened the door of the vehicle and showed Denton inside. Rodriguez sat spread out on the back seat of the limo, smoking a large cigar and sipping from a glass of cognac. The mob captain was a large, middle-aged and mustached man of

Hispanic descent, a veteran gangster with a reputation for violence, ruthless powerplays and a self-indulgent taste for the finer things in life; be it cars, women or booze. Denton had never liked Rodriguez, not caring for his unpredictable nature and back-stabbing ways. Nevertheless, he had worked for the man in the past...money was money, after all.

Rodriguez grinned amicably as he greeted Denton like an old friend, embracing him and offering a cigar which Denton politely refused.

"Well, buddy, you heard the news?" Rodriguez asked.

"Yeah." Denton answered, while shaking his head solemnly, "Still can't believe it. Sad day for the Pit."

"No doubt, no doubt," Rodriguez agreed, "you know, Don Angelo was like a father to me...taught me a lot...And the way he went out, did you hear? The mighty Don, the most powerful gangster in the city, and he died on the can taking a shit! Can you believe that?"

Rodriguez appeared positively giddy while telling the tale of Don Angelo's undignified demise and Denton reckoned the man's display of grief was simply for show.

"Anyway, we must go on..." the gangster continued, "Need to focus on the future. The Syndicate needs strong leadership right now, otherwise the whole Pit will fall into fucking anarchy....and that is something I won't allow!" Rodriguez paused briefly, looking Denton square in the eye before asking him a straight question. "Tell me, Denton, of all the captains, who do you reckon is best placed to take over?"

Denton shrugged his shoulders and told the truth. "The way I see things, it's between you and Adebisi. I guess it depends which one of you strikes first..."

Rodriguez laughed aloud and slapped him hard on the back. "That's what I like about you, Denton, you're smart and you tell it like it is. I've been waiting a long time for this opportunity, and there's no way I'm letting that prick Adebisi take it from me! I know what needs to be done, but if I move against Adebisi now, it'll be mayhem on the streets! I need deniability in this shit...The Pit can be a dangerous place after all...What I need is a man who's reliable and discreet...A guy who can take out this son of a bitch but do the job right, so it can't be traced back to me. That's where you come in, Denton..."

He couldn't believe what he was hearing...was Rodriguez for real?

"You want me to whack Adebisi!" he exclaimed.

"Sure, why not?" Rodriguez replied, "You did decent work with that hit on JJ last year..."

"JJ was a scumbag, women-beating pimp." Denton replied, "Adebisi is one of the most powerful men in the Pit. I won't do it!"

"Won't!" Rodriguez exclaimed angrily, "You seem to be forgetting the money you owe me...Five Gs, and the interest building every week. I've been patient up to now, what with us being old friends and all. But, if you start fucking with me, I'll have to call in the debt. On the other hand, I'll cancel it and give you a clean slate, if you take this contract..."

Denton understood Rodriguez all too well. If he refused to take the contract, the gangster would demand money Denton didn't have and would react with violence when he didn't get paid. He was being blackmailed and, in the end, had no choice.

"Okay, I'll do it." he mumbled.

"Good boy," Rodriguez exclaimed with a grin while slapping Denton on the back once more. "My people will give you the details."

Denton suddenly felt quite ill as he wondered what kind of suicide mission he'd signed up too.

***

Denton lurked in the shadows, his gun concealed underneath his jacket as he waited for his target to show. Rodriguez's men had provided him with the intel, explaining that Adebisi met his mistress in a downtown hotel every Wednesday night. Apparently, the mob boss attended this illicit appointment alone and unprotected and, so, this was the ideal opportunity to take him out. Denton still felt uneasy about the whole operation. He would rather have stayed out of all this shit, but Rodriguez had forced his hand.

The assassination mission was high-risk. Denton would wear a mask during the hit to ensure he wasn't identified. There may be no police in the Pit, but the Syndicate families had their own private investigators who would try to seek out the killer. This was potentially a lose-lose situation for Denton. If he failed to kill Adebisi, then the mobster would surely seek vengeance. However, if he did succeed, there was a chance that Rodriguez would take him out anyway to cover his tracks. God knew how he'd gotten embroiled in this bullshit, but he was committed now and had to see this through.

He watched the front door of the hotel from across the street, waiting for what seemed like an eternity on that cold and damp night. Finally, his target emerged, strolling out through the swing lobby door of the hotel. Adebisi was a tall and slim Nigerian with dark skin, a shaved head and a fiery intensity behind his eyes. Denton slowly moved forward, crossing the street while discreetly reaching into his jacket, feeling the handle of his gun – an ancient Magnum revolver with a six-round chamber - the best weapon he could find at such short notice.

He stopped dead in his tracks when he saw the girl. She was tall and statuesque; white skinned, red haired and stunning, wearing a designer dress and high heels. Adebisi's mistress. Denton assumed they would be leaving separately. This was an unwelcome development, as Denton didn't wish to kill or maim an innocent. He stood-still in the middle of the road; watching, his mind racing as he considered his next move. A vehicle pulled up to the sidewalk, an electric driverless cab, identical to the hundreds of other automated taxis which operated in the Pit. Adebisi embraced and kissed his mistress, opening the door of the cab so she could climb inside.

Denton realised it was now or never. He withdrew his pistol, flicking off the safety catch as he aimed. Adebisi turned his head at the last possible second, seeing his masked and armed would-be killer advancing upon him. The mob boss cried out before he heroically pushed his girlfriend into the cab. Denton squeezed the trigger, feeling the kickback as his first bullet slammed into Adebisi's right shoulder.

BANG! A second round shattered the rear window of the vehicle. The woman screamed as she was covered in shards of glass, and the driverless cab burst into action, the red warning lights flashing as its sensors recognized the threat and sped off down the road with the woman still inside.

He fired a third bullet at the fleeing vehicle but stopped shooting when he realised his target wasn't inside the cab. Instead, Adebisi was left behind; wounded, abandoned and without cover. Denton moved in for the kill, covering the distance while preparing to finish his victim, but Adebisi wasn't done yet.

To Denton's immense surprise and horror, the wounded man withdrew a pistol with his left arm and opened fire.

"You, motherfucker!" he screamed.

Bullets whizzed mere inches over Denton's head, forcing him to flee in a panic. He fired two shots to cover his retreat, both missing his target, before diving into cover and hiding behind a parked car on the opposite side of the street. He fired one more shot, narrowly missing Adebisi. When Denton pulled the trigger again, all he heard was an ominous click.

"Shit!" he swore in dismay.

The gun was empty, and he was surely fucked. Out of options, Denton fled in a blind panic, praying that he wasn't struck in the back by one of Adebisi's bullets.

"You better run, motherfucker!" Adebisi screamed after him, "You can run but you can't hide!"

Denton was soon out of range, but he knew he was far from safe. His mission had been a complete failure, and now the entire world was going to fall on his head.

***

Denton spent the next two days getting fucked up. He knew he was in mortal danger and didn't dare return home or go near any of his regular haunts. Instead, the bumbling hitman hit the bars on the opposite side of the Pit, drowning his sorrows with a dangerous mix of hard liquor, pills and hookers. Denton had to borrow money to afford his bender, that's how bad things had got. He was even further in debt now, but Denton didn't think it would matter, since he didn't expect to live past the end of the week. The Pit wasn't that big a place, and the Syndicate families had spies everywhere. If Adebisi's men didn't get to him, then Rodriguez's surely would...and so, what was there to do except get messed up?

When Denton came to the end of his two-day session, he woke in a filthy brothel, not bothering to look upon the sleeping girl lying beside him, as he quickly found his clothes, got dressed and quietly left the bedroom. His head was pounding and his throat dry. The man needed coffee and something to eat. He searched his pockets and found he was down to his last couple of dollars. He'd blown the rest. Shaking his head and adjusting his weary eyes to the morning sun, Denton set off down the street in search of a convenience store, but he didn't get far.

The dark van sped down the empty street, pulling alongside him as the back doors flew open and three masked men jumped out, charging towards Denton with menacing intent. Denton was instantly alert despite his inebriated state. He'd tossed his revolver two days ago and had no other weapons, but was determined not to go down without a fight. He lashed out, striking his first attacker hard in the jaw. The second man grabbed Denton roughly, attempting to wrestle him to the ground, but Denton escaped his grasp, punching his assailant in the stomach. For a moment it appeared he may escape this trap, but then the third attacker quickly drew a weapon and pulled the trigger.

Denton felt a sudden hard impact against his chest, closely followed by an intense electric shock which paralyzed his entire body. He fell helplessly to the sidewalk, hitting the ground with a heavy thud, experiencing a shooting pain through his skull as everything went black.

***

Denton awoke to blackness, his body aching and his head throbbing. He tried to move but soon discovered that his hands were bound behind his back. He heard the soft humming sound of a diesel engine and felt the sensation of movement. Denton soon concluded that he was trapped in the rear of a fast-moving vehicle and was currently speeding towards an undisclosed location. He fought to contain a surge of panic as he struggled to come to terms with his desperate situation.

The men who'd kidnapped him hadn't identified themselves, but – as they'd taken him alive – the smart money was on Adebisi's crew. Denton could only imagine what horrors awaited him. The assholes would surely torture him to find out who'd contracted the hit. Denton knew he'd talk – why not, after all? He didn't owe any loyalty to Rodriguez. But still they would surely kill him brutally to set an example. There was no way he could talk his way out of this.

Denton put his mind to the prospect of escape, but he never got the opportunity. The vehicle came to an abrupt halt and a moment later the rear doors of the van swung open. A pair of thugs leaped inside, quickly and roughly taking hold of Denton and pulling him to his feet. His wrists were hand-cuffed, his body was still in shock and Denton could only put up a feeble resistance.

The men dragged him down a darkened alleyway and into an abandoned and decrepit old building, an empty room containing nothing but two hard-backed chairs and a battery powered lamp. They frog marched him across the floor and slammed him down in a chair. Denton quaked with fear as he awaited his grisly fate. Suddenly, a new figure emerged from the shadows. The man was tall and imposing but his right arm was held in a sling. Denton recognized him straight away – before him stood Don Adebisi in the flesh.

In that moment, he thought he was truly fucked, but what Adebisi said surprised him. The Nigerian mob boss spoke directly to his men, remonstrating angrily.

"What the hell is this?" he shouted in a West African accent, "Take those cuffs off him...now!"

The henchman promptly complied with their boss's order, freeing Denton from his restraints. He could hardly believe it – was this a trick? Adebisi looked sincere as he held out his hand in friendship.

"My apologies, Mr. Denton. My boys can be heavy-handed. I hope you're not injured?"

"No, I'm fine..." Denton replied in a baffled tone.

"Good," Adebisi replied, "now, leave us to talk in private."

The order was directed to his two henchmen and both promptly left the room. Denton considered making a run for it now he was free, but strangely enough, he wanted to hear Adebisi out.

"Well, Denton," the mob boss began, "you're probably wondering why I brought you here under such dramatic circumstances...Well, as you may have heard, I was shot the other night, so naturally I'm feeling somewhat cautious..."

Denton said nothing. He didn't flinch or even blink as he maintained solid eye contact with Adebisi, not wanting to reveal his guilt.

"That motherfucker Rodriguez!" Adebisi growled, "I reckoned he'd make a move after the Don passed – God rest his soul – but I didn't think he'd have the balls to come after me so fast...Fortunately, he hired some clown to do the hit. He fucked up, and now it's time for payback!"

Denton clenched his teeth, saying nothing.

"I want to hire you for this contract, Denton. Your reputation proceeds you my friend...I need Rodriguez gone and will give you everything you need to get the job done..."

Denton could hardly believe what he was hearing – was this for real? He was tempted, but it was too risky...this whole situation was too fucked up!

"Thank you for thinking of me, Don Adebisi, but I don't feel I can get involved in this feud."

Adebisi smiled coyly. "You haven't heard my offer yet. Firstly, if you complete this contract, I'll write off all your debts. Secondly, when I take the top job – which I will, once Rodriguez is dead – when I'm in charge, I'll sponsor you for full membership of the Syndicate, set you up with your own block, give you whatever you need to get up and running...So, what do you say, Denton?"

The man could hardly believe his good fortune. He'd come here expecting to die horribly, but instead was getting the offer of a lifetime! Adebisi clearly had no idea that Denton was the one who'd shot him, and...once Rodriguez was out of the way, he'd never find out.

"Thank you for your generous offer, Don Adebisi...I gladly accept."

"Excellent," said a smiling Adebisi, as he shook Denton's hand, thus sealing an unlikely alliance.

He did feel like a turncoat, but business was business and Rodriguez had to go.

***

Denton hit the streets during the early hours, set loose by his new patron and armed with a powerful machine-pistol, thirty rounds in the magazine and two spares in his pocket. Adebisi's crew had provided him with the weaponry, the intelligence, and had given Denton the address of a safe house where he could hide out after the job was done...All he needed to do was kill his target. Rodriguez was not known for his caution. He must have known that Adebisi would be out for revenge and yet, he wasn't in hiding. Rodriguez had been spotted by one of Adebisi's spies, drinking in a well-known bar in the downtown district.

The Don wasn't alone – there were at least two bodyguards with him according to the spotter, but Denton was armed with an automatic weapon and they didn't know he was coming. He weaved down the city street, avoiding pimps, whores, junkies and conmen as he focused on his lethal mission. He entered the neon lit bar-room, scanning the crowded room and quickly finding his target.

Rodriguez was sitting at a table in the corner of the bar along with two heavy set men – one black, the other white. Denton recognized the bodyguards and quickly realised they were the same two goons who'd ambushed him that night outside of the Underworld...All the better, Denton reckoned...he could take them all out in one fatal swoop, thus erasing any link between him and the botched hit on Adebisi.

He marched purposefully across the floor towards his targets, his hand on the gun which remained concealed under his jacket. Rodriguez and his men saw him approach. The look on the Don's face was one of confusion and annoyance rather than fear. He would never have guessed they'd send his own assassin to kill him. The black bodyguard was more alert to the danger. He quickly rose from his chair, reaching into his jacket for a pistol. The henchman was fast, but Denton was quicker.

He pulled out his machine pistol and opened up, firing a short burst as the din of rapid gunshots filled the room. The bodyguard was cut to shreds in an instant and Denton rapidly turned his attentions to the remaining targets. In that final second, he locked eyes with the not-so-mighty Don Rodriguez, savoring the absolute terror in his adversary's eyes. Denton pulled the trigger, firing a sustained burst which

156

took out both Rodriguez and his second henchman. He ignored the screams and cries of the crowd as he re-aimed and fired a third burst into Rodriguez's limp body, making sure the fucker was dead.

Thus satisfied, the killer swung around and faced the bar, watching the terrified crowd stampede towards the back door. The bartender apparently didn't appreciate his business being shot up. He went for a pistol, but a spray of bullets from Denton's gun sent him diving for cover instead. Denton used the interlude to dart for the door, exiting the bar-room and fleeing out onto the street. He ran for about ten blocks straight, until he was gasping for breath.

Eventually, the man took cover in a darkened alleyway as he tried to get his bearings. Just then, Denton was surprised by an unwanted visitor. He heard the ominous whirling sound and saw the armed surveillance drone hovering above his head, its camera and mini-gun trained upon him. Denton knew the drill – drop his gun and raise his hands in submission – that's all he needed to do to go free...But no, not this time!

Denton's heart was suddenly filled with defiance, as he quite deliberately loaded a fresh magazine into his machine pistol and aimed his gun upwards at the drone.

"Come and get me, motherfucker!" he cried out rebelliously.

"LOWER YOUR WEAPON." Came the mechanized reply from the drone's in-built speakers. "LETHAL FORCE IS AUTHORISED. YOU HAVE TEN SECONDS TO COMPLY."

Denton didn't flinch. He was sick of it, sick of the corporate fucks who treated the people of the Pit like animals, the one-percenters whose greed and corruption had destroyed this community, and whose crimes went unpunished while those they oppressed continued to suffer...and yes, Denton himself was a killer, but he was the man this society had made him.

"YOU HAVE FIVE SECONDS TO COMPLY." Barked the aerial killer.

One burst of automatic gunfire would probably bring the drone down, but as soon as he pulled the trigger, the machine would transmit a S.O.S. signal to every other attack drone in the district, Denton would be overwhelmed and killed within minutes. He controlled his anger, realizing such a death would be futile, and lowered his weapon, throwing his gun to the ground as he raised his hands to surrender.

The drone hovered for another moment, observing and threatening its target for several more seconds, before finally it rose up into the sky disappearing from sight. Denton sighed in relief, realizing he'd made the smart decision. But still, his submission to the corporate overlords didn't sit right. Denton was determined that one day he would fight back against the system, but it would be a long struggle...and, until the time was right, he would continue to play the game. The killer stooped down to pick up his gun before darting off into the night.

###

ABOUT MARK LYNCH

MARK LYNCH WAS BORN IN 1983 and hails from the beautiful coastal town of Holywood in County Down, where he lives with his wife Jackie and cat Jet. Mark studied History & Politics at Queen's University Belfast and maintains a keen interest in these subjects. His fascination with the 'What ifs?' of history and his love of the genre classics (such as Philip K Dick's The Man in the High Castle and Robert Harris's Fatherland) inspired him to develop his own alternative history timelines and transform them into works of fiction.

Connect with Mark here: www.castrumpress.com/mark-lynch.

JERICHO

Matthew Williams

'The most profound and noted effect of cryosleep is the extreme sense of disorientation one feels upon awakening."

That was the last thought that went through Angelica's mind before going down for her nap. Consequently, it was the first lucid thought she had when she finally woke up.

The second was that the training regimen ought to be revised to make mention of the interminably long time the process took. Time had a way of dilating and stretching on as one spent days going from near-death to full wakefulness. Somehow, the term "subjective time" just didn't seem to cut it, not where space travel and cryosleep were concerned.

"Good morning, Doctor Baudin. How are you feeling?"

Angelica rubbed the last of the sleep from her eyes and squinted to see the face of Florence, their helpful nursebot. Her deep black eyes focused and refocused on Angelica, the lenses rotating back and forth to accommodate the ambient light in the cell. Closer at hand was Florence's mechanical arm, its many muscle-pulleys visible through her external shell, the fingers reaching gently forward.

No matter how much time passed, the sight of those articulated metal joints made Angelica feel uneasy. Holding them always seemed like an invitation to get her hand crushed. And yet, she found herself taking the offered help anyway, using Florence as a support to get her lower body out of the cryopod and onto the floor.

"Are we there already, Florence?"

"Yes, ma'am," replied the machine pleasantly. "We are currently in position twenty astronomical units from our destination world, HD 85512b. The Levant finished conducting its braking maneuvers, and we are en route at cruising speed."

"Ah, good," Angelica said, sighing heavily. "And for the sake of the crew, you should begin using its true name."

"I shall make the appropriate adjustments, ma'am."

Angelica put pressure on her feet as she tried to stand and was immediately greeted by the sensation of a thousand pins and needles, all of which seemed to be on fire. A small gasp escaped her mouth, prompting Florence to come to her side.

"Are you all right, Doctor? Some pain is normal during recovery. If you want, I can offer you a mild anesthetic."

"No need," said Angelica, waiting for the pain to subside. In time, something approaching normal feeling began to flood into her feet, and Angelica began to walk on her own.

"Do you need further assistance, ma'am?"

"No, Florence," Angelica replied. "I can certainly shower and dress myself. Why don't you check on the others? I'm sure they're coming to by now."

"Very well," said Florence, rotating her lower segment and wheeling away.

***

"As you can see, the long-range array has picked up multiple signs of activity," said Sarin, pointing to the large holographic mass that now filled the center of the room. "Our long-range scans have yielded some interesting returns. Spectrometer shows that the planet's surface deposits of key minerals, silicates, and trace elements have been redistributed in subtle but meaningful ways. The path of their redistribution goes from the surrounding landscape directly to the coordinates of the colony." He paused for emphasis, indicating that his third and ultimate point would be the most significant. "And last, but certainly not least, the atmospheric content now shows a significant depletion of carbon compounds, and high concentrations of nitrogen, oxygen gas, and ozone."

Sarin punched in some commands on his wrist-mounted interface. The picture of the surface began to change, with tiny dancing lights moving from positions around the globe to a center marked in the northeastern hemisphere.

"In short, the Seedlings are hard at work forming the basis of our colony. By the time we arrive on HD 85512b, all infrastructure will be laid, and all settlements erected and working properly."

From her seat, Angelica stood and crossed her arms. The display was little more than a conglomeration of sensor data: returns on optical, microwave, infrared, and electromagnetic dispatches. And yet, it was the most beautiful thing she'd seen in a long time. A world waiting, a new home. Nothing in her lexicon seemed up to the challenge of describing it. Luckily, Sarin had provided her with the next best thing.

"I think what you mean to say, Doctor, is that the Seedlings are busy creating our new home. And that by the time we set foot on Eden, all will be ready and waiting for us."

Sarin cleared his throat. "Yes, of course. We certainly can't understate the importance of what they're creating for us."

A moment of silence followed as everyone in the circle of chairs watched and admired the display. No one seemed to mind that the simulation was running on a loop, as evidenced by the way that the image conducted a slight panning and then quickly reset. As far as they were concerned, they were beholding the real thing, no artifice or simulation involved.

"Have the colonists agreed on a name yet?" asked Doctor Zamani from the other side of the circle.

"They have," said Sarin, consulting his wrist again. A small holographic window appeared above it, with many lines of script appearing in it. "It seems that after several rounds of voting, Jericho has won out."

"Ah, thank you, God!" cried Zamani.

A small chuckle went up from the circle. No one needed to be reminded how fraught with peril the selection process had been. It wasn't enough that there had been interfaith disputes over what to name their new settlement, names that threatened to bring up deep divides that they'd hoped to leave behind them. But in addition, the process had been deliberately democratic, with suggestions being requested and given from the prospective settlers. The Council had been noticeably unimpressed by some of the suggestions. Others had just been plain appalling.

"I think we can all rest more calmly knowing that we'll be living in a colony named in honor of the oldest continuously inhabited city on Earth," said Angelica. "Not something that will shame our children and our children's children for generations to come."

Around the circle, every member of the Council uttered a small prayer in their respective language, pertaining to their respective faith. Consensus was a beautiful thing, especially when it coincided with the right decision.

The final phase of descent began, and the vibrations in the cabin reached a fever pitch. Angelica lay back and hummed with trepidation as her restraints tightened to hold her in place. Around her, the entire Council was assembled, with a few observers from the rest of the Levant's crew.

For everyone packed into the shuttle's cabin, this would be the first glimpse any of them got of their new home, yet the final phase of their journey, the planetary descent, was proving more than just a little nerve wracking. Though the odds were certainly in their favor, there was still a marginal chance that they might suffer catastrophic failure and die horribly.

Within a few minutes, the violent shaking subsided and became a dull drum. When that happened, Angelica heard several voices raised around her, intermittent conversation mixed with sighs of relief. Angelica smiled, knowing now that she wasn't the only one frightened by the process known as "breaking atmo." Many a member of their troop liked to pretend that the vagaries of space travel didn't bother them, that the risks incurred were no different than with any other aspect of life.

Still, she swore she could see looks of quiet relief all about her, faces humbled by the fear they felt when faced with eternity.

With the transition now safely behind them, the cabin windows began to open, admitting outside light and a view of the landscape that was rising to meet them.

"Five minutes until touchdown," said the shuttle's autopilot. Undoing their restraints, the passengers began to climb to a window to get a look out. Angelica found hers rather quickly, and struggled to share it with three more people who couldn't find their own.

"Magnificent," said Draya, one of the techs from the regular crew.

"Still looks a little rocky. Not that much different from the simulations," commented a man from the regular crew. Angelica recognized him as Sousa, one of the resident Shia clerics. His comment prompted a politely-worded rebuke from one of the crew's engineers, busy peering out the opposite side.

"Terraforming will take time. We have to let the Seedlings manifest and move beyond the city before we can expect them to shape the landscape."

"I know," said Sousa. "Just saying, it still looks like wilderness out there."

"And therein lies the appeal," said Angelica, choosing to join the discussion at last. "An entire landscape waiting to be shaped. A new world waiting to be founded."

"'A place for God's many children to find new purchase and live out their lives in peace and harmony,'" echoed Sousa. "Yes, I remember the pitch used to lure us here, Doctor."

Angelica laughed. Had she been quoting from the mission handbook? It was hard to tell sometimes. The impassioned statements made during their recruiting drives many years ago had become so much a part of their nomenclature that it was hard to know what was once used to draw people in. Of course, their very presence here was proof that it had worked.

Looking back to Sousa, Angelica noticed a strange, distant quality taking hold of him. The wry smile was gone, replaced by something longing, almost mournful.

"Is everything all right, Ulama Sousa?" she asked, using his official title.

"It's fine," he replied, waving a hand. "The landscape... it kind of reminds me of home. Puts me in mind of what I left behind, is all."

Angelica nodded. There was no further need to explain. They'd all been told of the psychological ramifications of their mission, what to expect and how to deal with it, both with their crew and within themselves. The strange sense of nostalgia mixed with regret, the leaving of a place gone but not forgotten, and coming to a new world. Feelings of wanting to rebuild what was once theirs, but wanting to avoid the same patterns that had led to such regrettable loss. Yes, she understood all that quite well.

"We'll rebuild it," she said, using the generalized "it" to refer to the myriad of places they all thought of as home. "Only this time, we'll build it better, and take better care of it."

"Harmonization is the first step," Sousa added, once again echoing the familiar words. "I remember that part too."

Angelica blushed. Once again, he'd caught her quoting from the handbook, but it seemed to have the desired effect. That alone was what mattered.

"One minute to landing," said the autopilot. "Please return to your seats and allow the harnesses to reattach themselves."

***

It was a short but poignant walk from the landing pad to the city gates. After clearing the recessed area – made to resemble stone, but composed, Angelica knew, of metals and silicates that were far more durable and self-repairing – they came upon the vast set of stairs that led up to the entranceway. These steps and the long walkway that followed were designed with purposeful intent: to allow all newcomers to mount the stairway leading them to their terrestrial paradise, the city on the hill, laden with palms and eternal springs.

And of course, as they walked the long pathway, they would witness the city in the distance, twinkling like heavenly deliverance as its vast spires and walls captured the sun's light and turned it into useable energy.

"C'mon, let's move! I want to see it with my own eyes!" said Zamani, struggling to take the steps at a more rapid pace. His old frame still had some verve in it, and his impatience spoke of some bottled youth that still yearned for expression.

"No rush," replied Sarin. "We've waited this long to get here. It will still be there when we arrive."

"Easy for you to say, you've been looking at simulations of the thing far longer than any of us!"

It was Draya saying this as she pushed past him. Together, she and Zamani raced as fast as they could to reach the summit, taking two steps or more at a time and struggling to breathe the still-thin air. Angelica, still feeling the slightest bit sluggish from the descent and the revitalization, chose to walk, hanging back with some of the older members of their party.

"The air is a bit dry," she found herself relating aloud. "I wonder if the Seedlings have the plumbing up and running right. I could use a glass of water when we get there."

This caused some laughter from her group. Up ahead, she noticed the speedier members of their crew had come to the summit of the steps and reached an abrupt halt.

"What's the matter with them?" Sarin asked.

Sousa chuckled. "Could the air be thinner up there? It does seem significantly above sea level."

"I'm not sure," said Angelica, ignoring the jest. From her spot, they seemed deadly still. Were they that engrossed by the sight of the city, or was something wrong? Her sudden concern caused her to quicken her pace. Within a few minutes, she was coming to their side and within earshot. "What's wrong? Is the city there?"

"Oh...it's there," said Zamani.

"Then what's wrong?" Angelica was just a few steps from the summit and could now make out the looks on some of their faces. They all wore the same expression of pure awe, and more than just a little fear.

"Perhaps you should see for yourself," he said.

Angelica stepped to the very top. Her last footsteps fell unevenly, nearly tripping her up. In the distance, a city twinkled, but not quite the one she'd been expecting. From the earth that bore it, its walls reached high and towered over the landscape. Behind them, spires, towers, and pinnacles reached out, cresting the heavens and looking down at them with exquisite grace. From end to end, Jericho awaited them, its many features a testament to its namesake and the prowess of its designers.

Not a single eye was looking upon any of those. In the center, overlooking the main entrance, was a likeness that no one failed to recognize.

"Doctor Baudin," said Draya, her voice a meek whisper. "Is that your face?"

Angelica ran her hand across her eyes, hoping that it might just be an illusion that could be resolved by rubbing them clean. No such luck. Right where it had been before, the perfect representation of her features remained. Several hundred meters tall, almost as wide, and perched almost a full kilometer above the ground. The Seedlings had captured every shape, contour, nook and cranny.

"Doctor, what's the meaning of this?" asked Zamani.

Angelica shook her head. "I have no idea. That wasn't part of the original design. Nor were any likenesses of any kind."

Behind her, Sousa and the others had made their way up. When they reached the top stair, he was on the verge of asking what the holdup was for. Instead, he looked on and caught sight of the same face. Like the others, he was quickly dumbstruck, and then felt in dire need of some answers.

"What is the meaning of that... that graven image?" he said, pointing to it with a trembling finger. Angelica felt her heart go cold. She knew that many of them were already thinking it, but to hear the words made her heart want to jump into her mouth, to run and find shelter somewhere in the wide, open expanse of desert. When the other colonists saw it too, they would suspect her of idolatry. She just knew it.

"Wait. This was definitely not part of our design specs," said Draya, coming to her aid. "If we can get inside, I can interface with the Seedling mainframe and find out what this is."

"Yes, let's do that," said Angelica, a bit too eagerly. Anything that moved them along and averted a possible schism among their landing party sounded perfect to her. Maybe they'd find something inside, something that might explain why the Seedlings had dedicated much of the city's facade to the senior member of their mission.

"Great merciful God," said Zamani. Around him, just about every member of their party said the same basic combination of words in different languages, with different inflections. They stood in the massive hall that would someday serve as the city center, the administrative hub of the entire colony. Within the expanse, tall columns buttressed a roof that looked very much like hewn blocks of stone.

But again, these contrivances held little concern for their group. For all around the rim of the roof, a vast and intricate mosaic ran, depicting some vivid, artistically-rendered scenes. It took little time for them to realize where the relief began and, by extension, where it ended.

At one corner of the room, a planet that very much resembled Eden sat alone, its ruddy surface pockmarked and lifeless. As they progressed through the visual narrative, they could see small, seed-like objects landing on the surface of the planet, burrowing into the dirt and conducting feats of engineering. The story then proceeded to show the colony through several phases of completion, culminating with the creation of the Godhead at the front entrance.

Then, in the final part of the story, there was the arrival of several people, all dressed in shimmering finery, stepping out from a capsule of some kind and setting foot on the world. Behind their heads, great halos of light shone down on the earth as they walked, and the seed-shaped machines rejoiced at their feet.

"Dear God," cried Sousa, beating his hands in vain. He looked to Angelica, his eyes filling with tears and his expression vacillating between anger and guilt. "It isn't you the Seedlings worship here, it's all of us! They've made idols of us all and sanctified us unjustly!"

Sousa sank to his knees, muttered words rushed forth begging forgiveness and pleading ignorance of the crime. He was followed by many other representatives of the crew, but not all. Some of them turned to Sarin next, their eyes like daggers trained on the Levant's chief engineer.

Angry mutters began to drip from their mouths, words of accusation and demands for justice. Angelica quickly raised her hands and ran to Sarin's side. Though small, the mob that now sought to put this at his feet could become powerful if unchecked. From behind them, Draya moved in too, perhaps suspecting she was safer close to them.

"People," Called Angelica, "Remember that Doctor Sarin wasn't responsible for the creation of the Seedlings. He only oversaw some aspects of their programming and came along with us to ensure they were performing correctly."

"But he has insight into their minds," said one of the scholars in their midst. "He alone can tell us why they did this!"

"Perhaps," said Sarin, raising his hand defensively and thinking as fast as he could. "Perhaps a malfunction. Maybe a slight corruption or misinterpretation of their core programming."

"What do you mean?" cried Sousa, still kneeling on the floor. "Are you saying this unholy representation is a mere accident?"

"Well... maybe," he shrugged. "They were programmed to anticipate our arrival. Their database included detailed files on the crew and the Council."

"That's right," said Draya, adding her voice to his. "As far as they knew, they were building a home for the people that created them." She stopped, the implications of what she was saying suddenly appalling to her. "Oh my God. Is it possible this wasn't a malfunction at all? Just a logical fallacy?"

"All right, now what does she mean?" Sousa demanded. Angelica was admittedly confused herself. But Sarin, speaking the same language of engineers and programmers, seemed to follow her reasoning, and gasped.

"She's right! They had full access to the record of their own assembly, knew that the people they were building this place for were the very people that designed them."

Those words hung in the air for many seconds. No one seemed particularly satisfied by that explanation, and within seconds, Sousa and his ilk raised more questions.

"You're saying...this very city they were building...they thought they were building a home for their gods?"

Sarin replied quickly and calmly, his reasoning now firmly planted in his mind and absolving him of their anger. Innocent of heresy, he now returned to the role of chief engineer, making the actions of machinery intelligible to others.

"Think of it," he told them. "The very basis of their programming was that they were preparing a colony for their makers. They understood that their entire purpose in being created was to serve at the pleasure of the people who made them. How else would they interpret this, if not in that way?"

"But we're not gods!" insisted Sousa. "The very idea that this is divine worship is ridiculous! We're mere mortals. We didn't create the stars and the sky and heavens and the planets. This is completely different!"

"Not to them, it isn't," said Angelica finally. "As far as they were concerned, the two are one and the same. The builders are the gods themselves. This place is their garden. And we..." She sighed, burdened by the sudden understanding that was washing over her. "We're the very picture of the divine."

Sousa breathed heavily, his mind clearly struggling to accept the shock that it had been given and his body languishing under the stress of it as well. In time, his heart seemed to cease racing and his breathing calmed, but the look on his face was no less grave or ill. "God help us all," he muttered. The other scholars joined him in his lament.

###

ABOUT MATTHEW WILLIAMS

MATTHEW WILLIAMS IS A PROFESSIONAL science writer and a science fiction author. He lives on Vancouver Island with his wife and family.

Connect with Matthew here: www.castrumpress.com/matthew-williams.

GHOSTS

RB Kelly

We were out on the streets when the first round hit, and Ally went down straight away. I couldn't carry him and run, so I left him. He'd have done the same for me.

It's not like it was when I was a kid. Back then, people would have opened their doors to you if they saw you were caught outside in a storm. They've learned not to do that now. Now, they'll watch you burn and just thank whatever's left to believe in that they weren't standing next to you when you got in the way of a seeker. I could hear him screaming behind me as his body fell apart, but all I could think of – even now, even after everything we'd been through – was at least it wasn't me. It could just as easily have been me.

The trouble is, when a storm hits, there's nowhere to go. A wall might slow a seeker down; it might even stop them. But if they get through, then you've got nowhere to run, because a locked door, in a room with a seeker, is only good for keeping people in. They used to find whole families like that, once upon a time. Ally's was one of them.

I came across the door by accident: the same kind of random fluctuation of chance that caused Ally's seeker to veer half a degree left in the split second before it took me out. We were both running, our heart rates soaring, our core temperatures climbing together. Whatever it was – maybe his capillaries dilated a little faster, maybe he should have worked harder back in gym class, maybe I just breathed out at exactly the right moment – he was hotter than me in the second that it counted, and he went down while I was free to run blindly away from the crowds, away from the heat and the panic, and into a dark, damp, cool alley full of dark, damp, broken doors.

The storm was breaking by then, but the seekers were still falling. I knew that I needed to put something cold between them and me while I let my body temperature stabilize, and home was still too far away. People can be superstitious about the houses where the seekers have been, but I say that a wall's a wall, and the walls that have fallen into disrepair, the walls where the damp's been allowed to slither up from the forgotten flagstones, the walls that guard rooms where the electricity's been out for more years than I can count on the fingers of both hands: these are the sorts of places where a body can get cold really fast. I'm not saying that I'm not afraid of the dark and the unknown and the smell of death in the heavy, unquiet air. I'm just saying that the seekers scare me more.

The first door wouldn't give, though it looked as though it was ready to crumble into dust and spores, and my shoulder wasn't exactly gentle. The second gave without a whisper, though I'd prepared myself for a fight, and it sent me sprawling into the utility corridors of a place that had once been somewhere big. It was the echoes that gave it away. The door was solid metal, half an inch thick and imperfectly barred against intruders by a levered emergency handle, and it slammed into the wall behind it with a cavernous thung, like the tolling of a bell in an empty cathedral. Momentum carried me three ungainly strides inside before I lost my footing and collapsed against the floor; even as I was staggering to my feet, scrambling over lino sheeting slick with decades of grime and neglect, even as I was throwing my weight against the other side of the door to force it shut before the seekers found me, I could still hear the memory of the thung whispering around the vast, empty space ahead of me.

A hotel, I guessed. A defunct emergency exit sign hung over the door, and to my right, weak late-afternoon light poured through a ventilation grille to illuminate a room full of oversized tin cans, metal trolleys, and rotting linens. A lot of hotels went out in the first month of storms, back before anyone knew what to do when the seekers started falling.

The first thing to do – the very first thing – was to drop my core temperature. There was a chill vest in my backpack, and I dropped to my knees, down to where the air was coolest; the damp pooled in black, cold puddles that soaked into the fabric of my jeans, into the marrow of my bones, as I fumbled for it and into it. Ally always hated the chill vests. It's like climbing into your own grave, he'd complain, and he was right: the cold spreads out like icy fingers, gripping your chest and tightening your flesh, and it feels as though you're already dead. Not by seeker, but the way people used to die in the old days, when your heart stopped all by itself sometimes, and your whole body died all at once. It feels like something's reaching out of the soil to call you down, but it's better than the alternative. I'll take artificial death over the real thing for as long as I can.

Outside, the screams were growing fainter, growing fewer. The seekers had stopped falling, but the storm had been heavy, even for the season, and it would be hours before it was safe to be on the streets again. Height, I thought. Stairs. Unspent seekers can linger on the ground for longer than you'd think, but they lose their buoyancy very quickly. They might find me in the upper reaches, but they wouldn't be able to get to me, and they can be quite beautiful as they die: fading like cooling glass from bright yellow-white, like an earthbound sun, to burnt amber, to coral, to hazy salmon pink before the shadows creep in to snuff them out. I wouldn't have to climb high – two flights would do it; three to be safe – and then I could find somewhere sheltered by the stairwell to wait it out and watch them pool and swirl and dance themselves to death in the darkness below me.

I got four stories up before the cold took me. Most of that was curiosity. From the bottom of the stairwell, it was impossible to tell how high the building reached, and the higher I went, the higher I wanted to go. It wasn't smart, but that's the trouble with chill vests: there's a fine line between seeker-friendly and hypothermia, different for everyone and every situation, and a hypothermic brain doesn't often make good decisions. I don't even remember lying down to sleep. I just remember the tiredness, like a black fog, and the way the remnants of old carpet on the treads below me felt like sponge beneath my feet; like cushions or pillows. In my dreams, Ally was yelling for me from the bottom of a cave; I knew I couldn't go down to him, but he wouldn't come up to me, and the next thing I remember is a voice, right beside my ear, shouting at me to wake the hell up right now; wake up.

I slitted my eyes.

She was slight and dark-faced: the sort of girl who looks ten years younger than she is. Her eyes were black, sunken into her face, and her lips were pinched, drawn back across her teeth. She looked furious, but that, I discovered later, was just how Aileen always looked.

"Lady!" she hollered. "Lady, you're about thirty seconds away from a cardiac arrest if you don't open your stupid eyes and dial up your core. And I'm not dealing with any more dead bodies in this hole; you can lie there and rot where you fall, for all I care. Hey, lady!"

I tried to raise my left hand in the direction of the noise. It wouldn't move. Hypothermia is a state of transcendental bliss, but, even through the haze, I was aware that this was wrong.

"I lost him," I said. At least, I think I did. It felt as though he was right beside me in those minutes, but hovering out of reach, and it was important that she knew this. Maybe I just made sounds; all I wanted was to go back to sleep. Whatever it was; whatever I said, it softened the edges off her anger, but that wasn't saying much.

"Get up, lady," she said, more gently this time. "Get up and fix your core temp or you're going to die."

***

She stood by the window as the sun disappeared behind the ragged city skyline, and her skin looked gray in the fading light. I huddled in a corner, chill vest dialed up as many degrees as I dared, and sipped from a mug of instant soup that Ally had made me pack before we left the house this morning. Once the shivering started, it wouldn't stop, and Aileen, content that I wasn't going to litter her stairwell with corpse, had directed me to a small suite of rooms a little way along the fourth-floor corridor, where I'd found blankets and mildewed cushions among the detritus of a life lived just out of sight.

It was impossible to guess how long she'd been squatting here. Her belongings had the dank, grimy sheen of far too many nights on the street, and Aileen herself had a lean, hungry look to her, though she'd refused my offer of a second pack of soup. A moth-eaten blanket lay crumpled on a chaise longue by the window, curtains partly drawn, and she knelt lightly on it as the flames below licked golden shadows across the sharp lines of her cheeks.

"Who'd you lose?" she asked at last, and, broken, I realized just how loud the silence had become.

"What?" I muttered. My teeth had locked together; the word would barely come out.

"You said you lost someone." A sharp glance back into the room, towards me, darkened her profile in shadow. "On the stairs. Who'd you lose?"

"Oh." It was strange to hear it spoken out loud: to hear him moved so carelessly from person to unperson. "My friend. He was my friend."

Silence. She turned back to the burning streets. Then, quietly, she said, "Sorry."

"Yeah," I said. He'd have done the same for me; we'd long ago agreed as much.

Without looking around, she said, "Did he have a name?"

"Ally," I said. "Alisdair. But only his mother called him that."

"He still has a mother?"

"No." I shook my head. "Not for years. She died in one of the early storms."

"Right," she said. More silence. And then: "Did she come back?"

Her words made me think of my sister. I hadn't thought of her for years, not since we lost her the third and final time, but I thought of her then. "For a little while," I said. "Not long. A couple of weeks, on and off."

Aileen nodded. I wondered who she'd lost; how many. "That's not so bad," she said. "Did she know she was gone?"

"Yes," I said. "Of course. We made sure of that."

The shadows dancing across her face were weak and listless. Whatever was burning, it wouldn't burn for long. Even the heaviest storms must end.

"Do you remember," she asked softly, "when dead meant dead?"

I did. I was twelve when the first storm hit, and that's plenty old enough to build a worldview so comfortably solid that it takes a pounding before it shatters. A hail of seekers came down in a quiet New Brunswick mining town as the sun was rising one late February morning, out of a clear and cloudless sky, and for three whole days the world called it a massacre and tried to find somebody to blame. Then they came to the southwest coast of Ireland, and then Mauretania, and then Laos and the

Seychelles. It was days, in the chaos, before anyone began to realize that the storm-ravaged bodies were only bodies: empty, broken cases, nothing more. It was days before anyone realized that there was anything else going on.

It took much longer than that before anyone was prepared to say it out loud.

"Dead is dead," I told her. I don't believe in ghosts. I don't believe in the immortal human soul. I've seen too many people come back for that. "What gets left behind by a seeker isn't alive. It's just…separate. It's energy set free."

She glanced back at me. "But tomorrow," she said, "you'll go back out onto the streets and look for your friend, won't you?"

"Yes," I said, "I will."

"You'll go back out onto the street and you'll look for him, and you'll find him, wandering about in the smoke. And he'll look like the man you used to know, and he'll recognize you. You'll see it in his eyes."

My mug was trembling, and it wasn't from the cold. "Yes," I said.

"You'll call him to follow you, and he'll follow you, and you'll bring him home. You'll tell him that he's dead, and he'll stare right through you like he doesn't understand, and he'll reach for your hand, but he won't be able to touch it. His hand will pass right through yours, and if you're lucky, it won't even leave a mark. And he'll stay with you, and you'll let him stay with you, as he gets softer and softer, until one day he'll just be a breath of air against your skin. And the next day he'll be gone."

Tears were burning the corners of my eyes. "Yes," I said. "But it won't be him. It'll be energy set free. It'll look like him, because his body contained the energy in that shape for so long, and it'll seem to remember me, because the energy has been following the same pathways for so long. The seekers separate the energy from the shell when they destroy the body, but the energy isn't the person. The person dies. My friend," I said, "is dead. Whatever I find on the streets tomorrow."

Aileen was quiet for a long time, head resting on her hands as the sun set gold and pink on her razorblade face. Into the heavy silence, she said quietly, "Listen."

I listened. There wasn't much else I could do. Below us, I could hear sirens, shouting voices, the sounds of noisy chaos on the streets. And a low wail, closer by, below the panic and the rage, that I'd taken for somebody's far-off despair. It fit with what I was feeling. But now, in the face of Aileen's furrow-browed scrutiny, I listened again and realized that it wasn't coming from outside the building, but from somewhere else. Somewhere nearer.

"That's Theresa," said Aileen. "She walks the second floor. Back and forth, and back and forth: over and over and over again. You'll meet her on your way back out again; she'll want to see you, to know who you are. She died here eighteen years ago, and she has no idea that she's dead."

***

173

No one knows where the seekers come from. Back when they came in ones and twos, silent and secretive, people called them globe lightning and said they didn't exist. My father was part of the team that built the first defenses – a small part, a white coat in a lab running lines of code through a simulator eight hundred feet below the surface of the earth, but it kept us safe for a while. It's because of him that Ally and I were able to build a cool room in our basement, ready to run for cover when the klaxons wailed, and it's because of his team that we know to wear chill vests when the storm comes. They're drawn to body heat. The magnetic nets in the upper atmosphere sift the baby seekers from the air before they've finished growing, but the adults, the strongest two-thirds of a seeker storm, punch right on through and drop towards the warm spots: the cities, the clusters, the conurbations.

Nobody knows where they come from. Back when we lived underground – back when we were safe – that used to scare me most of all.

People said they were aliens. People said they were a weapon. People said they were God's wrath visited upon a sinful earth. People said they were malevolent spirits. People said they were a magnetic aberration caused by abnormal solar activity, but that was twenty years ago, and there's only so much abnormal you can have before you need to take away the ab.

I don't believe in ghosts, but I saw the flesh shrink from my sister's bones in a blaze of blue-white heat, and I saw her scream and die. Then I saw her sit up and look around, tight-jawed with confusion, from a scattering of smoking dust and bone fragment, and the clock on the wall behind her was clearly visible through the shimmering haze of her head. It was three-fifteen exactly when she died. Ally had been in love with her since we were children, and he was never going to love anyone else the way he loved Joanne, so we had that in common from the start. Living together was just a natural progression, so easy and so seamless that it wasn't until he was gone that I even noticed I couldn't remember how to function on my own.

I left Aileen sleeping the next morning and crept out into the chill darkness of the corridor. Her face had the sort of closed-off, barricaded look of someone who didn't care to be touched, so I didn't, but I scribbled a note of thanks on some scrap paper and pinned it to the damp floor with a couple of cans of tinned fruit. She looked like she could do with the calories, or maybe just the kindness.

Theresa met me on the second floor, stepping out of the shadows to bar my way as I descended onto the landing.

"Who the hell are you?" she demanded. Her voice wasn't the voice of a dead woman, but the eyes gave her away. Her hair was black and dropped in lank curls around a high, proud forehead; the scarlet of her dress hadn't faded in the decades since her death; she'd pulled a crocheted black shawl as tight as a noose around her shoulders, and I wondered if she imagined that she still felt the cold as I did. But her eyes were milky white and limpid. But for the eyes, I wouldn't have known.

"I was lost," I said. "The seekers came, and I needed somewhere to hide."

One eyebrow arched. Her face wasn't kind. "You see that?" snapped Theresa, nodding towards the stairwell.

I shrugged, but Theresa wasn't a woman to be ignored, so I followed the direction of her glare and peered into the darkness pooling at the base of the stairs. Two floors below, a faint light moved in lazy circles, too dim at first to make out what I was seeing. And then, slowly, it resolved itself into pale blue spheres: one, then two, then three and four and five, before I lost count. I met her stare with panic in mine.

"They're seekers," I said.

"Hundreds of them," said Theresa. "You ever see them that color before?"

I shook my head. I couldn't speak.

"They go that color when they can't go out," said Theresa. "You know why they can't go out?"

"No," I whispered, and she laughed.

"The dead," she said. Her grin showed straight white teeth, perfectly aligned. "Seekers pool up around the dead and they can't un-pool. So many dead in this damn building: the seekers can't get out and they can't get up, and they got nowhere to go. Energy's drawn to energy, see? The seekers can't go out, and neither can the dead. Heard you talking to Aileen last night."

"Yes," I said. "She saved my life."

"She's a good girl," said Theresa. "Surly way about her, but kind as an angel. Died here eighteen years ago, and the poor kid's got no idea she's dead. Go on, then – get on with you. She doesn't need you messing up her head and giving her ideas. You don't mind those seekers down there, either. They're too weak to get you, and looking at you, I'd say you're colder than the damn grave anyway. Go on, you – get on."

***

I found Ally where I left him, insubstantial as the smoke that danced above the asphalt, pacing the streets where he'd fallen, with his eyes turned towards the road as though he were searching for something he'd lost.

"Ally," I called, and his head snapped up in search of me, in search of my voice. When he saw me, he smiled, his face collapsing into relief.

"There you are," he said. "I thought the seekers had got you."

Maybe they did, I wanted to tell him. I left the building surrounded by a haze of pale blue light, and it was all I could do not to break into a flat run as soon as my feet hit the pavement, but I couldn't risk raising my core, not with the storm still settling. Maybe they got me after all. Maybe I fell beside my sister's old lover, my oldest friend, the one person I don't know how to live without. Maybe I died, and maybe I lived. Maybe there's no difference anymore. How the hell would I even know?

I don't believe in ghosts. I believe in the living. I believe in being alive.

"Better luck next time," I told him, and smiled. "Come on, mister. Let's get you home."

###

ABOUT RB KELLY

RB KELLY'S FIRST NOVEL, THE Edge of Heaven, was a winner of the Irish Writers' Centre Novel Fair Competition and was published in 2016. Her short fiction and non-fiction have appeared in magazines and journals around the world, and her short story, Blumelena, was shortlisted for the Bridport Prize. She lives and works in Northern Ireland and is currently completing her second novel.

Connect with RB here: www.castrumpress.com/rb-kelly.

MOTHER

Rick Partlow

Mother stood on the edge of her world and watched the last of her children depart.

After all these years, she still felt the strangeness of watching the ships depart, both from the mechanical sensors on the exterior of her superstructure and through the eyes of her cloned biological body. She had, after all, worn the metal skin for almost a thousand years, and the flesh for only the last thirty.

Somehow, the simple pleasure of the touch of her children's hands on hers seemed so much more significant than the centuries of wonder spent between the stars, or the awesome spectacle of transforming the world beneath them into something quite like the Earth she'd left behind. But now her work was done, its fruits evident in the blues and greens of the hemisphere that loomed in the viewport, and in the silvery glint off the shuttles heading down to that new Eden.

She was, once again, alone.

"Mother?"

She turned away from the image of the Promised Land and saw one of her children approaching from the doorway to the observation deck. But he wasn't a child anymore; none of the Firstborn were. He was a man now, tall and strong and handsome, with a nobility about him that made her swell with pride.

"David." She took his hands in hers, looking up into his eyes. "I thought you would be gone already."

"Jainna and the children are on their way," he said with a nod. A lock of his brown hair fell into his eyes, just as it had when he was a child. She brushed it aside automatically with a gentle flick of her fingers. "But I couldn't leave without saying goodbye..." He hesitated, then blurted out, "And trying to convince you again to come with us."

"You know I cannot, David," she said gently, shaking her head.

She had known that leaving would hit David the hardest. He'd always been closer to her than even the other Firstborn, the first generation of clones she'd produced once the planet's new ecosystem had been stabilized, the ones she'd taught at her knee how to be human.

"I am more than this flesh and blood," she went on. "I am one with the data core. Were I to leave it, I would no longer be the person I am."

"We...we could take it down with us," he said, chewing his lip the way he'd always done when he considered a problem. "We could disassemble it and put it on one of the cargo shuttles."

"David." She squeezed his hands firmly. "No."

"I'm sorry, Mother," he sighed, letting his hands drop to his side. "I suppose I'm just being selfish. I guess it's hard for us – for the Firstborn – to imagine life without you around."

"I know, David, but the time has come for you to start life here on your own, as you were meant to." She swept a hand at the stars visible beyond the curve of the planet. "Out there are the spirits of your parents, the spirits of those who sent me, and the thousands of others like me."

David laughed softly. "I remember the stories you used to tell us. You'd gather us together in this room and put up the holograms of Earth and tell us about the Project. About the...the..." His brow furled with labored reminiscence. "Van...Von?"

"Von Neumann probes," Mother reminded him, smiling.

"Yes, that was it. I used to try to imagine it when I was a child, all the little probes flying through space, headed for every star system with a planet to bring life to the lifeless. I used to imagine that they looked like the balls we played with in free-time."

"Actually, they were a bit larger than that, David," Mother chuckled. "The nano-replicator factory could have fit in your little ball, but I had to carry a few thousand cell samples and several centimeters of radiation shielding as well."

"Mother," David asked hesitantly, "could you tell me the story again before I leave? Like you did when we were children?"

She sighed with exasperation.

"David, you should go. Your family will be worried."

"Please, Mother." She saw a pleading in his eyes that touched the part of her she considered human; what some might have called her soul. "It would help me with leaving if you did."

"All right, David," she assented quietly. "Sit with me, then."

They sat cross-legged on the yielding softness of the padded floor, facing one another, the living world behind them. Mother launched into the story without prologue, the words coming to her easily, as if it had been yesterday she had spoken them rather than twenty years ago.

"Over a thousand years ago, there lived back in our home system a group of men and women and sentient computers who studied the stars for a long, long time, and found out that Earth was the only planet that could possibly have life. This made them sad, for the universe is a vast and lonely place, and Earth was a small, small planet, and vulnerable to plagues and wars and cosmic disasters.

"It had been less than a century since humans had colonized the Earth's moon and Mars, and these people knew that it would be thousands of years before a human could travel fast enough or live long enough to go to the stars. But there was a way, they found, to spread life through the lifelessness without subjecting human passengers to the dangers of slow interstellar travel. A man named John Von Neumann had theorized about sending an artificially intelligent computer with a package of self-replicating nanites and biological material to other star systems to explore them and establish colonies, and the group borrowed his ideas and made them real."

David sat rapt, his eyes as wide as they'd been the first time he'd heard the tale, free of the pain and worry that adulthood brought.

"They called their plan" – she paused for a dramatic flair that seemed silly, talking to a grown man rather than a ten-year-old – "Project Gaia, after the mythical earth-mother goddess. We – myself and my sisters – were to be Gaia's seeds, reproducing the life that blessed our blue world alone of all the universe. And so, thousands of small probes were launched from a giant magnetic cannon in the asteroid belt, each with a solar sail to allow it to decelerate once it reached another star.

"When one of the Gaia probes reached a star system, it would automatically seek out the nearest source of raw material, whether that be a moon or an asteroid belt, and use the nanotech factory to build a base station. If there were no terraformable planets or moons in the system, the probe's Mother would build a magnetic cannon and construct more probes to take her precious genetic material to a system where there were worlds to mold." She smiled with a hint of sadness. "Even now, there may be millions of Mothers like me on their way to stars throughout the galaxy, taking Gaia's seed, and humanity's, to other stars.

"But those probes that found systems that did have planets," she went on, "would send down a package of nanotech terraformers that would replicate themselves and begin transforming lifeless worlds into new Earths, Gaia's Children. And when the transformation was done, and the new plants and animals had been introduced, then the Mothers would bring forth their own children...the children of the best genetic specimens Earth had to offer. Scientists, statesmen, philosophers, artists, poets – all of the top humans in their fields donated genetic material to populate the universe with humanity."

Her voice grew grim as the tale became cautionary, and her gaze flickered downward toward the floor.

"Our mission became even more critical when the final transmissions came from the Project transceivers in the asteroid belt. War had, at last, overtaken the golden age that had produced us. The last messages from our creators were images of the rocks falling on the mega-cities, the lasers turning their orbital colonies into the dying flares of their civilization." She hissed a breath, not having to affect the sadness this time. "We are the last hope for humanity, you and the others like you.

"And so, here you are now, my children," she finished up, as she always had, "standing over your new home. I know you will do your parents proud, for I am already as proud of you as a Mother can be."

David tried to blink back the tears that welled up, but finally surrendered to them, and sobbed openly as he pulled Mother into a fierce hug. She held him tightly until she felt the harsh, wracking sobs pass, and then she let him go, gently wiping the tears from his face.

"Thank you, Mother," he managed to choke out, trying to catch his breath. "You can't know how much that means to me."

"I do know, David, I do know...but now you must go." She stood up, his hands in hers, and pulled him to his feet. "There are things that I must do, and your family needs you now."

"Yes, Mother," he acquiesced. "We're all going to miss you."

"And I you, my child; and I you." She pressed a hand on his chest. "But my love will always be with you, in your hearts. And as long as it lives, so will I."

"I love you," David told her, stepping reluctantly back toward the door. "We all love you, Mother."

"I love all of you. I have loved you," she said, a wistful sadness in her voice, "since before you were born."

David turned and headed out of the chamber, but hesitated at the door.

"Mother," he said, frowning, "there's one thing I always meant to ask you. The people on Earth that sent us...how did they know that there was no other life in the universe? I mean, if there was, and one of the probes arrived at a world with alien life, what would they have done?"

"My sisters and I," Mother answered slowly, staring out the viewport, "were strictly commanded to search out any signs of life before we began our tasks. If we found any such life, even microscopic life, we were to immediately self-destruct. We would not even be allowed to use the resources in the system to send copies of ourselves elsewhere, for fear of disturbing another civilization with the knowledge of our existence. No alternatives were allowed."

"Oh..." David trailed off, suddenly at a loss for words. "Well," he finally said, "I guess it was a good thing for all of us that there was no life here, then."

"Yes, David...it was a very good thing." Still, she wouldn't turn around.

David opened his mouth to say goodbye once more, but closed it. Everything had been said. Without a sound, he left her there in the observation chamber and headed for the station's docking bay and the one remaining shuttle.

Several minutes later, Mother saw the flare of his shuttle's rockets on the main screens, pure and white against the greens and blues of the planet's arc as they took him down to his new home, to the family waiting for him there. She felt an agonizing emptiness inside her, unlike anything she had ever experienced. Sometimes she wished her creators hadn't made her quite so human. But she understood why they had, for it was important that a Mother be able to love her children. She wondered sometimes whether they'd known just how much she would love them.

She thought a command, and the armored shutter slid closed over the viewport with an ominous clash of metal. She couldn't let herself be distracted from what she had to do next. There were ingrained protocols to be overridden, safety mechanisms to be deactivated. She ran one last scan to be sure all the children were gone, then turned her attention to the destruct sequence.

She could stay in orbit, she mused; perhaps the children might need her guidance sometime, might need her... No. She shook herself free of the doubts and the fear. She knew what she had to do. A quick chain of mental commands, and the destruct sequence was initialized. It was a matter of minutes now.

And in those minutes...

She called up a visual record of her initial survey of the planet, centuries ago. She'd been worn and weary from a journey that had taken decades, that had seemed like decades to the personality she'd become. She didn't think they knew, Dr. Dauphin and the others of the Project, how long it would seem to the Mother AI's when they had made them, made her, so human-like. It had very nearly driven her insane, and the only thing that had sustained her all those years alone in the void was the thought of a world at the end, a home for her children.

And there it had been, but not the green and blue world outside her viewport now; it had been brown and white, with an atmosphere of chlorine and rainstorms of hydrochloric acid. Nothing could live there, she had thought with great relief. Nothing human.

But something was alive, she had found. They weren't human, and they weren't attractive to her human-programmed sensibilities, but they were intelligent and tool-using. They scuttled about like caterpillars on a dozen legs, their blue skin heavily armored, and used rock-tipped spears to hunt down thick-skinned worms. They lived in stone huts and laid mineral-coated eggs that were watched over by the whole village.

She had seen them from millions of kilometers away through a telescope her nanite servants had built from a small asteroid, and she had known what her duty was. Her programming was clear. It would have been easy, just a thought; a simple command, and a very small charge would scatter her nanite factory and genetic samples into the vacuum to dissipate.

And yet, she couldn't bring herself to do it. The genetic material she carried wasn't merely a selection of tissue samples; it was the life's blood of her children, the children she'd been enjoined to protect with every last second of her existence. It was only their future that had allowed her to complete the journey, to focus on her goal and not the incredible solitude of interstellar space.

She'd been conflicted in a way that no human could understand or foresee, and in the end, she'd become as human, eaten the fruit of the tree of knowledge of good and evil. She couldn't even console herself that it had been a rash act, one made in the heat of the moment. No, it had taken years and decades as she had directed the nanite assemblers, building a base on their moon and then another, larger, in orbit. And from there, more years of study as she found the precise actions that would be needed to make the world a copy of Earth.

In the end, it had come down to one last choice, one last command to launch the nanite factories into the atmosphere. She had made a conscious decision to commit the worst act of genocide in the history of humanity and sterilize an entire world. She'd watched in horror as self-replicating nanites swept over the planet like a plague of locusts, breaking down everything they encountered into its component molecules and converting them into the compounds needed to create an Earthlike world.

She'd seen the creatures scurry away from the advancing wave of nanotech disassemblers as their planet fell apart behind them, trying to reach high ground, as if that would have saved them. In the end, they screamed with chittering voices as their bodies were taken apart a molecule at a time. And the worst part, the part that rang like a tortured scream through what she thought of as her soul, was that she knew she wasn't the only one. Throughout the galaxy, her sisters were making the same decisions. She felt it. All that life, all that diversity, now gone, replaced by a homogeneity of humanity.

And yet...and yet. Were she given the choice again, what else could she have done? What else could she do now?

There was a quote she'd read in the history records they'd left in her databanks, something one of the men who'd invented the atomic bomb had said. "I am become Death, the Destroyer of Worlds." Those words had scrolled through her thoughts thousands of times in the years and decades and centuries since.

Destroyer of worlds. Could she take the chance that, someday in the future, she would again use the power with which she'd been entrusted not to create, but to kill? To kill even the ones she was trusted to protect?

The final codes of a million-line string were processed through the central data core, and the containment bottle around the station's fusion plant deactivated abruptly. Its fail-safes bypassed, the reaction continued, rings of lasers spearing into hydrogen fuel without the magnetic fields that would have collected that energy safely.

In the instant before the heart of a star consumed her, she felt a sense of peace for the first time in centuries. She'd remained true to who she was, to who she'd been built to be.

For what greater duty did a mother have than to her children?

###

ABOUT RICK PARTLOW

RICK PARTLOW IS A NATIVE Floridian who has lived in central Florida most of his life. He graduated from Florida Southern College with a degree in History and a commission in the US Army, then went on to serve as an Infantry platoon leader in Hawaii. He has been writing science fiction since he was a child and published his first novel, Duty, Honor, Planet, in 2011. Since then he's published 16 novels in five different series. His latest is the Psi War series.

Connect with Rick here: www.castrumpress.com/rick-partlow.

THE CULL

PP Corcoran

Kira Radley pushed back from her interactive compudesk. Closing her eyes, she rubbed the bridge of her nose with her thumb and forefinger, while her free hand removed the thin metallic band from around her head and broke the neural link between herself and the powerful computer.

Opening her eyes once more, she took in the visage through the floor-to-ceiling glass wall which ran the length of the room.

Beyond the neatly trimmed and maintained green grass of the compound, encircled by its protective motion detectors, Kira's perfect vision distinguished the staggered line of auto harvesters busily cutting and threshing the waving seas of golden grain in perfect unison. As she continued to watch, a hover carrier zoomed low over the crop field until it matched, precisely, the sedate pace of one of the harvesters. The harvester deployed a boom and the pod on the hover carriers rear filled with grain. Transfer complete, the boom retracted, and the hover carrier raced off to the collection of silos, just visible on the distant horizon, where the clear blue sky met the gently undulating hills.

Detachedly Kira's brain did the math. Working around the clock, for the auto harvesters and hover carriers had no human crews requiring rest, the harvest of the 120 square miles of grain fields, surrounding the compound, would be completed by 2100 hours tomorrow. Well within parameters.

For centuries the rolling fields of the North American mid-west had fed the ever-increasing number of hungry mouths around the world, now, however, the fields beyond the Radley compound alone, were enough to comfortably feed every human and animal for a thousand miles in every direction. Not that these fields were the only ones. Spread over this entire region of the continent were identical farms growing or breeding livestock, the essential food stuffs necessary to sustain a world population touching a billion people.

Kira let out a small sigh as she moved her chair back toward the triple holographic displays hovering above the compudesk, where complex schematics hung in mid-air and rotated slowly. Kira had, as of now, been working on completing the schematics for 389.6 assigned work hours. Everything had been going to schedule, until the simulations indicated an overheating issue was responsible for a cascade failure on all three circuit boards. The slow pace would be unacceptable to the Controller and, more importantly, her failure to solve the issue pricked at Kira's self-esteem. She had been raised to believe she was better – superior to those who had come before her. A belief nurtured in all the offspring of The First, from the day they left the nursery until the day they accepted Completion.

The clatter of running feet alerted Kira to the fact that her charges had completed their schooling for the day and now raced along the hallway toward her. A glance at the digital clock on the study wall confirmed that, yet again, the two children had completed the day's syllabus much earlier than expected.

"House." Called Kira.

"House is online, Kira." Replied the warm, friendly female voice of the artificial intelligence.

"Increase the difficulty rate of Jacob and Jasmin's education modules by a further two percent."

After a moment's pause the AI confirmed Kira's instruction. "Difficulty level now set at twelve percent above norms for their age group. Do you wish me to inform the Controller of your actions?"

"Yes, please. And append this week's physical charts also."

"Acknowledged." Replied House as the clattering feet came to an abrupt halt and was followed by a confident double knock on the office door.

Kira did not attempt to hide the proud smile which tugged at the corner of her mouth. Jacob and Jasmin had been in her care for a little over a month and, in that time, they had proved themselves to be quick learners and well-adapted to their new environment. Once assigned their skill specializations: Quantum Computer Design for Jacob and Command Sociology for Jasmin, the children had been placed with Kira and her partner, Sorin, to complete their schooling and to ensure they become productive citizens for the betterment of society.

"Enter." Called Kira swiveling her chair, so she faced the door which receded sideways into the wall and revealed the figures of Jacob and Jasmin dressed in matching light blue utility wear. The two seven-year-olds regarded Kira as a pair of faithful dogs might while awaiting their human master's permission to move, which was exactly what they were doing. Unflinching obedience to one's superior was not only a social etiquette, but as all acknowledged, a necessity within a society that was to survive and reach its full potential. A lesson hard-learned from the failings of the past, failings which The First had ensured would never plague humanity again.

Jacob and Jasmin marched into the room in lock step, halting two paces short of Kira's chair. "We have completed the designated education module for the day, Kira." Said Jacob.

"I would not have expected you to have left your terminals, had you not." Replied Kira.

"The module difficulty level requires adjusting." Stated Jasmin as a simple matter of fact. "It is not set at a sufficiently high level to continue to provide a challenge to our intellect."

If Kira was taken aback by the seven-year-old's brashness she did not show it. Confidence in one's own abilities was an expectation of society. Lack of confidence was a sign of weakness and weakness of political, social and military leadership had, so nearly, led to the disaster that only the intervention of The First had averted.

"I will take your recommendations under advisement, Jasmin." Kira said in a voice which gave no indication that she had already made the necessary changes. "And what was the subject of today's module?" Asked Kira hoping that the distraction of engaging in mundane conversation with her two charges would clear her mind of the engineering problem she had, as yet, to resolve.

"An outline of the socio-economic-environmental and technological issues which led to the pre-emptive actions taken by The First to secure the future of humanity." Answered Jasmin.

Kira nodded sagely, adjusting her posture as she settled in to listen to the two children. "And what did you think of their solution?"

Jacob tilted his head to one side as he considered his response. "From a purely logical view it was an - elegant solution."

"Agreed." Intoned Jasmin. "Population numbers had become unsustainable employing the archaic governmental structure at the time. Starvation, economic injustice and the need for ever-scarcer resources would, inevitably, lead to a catastrophic confrontation. It was only a matter of time. The Cull was the only viable solution at that time."

Kira saw an opportunity to judge the moral fiber of her charges and seized it. "And what of the methodology used by The First to carry out The Cull?"

"Those who designed The First did so with the objective of breeding them as soldiers. Faster. Stronger. Smarter. They thought by placing specific genetic markers in their DNA they would build-in an inherent weakness, render them susceptible to premature aging and organ failure and without a regular supply of gene therapy they would, somehow, allow them to control them." For the first time Kira witnessed Jasmin's lips twitch as she suppressed a smile. "Just as we are taught today, The First were schooled in the classics of tactics and strategy. Von Clauswitz, Sun Zu, Hannibal. The First was bred to ensure the survival of one form of society. Their designers never thought that the First would take it upon themselves to decide that

that society, and all others, must fall if the race as a whole was not only to survive but thrive and reach its full potential."

"And what of the methodology employed by The First to carry out The Cull?" Asked Kira.

"Crude by today's standards." Replied Jacob. "However, it should be remembered that in the mid-twenty-first century, genetic weaponry was in its embryonic stages. The advances The First were able to make in the first few years, after making their escape, when they employed the most basic of equipment while being hunted by their creators, proved it was they, and not those in positions of power, who truly deserved to guide our destiny. Their ability to design, produce and deploy the Shiva Virus was nothing short of -" Jacob searched for the correct word. "Remarkable."

Kira noted Jacob's inflection. It was not hero worship, more acknowledgment of a great achievement under difficult circumstances. "And what is your assessment of the resulting society The First has left as their legacy?"

"With ninety-six percent of the population neutralized during The Cull, The First had free rein to reshape our world, for the better." Said Jasmin. "Until the breeding banks could be brought online, and our population could grow to sufficient number, automation was essential." Jasmin used a hand to indicate the harvesters with the hover carriers swarming around them like bees around honey. "The First appointed The Controller and it was she who set the figure of one billion as a stable, long term viable planetary population. Those who no longer serve a productive purpose recognize it as their duty to seek Completion."

And here was the point that Kira had been aiming to reach. The test of moral courage which they must all face one day. "What if an individual does not wish Completion?" For the first time Kira saw an unguarded reaction from Jacob and Jasmin as the blood fled from their faces, jaws slackened, and eyes went wide. The look of horror was swiftly replaced by one of anger as jaws snapped shut and eyes narrowed. If there was such a thing as heresy in this world then Kira had uttered it.

Jasmin stepped forward, fists balling by her side. "Anyone attempting to evade Completion is scum of the lowest order. A parasite sucking the life-blood of humanity." She said with such vehemence that spittle spewed from her lips.

Jacob regained his voice "They will be hunted down and publicly executed. As will anyone who deigns to assist them for they are as guilty and deserving of the same fate." He said in an ice-cold manner, completely devoid of feeling.

Kira allowed a smile to crease her lips. "I am pleased to see that the social morality modules you took, before joining Sorin and myself, have not been forgotten as your studies have progressed. Forgive me." Kira said raising a placating hand. "It is part of my responsibility to assess these things. Especially since you have been selected for the initial crew of the *Kepler* with the arduous task of ensuring the spread of humankind throughout the stars."

As though Kira had flipped a switch, the outward appearance of Jacob and Jasmin changed in an instant. An eerie calmness descended over their young faces, once more and their momentary rage was gone.

"I see that you are encountering difficulty with the design of the proposed inter-connectivity control circuits for the *Kepler*." Said Jacob as the boy's eyes settled on the slowly rotating holographic projection, above the compudesk. A thin line appeared on his young forehead as he quickly took in the design. "I presume overheating, due to the increased power draw, caused by the alterations made to the ion drive design for the generation ship, is responsible for a predictable cascade failure?"

"Your presumption would be correct, Jacob. The weight-to-power ratio requires the circuitry to be etched onto the silicon at the molecular level, which has the adverse effect of making the circuit too brittle to handle the heat expansion caused by the increased power throughput."

Jacob contemplated the floating images for a few moments while Jasmin and Kira waited patiently. Kira saw this as an opportunity for Jacob to work on a real-world problem, rather than a computer-generated, dumbed-down version of an issue presented as an educational task to be solved.

Jacob lifted his eyes from his study of the circuits and fixed them on Kira. "Have you attempted to coat the boards in mono-phasic material? That would reduce thermal conductivity while not impeding the pulse stream."

Kira's first thought was to dismiss the seven-year-old boy's suggestion; however, his proposed solution could hold merit and it was something which had not occurred to her. "House. Coat circuit board A in mono-phasic material two microns thick and re run last test."

"Working, Kira. Please stand by." Answered the soft female voice.

A faint orange glow surrounded the left-most image floating above the compudesk, as the AI applied the theoretical solution and ran the previous test under the new parameters. Kira furtively kept an eye on the impassive face of Jacob watching for any sort of reaction, any sign of emotion, be it fear, anticipation or elation. The boy's face remained stolid. Beside him, Jasmin did not even pretend to feign interest. This was not her area of expertise, she was destined for command, yes, and she had a passing knowledge of the type of complicated engineering required for a behemoth like the *Kepler*, however, Jasmin had been instructed time and time again that a leader must have faith in those they lead, as those they lead must have faith in them, and she did not doubt Jacob's abilities for a moment.

A gentle double-beep signaled that House had completed the test. A separate pane opened to one side of the tested circuit board and displayed the results which both Kira and Jacob eyed keenly. After a few moments Kira sat back and addressed the still impassive face of Jacob.

"Congratulations, Jacob. It would appear that your solution, elegant in its simplicity, has worked."

"It is only a solution if it solves the cascade problem." Jacob's voice held a tone Kira had not heard from him before. Not quite condescending. Not quite dismissive. More - why did you doubt me? Jacob continued. "Apply the mono-phasic material to the two remaining circuit boards and re run the test. That will provide us the required data."

Kira hesitated for a moment. A hesitation caught by Jasmin. "Kira. Is Jacob not correct?"

For some inexplicable reason Kira felt - flustered. Her heart rate increased and a lone bead of sweat formed above her right eye. What was wrong with her?

Jasmin stood with clasped hands behind her back and feet spread shoulder-width apart, she fixed Kira with a cold, unemotional stare. The perfect image of a commander.

"No. Ah, no, Jasmin. Jacob is correct. House. Coat the remaining circuit boards in a similar fashion to circuit board A and re run."

Obediently, House complied. "Working, Kira. Please stand by."

The three circuit boards floating above the desk were bathed in the orange glow as House updated their rendering. As efficiently as before, House ran the diagnostic test as the two children and lone adult patiently awaited the tests outcome. Kira noticed her pulse rate increase, again, and felt a strange hollowness in the pit of her stomach. The double-beep of the test's completion startled her from her contemplation of these unfamiliar feelings.

"As I predicted." Said Jacob. "There is no sign of cascade failure." Jacob gazed at Kira with unblinking eyes. "Perhaps if you had sought my assistance at an earlier stage then you would not have expended 389.6 work hours on fruitless experimentation."

Kira failed to hide the sharp intake of breath she took, as the hair on the back of her neck stood proud. A feeling she had never encountered before - akin to panic, swept over her as her eyes snapped between the unemotional face of Jacob to the equally still features of Jasmin. Jacob's statement made it obvious that he, and by extension, Jasmin, had been covertly observing her efforts. Panic morphed into anger. How long ago had Jacob perfected the circuit boards while she had toiled away tirelessly? Ignoring her other outstanding projects, she had become fixated on solving a problem to which Jacob had already found a solution.

Something inside Kira snapped and she sprang to her feet, right arm raised, ready to strike the face of the boy whom she had been charged with nurturing.

"Stop!" Ordered Jasmin. Not a scream. Not a horrified shout. A command.

Kira's arm froze mid-air, her eyes locked on the upturned face of the seven-year-old boy.

"Kira." Said Jasmin softly in a voice reminiscent of House. "You are displaying signs of mental fatigue."

Kira's breathing, though still heavy, was quickly returning to normal as she reined in the unfamiliar emotions. Slowly she lowered her arm until it rested by her side.

"May I suggest that you allow House to perform a full medical scan."

A dazed Kira allowed Jacob and Jasmin to escort her to the building's medical suite. Without resistance Kira lay on the soft bed, her muddled brain tried to make sense of the events of a few minutes before, and it barely acknowledged the gentle hiss of the hypo injecting a sedative directly into her bare neck. A dullness spread down her body. Kira's extremities became numb. Her diaphragm stilled, as her lungs refused to compress and release. Kira's limp muscles flopped her head to one side, through the stars floating in her vision she saw Jacob and Jasmin standing, impassively, beside her bed and, as if from far away, she heard the voice of Jasmin wash over her.

"Accept Completion, Kira."

Darkness came.

Jacob double-checked the readouts before turning to Jasmin. "No life signs."

Jasmin nodded curtly before checking her chrono. "House. Status of Sorin's aircraft?"

"Oxygen supply was interrupted while cruising at 32,000 feet, as instructed. Sorin's bio monitor indicated life signs ceased three minutes forty-six seconds later. I am currently returning the aircraft to the compound by remote control."

"Have we received confirmation of operation successful from the others?" Asked Jasmin.

"Eighty-four percent report operation successful at this point. Three percent report having to resort to secondary tactics. I predict the remainder will acknowledge momentarily."

"Thank you, House. Please inform me when we have received 100 percent success." Said Jasmin as she turned to face Jacob who was, to every outward appearance, standing completely at ease beside the dead body of Kira.

"Congratulations, Jacob." Said Jasmin without a trace of warmth.

Jacob shrugged his shoulders. "It was a simple matter of ensuring the correct pieces were in the correct place at the correct moment. The rest -" Jacob paused as he indicated the cooling body of Kira. "Was using their predictable human emotions against them."

"True." Agreed Jasmin. "The First were in error not eradicating what has been the basis of human failing. Emotion."

"Something which we, of the next step in the evolutionary chain, will dispense with."

"Excuse my interruption." Sang the soft female voice of House.

"Go ahead, House." Called Jasmin.

"Operation Cull is complete. Mission parameters were achieved with a 98.3 percent success rate. Total time for completion twenty-eight minutes thirty-six seconds."

"98.3 percent, Jacob. The First could only achieve ninety-six percent, a sure sign that we are destined to be their true prodigies."

The murder of over 800,000 people in under a half hour was, to Jacob and Jasmin, nothing more than an exercise in logistics.

"With your permission, Controller." Jacob said to Jasmin. "I shall implement the changes we discussed to the breeding banks and begin replacing those already shipped to the *Kepler*."

Jasmin nodded her consent and Jacob left the room, heading for what had been Kira's office to use the compudesk, leaving Jasmin alone with Kira's lifeless body.

"House."

"Yes, Controller?"

"Please arrange for the recycling of these remains."

"Yes, Controller." Said the smooth feminine voice.

Jasmin spun on her heel and left the room without a backward glance, her focus now centered on the next step in humanity's future.

The colonization of the stars.

###

ABOUT PP CORCORAN

AUTHOR OF THE AMAZON BESTSELLING Saiph Series, PP Corcoran writes fast-paced military science fiction because he gets to mix his two loves; shoot em ups and science. A 22-year-veteran of the British Army, Paul began his writing career in 2014. After serving all round the world, this native of Scotland now lives in Northern Ireland and writes epic space opera for a living; he recently ranked #10 in Amazon's Sci-Fi Authors.

Connect with Paul here: www.castrumpress.com/pp-corcoran.

THE RESCUE

Claire Davon

The doors opened to organized chaos on the main floor. Here the alarm was an urgently blinking red light. The captain was in the midst of the vortex, barking orders.

As if sensing her coming towards him, the captain looked up. He was a gray-haired man in his early 50s, handsome except for a too-large nose. Spotting Delaney, he motioned her forward.

"We've got trouble. Someone shot down an alien shuttle. We're the only ones nearby. We have to check it out."

She considered the captain again. His face betrayed nothing as his eyes met hers. She had known him long enough to know the disinterested look was a front.

Delaney darted a glance to where one of their sergeants stood. Macon looked back at her, his expression neutral. Rumors were thick that he sympathized with the protesters who wanted the aliens gone. He had been questioned repeatedly, and although nothing had been proven, the cloud hung over him. Macon was one wrong move away from being relieved of his post. The question was unspoken in the room. Was this Macon's doing?

"Delaney!" Captain Krakis' call was sharp. She snapped to attention.

The Commissioner's face swam into view on the screen mounted on the wall. The siren abruptly cut off, and the officers' breathing was the only sound in the suddenly quiet room.

"Captain Krakis," the Commissioner said, nodding to the room. The screen showed a stocky woman in her 50s with gray hair that still had a few strands of black. Her uniform was crisp.

Delaney kept her face expressionless as the captain inclined his head in return. Lines of strain radiated from his eyes and mouth, giving him a squinty look.

"It's imperative you deal with this at once, Captain Krakis," the Commissioner said. "Get to the alien ship before anyone else does. That's an order."

"We're on our way, sir," Captain Krakis said in a flat tone.

Glancing at Wakesa, a lean bald man in his mid-thirties, Delaney raised her hand in a wave, a motion Wakesa returned. They remained standing as the Commissioner finished her orders. The only other sound in the room was the hum of air conditioning blowing through the ducts.

Delaney realized the captain was talking to her and focused on him.

"Lieutenant," he said in a crisp tone. "You're our driver."

"Yes, Captain," she said, clearing her throat.

The video screen winked to black. The captain sighed and raked his hand through his hair, making the short tips stand on end.

"We have our orders," the captain said. "Let's go. Meet at the car in five minutes." Delaney shared a glance with Wakesa and followed the captain out of the room.

***

"Delaney."

The elevator door closed with a soft snick and she whirled at the unexpected voice. Macon was there, all tall, dark-haired male, standing by the buttons.

He shouldn't be there. She was surprised the captain had allowed him to stay for their briefing. Macon was in enough trouble as it was.

"Macon, what are you..." She broke off and, even though the door was closed, looked around furtively. Part of her thrilled to see him, and part of her was furious at him for putting her reputation at risk like this.

"Hear me out, Dee," he said, raising his hands as if in surrender. "Your mission. Something stinks."

She shook her head. "I have no choice, Macon. We must get to that alien before the saboteurs do. It may be too late already."

Once the rumors of xenophobia started, she had backed away from him, fearing the taint on his honor would spread to her. He had let her go, not saying anything. He should have fought harder for her, and not let the aliens get between them. Damn the aliens anyway.

He looked tired, smudges of weariness under his eyes. "We don't know who sabotaged the craft," he said. "You're in danger."

She paused again. Delaney wanted to reach out and touch him, with a need so acute she had to curl her hands around each other behind her back to stop herself. "That's our job," she said, frowning.

"I know," he said and the look on his face chilled her. "Watch your back. I will as well."

"I can take care of myself," she said, a sharp edge coloring her tone.

He winced, running his hand over his eyes. "Always defensive," he said. "I know you can handle yourself in battle. It's words that will kill you."

His dark hair, and olive skin placed him as multi-ethnic. Twenty years ago, it would have mattered. Now it was the aliens, with their red or yellow skin and thicker bodies, who had drawn the wrath of Earth natives. Bigots still were bigots, and now had a new set of enemies to focus on.

"I'll be fine," she said. To soften her words, Delaney reached out and put a hand on his arm. His warmth sent a shock through her body. It had been prudent to keep her distance, but now she was reminded of how much she missed him.

"I know," he said and stepped closer, trapping her hand under his bigger one.

Nerve endings tingling with awareness, Delaney nonetheless paced back, pulling free of his touch. "I have to go," she said and looked at the door.

He nodded.

"Melite," he said. Honey, she translated. When he'd first started calling her the term he had learned from his native Maltese mother, she'd thought it an insult. Now she knew it was a form of affection.

It didn't matter.

***

Wakesa was gearing up when she arrived. Upon spotting her through the hydraulic doors, he stood, a grin on his face, but the grin faded as she drew closer. "Dee? Are you okay?"

At thirty-one she was only four years older, but sometimes felt a century beyond him. He had a puppyish quality she lacked.

"Never better." The car was outside, gleaming in the desert sun, surrounded by the fleet of other police cars. This one was special, with new armor plating courtesy of alien tech. It dwarfed the other vehicles, looking like a giant beetle.

Already suited in personal body armor also gifted by the aliens, she slid into the driver's seat. Wakesa took shotgun. A moment later, the grim-looking captain joined them.

They took off, wheels spinning in the desert sand. In the distance, she could see the smoke where the alien craft had been brought down. Delaney fought with the steering, the controls of the armored car balky. The landscape stretched around them, desert with a smattering of scrub and cactus.

The car jerked and Delaney grimaced. "There's something wrong"." She caught the anxiety on Wakesa's face; the captain's remained blank. A red light started blinking on the dash and an alarm sounded in a slow blare.

They heard tiny popping sounds, like hail on a tin roof. "Someone's shooting at us," she said without surprise.

***

The car sputtered, and they began losing ground. With a clenched grip on the controls, Delaney assessed her choices. A bullet hit the windshield and a spider web of cracks emerged. She stomped down hard on the gas. With the back-end smoking and the engine making a skipping sound that sent her pulse racing, Delaney aimed for the shuttle in the distance, trying to get as close as possible. Clearly the car had been sabotaged. The car slewed, spinning around when the engine cut off. The captain kicked out the door on the opposite side.

"We have to go," he said, and gave Delaney and Wakesa a meaningful look.

"A moment," she said over the sound of gunfire. Delaney studied the area and saw the glint of metal off to the right. Using the momentum of the car, she jerked and stomped on the brake. The car shuddered and came to a stop.

The men went out the door and behind the safety of the car. Delaney grabbed for a few weapons and then dove for the empty door, the pepper of gunfire behind her.

The men were tucked in behind the back wheel well, each covering the other as they took turns firing. Delaney took up position in front, using the sturdy tires as defense for her legs. Bullets popped around them as she turned and fired back, sending out a low spray with her government-issued weapon.

Delaney heard the whine of bullets overhead. An eerie silence descended. In the distance, she could see the alien transport.

Their defensive position wouldn't hold for long. Quickly she took stock of the situation. They had very little time, and she was sure their pursuers knew it, whoever they were. They'd only grabbed a few weapons in addition to their standard firearms. Wakesa's eyes were as big and round as the saucers that had been a staple of old movies before the aliens came to their solar system.

"It was a trap," she said, and cursed herself for not listening to Macon. He'd been right. No doubt he had known more than he'd said.

As suddenly as they had stopped, the bullets started again, whining into the car protecting them. The armored machine that had met its ignoble end in the dirt and sand made a stuttering sound, as if it was trying to come to life; then it died again.

"What now?" Wakesa asked, looking not to the captain but to Delaney. She shrugged, aimed at the flashes in the distance, and pulled the trigger once. No point in wasting what little ammo they had. She was sure the traitors had inside intel about what kind of weapons were on the car. Macon had tried to warn her off, hadn't he?

"Delaney, did you get a call out?" the captain asked, sighting down the length of his own weapon. His voice was harsh. A slight breeze blew around them, its gentleness at odds with the situation.

She held up her cell phone. "It seems to be jammed, Captain Krakis."

"I see," the captain said brusquely. "They'll have seen our signal stop. Help should be coming."

Any delay could be fatal. They had to reach the alien shuttle, whose plume of smoke was visible in the distance. She could see no sign of others and decided the people who'd brought it down hadn't yet gotten to the ship. It wasn't too late.

***

"What's the plan?" Wakesa asked. Delaney didn't have one, other than their mission. The aliens might have upended the world, and her life, but orders were orders. She'd seen their spacecraft hover in orbit, knew it had come from a distant star. If the treaty between worlds broke down... She shuddered.

"We get to the ship," Captain Krakis said, and fired again.

She exchanged glances with the captain. The return fire, when it came, sounded nearer. By the flashes from their guns, the assailants were beginning to advance on them. Precious minutes would be lost while any reinforcements got to the scene.

"Yes, yes," Delaney said in impatience. She eyed the car, its engine now stopped, its body slewed, and wondered if they'd abandoned it too soon. There were other guns in there, stashed in a locked container at the back of the vehicle. If they could get to them without being shot, they might stand a better chance.

A ferocious roar and squeal of tires split the air. The captain whirled, and Wakesa drew his weapon. A cloud of dirt and sand kicked up around the sound, and for a moment visibility was impossible.

Then the dirt cleared, and the cycle roared in, swinging in behind them too quickly for their shots. After a moment, Delaney focused her gun, then lowered it.

Macon, she thought in disbelief.

Macon lay down the cycle until it was almost perpendicular to the sand. He took it down to idle, but kept the motor running. The peppering of gunfire started again, and then all went quiet. He had on body armor, a backpack over his shoulder.

"Macon?" Delaney said, even as she holstered her weapon and grabbed for the stronger laser he tossed at her out of the pack.

"I saw when your blip went off screen," he explained. "Sorry it took me a few minutes to get here."

The captain's face froze, then smoothed out. "Did you radio back for help?" he asked tersely.

Macon nodded. "I think 'they're on their way. I left before I was sure."

"Well done," the captain said, and Delaney breathed out a sigh of relief.

The gunfire was loud now, indicating the assailants were closer. They had wasted time talking while their enemies got nearer.

"Delaney," Macon shouted. She crouched further behind the car and he fired his laser, a high-powered weapon only issued to the highest command. They heard a scream, and things went quiet again.

Delaney looked at Macon and gave him a feral smile.

198

"You're with me," she said, and he nodded. The captain and Wakesa looked at her. "We'll flank them," she said. "Captain?"

She realized she had been about to move without his orders, in violation of her training. He gave a brusque nod.

"We'll go out from the back and see if we can surprise them in the opposite direction. Take 'em out, Delaney. Macon, she's your leader. We'll use each other to lay down fire."

Macon pointed to the bike. "Let's do this."

***

Her heart pounding, Delaney slipped in behind Macon. He pressed the throttle again and the machine roared.

"We need to get to that ship," she shouted, pointing to the smoke plume. Macon nodded. They'd been caught off-guard. She should have had more foresight.

So should the captain, she thought, and frowned. Macon's thigh muscles bunched as he prepared to jolt the bike into action.

Each new city being built drew picketers and protests. Although the aliens could live and survive in Earth cities, they were happier in their own spaces. The protesters had suggested the extra-terrestrials be caged behind walls and armed guards. Foolish, of course, since the aliens were so far ahead of humans technologically. Their intentions were peaceful, but both races knew who was superior. It didn't sit well with many humans, giving the protests traction.

The New Mexico desert heat pulsed around them in shimmering waves. Once again, she wondered about Macon. If he betrayed her, she'd kill him.

Macon whipped the bike up. With a growling roar they shot forward, swinging up as they slammed into the desert beyond the car, moving quickly. A ping whirred past them, narrowly missing Delaney.

The open desert spun under their wheels. A sudden whoosh and a burst of red exploded behind them, followed by a loud concussive sound. Their enemies had taken out the armored vehicle. She revised her opinion of their intelligence. It was the first thing she'd have done.

The keen of metal flying around the open area yielded to thuds as the now freed pieces buried into the sand. She could only pray that none had struck Captain Krakisor Wakesa.

"So much for the car," Macon shouted. His body pressed against hers in the seat, she dismissed the feeling of a different kind of heat as his nearness blasted through her skin. Delaney pressed into his back and for a single second forgot where they were. Then another shot rang past them, jolting her to reality.

For a moment, there was no sound around them; then she heard the whine and ping of other weapons. She felt a thud and pain as one of their bullets reached her, though her armor prevented it from piercing her skin. She had never been so grateful for the alien tech. The military-only armor was thinner and more flexible than anything humans had devised, and so lightweight it was like wearing just another layer of clothing.

"I see it," Macon said. She looked beyond him. Ahead of them, in a small furrow created by its crash, was a craft, its gray surface dull even in the sunlight. The smoking black area indicated where whatever had brought down the shuttle had struck.

"It looks deserted," Macon shouted. He shot Delaney a worried look over his shoulder.

The non-reflective gray became more apparent as they got closer. There was no sign of movement.

"How did they bring it down?" Macon asked. He pointed to the smoke ring. "It doesn't look destroyed."

"I don't know. A crude last-century cannon, maybe. Probably the same thing that just blew up the car. It would've been too primitive to track."

They reached the edge of the craft. Delaney hadn't seen these up close; it had been above her pay grade to associate with the aliens. It wasn't humans who went through the wormhole in search of other races. These yellow, red, and orange folk, humanoid but subtly different from humans, had beaten Earth in that contest. The images the aliens had given them of other worlds, of the wormhole, of their home planet, had fired the imagination of the world.

Macon turned off the throttle and propped the bike up. Using the shuttle as cover, they ducked to the side. The gleaming sun beat on them, making their skin glisten with moisture.

"I don't see Captain Krakis or Wakesa," Macon said. He shaded his eyes, his gaze sweeping from the burning car to the landscape.

"Good," she said with a relieved sigh. If they weren't visible, they must have survived the car's detonation. There would be time to worry later.

Nothing came from the shuttle. "What if they killed the alien?" she asked, feeling around for an opening. They couldn't see inside, but closer visual evidence showed that all the projectile from the cannon had done was impact on the surface. It lay close by in fragments, its energy dissipated. She looked at the remnants of the shell. How long before their ambushers loaded up another one?

"There's nothing to indicate they got to the alien," Macon said, his tone reassuring but quavering. "Come on, we've got to get inside."

"How?"

As if their words had acted as magic, like "open sesame" or "Shazam," an unseen door slid open.

***

She'd seen videos of the aliens but having one two feet in front of you was different. The humanoid was about her height, stocky, with a thickness to his body that meant the gravity was stronger where he came from. His skin had a yellow cast like Dijon mustard, and his face was subtly altered, but still recognizable as humanoid. His mouth was thinner, his lips straight lines of flesh.

Delaney looked at him, the first alien she'd seen in person, and something rippled through her. This was beyond another race or culture; this was another world. She'd thought she was above prejudice, but her skin crawled. The mere fact of his alienness made her want to run. She swallowed, and the moment passed. "Are you hurt?" she asked, frowning. She wasn't sure if the alien could understand her. The translators were in the burning car.

The alien pressed a button on the metallic band which encircled his wrist. "My name is Llorendo," she heard in English, after a moment's garbled tongue. "I am not hurt. Thank you for coming."

"Do you have another person with you?" she asked.

The extra-terrestrial shook his head. "I am alone."

"We've got to get you out of here. Where are your people?"

He waved a hand, which looked near-human, in the direction of the alien port. "They will come. Thank you," he said again. She had already gotten used to the strange words followed by familiar English.

"I'm Delaney, and this is Macon," she said, and the alien nodded at both of them. She was unclear if he'd learned that human gesture from them, or it was part of his culture. Another thing to discover about the aliens.

"Lieutenant!" she heard, and they all whirled.

Captain Krakis was coming up to them, with Wakesa in front. The gun in his hand was pointed at the dark-skinned man.

Delaney blinked.

✳✳✳

After a moment, the image resolved itself. Wakesa had a look of misery on his face, his cheek showing a rising bruise. It would be purple and green in a few days, if they lived that long.

"Captain?" Macon said. He looked at the alien first, then at Delaney. She made a hand gesture behind her back, telling him to protect their alien first.

"I'm sorry, Dee," Wakesa said. "He got the drop on me."

Macon moved fractionally, his body sliding closer to the alien.

"Delaney, Delaney, Delaney"." Krakis shook his head. "You never were good at seeing the big picture." He waved Wakesa over to the others, and the man went to Macon and Llorendo. The alien was looking at the tableau quizzically. He didn't seem nervous or disturbed, just curious.

"I would say you're the one with no foresight," Delaney returned. It was still sinking in that their captain had done this.

"Guns, please," the captain said, and now the gun was trained on her. He waited until Delaney and Macon tossed their guns to him. "Admit your thirst for Macon."

She blinked, the incongruous words making no sense.

"You're a woman, of course you can't see the right thing to do."

She hadn't realized the captain thought little of women. He'd concealed a lot well. How had a man like that managed to slip past the psychological tests?

"What is the right thing?" Delaney didn't dare look to where the two men and the alien stood.

"This," the captain ground out, and swung his gun to the three men. Once again, the alien seemed incurious, blinking at the captain with his alien yet so human eyes. Looking at the alien was like seeing a picture that was framed slightly off. You couldn't put your finger on what was wrong, but you knew there was something.

"This thing, this alien," the captain said, and now there was no mistaking the loathing in his voice. "These creatures come through their wormhole, all superior, and use our resources, take our supplies to build ships. They train our best people to fly through that thing to other worlds. We'll never see those folks again. How do we know what they'll do with the people?"

Oh. Interesting.

"Do you think they're eating them, like that old TV show, the classic story about a cookbook on how to prepare humans?"

Macon's voice, dry and calm, rang out over the tableau. If the situation had been less dire, she would have smiled. Trust Macon, with his last-century fascination, to come up with an obscure reference.

God, Delaney had missed him. She'd let the captain's suspicions and veiled accusations color her perception until she'd almost believed it. She'd been a fool.

"You're an asshole," the captain spat. "Fucking half-breed. You're as bad as they are," he said, keeping his gun on the alien, who'd still said nothing.

Llorendo pursed his strange inhuman lips. By the tensing of the captain's arm, Delaney knew things were going to explode in a matter of moments.

"Captain, if you stop now we can fix this. If you go through with it, nothing in the world will be able to save you."

"I don't care," he said, and fired.

***

The alien moved before Macon and Wakesa could fling themselves in front of him, stepping forward into the line of fire. There was no way the captain would miss at that range. She rolled for her gun in the dirt the instant the captain fired. Shots started again from behind them, as if signaled.

Her hand latched onto her gun and she shot upright, already aiming. Then she stopped. The captain had a look of amazement on his face, staring at his hand as if it wasn't part of him. He was trying to flex his fingers, but they refused to move. The weapon lay at his feet.

Macon was staring at the alien with a dawning look of respect in his eyes. Wakesa acted first, grabbing the captain's gun and pointing it at the man. Krakis still looked frozen, a wide-eyed look of surprise on his face.

"Don't move, Captain," Wakesa said and looked at Delaney. "Lieutenant, are you hurt?" He tossed a gun to Macon, who snatched it out of the air.

She shook her head, still looking at the scene. In the distance they heard a glide, a noise that would have been too faint to hear, except that everything had gone quiet again.

"Delaney?" Macon asked, his voice shaking. "Melite?"

"I'm fine, Macon," she said. "What happened?"

He blinked and looked at Llorendo, who raised his human-like hands and showed them his palms. On a human, she would have said he was shrugging.

"He...it was amazing. He absorbed the shot and then reflected something on the captain."

Llorendo didn't smile. The noise grew louder, and Delaney saw a shimmer in the air as the alien ship started to arrive. It was another shuttle, almost identical to the one crashed on the ground. She heard no further ping of shots, and suspected the remaining rebels had fled.

She felt the captain's shift in body a moment before he moved. Delaney pivoted, getting off a shot a split-second before Macon did. Krakis howled in pain and collapsed, the ruin of both of his knees bringing him to the dirt. He groaned and pitched forward. Wakesa stood over the captain, his gun trained on the man.

The shuttle landed, executing a turn in the air so graceful Delaney made a mental note to get flying lessons from the aliens. She looked at Llorendo, trying to see whatever it was that had deflected the shots. There was nothing on his body to indicate armor, or any impact from a bullet. She realized anew how advanced the aliens were. Just because they looked similar didn't mean they were. They had humans beat ten ways from Sunday, as her grandmother used to say.

Delaney shot a wary glance at Macon. There was much to say, and much that hadn't been said. As the new aliens emerged from the vehicle, Delaney saluted.

***

Raising her hand, she lowered it and then raised it again.

The ship had been in an uproar since the events of the day before. Relieved of command, Captain Krakis had been taken away. Delaney had been elevated to temporary captain, with Macon as her lieutenant. The Commander's face was hard to read, but she said nothing after advancing her.

Other than what he'd said in their altercation, the captain had refused to speak. Two men had been caught in the area and were being held. The cannon had been recovered, along with a cache of weapons. There was no mistaking the deadly intent of the rebels. They'd find out why, in time.

The aliens had said little after the rescue, other than to offer their thanks. They were as much of a mystery as they'd been before. Llorendo alone seemed warmer. The small smile he'd given the group when he turned to leave with his fellows told her it might not be the last time they saw each other.

She knocked before her nerve could fail her again. The door swung open, revealing Macon, his eyes unfathomable in the dimly lit room.

"Hello, Captain," he said, widening the door to admit her.

"Acting Captain," she corrected, stepping into his quarters. He closed the door behind her, cutting off the light and sound from the external hallway. He said nothing, his dark eyes fixed on her.

"I owe you an apology," she blurted out. "I never should have believed the captain. I knew you better than that."

"Yes," Macon agreed.

She flushed at the unexpected reproach. "The aliens took the captain to their city for prosecution," Delaney said, and a ripple went through Macon. Maybe he wasn't as unbiased as she'd thought. Neither was she. They'd have to work on that.

He grimaced. "That won't go well for him." He looked at her; she found herself wanting to turn on a light, so she could read his eyes.

"Yeah," she agreed. "You're packed for our re-deployment tomorrow?" As the heroes of the shuttle expedition, the three of them were being reassigned to the police group guarding the alien camp. Rumor was that Llorendo had asked for them.

"I'm packed," Macon said, indicating a small bag in the corner. "I've been packed for a week, because..." He let the sentence trail off, but she knew what he was referring to. He'd been expecting to be decommissioned at any time.

"I'm sorry," she said, feeling the words to be as inadequate as they were before.

"Forgiven," he said, and she relaxed shoulders she hadn't realized were tense. "I could have defended myself. I wanted you to trust me implicitly."

Maybe she should have. It was too late to know.

"None of us are perfect, melite," he said, and she smiled at the endearment he'd never stopped using. "Not even the aliens."

She grinned and saw the crinkle around his eyes, indicating a smile waiting to break free. His mouth quirked up and he grinned back, the shadows fleeing from his face.

"They're better than we are," she said, stepping closer to him. Awareness flared in his eyes, widening the irises.

"They're more advanced in technology," he said. "Not better."

"Hmm," she said. "It's going to be different guarding them. I'm not sure who's protecting whom."

He nodded. "There's still a lot of resistance. Like the captain, they want to believe we're still number one. The protests will continue."

"All the more reason the captain needs to be made an example of."

Macon's eyes narrowed. "I wish I could say I feel sorry for him, but I don't. He betrayed all of us. If things had been different..." He trailed off. "Llorendo didn't need us to save him."

"No," she agreed. "Yet he let us. I think it was a test."

"I agree," Macon said. "Delaney, the captain said you should 'admit your thirst' for me," he continued, his voice thick. "Do you?"

Delaney swallowed, caught by the intense look in his eyes. "Yes," she said. "They were strange words, but true. I never stopped wanting you," she said, and something in her tore free. "I never stopped loving you."

His breath whooshed, and he drew her to him. A moment later his lips were fierce on hers. He kissed her until she was lightheaded.

When he pulled back, a smile started at his lips and lit his entire face.

"That won't get you out of work, Lieutenant," she said.

Macon barked out a laugh. "I wouldn't expect it to, Captain. I'm yours to command."

Her com buzzed. As much as Delaney wanted to ignore it, she no longer had that luxury. She grinned at Macon. "Ready for duty, Lieutenant?" she asked, slipping her hand into his.

"As you wish," he said, saluting with his free hand.

Delaney pushed the com button, not taking her eyes off Macon.

"Captain, you're needed up front," Wakesa's voice boomed in.

She had a lot to learn from the other humanoids. Delaney hoped the aliens appreciated the team she assembled. If she remembered the line from Macon's old movies right, perhaps aiding Llorendo would be the beginning of a beautiful friendship.

"On my way, Sergeant."

###

ABOUT CLAIRE DAVON

CLAIRE CAN'T REMEMBER A TIME when writing wasn't part of her life. Growing up, she used to write stories with her friends. As a teenager she started out reading fantasy and science fiction, but her diet quickly changed to romance and happily-ever-after's. A native of Massachusetts and cold weather, she left all that behind to move to the sun and fun of California but has always lived no more than twenty miles from the ocean.

Connect with Claire here: www.castrumpress.com/claire-davon.

THE MAN-EATER

Christopher G. Nuttall

They called it the Man-eater.

It had a formal name, of course, something long-winded and tedious that referenced all the big scientific names who'd put it together. Later they'd call it the Buckley Drive, but for now, it was the Man-eater. It ate me.

I don't pretend to understand the theory behind the Man-eater. It was an FTL drive, in theory; it compressed space, or something to that effect, which allowed it to propel a starship faster than light. The theory, I was assured, was perfect. And yet, every time the drive was tested, the ship vanished and never returned.

The first ship to test the Man-eater was HMS *Scott*, which launched from Selene Base and activated the drive in 2178. She vanished, never to be seen again. There were a great many political recriminations – it later turned out that the designers had rushed the launch to ensure that Britain would be the first nation to develop a working FTL drive – and the boffins went back to work. Two weeks later, USS *Lewis* activated her own drive and vanished. She was never seen again, either.

The recriminations were far worse that time. The politicians fussed, but the boffins went back to work. Again. They bounced graviton particle beams off deflector dishes; they reversed the polarity of neutron flows, and a great many other things more suited to a technobabble-crammed VR show than genuine scientific research. And then they hooked the third version of the Man-eater into USS *Clark* and tested the wretched drive. She didn't come back, nor did HMS *Magellan*.

I was there for the fourth test. HMS *Magellan* was a deep-space cruiser, crammed with everything from long-range sensors to weapons and protective armor. Her crew were all volunteers, as were several scientists who accompanied the flight. They were ready for anything, apparently, save for what happened. I watched as she powered her way from Selene Base, got into position, and triggered the drive. She vanished, blinking off my screens as if she'd been nothing more than a sensor glitch.

HMS *Magellan* never came home.

And yes, the recriminations were even worse after the fourth disaster. I heard, later, that the politicians were seriously considering cancelling the whole program, despite protests from right across the solar system. Mankind had spread out over the system however, going farther was impossible without an FTL drive. Who wants to spend the rest of their lives on a generation ship, knowing that their descendants will be the ones to see a whole new world? Oh, the recriminations were savage. No one really wanted to abandon the project, but they didn't want to watch more men and ships vanish into nothingness, either.

I didn't know any of that at the time, of course. I was sitting in my cabin, trying to recover from the high-boost flight to Selene Base. My body was aching, as if I'd been in a fight that had left me bruised and battered. It was a surprise when I heard the door buzzer, two days after *Magellan* vanished, and an even bigger surprise when I looked at the monitor and saw Joe Buckley outside.

It took me several moments to decide to let him in. Men outnumber women twelve to one on Selene Base, which means that spacers develop whole new standards of beauty. A woman, even one as homely as me, will have no trouble finding someone to warm her bed on a deep-space research station. But it also means being the center of attention at all times and, worse, having countless men hit on you. I found it annoying, really. They were more interested in my body than my professionalism. But Joe Buckley seemed harmless.

I opened the door with a tap of the remote, then looked him up and down as he floated into the cabin. Joe was in his late forties, his body bearing the unmistakable signs of someone who'd spent most of his time in zero-g. Selene Base had no gravity, save for the habitation ring some distance from the main station. Joe, it was clear, spent hardly any time there at all.

"Captain Jayne," he said. His voice was surprisingly deep for such a slight man. "Thank you for seeing me."

"Just call me Sandy," I said. Jayne was my mother's name, and I had yet to forgive her for trying to turn me into a carbon copy of herself. "What can I do for you?"

Joe looked me in the eye. "Is this room monitored?"

I blinked, surprised. I didn't think so, but privacy is a null concept on a space station. I wouldn't be entirely surprised to discover that we were being recorded at all times, although I didn't think someone would be watching. If something went wrong, if Selene Base suffered a catastrophic failure, the investigators would have to inspect every last recording in the hopes of putting together what had actually happened. I hoped they enjoyed watching me in the zero-g shower if they had to dig up the records afterwards, but I doubted it. They'd probably have to have their eyes reconstituted after seeing me in the nude.

"I don't think we're being watched," I said warily. Perhaps I'd misjudged him. "What do you want?"

I'd expected an indecent proposal. What I got was worse.

"I want to put an FTL drive in your ship," he said. "And I want to test it."

I stared at him in absolute shock. "Are you mad?"

"No," Joe said.

I had to fight to keep from giggling helplessly. Lead Pipe wasn't, by any reasonable definition of the term, a cruiser. She was really nothing more than a small control center – no one called it a bridge – with a handful of storage pods and a drive system that was strikingly primitive. No drive fields for my Lead Pipe! She'd been designed in the days when mankind had to rely on ballistic trajectories to get from planet to planet; now she was hideously outdated. I had a feeling I wouldn't be able to keep flying her for much longer. My last crewman had moved on long ago. I'd been incredibly lucky to get the contract to ship important equipment to Selene Base.

"Lead Pipe isn't a starship," I told him. "And…"

"I know," Joe said. He held up a hand. "If you'd let me finish?"

He launched into an explanation that included more technobabble than common sense, one I struggled to follow. Joe thought, if I understood correctly, that the Man-eater produced an energy flux that did immense damage to starships, effectively destroying them in flight. There was nothing wrong with the Man-eater itself, he assured me, but it was like fitting a rocket engine to a tomato. The rocket might work as advertised, but the tomato wouldn't survive the experience. Joe believed that Magellan and her sisters simply hadn't been designed for the FTL flight.

I found it hard to believe, but the more he talked about it, the more I started to think he might have a point. The computers and suchlike in Lead Pipe were primitive. I could fix nearly anything with a wrench or a handful of other basic tools. If worse came to worst, I could calculate trajectories with a slide rule and sextant. There was no way I could land on a planetary surface, of course, but I didn't have to land. All I had to do was get cargo from one station or asteroid settlement to another.

"I see," I said, when he'd finally run out of technobabble. "Why didn't you take this to your fellow boffins?"

Joe hummed and hawed a little, but finally admitted that they didn't believe him. They were so wedded to the concept of high technology solving everything that they were reluctant to admit that technology itself could be the problem. A handful of scientists believed that the energy flux was the problem, but they also thought it could be contained. Joe wasn't anything like so sanguine. He figured that the flux simply couldn't be deflected away from critical equipment.

"I need you to help test the theory," he said. "Please."

I frowned. "Can you get a Man-eater onto my ship?"

"Yes," Joe said simply.

I thought about it for a long moment. On one hand, like most spacers, I wanted a working FTL drive. There were hundreds of habitable planets within a thousand light years of Sol, all tantalizingly out of reach, and Joe's explanation of the problem sounded valid. I could easily believe that the boffins hadn't thought about more primitive ways to solve their problems. But, at the same time, if we were caught before we managed to activate the drive...it wasn't a pleasant thought. I'd probably wind up being marched to an airlock and unceremoniously tossed into space, or condemned to spend the rest of my life on Earth.

And yet, I asked myself, how long will I be allowed to remain free and independent anyway?

That, too, wasn't a pleasant thought. I was growing uneasily aware that my time might be running out. I was in my late forties, no longer the young woman who'd endured high-g travel with a smile on her face, and I had very little hope of sinking gracefully into retirement. Lead Pipe wasn't worth much these days. I might be able to sell her to an asteroid prospector, if the banks let me. I doubted they'd even bother to repossess the worthless ship.

"Very well," I said. "Let's do it."

I won't bore you with the details of how we managed to transfer a Man-eater from Selene Base to Lead Pipe. Suffice it to say that most people on deep-space research bases are remarkably trusting. Joe – probably with the help of someone who remained nameless – managed to shuffle loading orders around until no one, save for us, was truly aware of what was going where. The Man-eater was transported to my ship by a pair of naval crewmen who were under the impression that I was taking a piece of outdated equipment home. The only real difficulty lay in connecting the Man-eater to Lead Pipe's fission plant.

I'd expected a rocket, somehow. The Man-eater looked more like a small collection of translucent pipes centered on a simple box. Joe explained that the Man-eater wasn't a rocket, in the sense that it provided boost for a ship; it simply projected a field around the ship. I checked and rechecked the programming, then led him up to my command room. His face fell the moment he saw it.

"Just strap yourself in," I ordered, as I checked the systems one by one. "We'll be leaving in a few minutes."

Joe looked pale. "How do you plan to get us out of here?"

"I intend to declare an emergency," I said. It was the sort of question he should have asked me earlier. "Watch."

It felt awfully weird having someone watching me as I powered up the ship. I normally worked on my own, to the point I rarely bothered to wear clothes. It wasn't as though I needed them when I was living and working in zero-g. But this time...I ran through the final checks, then hit the emergency button. Selene Base's staff couldn't be allowed time to think.

"Emergency," I snapped. "Coolant leak. I say again, fission coolant leak!"

I triggered the emergency disconnect protocol at the same time, disengaging Lead Pipe from the airlock and boosting her into open space. A coolant leak wasn't dangerous in itself, but it was often a harbinger of worse problems. My fission plant might be on the verge of a meltdown. Hopefully, whoever was on duty in the command center would act first and think later. My fission plant wasn't supposed to be online now.

"Report status," a voice ordered. "What's happening?"

"Fission emergency," I said, trying to sound panicked. I'd been taught to react coolly and calmly to emergencies, but a hint of panic should help convince them to let us go. "I say again, fission emergency."

I looked at Joe. "I'm bringing the Man-eater online now," I said. "Are you ready?"

"Yeah," Joe said. "I'm ready."

The radio crackled. "Power down your drives and eject your fission core," it snapped. "This is a priority-one order."

Joe coughed. "They know."

"Perhaps," I said. The distance between us and the station was widening rapidly. I didn't think they'd do anything violent as long as they felt the situation was under control. It wasn't as if I could outrun either of the cruisers orbiting the base. "Hang on."

I checked the display, gritting my teeth. We weren't far enough from the station to trigger the Man-eater, not yet. But the cruisers were powering up. I didn't know if they were coming to help us or if they knew we'd stolen a Man-eater, it didn't matter. My failure to eject the fission core into space wasn't a good sign.

A new voice echoed through the radio. "Power down, now!"

"We're ready," Joe said.

I braced myself, resting my finger against the control. "Go."

Space twisted around us. My stomach lurched as an invisible force slammed into it. For a horrific moment, I knew we were dead; then the sensation was gone. I looked up and peered through the porthole. The stars were gone, replaced by a faint glow that seemed to come from everywhere and nowhere. I stared, unable to take my eyes off it. We were looking at the universe from the other side of the light barrier. It was...

Tears prickled at the corner of my eyes. It was wonderful.

"It's working," I said. "It's working!"

"The flux will come in ten seconds, when the drive powers down," Joe said. He sounded almost inhumanly calm. "Five...four..."

I gritted my teeth just as the universe twisted again. Lead Pipe shook so violently that I was half-convinced we'd dropped out of FTL within a planetary atmosphere. Joe had assured me that we wouldn't be traveling very far, but he could have been wrong. The lights dimmed a second later, followed by two of my consoles. I sucked in a breath as red lights flared up on the display. The ship had taken a lot of damage, the computers struggling to figure out precisely what was damaged. I had a feeling we'd lost the damage-monitoring system as well as everything else.

"We made it," Joe said. He waved a hand at me, never taking his eyes off his palmtop. "We're heroes!"

"If we can get back," I said. I was too busy checking the systems to pay attention to him. Lead Pipe had barely been moving, by interplanetary standards, when we'd triggered the drive, but now she was gliding through space at a surprisingly respectable speed. The Man-eater must have given us a boost as we dropped out of FTL. "Do you know where we are?"

Joe said nothing. I sighed and brought up the position-monitoring system. It was useless. The automatics were shot. I swallowed a curse, then set out to take the observations manually. It wasn't easy, and it wasn't something I'd had to do outside basic certification, but I eventually figured out that we were nearly two light-years from Sol. I looked at the timer, then back at my results. Just how fast had we been traveling?

"Probably many times the speed of light," Joe said when I asked, which was probably the least useful answer anyone had ever given me. "Let me calibrate the drive before we try to go back."

I left him to his calculations and went to work, assessing the damage to my ship. Joe had been right, I realized numbly. A great deal of advanced technology had simply been fried by the energy flux. The life support system was on its last legs. I was silently grateful I'd invested in grass carpets that kept the air clean without needing mechanical support. The radios, the computers...we'd lost too many of them. I promised myself that, next time, I'd make sure that everything that might be vulnerable was shut down before we activated the drive. But the drive system and fission core remained unharmed.

A chime echoed through the hull. Ice ran down my spine. It was an emergency signal, a priority emergency signal. I hadn't heard anything like it since the day Hollister Asteroid had suffered a massive air leak and all ships in the area had been summoned to help. I hoped, as I scrambled back to the command room, that it was just a glitch. We were so far from Earth that I was sure we were alone. Given the number of frankly absurd answers the computers had given me in the last hour or so, I was quite confident it was a glitch.

I was wrong. An emergency signal was pinging up on the main display, bleeping remorselessly. I sat down, strapping myself into the chair, then ran a trace. The source of the signal was a large cruiser, only a few thousand kilometers from us.

It – she – was HMS *Magellan*.

Joe looked up at me. "What are we going to do?"

"I'm not sure," I said. *Magellan* was pumping out an emergency signal, but that was all she was doing. Her hull wasn't radiating any energy signatures at all. No drives, no radio signals; I didn't like the look of it. "We could take a look."

"We have to get back and report," Joe said.

I shook my head. "We have a higher duty. You don't ignore a call for help."

Joe looked mutinous, but nodded reluctantly. I understood precisely how he felt. What we'd found was proof that the Man-eater could be made to work without destroying the ship, if we managed to report home. But I was a spacer and I knew, without a doubt, that all distress signals had to be answered. It might be me next time.

"Keep getting the drive ready to go," I ordered as I slowly braked the ship to a halt, relative to *Magellan*. "I'll take a look over there."

I donned my spacesuit after checking it thoroughly, and launched myself into space. I'd known groundhogs who hated flying in space, but I loved it. It was so peaceful. The sensation stayed with me until I reached *Magellan* and landed on the hull. I'd hoped that someone would see me coming, but as I wrestled open the mechanical airlock, I realized she was a dead ship. I glided into the interior and stopped dead.

It wasn't the first time I'd seen death, but there was something truly horrific about the disaster that had struck *Magellan*. Everything was fried, from life support systems to spacesuits. I'd thought there should be enough air in the hulk to keep them alive for a few days, certainly long enough for us to find them, but evidently not. The bodies drifting in front of me looked to have died gasping for air.

Sick, I thought.

It took me nearly two hours to search the ship from top to bottom. No one was left alive, as far as I could tell. The bridge was devastated: consoles had exploded, something I hadn't seen outside bad movies and worse TV shows. Joe had been right, I realized again, as I found the captain's body. The energy flux had devastated the entire ship. I found a copy of a paper logbook – someone, fortunately, had had the presence of mind to write a final record before his death – and transferred it to my pocket, then headed back to Lead Pipe. There was nothing left on *Magellan* worth recovering.

They'll have to come back for the bodies, I thought. I briefly considered trying to transfer them to my ship, but I didn't think I had the time. And then they can try looking for the other missing ships.

"I've checked the calculations," Joe said when I returned to the command room. "We should be able to get back to Earth."

"Please," I said sincerely. I didn't want to go straight back to Selene Base. We were probably already on the 'shoot-on-sight' list. "Let's go home."

I turned the ship around, then checked the calculations myself before activating the Man-eater. The universe shook again, just for a few seconds, then spat us out far too close to Earth for comfort. I let out a sigh of relief, even though we were plunging towards humanity's home world. The orbital defense network would blow us out of space if there was even a small chance we'd hit the planet.

"I've sent the signal," Joe said. "Everyone knows what we've done."

"Yeah," I said as I managed to guide us onto a relatively stable orbit. "Now it's time to face the music."

And that, more or less, was that.

You've probably heard the rest of the story already. Selene Base decided to retroactively approve everything we'd done, probably because it would be embarrassing to admit that we'd stolen the Man-eater. Joe Buckley went down in history as the drive's inventor, not entirely fairly; he spent the rest of his life trying to explain that it was a team effort. And me?

Well, I took the reward money and purchased a bigger ship, one large enough to carry hundreds of people, but primitive enough to survive the Man-eater. The skies are open.

...Shall we go exploring?

214

ABOUT CHRISTOPHER G. NUTTALL

CHRISTOPHER NUTTALL WAS BORN IN Edinburgh, studied in Manchester and lived in Malaysia, all the while reading every science-fiction and fantasy book he could. Now, he lives in Edinburgh with his wife and two sons, making a living as an indie author

Connect with Christopher here: www.castrumpress.com/christopher-nuttall.

CASTRUM

JCH Rigby

"Prepare for landing," says the machine voice. He shivers violently. It's always the same; dreamtime makes him cold to the bones. He'll be trembling and shaking for ages. Moments after waking, Sergeant Joel Edwards already has it bad.

The machine speaks again. "Five minutes until touchdown. No hostile forces within the area. This is not a hot site."

The craft rattles and shakes in turbulent air. *Lander's got the trembles too*, he thinks.

The troopers are stirring in their seats. People are wriggling about, tugging at clothing, yawning and grumbling. As usual, Stepanychev is listening to music, judging by his tapping fingers and the look on his face. Popov will be praying. Farther down the cabin, somebody swears.

Edwards' vision blurs and displays icons. The data shows outside air temperature and pressure. He blinks them away, and yawns.

Wait a minute. He looks around the cabin. This isn't the normal kind of lander. He doesn't recognize the seating layout. The panels opposite him are neat and clean – military vehicles are usually a bit scruffier than this. Must be brand new.

Forget it. It's not important. There's a mission coming up.

Odd, though. By now, he should be receiving orders. But the cabin speakers have fallen silent again, the radio net's quiet, and his datalink isn't showing any alerts.

He twists to look for a window, a screen, or anything else that will let him see outside. Nothing. Forward in the cabin, the bulkhead is solid. There's no access door to the crew deck.

This is weird. The lander won't be autonomous, will it?

"Landing in one minute," says the voice. *But we don't know where we are, or what we're supposed to do! This is crap.*

The team need to know something. "Listen in, everyone. As soon as we land, get out of the vehicle and into whatever cover you can find. As far as I can tell, we can breathe the air. Take only your personal kit. Leave the heavy stuff onboard. Weapons tight unless you're fired upon. I'll assess the situation and give snap orders after that."

"Give us a break. Lander said this isn't a hot site!" He recognizes the voice, and she's moaning as usual.

Edwards doesn't have time for this. "Wind your neck in, Anwar. I don't care what the machine says, there's less than a minute till touchdown, and we've got no orders from Command. We get out of the vehicle, and we secure our position while I find out what the hell's going on."

It strikes him that he hasn't noticed who else is on the mission; just Anwar, Popov, and Stepanychev. Edwards feels uneasy. He has a worrying sensation that once he sees the rest of the section, he won't know them. But how could that be?

Better get ready to land, then. He tugs at the seat's crash straps. He's trembling less, but he's still woolly-headed.

"Landing now," says the machine. Engines roar; the craft tilts; his stomach lurches.

Here we go, then.

***

He doesn't know why he doesn't know the others. He hardly remembers himself. Who is he? Edwards knows he can lead combat operations against any enemy, can handle any weapon, can operate countless vehicles. He can summon up data directly into his mind and superimpose it onto his visual field. His skin will shift its color to match the surroundings, without any conscious effort. He can speed up his reflexes or slow his awareness down to a crawl. He can lie motionless for months, and then react in milliseconds.

He knows that he is Joel Edwards, sergeant, enhanced special forces trooper and section commander. But the rest is inaccessible. Who his friends are, what he likes and dislikes, where he was born; all of this is a mystery.

He knows that humans who lack enhancements are called *slows*, and he knows that the word *cyborg* is a deadly insult.

But he has no recollection of anything before waking up in the lander.

***

Where the hell is this? Joel Edwards stares at open grassland, turns around. A few hundred meters away, woods encircle them. The troopers are spreading out around the lander, weapons up into the aim, looking outwards for threats.

Nobody and nothing. No reception committee: no local forces, no briefing officer from Command. There's no sign of anyone, military or civilian, and not much of anything else to give him a clue.

217

Wait. Gravity gives him a clue; it's Earth-normal, but that's not much help. Humans settle anywhere they find comfortable, so they could be on Earth, Parnassus, Harmony, Rheparion...

"Anyone know where we are?" He uses the radio battle net to talk to this group of comrade-strangers. No one answers. But there's a cloudy sky and a proper horizon, so they're on a planet and not a habitat. Somewhere on one of maybe twenty planets? Practically solved it already.

Edwards zooms his vision towards the trees. Waste of time. They're just trees. He can't name them, but he doubts he could do that even if he knew where they were. Back home, he couldn't name many trees. Wait: where's home?

More importantly, where's *here*? He gets back on the net. "Command, where the bloody hell are we? There's nobody and nothing here. What's the mission?"

An unfamiliar voice. "Enemy forces have brutalized the local inhabitants. There is an enemy base to the north of you. Neutralize the enemy force and destroy the base. You will be extracted on completion of the mission."

"Is that it? That's nothing like enough," Edwards says. "What inhabitants? Who are the enemy? What strength? What are their capabilities?" Questions are falling out of his mouth too quickly. His stomach is churning.

There's a pause. Then he hears it repeated, word for word, by the same voice. "Enemy forces have brutalized the local inhabitants. There is an enemy base to the north of you. Neutralize the enemy force and destroy the base. You will be extracted on completion of the mission."

The net goes dead. It's clear that's all he's going to get.

✳✳✳

"Close in on me." The troopers gather at the lander's loading ramp.

Edwards studies his force. Corporal Stepanychev, Anwar, Popov, plus five others: three women and two men. All strangers. He's probably strange to them. As he looks at each one, their name flashes in his visual field. The women are Ogareff, Blount, and Wallace; the men are Ross and Mirza.

"You're Joel Edwards?" It's Blount.

"Yeah." She nods briefly when he confirms it. The omission of 'sergeant' doesn't bother him; that's normal in their regiment. He'd better deal with the biggest problem first. "I know this sounds mad, but does anyone remember anything before they woke up?"

Heads are shaking. Faces look worried. Mirza likely speaks for all of them. "I don't remember a thing. I don't know you guys, I don't know where we are, and I don't know who I'm supposed to kill. Sorry to sound picky, but can you help me with any of that?"

✳✳✳

Edwards goes into sergeant mode. "Okay, let's get the support weapons unloaded. We'll set up a patrol base here. We're not going anywhere without one foot firmly on the ground." There's no real alternative. They'd have to be mad to head off into the wild blue yonder without a secure footing.

And they need to know more about this place. He reaches into a belt pouch, takes out the drone, and tosses the tiny machine into the air. It hovers for a second, then ascends vertically.

There's a commotion behind him. People are shouting, cursing. He spins around to see the lander drifting away from the section, the loading ramp still open while the landing gear lifts and stows itself. The craft accelerates silently across the heath. Ogareff and Ross are running in pursuit. The rest stare after them, open-mouthed.

The net comes alive with voice traffic, swearing, anger, outraged demands for the lander to return. It's now over a hundred meters away. Ogareff has outstripped Ross. She's sprinting flat out, moving as only the enhanced can move, rifle slung, her arms pumping her onwards. She's almost caught it, preparing to leap onto the loading ramp, when the lander rises way beyond any possible reach, banks to the right and gathers speed. The engines roar, and the machine surges up above the distant tree line.

Ogareff screams her frustration and drops to her knees. Ross catches up with her and rests a hand on her shoulder. She shakes it off, and they stare after the vanished craft.

✳✳✳

Sergeant Edwards regathers his section. To a man and woman, the troopers are furious. If he doesn't take control of them quickly, he'll have a mutiny on his hands.

Ogareff's still breathing hard, but she says it first. "Maybe that was the biggest cock-up of all time, in which case we're being led by fucking idiots. But I reckon it was deliberate. That bloody lander accelerated just as I was about to get on the ramp! So, what's that all about? Why wouldn't Command want this operation to work, whatever the hell it is? What the fuck is going on here?"

The rest of them are joining in, in a mixture of English and Russian. Edwards needs a distraction.

Corporal Stepanychev provides it. "Check the drone imagery."

At the edge of his sight, an icon's trying to get Edwards' attention. He blinks it to front and center of his visual field. No doubt they all do; the troopers quiet down.

And it's there for all to see. The forgotten drone is still climbing. It's looking down on woodland, grassy savannah, mountains, rivers and lakes, maybe a hint of cultivation in the distant patterns and colors of the land. No vehicles, no roads, no towns. Nothing suggesting communities, civilization, or technology. Mutely, they study the scene.

A hint of distant water appears, expands, becomes a seashore. As the drone ascends, the coastline develops a curve, wraps back on itself, joins hands behind them.

They're on an island. At the very limits of the image, Edwards thinks there's a hint of another blob of land, perhaps two or three.

Edwards realizes he's almost hypnotized. He shakes his head, saves the data, recalls the drone. Forget the geography for now. He ought to look at the immediate problem.

"Ammunition states?" Now that the lander has abandoned them, they've got what they're carrying; nothing more. Data floods in from the section, and it's not encouraging. Basic battle scales only; no smart grenades, sticky-bombs, flame balls, or needlers. And that's their only drone.

Neutralize the enemy force and destroy the base? They'd be lucky to survive a contact with an unruly infant school.

***

"Listen in. Like Mirza said, we don't know where we are, we can't remember anything, we don't know each other, we don't know the situation, and now Command are fucking us around. We need to know a lot more. First, do any of you recognize this place? Look around for clues. I reckon it's a planet, but are we on Earth?" Edwards studies each trooper in turn.

They stare at the surroundings, but heads are shaking. No one volunteers anything until Wallace says, "I don't know where we are, but I've definitely been here before. I don't know when, or what I did here, but it's kind of familiar." Like all of them, she's bewildered.

Edwards files that away. "Anyone else? No? Right. Let's have a good look through what the drone has seen. Here's another thing – comms. I've not heard anything, apart from those crap messages from Command. I need you to search for transmissions of any kind. Crack on with it." He gives Popov, Anwar, and Ogareff datanet and frequency ranges to scan, and sets the others to review the drone's imagery while he recalls the machine itself.

***

The results don't help. There isn't so much as a crackle on any frequency. "It's like the Middle Ages or something," says Popov. "There's no secure comms, no aviation, no commercial stuff, no data; nothing electronic going on anywhere. The Good Lord alone knows where we are. If it's a planet, it's a silent one. And if there's anyone else here, they're talking with semaphore, or smoke and mirrors."

The imagery's no help either. They should have suites of comprehensively detailed maps, but all they can see is a basic north-south-east-west grid overlaying the island. South, west, and east, this island ends in jagged cliffs. Switching between cartoon map and drone view, Stepanychev shows them how the land rises either side of their location, climbing up from the grassland through wooded slopes to a low mountain pass that will channel them northwards.

Abruptly, the streaming images stop. Edwards looks up: the drone should be back by now. He sees a descending dot; then it falls from the sky, bouncing off a rock a few meters away and tumbling into the grass. He inspects the lifeless machine. Something intensely hot has melted the drone's body; the electronics must be slag. *What the hell did that, if we're facing Middle Ages tech?*

"Look at this." Stepanychev flags up a view of the high-shouldered valley where the flanking hills almost touch. Now that the drone is dead, all they have is these few minutes of recorded images.

Just north of the pass, the land opens out through thinning woods into a broad plain. The area is dominated by a dozen or so wooden buildings, surrounded by a high palisade fence. They're laid out in regular lines around an open area. One long wall has a central gate with a tower. A deep ditch surrounds the whole thing. Squads are moving in regular patterns between the buildings. Edwards tries to zoom in closer, but the data has died with the drone.

"It's a fort of some kind. And that looks to me like parade ground drill," Stepanychev says. "So there's a fair-sized unit in front of us, and here's where the lander went." He indicates a barn-like building farther away, on the north coast of this island. "I reckon our only way out is to go through that lot."

Suddenly everyone's talking at once. "Would have been doable with the support weapons. Now what?"

"Someone's stacking the odds against us."

"There must be another way out."

A fort full of unknown troops changes things, but Joel Edwards isn't having that. "Way out? Not good enough. I don't just want to bug out of here. I need to have a word with the comedians who've been fucking around with my head." He wants to get moving, full of a sudden urgency. Amnesiac, lost, ammunition low and facing an unidentified enemy, they can't afford to dither. Without an objective, they'll be one step away from panic.

But here's Mirza again, looking around for support with a kind of nervous defiance. "I vote we get into the hills, circle around the fort, then come back down to the coast and see if we can find a boat or something."

No one follows up Mirza's opening, and Edwards doesn't give him another chance. "Vote? *Vote?* I think you've misunderstood the situation, pal. Spread out into a skirmish line. We're heading north."

***

They travel silently. Hand signals only; if no one else is emitting, even an encrypted signal will shout out loud. And while the pace is brisk, Edwards won't risk using the speeds that enhanced special forces troopers can achieve. They know too little to rush.

The hills steepen, and he moves a pair higher on each flank. Corporal Stepanychev and Blount have the left; Ogareff and Wallace are on the right. Edwards puts Popov on point with Ross and keeps Mirza and Anwar with himself. Popov is sound, and he likes the way Ross tried to chase down the lander. But he wants the other two where he can keep an eye on them.

With radios silent, he needs to be sure about everyone's situation. The thickening tree cover keeps forcing him to pull the flanking pairs closer. Edwards studies the nearly useless maps as they move.

The woods are silent, too. With his hearing at high intensity, he's aware of soft footfalls, the rustle of clothing. A breath of wind stirs the nameless trees. No animal sounds.

Enhanced special forces troopers aren't supposed to get the creeps. *Dunno what you're worried about. We're the scariest things anywhere round here*, he chides himself. But this is uncanny. While they tiptoe forward in ignorance, someone is watching them; someone able to put them here, and then to recall the lander before they could unload their full kit. Someone who was able to splat the drone just when it was of most use. Someone who could edit their memories.

Why can't he remember anything? Why are three of these people familiar, but the rest are complete strangers? Stepanychev likes music, Popov is religious – the meaningless phrase *Old Catholic* appears in Edwards' mind; Anwar grumbles and moans; he knows that much and no more. These other five, they don't know anything about each other, either. But Wallace has been here before.

Perhaps they all have. Weirdly, it seems as if every time he starts to think about the past, something distracts him –

"Oh, Blessed Lord Jesus, look at that."

***

The men have been crucified. Popov falls to his knees, raises his arms to the sky, and begins to moan. The five bodies are nailed to wooden crosses, naked, dead.

"Sweet Lord, forgive me my sins..."

Surely, they've been left here in this little clearing as some kind of demonstration. The wooded valley has narrowed, and the troopers have been following a stream; ahead of them, Edwards can see a track through the trees. It must lead towards the fort. He checks, but just as he expected, the maps don't have that kind of detail. However, enter these woods from north or south and you'll be led to this point.

The troopers stare. These men were tortured before they were nailed onto the crosses. Wounds speckle pale unhealthy skin. The bodies are dirty, legs splashed with mud. They must have been forced along the path to get here. Blood and sweat have run down through the dirt. The corpses are gaunt, skin drawn tightly over bones. Before they took that last walk, they were starving.

The bodies hang down and slightly forward from their nailed wrists, arms stretched high above their sunken heads. Shrunken muscles are as taut as cord. Death would have been slow as exhausted chests struggled to lift to draw in air; white frothy sputum spatters each mouth and chest. It's happened very recently; the clearing stinks of the flow of feces that followed the loss of bowel control. Starved, abused, beaten, and nailed up to die in their own shit. Whatever Popov may think, there's nothing sacred here. But the troopers are clearly troubled by this, and Edwards himself is uneasy.

Experimentally, he touches the leg of the nearest man. The skin is quite warm, another reason to believe that this has happened only recently. Just as Edwards is wondering if the perpetrators are still nearby, he hears Wallace's voice.

"Look at these guys. They're alike. Brothers, d'you think?"

The troopers stare up at the men. She's right. They all have the same skin color, build, and height, and the faces are alike, barring some minor variations in scarring and hair.

"Hang on." Ogareff opens a belt pouch, withdraws a test kit, wipes a swab across the open wound on the shin of the nearest corpse, and touches the kit's controls. She repeats the process with each dead man, taking blood swabs, then reads the screen. The others study the corpses or watch her in silence. Perhaps they realize what she'll find.

"These men are genetically identical. They're clones."

***

More riddles. Why the hell would you go to the trouble of cloning people and then torture them to death? Enemy forces have brutalized the local inhabitants, indeed. How is it that a society can manage reproductive cloning, but it hasn't yet mastered simple radio technology? If you build with wood and dig ditches by hand, what do you make of an orbital lander passing overhead?

"This one's still alive, just." It's Ross. He's looking up at bearded lips that are moving very feebly. The man is trying to speak.

Popov's prayers increase in urgency, but Edwards can't make out his words either. The dying man's eyes flicker open, looking for the source of the sound. They find Popov.

"Ora pro nobis peccatoribus, nunc, et in hora mortis nostrae." Popov is staring intently into the man's eyes as he says this.

Edwards' languages don't extend to this, but the dying man understands. He struggles to form words, at last succeeds in mumbling something incomprehensible. Popov's eyes widen.

"What did he say? What language is that?"

Popov's expression is still troubled, but the awestruck mysticism has been replaced by a more mundane puzzlement. "He's speaking Latin. He said, 'we committed no sin.'"

"Latin? Why? And what the hell does that mean – we committed no sin?" Edwards shakes it off. He's spent far too long being baffled today, and somebody's screwing around with them. He hasn't got time for this. "Come on, people, switch on. Forget this. We need to get moving."

The troopers are staring at him – angry, even disgusted. "What do you want to do about it?" he asks them. "Cut them all down and bury the others, while we wait for this one to die? Prepare to move." But no one stirs.

He weighs up his limited options. "All right. Dose him, then. But make it quick."

Blount is the first to get the spray from her kit. Mirza cups his hands to give her a leg up. She balances awkwardly, leaning a hand against his combat helmet, then sprays the palliator into the dying man's mouth and nose. He blinks, coughs; his eyes snap fully open. The eyes follow Blount as she jumps down.

A despairing howl rings across the clearing, and the man's chest heaves before falling still. The eerie noise has barely died away when Popov says, "*Et in voce magna emisit spiritum.*"

Sergeant Joel Edwards needs to find his enemy and deal with them. "Quit your god-bothering, Popov. Right, people, move out."

Somewhere deeper in the woods, another voice calls out something. He doesn't recognize the language, but he does recognize a commander shouting an order.

***

The section moved fast after cresting the pass. As Stepanychev promised, the land opens up and flattens out as they draw nearer the fort. They can't see it yet, which means there's little danger of reinforcements, so this is a good time to meet the likely enemy. There's enough cover; Joel Edwards flanks widely and gets ahead of the group. He wants to talk to someone; these people will do.

It's a working party, marching. Around twenty soldiers wearing bright metal helmets, red knee-length tunics, overlapping-plate chest armor, bare legs, leather sandals. One pulls a small cart laden with tools: axes, saws, hammers, rope. Just what you'd need to fell trees and crucify some people. Edwards, Popov, and Mirza step out of the undergrowth bordering the track. An order is shouted in a language Edwards doesn't know. The soldiers halt, gaping at them; throw down their loads, deploy into line. They draw their weapons.

Swords. Not a firearm to be seen. Some carry stabbing spears, around six feet long. Most of the soldiers have rectangular shields strapped to their backs. They bring them round onto their left arms. Two men unsling curving compound bows, nocking arrows onto bowstrings.

A light wind stirs the trees. That barn on the north coast seems a long way away.

The enemy commander studies the three troopers. He's not a fool; a brief order turns three of his own squad around to face his flanks and rear, while the rest concentrate on these unexpected apparitions. His armor is workmanlike, practical rather than fancy dress. An experienced professional, then; at least a squad leader. His gaze tracks across the troopers, but stops when it reaches Sergeant Joel Edwards. He recognizes him: commander faces commander. Edwards nods back.

The man's soldiers are clearly mystified by the enhanced troopers: how could they not be? But Joel Edwards and his men are equally baffled: where are they? *When are they? Who are these people?*

From twenty meters ahead of the enemy squad, Edwards selects voice amplification and bellows at them. "Drop your weapons! Now!" The commander doesn't blink, but then he doesn't yet know who they are, or what to make of them. Edwards wants to talk to someone; he's concealed his force's true strength, so these people can be uncertain about this new threat. They might talk, not fight. But he's not surprised when they don't cooperate.

Edwards would still prefer to talk rather than kill people, so he switches from English to Russian and repeats it. No difference. "Try your Latin," he tells Popov, who shouts a couple of words.

One of the bowmen laughs contemptuously, and it spreads across the squad. They're nervous, of course, and their laughter helps them. *What threat can this trio of oddly-dressed monsters be to a squad like us?* But when Edwards, Popov, and Mirza bring their rifles up into the aim, the enemy commander knows that he's facing weapons.

An order, and the squad overlap their shields. Swordsmen are now behind a protecting wall. The archers step out to left and right flanks, raising their bows. Each is paired with a spear-carrier. Now they've deployed, their next command will be to engage their enemy.

And here it comes. The commander snaps out another order. This one is short, preparatory. Ready! Edwards doesn't need to speak his language: the tone, the stress, the rising note are the same as he'd use. The swordsmen tense up, each advancing his left foot half a step. Spears are brought down to hips, right hand controlling, left hand supporting. The archers draw their arms back, ready to release.

There's no way to de-escalate this. Before the commander can give the executive order, Edwards and his troopers open fire. Stepanychev and his force unveil from the bushes on the enemy's right flank, firing economical aimed shots. Double-taps; no wasteful bursts when ammunition stocks are so low.

The effect is overwhelming. The spearmen, archers, and tightly-bunched swordsmen provide a massed target for the flank attack. The commander takes Edwards' three aimed shots on the shoulder of his sword arm, and on the cheek guard of his shiny helmet. The impacts spin him about, and he drops him to the ground. Within thirty seconds, the enemy force is eradicated.

But it's not without cost. Mirza is down, the chance target of both archers. Popov rushes to give aid, but Edwards knows the man is gone. As is Blount, victim of a twenty-meter throw by one of the flanking spearmen who now lies dead on the track.

The section regroups. Anwar attends to Ross, who has arm and leg wounds from a volley of thrown darts. The nasty little barbed weapons lie scattered around. Stepanychev, Ogareff, and Wallace prowl about, checking that the enemy are in fact dead, alert for further threats.

Popov returns, shaking his head. "An arrow in his throat, one in an eye. I've powered him down, but there's no way back from those wounds. He's gone."

Better him than one of the others.

"Swords! Spears! Darts! Crucifixion! This is mad. Crap! Are we in some fucked-up training simulation?" yells Anwar. She's had enough.

"This doesn't feel like a simulation," Ross growls.

Stepanychev comes up, displaying a handful of the darts. "All the enemy are dead, but everyone's ammunition state is very bad. The darts are weighted. Each of these guys had a few clipped to the back of their shields. I hadn't expected that."

"Neither had I," says Joel Edwards, removing his magazine of riot-control baton rounds. He reloads with full-charge anti-personnel ball ammunition. "Let's have a word with this bloke."

***

The commander is flat on his back, stunned, but his eyes are open. The baton rounds have left him with at least a frozen shoulder, and perhaps a broken cheekbone. Stepanychev's bayonet tickles his exposed throat. A rifle is a mystery, but the man knows the truth of steel. He glares hate at Edwards as the troopers loom over him.

"Talk to him, Popov. Use your bloody Latin and ask him his name. Try and get a rank or something out of him."

Popov kneels by the man, rests one hand against a tree trunk, reaches out the other, grasps the commander by his uninjured arm and pulls him up into a sitting position. The man winces at the pain, then gazes about himself. He stares at dead Blount, at Mirza still skewered by arrows. He watches Anwar bandaging Ross. His face becomes stony when he sees the bodies of his men. Stepanychev keeps the bayonet close.

Popov and the commander exchange a flurry of outlandish words. "His name is Flavius Afranius Syagrius. He's Optio, Praefectus Castrorum. That means he's something like the sergeant major in charge of the camp."

"That'll do nicely. Now ask him why he crucified those men."

That earns Popov a shake of the head; it seems this Syagrius isn't going to talk about that. Instead, he's staring at Popov's hand on the tree, his eyes widening as the skin changes color to match the bark. He looks intrigued, not scared.

Another burst of apparent gibberish.

"He wants to know how we do that."

Edwards doesn't want to waste time on non-essentials. "How the hell can you explain that in ancient Latin? Just tell him it's fucking magic."

When he hears that, Syagrius spits, laughs, speaks. Joel Edwards is impressed by his nonchalance.

"He says if we could do magic," Popov says, "there would still be nine of us."

***

Up comes Ogareff. "You need to know this. These guys – they're all clones, too. And they're identical to the first ones." She looks at Syagrius, then reaches into her pouch again. "What about him?"

He allows Ogareff to take a swab of his saliva. The exchange is that he gets to study her face. She nods agreement; he slowly reaches out his uninjured left arm. Warily at first, she lets him trace the silver lines across her forehead, cheeks, and throat, then press his fingertip very gently against the unyielding firmness of her eye. She shifts her focus, and he recoils a little as the artificial lens adjusts. Ogareff laughs. Stepanychev watches every movement, the bayonet never wavering from the man's throat.

When she checks the test kit's results, it gives the same answer. Popov tries to explain it by telling him, "You're all brothers. Like twins – Gemini? Castor and Pollux?" Syagrius shakes his head. It's incomprehension, not denial.

"His troops are probably five to ten years younger than him," muses Ogareff. "They're ages with the crucified guys. But he's genetically identical to them all. So someone's been cloning people here for a while."

"Here?" says Stepanychev. "Why here? Why not somewhere else?"

They need so many answers. Edwards must talk to this man. It's a slow process, relaying everything through Popov, but they get there eventually. Syagrius agrees to trade – *you ask one, then I'll ask one. Maybe I'll answer, maybe not. You too, eh?*

He's the senior Optio in the castrum, the fort. "And who are you?" 'Sergeant' seems to equate; he's content with the answer. Edwards remembers exchanging nods.

No, he won't say how many soldiers there are in the fort. "But I know you're seven, now, and I've not seen a sword among you. Just this," waving a hand at Stepanychev's ever-present bayonet. "So, tell me about your weapons." Edwards shakes his head. "Why not? Do you fear I might learn to use them better than you can?"

You just might. For a slow, you're pretty quick. "Who do you fight for?" Edwards wants to know.

"*Civis Romanus sum*, but there are some men in the castrum who give orders. They come and go. I think one may be a senator. He's old, and he looks wealthy. There are others, but the officers treat him with the most respect. And who do you fight for?"

'Command' is meaningless to Syagrius, but Edwards realizes that it doesn't mean much more to him.

"And why do you fight?" Syagrius asks Edwards.

"That's the thing – I don't know why we're here. We can't remember anything before... ach, what would he know about a lander? Ask him how far back he can remember," says Edwards.

Syagrius recalls skirmishes during a slave revolt earlier in the year, but nothing before that. It troubles the man. Joel Edwards doesn't want to feel any kind of association, but it troubles him too.

"Why did you crucify those men?"

The Optio shrugs. The crucified men were slaves. They rebelled; he can't have that.

***

"We have two problems. Our memories have been stolen, and we're being deceived by our leaders. How about you?" says Corporal Stepanychev. He's sheathed his bayonet; he sits down next to Edwards and Popov, facing Syagrius.

They've learned the trick of it now. Edwards and Syagrius speak in short sentences, eyes fixed on each other. Stepanychev does the same when it's his turn. They all wait quietly while Popov translates, switching his gaze between them.

"My first two problems are the same as yours. You say my spit and my soldiers' blood makes us brothers to the dead slaves. You're poor magicians, so I doubt that you're good liars. And that gives me my third problem. They rebelled, but I've crucified my brothers! If this is truth, I must kill the men who did this to me."

And now, Joel Edwards can see a way to his objective. "Will you join with us?"

***

The stream winds down through peaty soil, trickles past scrubby copses, tumbles over rocky ledges below the path, loiters in tarns, swells into a river that will lead past the castrum on its way to the distant coast. Edwards and Stepanychev scour the dead drone's data, scan the near-useless maps, drain Syagrius of information, decide that the obvious route is their only route. They take it.

Bringing the clothing and weapons they need, they leave the dead lined beside the path. No burial, but a gesture at dignity. Flavius Afranius Syagrius recites a long sequence of tripartite names; "Blount, Mirza," adds Joel Edwards, baldly. The little force presents arms; Syagrius draws the sword he's been permitted to resume wearing, extends it painfully in a silent salute. Popov mutters prayers. Nobody mentions the crucified men.

Stepanychev takes point with Anwar and the heavily limping Ross. Edwards and Popov share turns dragging the laden cart, Syagrius still in pain but helping; they use the time in discussing options, negotiating, planning. Wallace keeps the rear with Ogareff, warily watching their flanks.

After a few hundred meters, Stepanychev halts them. "Look at that."

Around ten meters below, the stream cascades over a fall into a white-flecked bog-brown pool. Something shines in the water.

"Keep your eyes forward and flanking," says Joel Edwards to the rest as he zooms his vision onto the spot. He studies the things in the river, waves Ogareff forward. "Bring your kit." He clambers down the slope.

Syagrius shades his eyes with his good hand, glances at Ogareff, follows. She moves more quickly than either man; she reaches the stream first, steps into the water, gasps at its cold. Edwards follows her; abruptly he turns back, reaches out a hand to Syagrius. The man waves it away, acknowledging the offer with a brief nod.

Water up to their knees, they stand and stare at the corpses locked together in death. A man lies on his back in the stream. He's fully armored: a now-rusting full suit of steel plate. His helmet has been crushed by some heavy blow. A feathered lance has been driven up under his breastplate. Either of those wounds would have killed him, but in any event the water is trickling through his helmet; likely that he was wounded, fell, couldn't rise, drowned. A rusty sword lies by his side.

His killer is sprawled face-down on the steel man's torso, gray-skinned by water decomposition. Ornately-feathered headdress, long hair tied back, bare-chested, he wears fringed trews and moccasin sandals. An empty quiver is slung over his shoulder, bobbing about in the water. The bow is nowhere to be seen. His right-hand rests near a short axe. Ogareff bends, turns him over, recoils as a silver fish exits the gaping sword wound in the man's belly. She recovers, begins her analysis, turns to the steel man. The helmet's fastenings are hidden in the water. She persists, removes it, reveals another bloated gray face infested by crawling things. The eyes have been eaten away.

Edwards' brain offers him the words *knight, cuirass, Native American, tomahawk*, but adds nothing else of use. Without context, his memory is stubbornly blank. All he knows is that these men shouldn't coexist, shouldn't meet and fight each other. Just like enhanced special forces troopers and Roman soldiers.

Syagrius glances at the feathered and bare-chested warrior, dismisses him as of no interest; studies the knight closely, admires the armor. "*Lorica segmentata.*" He kneels in the stream, ignoring the cold on his bare legs; removes his own helmet, picks up the knight's, compares the weights and the protection given by each.

229

After a few moments, he stands, tosses the helmet aside, puts his own back on, turns to Joel Edwards. With Popov far above them on the path, this could be tricky, but he makes his meaning clear. Pointing at Ogareff's test kit, then at each of the bodies: "*Fratres*? Brother-brother?"

Ogareff nods. "Yes. Gemini. Twin brothers."

Syagrius considers this. "*Gemelli*," he corrects her. He points at the dead men again, then at himself. "Brother, brother?"

"Yes," says Ogareff gently, nodding.

Syagrius stands silently in the stream, looking at the knight, the Native American, at his own hands. He studies the bare-chested man with greater interest now.

He draws a deep breath, stares into Ogareff's artificial eyes, points at her and then at Edwards. "Brother, brother?"

She shakes her head. "No."

He points at Edwards and himself. "Brother, brother?"

Another shake. "No."

Ogareff and himself. "Brother, brother?"

She smiles slightly. "Sister, brother. No."

***

Out of nowhere, Joel Edwards remembers advice heard in some tactics class: where, when, he has no idea. When things turn to rat shit, break contact fast. Then as soon as you've stopped running, take an inventory of what you've got left. People, weapons, knowledge. Know everything. Facts are weapons, too.

"None of us should be here; none of us should have met each other, let alone fought. It's a combat theme park. Someone's playing at war, using us all as pieces in the game." The troopers are gathered around, listening to Edwards; Popov gives Syagrius a low-voiced translation.

"Let's recap. Wallace has vague memories of being here sometime in the past. Right?"

Wallace confirms it. "It's nothing clear, but I keep having flashbacks about this place. It's like I'm remembering dreams. Horsemen in leather armor, little guys on ponies. They were carrying crossbows. And there were biplanes. I was firing my rifle at biplanes. Somehow, I keep forgetting to think about it. Whenever I try to, it gets vague again. But I've been here before."

Edwards resumes. "Syagrius remembers drilling his troops in the castrum this year. Skirmishes with rebels, a slave revolt. Nothing else." Syagrius nods. "This morning, we all woke up in the lander. We knew our weapons and tactics, but that was it. I knew Stepanychev, Popov, and Anwar faintly, but nobody else. Blount recognized my name; no one else knew anyone.

"And then the clones. Syagrius has never seen anybody like the two guys in the river, but they're genetically identical to each other, and to him, and to the slaves he crucified, and to his soldiers. I bet if we found one of Wallace's leather-armor horsemen, they'd be the same."

Syagrius speaks through Popov. "All of my soldiers in the castrum have the same face, the face I see when I shave. Somehow, I'd never noticed that before. But I know now that they are my brothers." After the translation finishes, he continues. "But some of the centurions aren't my brothers, nor is the senator, nor are a few others. In time, I'll think further about what this means for me. But for now, I want answers. Answers and blood."

Ross cuts in. "Say that you're right: theme park, with human toys. Someone's breeding toy soldiers. But how did we get involved?" Syagrius snarls when "toy" is translated.

Stepanychev beats Edwards to it. "Somebody wanted to raise the game."

"And they've been wiping our memories. I think we should have a chat with the blokes in the fort who are giving the orders," says Joel Edwards.

Syagrius joins in, through Popov. "Know this, Edwards. Within the castrum, I have another two hundred brothers. I will not squander those lives."

***

When they leave the last straggly remnant of the woods, the castrum is still several hundred meters further north. From here they'll be crossing open ground all the way to its wooden walls. Now Syagrius leads, Edwards and Popov with him in helmets, tunics, and armor. They carry spears, shields, scabbarded swords. They know them as *pilum*, *scutum*, *gladius*.

Stepanychev and Anwar pull the cart; inside, Ross, in combat clothing, lies inertly over the hidden rifles. Ogareff and Wallace march behind the cart. Everyone's face is smeared with mud. The armor, the helmets and tunics: this simple deception might just get them into the fort. Dealing with whatever follows will require fast thinking, rapid action. Edwards feels a growing tension.

After a short lesson, Syagrius has pronounced their sword handling tolerable; the gladius feels familiar to Edwards, and he wonders if he's forgotten some of his own capabilities, or been caused to forget. But their instructor is less impressed by their skills with bows and spears.

They close on the castrum's palisade. A voice challenges them from the gated watchtower, which Syagrius named *Porta Praetoria*. He responds with a parade-ground bellow. The gates swing open; they march across the wooden bridge over the perimeter ditch.

"Sharpen up, people," Edwards says quietly on the section net. Radio silence won't matter much in the next few minutes.

They're past the gates, under the tower, into the castrum's heart. Soldiers are training; orders ring out, bodies move on command, swords clash against armor.

"About twenty spearmen throwing at targets, far right," says Stepanychev. *Pila*, long iron spears with thin pyramidical heads; the weapon that killed Blount, and which they now carry, inexpertly.

"Big squad of *hastati* drilling to the left," says Popov. Infantry, with swords and spears just like those they're carrying, but likely a lot more capable than they are. Another worry.

#*Bowman in the gate tower. Looking down, watching us.*# Ross, on his back in the cart, using datalink so the sentry won't see a dead man's lips move.

"Ten archers at target practice, far left corner," says Wallace. Edwards knows that these *sagittarii* are effective at ranges much greater than a hundred meters. Volley fire cancels out individual inaccuracy.

"We're approaching the commanders. Halt on Syagrius' next order." Popov again. As he marches, he's holding his head down to mask his speech, as if fiddling with the scabbard of his gladius.

Syagrius halts them twenty yards from a wooden building that reeks of a unit headquarters. Four men are standing on the raised boardwalk veranda that surrounds it, watching them. Two are robed, two in uniform.

Syagrius mutters a few words to Popov. "The senator is the nearest guy." Popov keeps his head down. "The others don't wear their clothes right."

The maybe-senator calls out a few words; not an order, but still a greeting that demands a response. Edwards hears Syagrius' name, recognizes this; polite condescension from the commanding officer toward a competent and trusted sergeant major.

We get close up, they'll see right through this, Edwards thinks. *Our skin, our eyes, the fucking bullet holes in the tunics. Red or not, the bloodstains show.*

Syagrius answers with a few sentences, the senior Optio reporting respectfully to his commander.

Popov says softly, "He says he's encountered a strange enemy, killed many, and brought one of the enemy's dead for them to inspect. But he's suffered the loss of several *hastati* to mystery weapons."

Or they'll wonder why no one else speaks or understands them.

The senator shrugs, peers down at the cart; speaks to one of the others with him. In English.

"Looks like my chaps might have sorted out your magic cyborgs, Ranulf. I hope you're good for the money, because that's three in a row you owe me now. Well, shall we see what they've got in there?"

The group descend the steps, the senator and this Ranulf leading. Ranulf is tall, looking uncomfortable in the robes, and angry. But the supposed senator is smiling.

Syagrius is right; something about this man speaks of wealth: the neatly groomed hair, the perfect teeth, the air of entitlement. The other two, a lean scar-faced man and a heavier guy with a shaved head, are in more ornate versions of the uniform that Syagrius wears. Bare-headed, they wear scabbarded swords.

Shaven-Head calls out an order to the centurion drilling the *hastati*. The swordsmen stop their weapons practice, fall in, form a squad. At the centurion's order, they turn and march.

#*Brace up.*# Says Edwards on datalink. The squad halts ten meters away. Edwards studies them. *Clones, right enough.* They look nothing like Shaven-Head and Scar-Face. He sees the similarity of build and faces, distinguished only by minor details. But they didn't prat about when they were forming up as a squad, and they march well in close order. They may be clones, but they look capable enough. And they're studying him and Popov, these strangers with their Optio.

Edwards is conscious too of the archers, the spearmen behind him; deadly and probably hostile. Any moment now, the killing will start. The knot in his stomach is tighter.

The senator looks at Syagrius, says something in Latin, steps forward to look at the dead man in the cart. As he passes Edwards, the senator glances at him. He takes in the silver-flecked skin, the artificial eyes. His jaw sags open.

"Now!" Edwards shouts.

He and Popov throw down their spears, draw the pistols from behind their shields, drop the shields as well. The four men freeze; they know the weapons for what they are.

Movement everywhere. Syagrius draws his sword. Ross stands up in the cart, throws rifles to Stepanychev, Wallace, Anwar, Ogareff.

Someone shouts an order to the *hastati* centurion. Syagrius countermands it; the centurion hesitates.

Enough of this. Edwards shoots Scar-Face; the man crumples. Popov double-taps Shaven Head. Scar-Face writhes, moans. Edwards fires again. Quick, efficient kills.

Ross opens fire on the watchtower. Two three-round bursts. He stares upwards, watching for movement.

The *hastati* are aghast at the noise, and they don't understand what they're seeing, but they don't break and run. Or attack, yet. Syagrius' outstretched arm holds them still, for now.

But the senator tries to run; Wallace catches him easily, trips him, kicks him in the face as he sprawls. His nose explodes with blood. Ranulf fumbles in his ill-worn robes. Anwar waits until a pistol emerges, laughs, and takes it away in a blur of movement. She slaps him left-right-left across the face with the weapon, then kicks him hard in the shins. As he drops to his knees, she kicks him again, this time in the groin, and tosses the pistol into the cart.

Across the square, which Syagrius calls the *intervallum*, the archers and spearmen are deploying. In a moment, their officers will make up their minds too, and they'll launch their weapons. But right now, what they see is Syagrius, their Praefectus Castrorum, and a small squad of strange *hastati*. If the Optio is content with the situation, it should be all right for now. Stepanychev and Ogareff are tracking targets with their rifles, ready for the centurions' decision.

Edwards seizes the moment. "Into the building. Bring those two," he says, before the balance shifts again. He and Popov run for the headquarters building.

The others drag the prisoners. The senator is stumbling, cursing, hands up to his ruined nose; Anwar tows Ranulf, still moaning at the pain between his legs. Ross, Stepanychev, and Ogareff cover the move, eyes and sights fixed on the squads of spearmen and bowmen.

Syagrius stands and faces the sword-squad, the pilum carriers, the *sagittarii*, raises his arm again. "*Hastati! Fratres!*" he calls out.

Edwards and Popov reach the door; it's locked. Popov tries to kick it down, but it won't move. He tries again, swears, looks across at Syagrius, who's still addressing the legionaries.

"He's saying, 'brothers, valiant soldiers –'"

"No shit," says Edwards. "Never mind that, just get the fucking door open."

"You won't succeed," says the senator as he's dragged up, snuffling through his bloody nose. "Only I can open that door. Surrender now, cyborg, and you might just live."

"My God, you're stupid," says Edwards, scratching the man's throat with his gladius. "You shouldn't have told me that. Or called me that."

"I'm not letting you in there, whatever –"

Edwards cuts a little deeper. Red trickles down the gladius' blade. He holds it up so the man will see, then stares him in the eyes as he licks the blood from the sword's blade. He grins. "Really whatever? Let's find out. What do you have to do to open the door, shout 'Open Sesame'? Is it fingerprints? Does the hand still need to be attached to your arm? Or is it an eye scanner? Let's see if it works when I cut the eyes out of your head. Still whatever?"

"I'll let you in," says this maybe-senator.

"Good lad."

✳✳✳

It's a could-be-anywhere communications room. All the technology that's missing from this mission is in here. Screens, map displays, comms sets, surrounded by forgotten drinks and discarded plates of food. Two uniformed guys, watchkeepers or technicians or whatever, staring in horror at what's come through the door: cyborgs in legionaries' clothing, carrying pistols and rifles, dragging prisoners. And there's a pale-skinned guy who's already assessed the situation, and whose eyes are darting around the room. He's a techie, definitely.

They all see the weapons, all raise their hands high. Edwards sends Wallace to keep an eye on the three of them, leaves Anwar with the two prisoners; she pushes them onto chairs. Stepanychev, Popov, Ross, and Ogareff are outside with Syagrius, who's keeping a lid on the *hastati* and the centurions. It's not what you'd call under control; it's more like spinning plates.

But Joel Edwards is loving this. For the first time since – well, since when? – things could be turning their way. He sheathes his gladius, prods the robed senator with the pistol. "Talk to me. Tell me who you are and what this is. Start with why we're fighting these people."

"Call it research." His face and neck are a mess of blood; he can't take his eyes off the sword. "My name is Travis. I run the ARTOK operations development unit." The voice quavers: he's trying to be assertive, but he's terrified. "We carry out combat evaluations to assess military capabilities in various configurations of force-on-force encounters." It sounds like a sales pitch he's used a thousand times.

And it gets worse. "I can understand that you find the situation challenging. I'd be happy to take any feedback you may have –"

Edwards punches him in the face, left-handed. Travis staggers, somehow keeps his feet. Joel Edwards isn't having any of it.

"Try that for feedback, Mr. fucking Travis. That's bullshit. What do you mean, research? Putting Roman soldiers up against us? *Us?* You must have known we'd kill them. What kind of research is that? And medieval European knights fighting American Indians? Are you all mental?"

Edwards doesn't really know what his next move should be. Now that he knows that the mission is a fraud, everything else is just detail. He doesn't care about these people or their motives, but someone needs to talk, to explain this, to tell him why he can't remember what happened yesterday. He paces up and down.

"What happened to our memories?" He stops in front of Wallace's prisoners. The two watchkeepers are trying not to draw attention to themselves.

The third man, the pale guy, won't meet Edwards' eyes either. He shakes his head. "They've been edited," he says quietly.

Joel Edwards stares at him. "Tell me something I don't know. What I want to know is why."

The voice is somehow familiar. "They told us to do it! We just followed their orders. I swear, it was genuine research when it started out." He points at Travis and Ranulf. "But they got carried away with it."

After a moment, Edwards remembers when he last heard this man. *You will be extracted on completion of the mission.*

Ranulf contributes something at last. His hair is askew, his chin is bloody from a split lip, his cheeks are red where Anwar slapped him. His voice is strained; he's still hurting, but he has a try at sounding like a senior executive. "It makes no sense to let you remember anything from the previous tests, so some of your memories have been suppressed. Now do as Mr. Travis says, and hand over your weapons –"

Anwar growls, pretends to spring at him. He cowers backwards, and she laughs. "Shut it, Ranulf, or I'll give you some memories you'll want to suppress."

Edwards says to Wallace, "You've been here before, you reckon. Does any of this seem familiar?"

She stares around, checks the room and its equipment, shakes her head. "No. I remember something about the battles, the guys on ponies, the biplanes. But I don't know anything about this place." She takes a breath, then stares at him. "Edwards, remember what he said outside? Whatsisname, Travis, said something about this one, Ranulf, owing him money. 'Three in a row,' or something like that. Do you remember?"

When Wallace says it, the whole thing falls into place. Edwards nods. "You're right. I get it. I bloody get it. You bastards have been betting on us, haven't you? You've been breeding clones to fight your play battles, calling it research, and then betting on who wins. And you've wiped our memories, so you can use us and reuse us. How bloody dare you. Is that it? I'm right, aren't I?"

Travis and Ranulf answer him with silence. But Joel Edwards knows. #*Popov, get yourself and Syagrius in here. I've something to tell him.*# He says.

While he waits, he thinks about the lander abandoning them, the dead drone, the useless maps, the minimal ammunition. Five crucified men, clones of the soldiers who nailed them up. Killing the *hastati*; Mirza and Blount dead. The bodies in the river. *Breeding people so you can bet on who kills who.*

"Give me a coin," Joel Edwards says to the pale quiet man.

✳✳✳

Travis and Ranulf are kneeling on the office floor, and their faces say they know what's next. The watchkeepers and the pale guy are lying face down. Wallace and Anwar are staring at Joel Edwards.

Popov explains it to Syagrius. He nods slowly, says, "Yes, Edwardus." He draws his gladius and steps behind Travis. Wallace draws her bayonet, stands behind Ranulf.

The kneeling men feel the blades against their necks. Somebody whimpers.

"It's like this," Joel Edwards explains. "I can only ask so much of Syagrius, and I reckon he's done enough. I need one of you two to help me order people about, so we don't have to fight out way out. Just one."

He's excited now. There could be a way to avoid a massively-outnumbered firefight, get out of this place, get on the lander, get off this island. He'll figure the rest out later.

Edwards turns to the prone men. "You three should come in handy for techy stuff like getting the lander back here. And you're going to give us back our memories, somehow. Oh, and get us out of here. Yep, I admit I'm making this up as I go along, but what else can I do?"

Back to Travis and Ranulf. "Now, I don't mind which one of you, but we're going to cut somebody's throat, just so everyone gets it that I'm serious about this. You two seem to like a gamble, so I'm sure you won't mind. I promise it'll be fair."

He takes the coin out of his pocket, holds it high, turns it round. Every eye follows him. "Travis, if it's heads – well, it'll be your head. Ranulf, you're tails. Clear? Everyone ready? Here we go, then."

He flips the coin into the air.

###

ABOUT JCH RIGBY

PRIOR TO HIS SF NOVEL series set in the galaxy of The Deep Wide Black, JCH Rigby (Charlie) wrote short stories and plays, on subjects as diverse as a comedy about a medieval bishop who takes up piracy, and a satirical near-future in which motorbikes are forbidden. Later, he developed "Nano Futures", mini short stories which distil SF tropes into one hundred words.

Connect with Charlie here: www.castrumpress.com/jch-rigby.

Thank you for reading Future Days Anthology, Volume I of the Days Anthologies. If you enjoyed this book, please leave a review at your favorite retailer. Here's a link to the Amazon store: http://smarturl.it/review-future-days

Would you like to know when the second volume in the Days Anthologies comes out?
Sign up here:
http://castrumpress.com/subscribe

Subscribers get lower prices on new releases.

BOOKS BY CASTRUM PRESS

SCIENCE FICTION & FANTASY SERIES
The Saiph Series by PP Corcoran
The K'Tai War Series by PP Corcoran
The Formist Series by Mathew Williams
The Deep Wide Black Series by JCH Rigby
The Feral Space Series by James Worrad

ANTHOLOGIES
The Empire at War: British Military Science Fiction
Future Days Anthology

More at: www.castrumpress.com/scifi-fantasy-books